The Case
Has Altered

Martha Grimes

The Case Has Altered

A RICHARD JURY MYSTERY

HENRY HOLT AND COMPANY • NEW YORK

Henry Holt and Company, Inc.
Publishers since 1866
115 West 18th Street
New York, New York 10011

Henry Holt® is a registered trademark
of Henry Holt and Company, Inc.

Published in Canada by Fitzhenry & Whiteside Ltd.,
195 Allstate Parkway, Markham, Ontario L3R 4T8.

Library of Congress Cataloging-in-Publication Data

Grimes, Martha.
The case has altered / Martha Grimes. —1st ed.
p. cm.
ISBN 0-8050-5620-3 (hc : alk. paper)
I. Title.
PS3557.R48998C37 1997
813'.54—dc21 97-20791

Henry Holt books are available for special promotions
and premiums. For details contact: Director, Special Markets.

First Edition 1997

Designed by Victoria Hartman

Printed in the United States of America
All first editions are printed on acid-free paper.
1 3 5 7 9 10 8 6 4 2

To the memory of
Lucille Holland

and to Christine,
whose case has altered

Contents

Part I

DORCAS IS WILLING 3

Part II

THE COLD LADIES 77

Part III

THE RED LAST 195

Part IV

HELLUVA DEAL! 323

The Case
Has Altered

Part I

Dorcas Is Willing

1

Dorcas hated the fens.

A no-man's-land once you got beyond the pub, whose cold window-panes behind her glowed like a row of golden fingerprints, and the only other lights were those of the occasional car moving along the A17. The endless monotony of the fens was bad enough in daylight, and worse at night because at night it got really spooky. Dorcas kept looking over her shoulder, seeing nothing but a vast black flatness and the tiny lights of the pub.

It was a little after eleven o'clock on a cold February night, mid-February it was, that found Dorcas walking across Wyndham Fen. She set her feet down in the sopping field, made spongier by the incessant rains. She should never have worn these heels, inch and a half they were, but they made her legs look ever so much better. She was convinced that there must be quicksand about, despite people's telling her this was marshy land, the fens, and though it might be soggy and spongy, it wouldn't suck you down. There was always a first time, she thought.

The pub was well behind her, probably a half-mile, its lights still visible. Now they looked as far off as stars, and nothing lay between her and the rim of the sky, black and blank. She especially hated Wyndham Fen because of the tourists who came into the pub and asked stupid questions. It gave her a kick to give them stupid answers sometimes and watch as the puzzlement grew on their faces. It was really a laugh how many tourists were actually eager to be separated from their two or more quid to have the experience of seeing a fen as it used to be hundreds of years ago. God, wasn't it bad enough to see it now without pining over what it was? It was like her own mum poring over old photos, snaps of them all at Skegness, places like that.

The dark shape of the Visitors' Center drifted like a ship on the unsteady ground. The fens lent everything around a curiously breathing life—objects appeared bigger, trees grew larger, the spire of a distant church spiked higher, stumps engorged. Bright light would return these objects to their natural shapes, but even in the light of day the overwhelming flatness of the fens could make what appeared in the distance more distant, and at the same time, things that were closer looked closer still. It was as if there was never a time, day or night, when you could depend on the evidence of your own eyes.

Her shoes sank in the spongy ground. There was peat beneath the grass and for some reason that always made her feel the ground was not secure. As if the ground itself floated on a raft through fog.

The Visitors' Center was the only building around, so the only place that offered cover. She was making her way to its porch, thinking it a very odd place to choose for a meeting. Why couldn't they have just as easily met inside where there was warmth and light? The only light here was her torch spiking the ground, and she soon turned that off. Looking to her right where the boardwalk began to weave its way through the canals, she remembered how she hated water, had done ever since she'd been left in the tub alone as a tyke and slipped under and almost drowned because her tiny hands couldn't get purchase, couldn't find anything but slippery enamel—the very thought made her sick, even now. When the family went to Skegness every summer, she wouldn't get any closer to the sea than halfway down the strand where she'd sit with her private hoard of film mags and sexy novels. She'd taken off the original dust jackets and replaced them with others. They were now entertaining her cloaked as *Jane Eyre, Adam Bede, David Copperfield.* Mum and Da would think that was what she was reading. *"Improving your mind are you, Dorcas? Good girl, just don't go getting too smart to get a paying job. Hah hah,"* her father would say. Not much of a laugh her father wasn't, but at least he wasn't always at her like the ones some of her friends had.

One of these books, *David Copperfield* it was, she was supposed to have read in school. She never finished it. The boys at the comprehensive seemed to have read Dickens for the sole purpose of taunting poor Dorcas, who had, at age thirteen, already something of a reputation. The boys had quickly put to use a slightly revised version of Barkis's message to Nurse Peggotty, which became in their mouths: *"Dorcas is willin', Dorcas is willin'."* She pretended she couldn't be bothered, but the taunt stung, and her reputation gained momentum with no help from Dorcas. The primary reason that Dorcas *was* willing was because she wasn't pretty; she had nothing that would attract men except for being willing. And that had gone right round the comprehensive like wildfire. Dorcas hated Charles Dickens.

For more than twenty years she'd been inwardly raging about her looks, not one feature she could be proud of except maybe for her teeth, but did any man ever tell a girl he loved her teeth? Not likely. And her shape didn't make up for her face, either. Lying on the warm sands of Skegness she was painfully aware that the spandex of her bathing suit was girdle-tight and showed the rills and ridges around her middle. Her hair was rusty-red and stiffish, like one of the scouring pads she used for dishes. The only color in her round face came from the freckles that almost covered it.

Well, her da couldn't accuse her of not working, not with her two jobs, at the house and at the pub. Of course, if he knew why she was working two jobs, wouldn't he be surprised? She'd already got her "going away" outfit: a washed-silk brownish gold suit that made her eyes look more honey-colored than just plain brown—worse than brown, a silt-color, muddy brown.

As she hobbled along the path—she really shouldn't have worn these shoes—she felt the burden of her plain looks lift a little, for they hadn't done her any harm in the last analysis; they were not important. She had found someone who could see her inner beauty. For Dorcas had always been convinced that here she shone.

She walked up the few steps, her feet killing her, and at the top took off her shoes and knocked off the mud. With shoes dangling from her fingers, she stood and looked out over Wyndham Fen and sighed. Here was history. She thought about that with absolutely no enthusiasm. Back in school she had been forced to go with her classmates to hear a boring lecture about how the fens were drained. And other boring details about the Levels. Did anybody really care except for the people who grew all of those acres of tulips and daffs?

What she was looking out at—except she couldn't see with the torch off—was what Wyndham Fen had looked like a hundred years before. Or was it a thousand? How could a person remember all that history? Then they'd drained all of the fens—she was unclear as to who "they" were, the Vikings maybe? No, that was too long ago. That Dutch yob, Vanderbilt? No, he was that American billionaire. Vander . . . Van Der—something? Anyway, he'd got this idea one fine day that you could make the fens produce crops and so forth if you went and drained them. This was good news she supposed if you wanted to be a farmer, maybe the dullest job in the world, but there it was, there's men liked it. Then after they drained the whole of Lincolnshire, nearly, someone else—the National Trust, she guessed—got the idea that it would be nice to have at least one of the fens looking the way the fens had looked before. Why, she couldn't imagine. So they de-drained this one where the Center was. Flooded it back or something with water. Dorcas stood there with her shoes dangling from her fingers thinking, My God, look at all the trouble for nothing. Bugger all, it was a bigger waste of time even than sixth form had been. Anyway, you can't bring things back the way they were.

That was a deep thought for Dorcas, and this pleased her, for she didn't much like thinking. She meant to file it away to repeat when the two of them were talking. He'd be pleasantly surprised to know he was going to marry a woman who was good in bed and a good cook *and* a thinker of deep thoughts. She stood in the frigid mid-February air absently humming and wishing another deep thought would come her way. Maybe she should go read *David Copperfield* again.

She wrapped her heavily sweatered arms about her. She chided herself for not wearing a coat because the sweater was prettier and the coat was black and awfully old. She shivered but not from the cold this time. No, she refused to think about the dead woman. She would not think about her, would not name her name, not even in the privacy of her own mind; she would set her aside. If she were nameless then she would lose her power to disrupt and unnerve. The police would or would not take care of that; they'd talked to everyone at the house, her included, till she was blue in the face.

Dorcas hunched her shoulders and huddled down into her heavy sweater and looked out over the dark tangle of trees and tall grasses and canals that was the old fen. She'd rather save her two quid, ta very much, for her trousseau or a good cookery book.

She heard a sound behind her, a creaking board. And then the arms encircled her waist. *Romantic* was her first thought. *Something's wrong*, was her second thought, and she barely had time for the third before she felt the breath being squeezed out of her, not by hands but by a soft, silky thing tightening round her throat. For a few moments she tried to claw it away as she opened her mouth to scream, but there was no voice to do it.

Dorcas ain't willin'. Dorcas ain't

2

Chief Inspector Arthur Bannen of the Lincolnshire police was in his late fifties, but looked ten years younger. His age was as enigmatic as the rest of him. If he resented Scotland Yard's turning up in Lincolnshire, he didn't show it. He was a man so soft-spoken one might wonder if anything could excite or harrow him. He said what he said with a smile, a small one, even a hurt one sometimes, as if it pained him his listener didn't quite agree. He was presently engaged in folding a length of paper accordion style, like a map.

"We haven't asked for your help, Mr. Jury," said Bannen, finally, but in a perfectly friendly way, while snipping away at the folded paper with his scissors. His feet were up on the edge of his desk, giving the impression of lethargy. Jury thought he was probably anything but lethargic.

"I know you don't need mine. I'm asking for yours."

They were discussing the murder of a guest who'd been staying at a small estate some forty miles away, called Fengate.

Bannen started cutting the paper carefully with scissors and, when he turned his attention to Jury, apparently found Jury the less interesting and turned back to his cutting. "I see. Well, then, how can I help you?" He didn't sound enthusiastic.

"From what I've heard, Lady Kennington's role in all of this is only—peripheral."

"If you mean by that she's on the fringe, or, as they say, 'out of the loop,' I'd say, no, she's definitely *in* the loop." Bannen smiled slightly, as if delivering this news was not unpleasant. He continued cutting tiny triangles out of the paper.

"You're not saying that she's a suspect, are you?"

Bannen's eyes were a mild and unengaging shade of gray, the color of the brackish water in the drains Jury had passed on his trip from London. "Everyone's a suspect who was present at the time."

"I expect I'd use the word 'witness.'"

"Use whatever word you like," Bannen said pleasantly, continuing to snip his design into the strip of paper. "She had opportunity; she and the Dunn woman were outside when the others were inside the house. Add to that, Jennifer Kennington and Verna Dunn were quarreling. Add to *that* your friend Lady Kennington was apparently the last to see the victim alive. After she'd left the Dunn woman, Jennifer Kennington was quite by herself, taking a walk." He paused, considering. "Or so she says." He snapped the scissors a few times, like crocodile jaws, and looked coolly at Jury. "Now if you were I, Superintendent, would you place Jennifer Kennington out of the loop?" Slowly, Bannen shook his head. "I don't think so." *Snip.*

✧

In the dream, Jenny was moving across the fen; others joined her, forming a procession. He heard the barely audible bells of a censer at a service in Lincoln Cathedral.

The telephone was next to his ear. Jury knocked it over groping for it. In his attempt to shake himself from sleep and retrieve it, he felt he was gulping down great droughts of air. His chest hurt, ached. A coronary? In a Lincoln B & B? If he was on his way out, he preferred to go in his own digs in Islington with Mrs. Wassermann and Carole-anne teary-eyed at his bedside. At last his groping hand found the receiver. "Yes?"

"Bannen. Thought you'd never answer. You still sleeping? I've been up for hours."

Jury gritted his teeth. "Good for you. But what's taxing your Lincolnshire police at six A.M.?"

"Get your skates on and I'll take you somewhere interesting."

"Where would that be?" Jury was rubbing what felt like glass dust from his eyes.

"Wyndham Fen."

"Where's that?"

"I can pick you up in twenty minutes. Be ready."

"I'll be ready." This fell on empty air, as Bannen had already hung up.

The bedside clock stubbornly refused to advance its hands to a decent hour. It was six-ten on this February morning and dark as the grave.

જી

Jury hadn't expected they'd be driving forty miles southeast toward Spalding. But that's what they had done. "National Trust Property," Bannen had told him and not much else.

At seven-thirty in the morning, Wyndham Fen was steeped in gray silence, except for the occasional hoot of an owl or saberlike rattle of the tall reeds in its narrow canals. Crystal cobwebs hung between post and rail of the boardwalk; out in the distant pastures, the rime-caked sheep looked as if they were dressed in glass coats. Morning might have been the time when the fens were most picturesque; Wyndham Fen would have been, except for the body.

She was lying face upward in one of the canals, around her neck a blue bracelet of skin that told the manner of death—she'd been garroted. Floating there, her body moving gently, she was surrounded by rush grass and water violets, and Jury thought of the Burne-Jones painting of Ophelia. But unlike the beautiful Ophelia, this young woman was anything but pretty. Her face was engorged and blackened with blood; the eyes and tongue protruded. But he could tell, even before this disfigurement, she probably hadn't been pretty. The face would have been pudgy, the body more so. He bet she hadn't had many chances in her short life and now she'd have none at all. She might have bloomed later in life, but there would be no later life for her.

Bannen walked back along the narrow boardwalk that spanned the canal to consult with one of his men. A dozen cars and a couple of vans were pulled up near the small building which served as a tourist center, a place to disseminate brochures and pamphlets about the fens. Police who'd been in the cars were now fanned out over the spiky, frozen grass and the dirt road.

It was cold; Jury shivered. He wasn't dressed for a February morning in the Lincolnshire fens. Jury couldn't take his eyes off the girl floating in the water. Bannen returned with the medical examiner, who set about getting his bag open. Jury thought he was probably not on the payroll of the constabulary, but was a simple country doctor.

Bannen rocked back slightly on his heels and said, "Dorcas Reese." He sighed and puffed out his cheeks.

"Did you know her?"

"I knew her slightly. She was housemaid and vegetable cook at Fengate."

Jury stared at him, shocked.

Bannen frowned as the medical examiner directed the removal of Dorcas Reese's body from the water. "You couldn't do that *in situ*, could you?" When the doctor gave him a look, Bannen added, "No, I expect not." He sighed. These provincials.

Jury was dismayed by Bannen's apparent sanguinity. "You're saying that this is the second death connected with that house."

"Um. Yes, it is, isn't it?" Bannen was still looking down at the water closing over the place where Dorcas Reese had floated. Bladderwort and water violets swayed on their delicate antennaelike stems. "She should have been looked at where she lay." Bannen's tone was disapproving, as if it were really difficult to get good help these days. "Strange, isn't it?" he said, ambiguously. They were hoisting the body onto the board for the doctor's examination. Bannen walked round the body, studying it, exchanging a few words with the doctor.

Back with Jury, he said, "He thinks it was a length of material, a scarf perhaps. She was garroted. Beyond dumping her in the canal—or she could simply have fallen in after death—no attempt was made to hide her."

Jury looked behind him at the Visitors' Center. "Is this open now? Middle of February? I expect in the warmer weather there's quite a lot of tourists."

"It's open, yes; that is, would be, if we weren't shutting it down." Bannen looked off into the distance. "The fen is about halfway between Fengate and—" He turned to look behind him. "—the pub where she worked some nights. Just away off there on the main road. Called the Case Has Altered. . . . Um." He ran his thumb across his forehead, reflecting.

"You don't appear especially surprised." Jury thought Bannen probably never appeared surprised.

He turned to look at Jury out of his cool gray eyes, smiling slightly. "Oh, I'm surprised. Yes. I'm surprised she was strangled. Verna Dunn was shot."

"Killed by the same person, you mean?"

Bannen turned his head slowly to regard Jury. "This is Lincolnshire, not London. That we would have two murders in the space of two weeks, both targeting women from one house—" He shook his head. "Yes, it would be hard to think two killers were moving about the fens." He ran his finger under his collar as if the collar was too tight. "Usually it's the same method. When one's compelled to kill, it would be in such a way and by such means as would relieve some sort of anxiety . . . You think that's funny?"

"You sound like a psychiatrist, Chief Inspector. I expect I don't believe much in solving murders with mind-games. Basically, it's all plodding—" Jury caught himself, thinking, My God, I'm beginning to sound like Chief Superintendent Racer: *"It's one foot in front of the other, police work is, Jury; it's plodding, Jury, not your slippery-minded conundrums. . . . "* And here he was with this detective chief inspector, whom he hardly knew, and who had, clearly, solved cases in just the way he said—or he wouldn't be saying it. Why was Jury adopting this condescending manner?

Yet Bannen didn't appear to take offense. Perhaps he thought there were more important things to think about. He looked around him at Wyndham Fen. "It was all like this once." Bannen looked at the ground, at the wet grass and the scarves of silver cobwebs stretched across it. With his foot he separated the tall reeds. A field mouse skittered off. "I'm driving along to the Wash now, to have another look. I expect you might like to see it."

Jury was surprised by the invitation. "Yes. I certainly would like to." He wondered if Bannen were, indeed, soliciting the help of Scotland Yard. The Wash had been the site of the first murder.

"There's a public footpath that borders this part of the fen, and she probably took that because it goes right past Fengate." He turned his head to the tree above them, where starlings whicked upward from the branches and knit a black pattern across the whitening sky, then vanished in the seconds it took to mark their flight. Bannen watched them. "Always makes me feel rather sad, the flight of birds." Then he continued talking about the footpath. "On the other end, it passes the Case Has Altered. The Owens were surprised she had this job moonlighting. Is that what they call it? Moonlighting?" He smiled. "Pretty word." Bannen scratched his neck again, seeming to afford this point as much deep thought as any other that had come up that day.

They turned from the drainage ditch and made their way back along the boardwalk to the small car park.

Bannen said, "My sergeant is down with some godawful allergy. He's violently allergic to whatever the stuff is that comes off the alder and hazel trees."

Jury smiled. "Your sergeant would get on with my sergeant like a house afire."

"Oh? Is he allergic to the stuff?"

"He's allergic to all stuff."

*

You can see the difficulty," said Bannen, with his characteristic gesture of rubbing a thumbnail across his brow. As if he'd spent the last two weeks seeing the difficulty.

Jury could believe it. They stood together on the saltings, looking out over that part of the Lincoln-Norfolk coast called the Wash. The public footpaths only went so far, stopping before the seawall. They had walked farther—up over the seawall and down again. Bannen had said there was no danger here of quicksand, as there was much farther out. Like an interior shoreline, the saltings, composed of mud and silt, stretched to meet sand that formed the protective barrier between land and sea. Bannen had pointed out the narrow, choked end of the River Welland where it ran no wider than a stream, into the waters of the North Sea.

There were a number of "danger" areas, legacy of the war. "Mines," said Bannen. "The Wash is littered with them." He pulled the collar of his windbreaker tighter. "This is where we thought the invasion would come." He nodded toward the North Sea. "There were gun platforms out there, big things, like oil rigs, garrisons with heavy artillery. Still there, some of them."

Jury looked at him, speculatively. " 'We'? You weren't in that war, surely. You must have been a kid."

Bannen smiled. "I was, but old enough to remember how the beaches were mined, and we weren't to get near them." They stood in silence for a minute. Then Bannen said, "Difficult. Our M.E. put Verna Dunn's death down to between ten the night of February first to one A.M. the morning of the second, Sunday. Though she wasn't found until afternoon. So the body'd been lying here in all of this muck. Hellish cold and windy. Brutal." He made it sound as if Verna Dunn had been alive to suffer through this exposure. "She might not have been found at all if the sands had shifted a certain way. They do, you know. We're still finding wrecks, hulls of ships. Over on Goodwin sands they found the propeller of one of the Sword bombers. Sand covered it up for all of these years."

"You think that was her killer's intention? To bury the corpse?"

"I would do, only it's a bit iffy. He might have been counting on high tide. Spring tide's twice as high, and if you noticed the seawalls behind us"—Bannen hooked his thumb back toward the walls—"that's one of the reasons for them. Neap tide—low tide—comes twice a month and the moon was in third quarter that night. It's the pull of the moon . . ." Bannen grew contemplative.

Jury held up his hand, palm out. "You've lost me."

"One simply has to look at the tide chart. I did. The killer might have been planning on high tide, the tides and the sand. But he must have miscalculated. Tide wasn't all the way in when the body was found." He rubbed his thumbnail across his forehead. "That's the trouble with murder, wouldn't you say? Counting on the moon?"

Depressed as he was, Jury wanted to laugh. "Somehow I can't imagine Jenny Kennington counting on the moon. And the thing you seem to be forgetting is that counting on it implies a great deal of calculation, not impulse."

Bannen smiled slightly. "Oh, I'm not forgetting, no."

"Who found the body?"

"Coastguard. Otherwise, God knows when she'd have been discovered. I mean this isn't Skegness by a long chalk. As I've said, this area was heavily mined in the war and a lot of mines went missing. Shells, too. The danger areas are clearly marked. Nobody'd be strolling along the Wash for the pleasure of it. It was quite deliberately chosen." Bannen paused. "I narrowed time-of-death down a little more because I think it's quite a reasonable assumption to say she must have been shot between ten-thirty Saturday night and twelve-thirty early Sunday morning. It was close to one A.M. when the gardener said he'd seen her car parked at the end of the driveway, and it would have taken at least fifteen minutes for whoever drove to get back. No one heard the car return." Bannen sighed.

"No one at Fengate called when she didn't come back to the house with Jenny Kennington?" Jury frowned.

"Oh, I expect someone would have done, only, you see, they thought she'd simply taken it into her mind to drive off, or even drive back to London. Since she wasn't with Kennington, they just made that assumption—that she'd driven off. She was like that, apparently, Verna Dunn. Very mercurial, very impulsive. And here she lay." Bannen bent down and scooped up another handful of silt. "You can imagine what it's like trying to find anything in this stuff. My men were down on hands and knees, must have gone over a good quarter mile. Well, you can't cover the whole area, I mean, look at it. A bullet could have traveled for half a mile down there."

Jury followed his gaze across the shining mud, starry with reflections from the weak sunlight. "Yes, I can see that. Wind doesn't help, either, does it?"

"Infernal banshee-winds." He dusted the shale from his hands and shoved them in his coat pockets. "We found a casing pretty much buried, one in the victim." He looked behind him. "Cartridge from a .22 rifle."

"Nothing else?"

"The shell, the gun, the car—? I'd say that's quite a lot."

"You mean you matched the bullet to a gun?" Jury was getting more anxious moment by moment. They did have a lot.

"Max Owen's. He's the owner of Fengate. Jennifer Kennington was the Owens' guest, as I've said."

Jury looked away, out to sea, said nothing.

"There are a surprising number of rifles standing about in the vicinity of Fengate. We gathered up four. Owen's, Parker's, Emery's—Peter Emery's a kind of groundskeeper for a Major Parker. Emery's blind but that doesn't mean someone else couldn't have used his rifle. So we got them all. Oh, and Jack Price even had one. He's an artist, a sculptor or something like that. Why would he need a rifle? And how they all managed to get licenses for these guns, I've no idea. You know how difficult it is. Except for Emery, of course, they're all fair shots, Parker especially."

"You haven't mentioned the women. Somehow, I can't see Jenny Kennington getting off a shot. I don't think she's ever handled a gun in her life."

"Afraid you think wrong, then. She used to go out with her husband occasionally, and Price along with them." Bannen studied the shifting expressions on Jury's face. "You didn't know she knew this man Price before?"

All Jury could muster for an answer was the briefest of headshakes.

Bannen pursed his lips, blew out breath in a soundless whistle. Mildly, he said, "You thought you knew her perhaps better than you knew her."

"Apparently." The Jenny he had fantasized about was a Jenny who, in awful trouble, blurted everything out. Well, why in hell *hadn't* she blurted it out? Because he was one more copper?

". . . tire treads."

Jury had been only dimly aware that Bannen was speaking of the Porsche.

"It did narrow things down a bit. Verna Dunn's Porsche had distinctive treads. The car, with Dunn in it, presumably, and with a passenger— whom of course they assumed to be Jennifer Kennington, but she says not—at any rate, the car drove off about ten-twenty or so—which is when the Owens and Parker heard a car. Price had gone to his digs, his studio, he calls it, and heard nothing."

Jury hunched down in his coat, wishing they could leave this place. The water was lead gray, and looked just as heavy. The sensation Jury felt

in his chest was like descriptions he'd heard of heart attacks, or the pre-
monition of one. The intractable wind, the sand, shale, and mud served
only to remind him of his powerlessness. But he went doggedly on, trying to convince Bannen—or himself—that Jenny Kennington was the
wrong suspect. "You assume Verna Dunn had a passenger. But you don't
know that."

"If she didn't, then how did the Porsche get back to Fengate?"

The question was rhetorical. Of course, he was right. Jury said, more
to fill the alien air with words than anything else, "But now there's this
Reese woman dead. How can you link Jennifer Kennington to *that*? Was
she here?"

"She went back to Stratford-upon-Avon on the Tuesday—that would
have been the fourth—after Verna Dunn was murdered. Stratford, of
course, is only a two-hour drive from here."

What he implied was not lost on Jury, who had no answer.

"Seen enough?"

To last the rest of my life, Jury thought, looking across the Wash and to
the North Sea. On the horizon, a black ship hung motionless.

"You can see the difficulty," said Bannen, again, running his thumb
across his forehead.

3

The two miles between the fen and Fengate were as empty as a map of the Hereafter. No woods, no hedge rows, hills or spinnys. The only dwelling Jury could see was a house far in the distance whose front sat behind tall, thin trees that looked more like bars than trees, straight and evenly spaced. And even this was much like a mirage that remains at the same distance no matter how much closer you think you're getting. Jury felt a little like a runner always running in place; they drove but seemed to get no nearer, in the way that one never succeeds in gaining on illusion.

Jury could not imagine himself living in such a country. The quality of the light added to this static dreamlike landscape, for it made the scene appear almost translucent—a light behind frosted glass. "Is it all like this, this flatness? It seems to go on forever." They had at last passed the farmhouse behind its row of pencil-thin trees. Not an illusion, after all.

"Lincolnshire?" Bannen turned to look at him. "Oh, no. No. You've got the wolds, haven't you, farther north? A lot of people don't like South Lincs, they find it bleak. Too much of a sameness."

Bleak it was. No place to hide.

"Fengate is buried in its own little copse. Used to be a virtual wood." Bannen sighed. "But there again, we've lost our woods, haven't we? Land was needed for crops. Fens were drained for farming. I expect the land had to be managed to sustain human life, but one begins to wonder—will the fens be managed right out of existence? They're a new aristocracy, the farmers. They have the land and that gives them power. You can see how the soil is, unbelievably rich and black. In Cambridge, they're called the

Black Fens because of that rich soil." He sighed. "They don't plow the fields with horses; it's tractors now."

Jury smiled. "Tractors—that's pretty low-key and hardly newfangled. You're waxing romantic, aren't you?"

"Um. Yes. I expect so." But he seemed not to care if Jury found him romantic or found him anything else.

A few cottages straggled by before they turned onto one of the narrower B roads. Jury said, "I can't see Dorcas Reese walking all this distance to go to the Case Has Altered. Didn't look the athletic type to me."

"She'd have taken the public footpath. That cuts off a mile, you see."

And then, as Bannen had said, they came to trees and a road—rough but graded—leading back through the trees.

Fengate was a large but architecturally unimposing house, flat-fronted and square, of no discernible period. It was more stout and sturdy than it was delicately cressellated or turreted; it might have graced the pages of a study on yeomanry. Bannen had suggested what it looked like: the house of one of those "aristocratic" farmers. Behind it and to one side was a large outbuilding that might have served as garage or barn. It had been converted to a dwelling, to judge by the painted window boxes and yellow door.

Bannen stopped the car in a circular drive that enclosed a bed of early-blooming crocuses. An elderly man, presumably the gardener, was tending them. He stepped over to the driver's side after Bannen called to him, leaned down, and pulled at the tip of his cap with his fingers by way of a greeting.

"Are Mr. and Mrs. Owen here, Mr. Suggins?"

"Not him, no suhr. Said what he had to go up t'London." The look on Mr. Suggins's face was almost sad, as if that's the sort of thing these landowners got up to. When Bannen introduced Jury—"Scotland Yard CID"—Mr. Suggins stepped back from the window rather smartly. *Scotland Yard!* This was an altogether different kettle of fish.

"Would you tell her—Mrs. Owen, I mean—I'd like a word with her." Bannen and Jury got out of the car. Mr. Suggins, seemingly at a loss as to what to do with an unexpected visit from both Lincoln and London police, pulled off his cap and motioned them up the front stairs. There was apparently little standing on ceremony or place, for Mr. Suggins preceded them through the front door.

Once in the large entrance hall, he took his leave, saying he would search out Mrs. Owen, and that he would send "the missus" in to them in the meantime. Again he snapped his cap brim by way of taking his leave.

"Who's 'the missus'?" asked Jury.

"Cook. Senior of the staff, I expect. Not that there's much staff, considering the size of the place; cook, maid, kitchen helper—well, that was Dorcas, who did both—then Suggins, who does the grounds, and another chap to help Suggins. He looks a bit arthritic, I'd say. Max Owen is certainly rich enough to keep a dozen servants if he wanted. Look at that chest over there, would you?" Bannen nodded toward an elaborately lacquered domed chest or trunk. "Cost me several months' salary, that lot would."

"You know antiques, do you?"

"No. Max Owen pointed it out to me. Says he's not sure what it's worth because he's suspicious of the lacquering. Needs to have it appraised, he says." Bannen shook his head again. "Imagine being able to put out nine or ten thousand quid for one piece of furniture, and not even a practical piece, at that." Bannen dolefully regarded the chest, apparently imagining what he could buy with the nine or ten thousand. "That'd buy me a three-piece suite several times over, wouldn't it you?"

Jury smiled. The homes of the rich, a number of which he'd seen, didn't register on Jury in terms of what use he could put the money to. Oh, yes, he could certainly do with more money, but the belongings of others were interesting only in terms of what they said about their owners. To what lengths would they go to get them or keep them?

Somewhere in the distance a door banged back and Jury heard what sounded like a tray of crockery approaching. Whoever it was made a noisy and clattering exit from the one part of the house to the other.

It was (he supposed) Mrs. Suggins who came into the room like a stiff breeze, her white apron crackling, with a large silver tray in her hands. The tray she set on a rosewood table and offered them coffee. Both said yes with enthusiasm, and she poured. She was a small woman with well-muscled arms, testament to all of the heavily laden trays she had carried, all of the whippings, stirrings, and mashings she had given all of the cream cakes, potatoes, and puddings over the years. Her gray hair was pulled back from her face, stuck about with pins in some version of a chignon. It was probably a permanent flush that had settled on her cheeks from steam. Indeed, Mrs. Suggins seemed to exhale the steam of the kitchen.

She greeted Chief Inspector Bannen with a no-nonsense authority, and pointed out she'd brought plenty of sugar. "Mr. Bannen here likes his sugar, he does." Her smile was close to possessive as she handed him the bowl and the sugar tongs and watched as he plinked four cubes into his cup. Mrs. Suggins was one of that marvelous breed of kitchen personnel who assume that every visit, every occasion is a signal for the kitchen to tuck up its skirts, tie on its apron, and get to work. Then, realizing that Mr. Bannen had probably not come simply for a well-sugared cup of coffee, but for her master and mistress, she said, "Suggins is looking all over for Mrs. Owen, but we can't think where she's got to." Stoutly, she drew herself up, clucked her tongue, and shook her head. Mrs. Owen might have been a pet or a child, an intractable one at that. Mrs. Suggins went on: "As the master's in London, I'm the only one in the house, except for Suggins. Mr. Price is off in Spalding. Don't tell me something *else* happened."

"Something has, yes. It's your kitchen girl, Mrs. Suggins. It's Dorcas Reese."

As if she'd guessed the errand, Mrs. Suggins took a step backward.

"I'm sorry to have to tell you, but Dorcas was found this morning, early, in one of the dikes in Wyndham Fen. I'm afraid . . . well, I'm afraid she's dead." Bannen stumbled a bit in his reporting.

Mrs. Suggins, Jury thought, had that effect upon one; she was the image of the bountiful but strict nursemaid of one's childhood, who would not put up with silliness and made-up tales.

She looked as if she'd just been slapped. Her face reddened and she put a hand to her cheek. "Dead? *Dorcas?*" Her eyes were wide; she had to lean on the arm of the sofa. "*Dorcas?*" she repeated. She looked up at Bannen as if she hoped he might refute this.

Bannen drank his coffee, looked at her over the edge of the cup, looked as if wishing he could take it all back. But he didn't. He waited for the cook to compose herself a bit, then asked, "Did you see Dorcas around dinnertime last evening?"

"Well, of *course* I did." Back to the business of running a house. "She peeled the vegetables, cut them up, like always. Then we had our tea and she did the serving."

"Did Dorcas tell you whether she was going to the Case Has Altered?"

"No, she didn't. But that's where she usually does go. Too often, to my way of thinking." The chiding mentor part of her nature took firm grip and she drew herself up again, hands folded over her ample stomach. "Last I saw of Dorcas—nineish, it was. I was just arguing with her about the washing up, for dinner would soon be finished. More like nine-thirty, then. That's supposed to be Dorcas's job, but—" Mrs. Suggins's face flushed brightly and she put her hand to her cheek. "Dead? I can't quite take that in. Anyway, Dorcas was eager to leave, well, I didn't mind doing it. There was only the three of them—"

"The Owens and Mr. Price?"

She nodded. "When I was finished, I went up to bed. I'd promised my-self an early night." Then, apparently in anticipation of Bannen's next question, she went on: "There's no use asking me what they did, for I've no idea." And of yet the next: "And, no, I've no idea of anyone who dis-liked Dorcas, disliked or liked. She was so *bland*, Dorcas was. Not much starch to her; not much ginger. She whined a lot, you know, kind of felt sorry for herself."

"What about boyfriends? Anyone serious?"

"Dorcas?" The cook gave a humorless laugh. "Nothing much going there. I hate to say it, but Dorcas wouldn't be the type to attract the men. No, too plain, not pretty at all. Oh, she talked about men, her being just a mite man-crazy, but I didn't listen to half. Except—"

"What?" prompted Bannen.

"It was just that lately, she'd got into a real good mood, but that changed all of a sudden and she went sour. Depressed, or like that. Well, that made me think there *was* some man in the picture." Mrs. Suggins shook her head. "Oh, but to see the poor girl murdered. Well, it doesn't make sense."

"I didn't say she'd been murdered," said Bannen, with that off-centered smile.

Mrs. Suggins looked at him blankly.

"Thanks very much, Mrs. Suggins. Now, if you could have another look for Mrs. Owen, I'd very much appreciate it."

The cook sighed and turned away. "I'll try. But if Suggins hasn't found her by now, no telling where she might have got to."

As she left, Bannen drew a small notebook from his pocket and was thumbing the pages. "I want to call HQ. If you'll excuse me."

Jury took this as a request for privacy and wandered out into the hall.

જ

While Bannen was speaking to someone at headquarters in Lincoln, Jury looked at the bronze busts set into alcoves, a Sheraton escritoire, and a large semicircular sideboard with a mahogany veneer.

Directly across from the doorway through which he had come was another with the same wide double doors, open. The room was bathed in shadows because the curtains were drawn. He supposed it was a sort of gallery; given the paintings lining the left wall. But the most interesting thing about the room was the collection of life-size statues assembled in no particular way. They were marble, the sort of thing one found ordinarily in a garden or at the end of a trellised vista or a columned corridor. Their marble wardrobe ranged from a mere drape around the hips to a full-skirted dress and bonnet. Jury assumed they were part of Owen's collection, or else he'd inherited these modestly smiling women together with the house.

Enough daylight seeped in through chinks in the curtains that Jury could see details that he was sure were not part of the sculptor's vision: as he moved from one statue to another, he saw a slender rope of tiny silver links around one neck; around another's wrist was a silver bracelet; and wound through another's marble curls was a blue ribbon. A long-stemmed blue flower, a hyacinth, he thought, had been placed so as to seem part of one statue's marble bouquet. He doubted these adornments were provided by Max Owen.

"My lord! You weren't supposed to be here until next week!"

Jury whirled at the sound of the voice.

She walked through bars of light made by the narrow openings of the curtains and undid the ornaments, one after the other, all the while keeping Jury in her line of vision as if he might pull something tricky if she didn't watch him. Removing the silver bracelet from one lady, she said, "It seems silly, I know, but I sometimes feel as if they should be compensated for having to live so much of the time in the dark. Max doesn't like opening the curtains because the window's east-facing and the morning sun might damage the paintings. To tell the truth, I think Max has forgotten what he ever intended to do with either the paintings or these ladies." The ribbon and costume jewelry now removed, she went to the last statue and scooped some coins from its upturned hand. "For the launderette. Our machine's on the blink." Then she stopped and studied Jury's face.

"You aren't Mr. Pergilion, are you?" A suspicious note crept in here, as if Jury had misrepresented himself.

"I'm not Mr. Pergilion, no."

Now, as if she'd lost interest in the transaction, she moved back and dumped the coins into the upturned palm of one statue, rewound the ribbon carelessly in another's hair, draped the bracelet back over a wrist, set the hyacinth back on the marble flowers. It was as if she were announcing Jury could take her as he found her, or not at all.

"But I *am* somebody." He smiled.

This didn't seem to stir her curiosity, for she only wanted to talk about who he wasn't. "Mr. Pergilion is the appraiser, you see. Max is always getting one appraiser or another in to value his paintings and furniture. He's thinking of selling off a few pieces, I can't imagine why, we don't need any more money. It's all just his excuse to get somebody in here to talk about his collection. He does it all the time. He exhausted my small store of knowledge long ago." She pointed to a fragile-looking writing desk and said, "This is one of the pieces Max wants to have valued. I love it. It's *bonheur-du-jour.*" The satinwood table sat on long narrow legs, with small

painted doors decorated with birds and flowers. "It's worth a few thousand, but a lot more if the painter was famous. I imagine Max hopes he'll
find out the painter's name."

She stopped in the act of replacing the silver necklace and held it
twined in her fingers, lost in some sort of difficult thought, judging from
her expression. The necklace looked much like a rosary and she looked
meditative as a nun. A dove gray dress with a soft white lace collar, straight
and shining hair, and that imperturbable face. Now she moved over to the
windows. "Whenever Max goes up to London, I open the curtains,
which is why I'm here—" It was almost as if she needed to justify her
turning up in her own house. Saying so, she pulled the cord on the curtain nearest her. "—because I think it's sad always having to stand in
shadow." She proceeded down the wall, opening each curtain in turn.
Until she stopped in front of him. "I'm Grace Owen." She held out her
hand.

Grace Owen could only improve with light and proximity. "Richard
Jury." He took her hand, cool as marble. Then he removed his identification and held it out. "Scotland Yard CID."

Her smile disappeared and it made him feel oddly sad. "You mean
Scotland Yard's investigating Verna's death?"

Jury shook his head. "I'm here only at the sufferance of Chief Inspector Bannen. It's not my case. I just happen to be a good friend of one of
your guests—your guest when it happened, I mean. Lady Kennington?"

"Jennifer Kennington. Oh, yes. This awful business about Verna has
been—hard on her, I'm afraid." Speculatively, she regarded Jury, as if
wondering whose side he was on. "But she's back in Stratford-upon-
Avon. It's been two weeks since—" She pulled a tissue from her skirt
pocket and was rubbing at a spot on the statue's arm. "The inspector
talked to everyone; what else is there to discover?"

"What happened."

Again, her look seemed to be assessing the situation. "Didn't Jennifer
tell you?"

Jury almost started himself to rub at a place on the statue's other arm.
"We've not—I haven't seen her actually, I mean—well, police work. You
know."

No—he thought her look said—she didn't. That this *detective* friend hadn't gone to the trouble of at least *asking* Jenny what had happened . . . Jury imagined this particular guilt-trip to be one of his own devising.

But Grace Owen made no comment; she dampened the tissue with her tongue and rubbed at the arm again. It was strangely erotic. "I can tell you what I know, if you like." She pocketed the tissue and walked over to the window. "They'd both gone outside, to that little wood—" She stopped. "Isn't that him? The chief inspector from Lincoln police?"

Jury joined her at the window. Bannen was standing at the edge of the trees, talking to the gardener.

"Why is he here, anyway?" she asked.

Jury suddenly realized that he hadn't told her about Dorcas Reese. "He's here because he has some bad news, I'm afraid." Having said that, he felt he could hardly refuse to tell her. "One of your staff, a woman named Dorcas Reese, was found in one of the canals on that National Trust property. Wyndham Fen, I think the name is. She's dead."

"What?" Her hands flew to her face. "That poor girl. But how? What happened?"

Jury hesitated. It wasn't his place to supply details. "We're not sure. The pathologist isn't finished. Chief Inspector Bannen came to talk to you and your husband."

"I expect he wants to ask me more questions."

Jury nodded, relieved that "more questions" didn't appear to cause her any anxiety.

She said, "Well, I expect I must go and talk to him."

As they started for the door, Jury looked again at the *bonheur-du-jour.* He smiled a little, thinking. "Are the other pieces as nice as this? That your husband wants valued?"

"What?" Muddled, she brought herself back from the death of her servant and said, "Oh, yes. I don't know all of what he says he wants to sell— he won't sell them, of course—it's all a kind of ritual he goes through when he gets bored." They were at the door and she pointed at an escritoire. "Here's another. Do you like antiques, then? Old rugs and things? There's an Ispahan carpet in the living room that's apparently 'of doubtful provenance,' as my husband would say."

"Don't know a thing about them. I have a friend who lives in Northants who's an appraiser, though."

"Don't tell my husband or he'll have him down here in a heartbeat."

"Really?"

"He threatened once he was going to sell off the cold ladies."

"Who?"

"This lot." She looked back at the marble statues. "That's what I call them, 'the cold ladies.'"

4

The day was cold and monochromatic, which suited Melrose Plant perfectly, for he wanted to brood. As much as he looked forward to seeing Richard Jury, Melrose simply couldn't think of the right approach to take regarding Jenny Kennington.

For the last twenty minutes or so he'd been walking through the grounds of Ardry End, pondering the call from Jury, and was now surprised to find himself far from his house in a stand of sycamore trees that were part of the woods Ardry End shared with Watermeadows. Difficult to know where one stopped and the other started. He stopped and looked at Watermeadows through the openings in the trees and thought of Miss Fludd. For the last couple of days, he'd been almost wholly caught up in this Lincolnshire business, but she'd been tucked away behind some door in his mind which she only occasionally opened to see if he was occupied—He was? And the door closed softly again.

He shook his drooping head.

A shot rang out.

Melrose turned quickly: what the devil? He thought he'd caught a glimpse of a dark-coated figure making a dash through those pines over there. He knew who that was, all right. It was Mr. Momaday, Ardry End's self-appointed "groundskeeper." The man had actually been hired to do what gardening there was; but Momaday insisted on calling himself "groundskeeper." He'd done precious little "keeping" if one were to judge from the weedy flowerbeds and the untrimmed herbaceous borders. What Momaday did do was patrol the grounds like some damned

Nazi and let off salvos at squirrels, rabbits, pheasant—whatever came within his gunsights. Melrose had told him to stop it. He did not believe in shooting for sport, and the Ardry End larder provided enough food that they didn't need to kill it on the hoof or on the wing. But the property was so extensive that Momaday knew he could blast away without anyone's being the wiser, since Melrose rarely roamed his distant acres or sought shelter in his darkling wood.

Fortunately for the animal life, the man was a wretched shot. Melrose had decided the only way Momaday would ever pick off squirrel or rabbit was if one was bent on suicide and strode purposefully into the gunman's path, shouting, "Come on, Momaday, you'd be doing me a favor, man!" Only then would he (who seemed to consider himself a killing machine) bag any game.

Melrose sighed and continued his walk. He was not sure why walking in the open air was more conducive to sorting things out than sticking to one's armchair and fireplace and port. Perhaps the thoughts themselves being punishing, the body must follow suit. Thus a frigid, sunless day was a better environment for troubled thoughts than a soft, sunny one. One must dress for the occasion, too. Stout boots were a must, and his green Barbour jacket. And it was always a point scored if one were to carry a shotgun broken over one's arm. Mr. Momaday had the only shotgun, though, and he was using it.

He stopped to inspect a tiny white flower, a mere drop of a flower, and wondered if it was a snowdrop. The name made sense. A bit farther along, he paused to run his finger along a long tendrily vine growing up the side of a tree. Was it ivy? Most vines were, so he left it at that and went back to brooding over Jury's impending visit.

The next moment he heard his name—*"Melrose!"*— being bruited about in the dim distance. He knew it was Agatha, no doubt come for her tea. There was one thing Melrose had learned long ago: Never underestimate his aunt's skill in ferreting out information. His butler Ruthven was total proof against wiliness, threats, and lies, so Melrose's whereabouts were safe with him. Might she decide to enlist Momaday's aid—?

Another shot rang out.

He was going to kill someone some day, Momaday was.

What a lovely fantasy.

_ஸி_

The all-clear having been sounded by Ruthven (the old dinner-gong put to this use), Melrose found himself back in the sitting room with the port and walnuts he was sorry he'd left in the first place. Agatha had, of course, left more than one message in his absence, none of which he paid any attention to.

For now he was much more interested in Richard Jury's forthcoming visit. And what he would have to say about Jenny Kennington. He felt guilty, he supposed, about that day in Littlebourne, innocent though it had been. Besides that, he'd given rather short shrift to Polly Praed, whom he hadn't seen in years. He sighed. Was this the sort of man he'd become, ogling every good-looking woman, flitting from one to another like a bee or a butterfly? He sat there feeling morose, picking at the paper napkin beside the dish of walnuts. Finally, he took out his pen and, unfolding the napkin, wrote a list of names:

> VIVIAN RIVINGTON
> POLLY PRAED
> ELLEN TAYLOR
> JENNY KENNINGTON
> MISS FLUDD (NANCY)

He tapped his pen, thinking for a moment and then added

> BEA SLOCUM

The nib of his fountain pen caught as he put brackets around Jenny's name. She should not be on any list of his. Neither should Bea Slocum, if it came to it. So he had written her name very small. She was much too young for him. He looked at Jenny's name again and, reluctantly, crossed it out.

On the right-hand side of the napkin he wrote "Comments." This was always the best way, wasn't it? Make a list and write down the "fors" and "againsts"? It was supposed to help clear the mind and get one's perspective right. He had his head in his hands, trying to think what to write down for Vivian (either for or against) and all he could come up with was Count Dracula, her fiancé. Otherwise his mind refused to respond. His concentration on the name *Vivian Rivington* was so intense that he didn't hear the approaching footsteps, and was surprised by Ruthven's voice.

"It's Superintendent Jury, sir," said Ruthven, from the doorway.

Melrose started up as Jury came through the door. Even though he didn't know quite what to say to him, still, he was delighted to see him. "Richard!" They clasped each other's hands. "But . . . how've you been?"

"Passable."

"Good lord, it's been so long since I've seen you."

Jury arched an eyebrow. "Two weeks?"

"Yes, well, it seems so long. Let Ruthven get you a drink. Sit down!"

Jury told Ruthven he'd like some whiskey and sat down opposite Melrose.

Melrose told Ruthven to top up the decanter and then they wouldn't have to bother him again. He sat back and allowed himself to hope that the subject of Jenny wouldn't come up. Stupid. How to avoid her coming up? She was in the thick of a murder investigation.

But Jury seemed more interested in the paper napkin that Melrose had left on the table, gathering up droplets of condensed water. "What's this, then?"

"A list." His hand moved to pick it up but Jury was too quick for him.

"I think I know some of these people," Jury said, straightfaced. "Not Miss Fludd, though. I don't know her."

Since he didn't, that subject was at least safe. Melrose expelled his held breath. "A neighbor. You remember Watermeadows—" He cut himself off. Watermeadows had marked an especially unhappy period in Jury's life. God, talking to him about women was like negotiating a minefield. The worst things happened to Jury's women.

Jury's expression betrayed nothing, however. He said, "A neighbor you don't know very well, I take it. Hence the 'Miss.'" Jury smiled. "And here's Bea Slocum, of all people. Hmm. Interesting to speculate on what these women have in common."

Good grief, was anything worse than to have written something exceedingly personal and have someone else come along and read it? Melrose was damned glad he hadn't yet filled in the "Comments" column.

Ruthven swanned in with their drinks. Jury thanked him and then went on, relentlessly. "Could these be the women in your life?" His smile was wicked.

"What? Of course not." Melrose let out a snort, dismissing this idea.

"Oh. Well, since I know them, then it must be a list of the women in my life. Except for Miss Fludd, of course." He held up the napkin. "Nancy. That her name, is it?"

Melrose adopted a superior tone. "Tell me, Richard, is this what you came to see me about? Is this what you traveled all the way from Lincolnshire for?"

"No. Look here, you didn't put anything down under 'Comments.' Are all of these women comment-less, then?"

Melrose faked an easy smile. Jury could stick to a subject like glue when he wanted to. He was apparently set to grill Melrose on this napkin list until he came up with some acceptable explanation. This was the way Jury handled befuddled and guilty suspects. "Oh, that." He waved a hand, brushing aside Jury's questions with feigned self-assurance. "Well, I hadn't got around to it, had I?"

"Let's."

"Let's what?"

"Make some comments." Jury took a ballpoint pen from his pocket and clicked it several times in a most annoying manner.

Melrose coughed. Why wasn't he better at thinking on his feet? Why didn't ideas come hurtling off the top of his mind? "I was just noting down their names as witnesses. They've all been witnesses at one time or another; I was just pondering who'd make the best witness. You know—which one would be the most reliable." *That* was quick thinking! He was pleased with himself.

"Why'd you cross out Jenny?"

Melrose studied the jumping flames of the fireplace. He shrugged. "Well, I wasn't sure she *was* a witness."

"Yes, you are. You wouldn't have had to go looking for her otherwise."

Jury was just stitching him up, he knew that. Jury with his poker-face. No wonder suspects wanted to confess. Yet, he did seem to be in a good mood and ready for a joke. "We haven't met since—" He was bringing it up himself, that fatal meeting in Littlebourne. Oh, hell . . . but the words were out now "—since you came back from New Mexico." He kept his head down, making wet circles with his glass on the little rosewood table, ruining the finish. "I mean that we've actually been sitting down talking . . ." he added lamely.

Jury merely nodded. Then he said, "I never thanked you. Macalvie told me you'd been a real help. And God knows Wiggins appreciated it."

Melrose was surprised. He laughed. "Wiggins didn't need me. He loved that hospital. That nurse—" Melrose snapped his fingers. "What's her name—?"

"Lillywhite." Jury smiled, drank his whiskey. His glance strayed again to the napkin.

Melrose wished he'd stop eyeing it. "Nurse Lillywhite. That's the one. He had her running all over London looking for books."

"And still does. Apparently she's 'done wonders'—his words—for his health. And his temperament. Both of which have always been perfectly sanguine, far as I'm concerned."

They spent some moments speaking of the case that had taken Jury to New Mexico. They talked until the subject was fairly well exhausted. Melrose had taken out his cigarette case and offered one to Jury, who refused. "Thanks, but if you remember, I quit."

"That's right. I didn't expect it would last. Good for you."

"It's only been eighteen and a third days, but who's counting?"

"I doubt I could do it for eighteen minutes. I'd sooner give this up"— and he raised his whiskey glass—"than cigarettes."

Jury laughed. "You need a confederate; someone who's trying to stay stopped too. Whenever I think I can't stand it one bloody minute longer, I ring up Des."

"Who's Des?"

"Young lady at Heathrow. She works at one of the cigarette and to-bacco kiosks. Hell of an environment if you're trying to stop smoking. We got in a conversation about it, and I told her I'd stay stopped at least as long as she did. It was a pact, I guess you'd call it. Like the ones you made when you were a kid, you know, never to tell on the other one, that sort of thing."

"Oh, nobody trusted me, none of my little friends."

Jury laughed. "No wonder."

"I always had to put up cash. It was a damned racket with them." They both laughed, and Melrose looked at the coal end of his cigarette. "But it's a good idea, that. A pact. Who could I make one with? Marshall True-blood? Anyway, I can't imagine Trueblood giving up those candy-cane Sobranies."

"It's part of his rap."

"Rap?"

"You know, his game. His persona."

"For Trueblood the rap's all there is. Now, what is it you want me to do? What dire plot? What exquisite scheme have you in mind?"

Jury slid down in his favorite soft leather chair, balanced his drink on his knee, and studied the ceiling. "Remember the Lake District? The Holdsworths?"

"Oh, ha! I'm not going back there!"

"Don't tell me you didn't enjoy it because I know you did."

Melrose hemmed and hawed, vastly moderating his enjoyment of it. "If you want me to be a librarian again, forget it."

"No, nothing like that."

"Thank the lord."

"I want you to be an appraiser."

Melrose frowned over the rim of his glass. "A what?"

"You know. Some bloke who goes round telling people what their old stuff is worth." Jury finished off his drink and held out his glass. "You're the host."

"I don't *know* what anybody's old stuff is worth." Melrose took their glasses to the sideboard where Ruthven had set the decanter. He poured two fingers of whiskey into Jury's glass, held it out for him. "I don't even know what *my* old stuff is worth." He splashed whiskey into his own glass, returned to his chair.

"I just want you to be an antiques appraiser. Hell, you can cardshark your way through this assignment. You did with the librarian act."

"For God's sake, that was *books*. *Books*! Of course I know something about books. I know sod-all about antiques. Send Trueblood."

Jury ignored that. "I need someone inside the house. Fengate. It's near Spalding."

"Near Spalding is it? Oh well, that makes all the difference! Where in hell's Spalding?"

"South Lincolnshire. Little Holland."

"Little *who*? Anyway, these people with their unvalued antiques would hardly want a strange chap actually staying with them." Melrose took a hearty swig of his drink, having put paid to Jury's idea. "A boarder. My, doesn't that sound a treat of a role? I'll shuffle into breakfast every morning in my out-at-elbow brown cardigan and hairy jacket." Melrose reflected for a moment. "Tattershall. Isn't that castle up there someplace? You know, the one that what's-his-name—Lord Curzon?—was so fond of and gave a lot of money for restoring?"

"Don't be daft."

"Me? You're the one that's daft, expecting me to masquerade as a . . . Truebloodian."

"I'm not suggesting you masquerade at all. You're to go as plain old Melrose Plant. You'll just know a bit more about antiques than you usually do." Jury's smile was brief and bright.

"Well 'plain old Melrose Plant' doesn't know *anything*."

"All right, so you're not an expert and it's true you might not know enough to fool Max Owen—"

Relieved, Melrose sat back. "Glad you've come to your senses."

"—so you can take lessons from Trueblood."

Melrose sat up straight as a stick. "Lessons from *Trueblood*? A ha ha ha." Melrose slapped his thigh in this pretense of wild laughter. "Oh ha ha ha ha."

Jury ignored this outburst. "It wouldn't take long at all. That's because I know the particular pieces—at least the ones he has in mind now—that he wants valued. So, you see, it's not a matter of your knowing *everything*."

"It's a matter of knowing *nothing* that bothers me. Send Diane Demorney. She's the *perfect* choice, since in her uncluttered mind is but one little fact about nearly everything in the world, from Stendhal to baseball. She could flummox this—what's his name?"

"Max Owen. There've been two murders. So far."

Melrose swirled the whiskey in his glass. "Really? Well, who's in charge of this case?"

"Detective Chief Inspector Bannen. DCI Arthur Bannen. Lincoln police. Not your typical village yob. He's too smart by half."

"He'll see through me in an instant."

"Of course he won't. He doesn't know anything about the value of *bonheurs-du-jour*."

"I don't even know what it *is*, much less what it's worth!" Melrose snorted. Then he said, "Two murders." Melrose seriously thought this over, then gave it up. "I revert to an earlier point: the family wouldn't want a stranger moving in, not on top of that. How would they know I'm not the Fiend of the Fens who'll strangle them in their sleep?"

"I think they'd be delighted to have a bloke around. Grace because she's very friendly, her husband because he's got a weakness for a title."

Melrose sat up again. "I beg your pardon. I do not have a title."

"You're an earl."

"*Ex*-earl! Ex-!" Melrose got to his feet. Swayed a bit. "E-X, extinct. I'm the brontosaurus of earldom."

"You've still got some of those old cards. Calling cards with crests on them." Jury smiled. "I've seen you use them, haven't I? So it isn't as if you've never done this before. It's not as if you've never thrown your earldom or earlhood around to suit yourself. Once an earl, always an earl. It's like being Catholic."

"*Your*self, you mean. Not once in a dozen years have I become an earl again except where it suited *you*, old bean."

Jury held out his glass again. "As long as you're up."

Melrose went to his Waterford decanter, fuming. He splashed more whiskey in both glasses. A lot of it. "Those occasions—precious few of them, last time was in Dartmoor, wasn't it?—have always been to help you out. Here—" He handed Jury his glass. "But wanting me to be—"

"This is to help me out again. And Jenny—"

"—an antiques-expert besides—"

"—Kennington."

Melrose fell silent. As Jury looked at him mildly, he sat back down in his wing chair, stared into the fire, said, finally: "Jenny? Be serious, will you?"

"I am being. Jenny's a witness."

Melrose gave a short bark of laughter. "I should know. I was all over hell's half-acre looking for—" He could have cut off his tongue, bringing that up again.

"And prime suspect."

"*What?*" Melrose sat forward.

"DCI Bannen seems to think so. At least that was the strong implication." Jury told him about the murder of Verna Dunn. "The ex-wife, shot with a .22 rifle."

Melrose felt a little ashamed of himself. He was more intrigued than disturbed. "What in heaven's name is gained by killing off the *former* wife?"

"Especially in view of the more recent murder. One of the staff. A kitchen helper."

Melrose put down his glass. "A second murder?"

Jury told him what had happened.

"Wouldn't that obliterate any motive for killing the ex-wife, though?"

Jury shrugged again. "That depends, doesn't it? We don't know the motive for either murder. There's also opportunity. The two of them, Jenny and the Dunn woman, were outside, arguing. This was the last time anyone saw Verna Dunn alive."

"Good lord . . . well, in view of this kitchen-help getting murdered too—obviously your DCI Bannen thinks it's the same person."

"Probably."

"Well, then." Melrose studied the fire again. "Jenny isn't there now, is she?"

Jury shook his head. "She's in Stratford again."

"So if Bannen thinks it was the same person, that lets her off, anyway." Melrose picked up his glass again.

"Except for where she was the night of the fourteenth. It's only a couple of hours, three at best, from Stratford-upon-Avon to Fengate."

"God, but you sound like prosecuting QC."

"It's absurd without a motive. Only . . . I think DCI Bannen knows a lot that he's not telling me. Still, I find it too difficult to believe . . ." Jury slid down in the leather chair, eyes on the ceiling again.

In spite of the unhappiness of the subject, Melrose felt how pleasant it was, sitting here talking with Jury, how much it felt as if the clock had been turned back. Only it hadn't, and he had to get this off his chest. "Look, Richard. That day at Stonington—"

"What about it?"

"You left in such a hurry. . . . Well, I've always felt pretty rotten about that. I mean I thrust myself upon the scene—"

"But you were there only because I asked you to help find her. That's all. So how can you say you 'thrust yourself upon the scene'? A noticeably archaic manner of speaking, I must say." Jury smiled and drank his whiskey and held up the napkin he'd left on the chair arm. "That's not the reason you crossed her out, I hope. I'd say the decision here is monumental."

"What decision?"

"I mean, if this were another kind of list. Such as a list of women you might possibly love. Or even marry."

"*What? What?*" Melrose sputtered. "Marry? *Me?* Who in hell would I be marrying, anyway?" Melrose uttered a short bark of laughter.

Jury waved the napkin. "One of these, presumably."

"*Don't* be daft!" Melrose fell silent again. "I just didn't want you to get the idea that I was—" What? he wondered. "Lady Kennington and I aren't especially . . . compatible."

"Funny. I'd have thought the opposite."

"That's where you're wrong. I find her, well, a bit . . . dry. Do you know what I mean?"

Jury shook his head. "No. Dry like a twig?"

Exasperated, Melrose answered. "No. Of course not."

"Like a leaf? Like a Diane Demorney martini? *There's* the quintessence of dryness for you."

Melrose plowed on. "Jenny is not my type at all. I'm not criticizing her, understand. It's just that different people get on with . . . for instance, I can't imagine you and Ellen Taylor really hitting it off."

"I can." Jury took another gulp of his drink. "As a matter of fact, I can imagine hitting it off with any one of these women. Excepting Miss Fludd, naturally. Whom I don't know."

"I mean, relatively speaking. Oh, hell—"

Jury's laughter was sincere and hearty. "You're a terrible liar. Anyway, it's all forgotten, that episode at Stonington."

Melrose found this difficult to believe. "You're sure?"

"Absolutely. I mean how could I hold that against you when you're about to do me this tremendous favor. Being an antiques expert and an earl and going to school to Marshall Trueblood. Hell, you'd have to be a great friend to do that." Jury smiled expansively.

"Blackmail."

"Who? *Moi?* Surely you don't think I'd stoop—"

Melrose regarded him through narrow eyes. "To anything."

"Okay, I will certainly admit I was very upset—mad as hell, I expect, that day at Stonington. I drove all the way to Salisbury to wander around Old Sarum, that godforsaken ruin. Well, that was the case we were working on then. And I met this chap who works there. He reminded me of Othello's rush to judgment over Desdemona. All Othello saw was a handkerchief." He smiled at Melrose. "You can't rush to judgment over a handkerchief, can you? Or a napkin?" Jury waved it back and forth, at the same time running his eyes over the ceiling, one corner to another. "And we're forgetting something, aren't we?"

"What?"

"It's not our decision. It's hers. Whether she fancies one or the other of us—or even Max Owen. That's her decision. We're being pretty macho if we think it's ours."

Melrose felt a great weight lift; he breathed more easily. For that was true. It wasn't their decision. He raised his glass. "Friends again?"

Jury raised his. "Always have been, far as I'm concerned. But there's one thing I do have to say."

Jury's expression was grim as he sat looking at the ceiling, and Melrose felt a frisson of anxiety. "Yes, what?"

"For an earl you've got a hell of a lot of cobwebs up there."

5

"A drop of this and I'll be right as rain," said Wiggins, tap-tapping a spoon against his cup.

Richard Jury looked up from the small pink message slips scrambled on his blotter and wondered what on earth had brought his sergeant to this state of sanguinity. The sergeant had never been "right as rain" in all the long years of their association. He was getting smug, really. Wiggins could be insufferably smug. Well, there wasn't going to be any *con*-sanguinity on the part of Jury. He flicked a glance the sergeant's way and saw Wiggins was stirring something in a glass, something thick, amber, and medicinal. Wiggins stirred slowly and thoughtfully.

Waiting for him to comment, thought Jury. If there was anything Jury didn't feel, it was "sanguine." Still sorting through his call slips, he could feel Wiggins's eyes on him, boring into his carefully constructed silence. Of course, Wiggins's announcement—for it had all of the gravitas of an engraved card or a black-edged telegram—was supposed to call forth an astonished gasp, or at least an eyebrow raised in query.

Getting neither, Wiggins stopped stirring and tapped his spoon again on the rim of his cup in regular beats that had the curious effect of sounding like a censer, shaking down clouds of bells or raindrop tinkles. Jury wouldn't have been too surprised to find the air perfumed with incense. Wiggins's complaints usually took on the tincture of ritual and religiosity. Now, he was sighing. Heavily. "So what's got you in such a life-affirming mood?" asked Jury, giving in.

Wiggins gave him a smile like the weak crescent of a waning moon.

"Life-affirming? Oh, no, it's just Vera has made me see that sometimes I talk myself into feeling under the weather."

Vera? Jury looked at Wiggins. "Vera?"

"Vera Lillywhite."

Jury frowned. *Nurse* Lillywhite? "You mean Nurse Lillywhite?"

"Well, she *has* got a first name." Wiggins seemed affronted.

"Yes, but you never use it." Did this mean the relationship had shifted to ground farther up?

From a thermos Wiggins poured an amber-colored, thickish liquid into the cup to which he'd just dropped some feathery-looking stuff and assured Jury that yes, he and Vera had got to know one another rather well.

Jury remembered Nurse Lillywhite as a plumpish, rather pretty woman of unfailingly happy temperament. Well, you'd have to have a pleasant temperament, wouldn't you, to take on Wiggins's ills. Taking care of Wiggins was no small matter. There were, to begin, his complex ailments; that is, what Wiggins thought were his ailments—all of them fairly minor, but in such numbers they would war with one another, so that a flare-up of catarrh would exacerbate a fit of ague. Wiggins claimed to suffer from these medieval conditions, ones that Jury thought had been stamped out with the Black Death.

Jury quoted: "'Oh, Gertrude, Gertrude, when ailments come, they come not single file, but in battalions.'" At Wiggins's deep frown, Jury said, "Just quoting Claudius. You know, *Hamlet's* Claudius. Except there it was sorrows. 'When sorrows come.'" But Shakespeare only served to remind him of Stratford-upon-Avon and Jenny Kennington. He turned glum again.

Then Wiggins said, "Anyway, Vera's got me off a lot of my medications—"

Oh really? Then what's in those two bottles and what's that orange swill in your thermos?

"—and onto a health regimen. Vera believes in a holistic approach, you know, treating the whole person."

"Were you only treating parts before?"

Wiggins uncapped one of the bottles and dropped something into the stuff in his glass that made it fizz. Bromo-Seltzer, probably, thought Jury. He'd been addicted to the stuff ever since the Baltimore trip.

Wiggins said, "I'm trying to be serious, sir."

"Sorry." Jury watched him twirl the cap back on the bottle, the movement of his fingers annoyingly lithe and balletic. A man without woman problems. Jury felt even more depressed.

"I'd think you'd be pleased. After all, it's you who've suffered as much as me."

Nobody could suffer as much as Wiggins. But Jury was touched by his considering the possibility. "Holistic. Is that the medicine made of beet tops and things like that?"

"You're thinking of 'homeopathic.'"

Psychopathic was more like it, he thought, as he watched Wiggins's glass sneeze up a spray of bubbles.

"Homeopathic's this sort of thing." Wiggins held up a small tube. "Natural medicine is what it is."

Jury nodded toward the amber glutinous stuff. "What's that, then?"

"Apricot juice with seafern." Wiggins held the glass up as if toasting or blessing the office and tossed the lot back. He set down the glass with an *aaahh* as if he were a sailor who'd just had a shot of overproof rum.

Jury had to admit listening to Wiggins was in itself pretty good therapy. It took his mind off things, since he felt like strangling him a lot of the time and that used up energy that might instead have been consumed by brooding over Jenny Kennington.

This morning he had had a message from Jenny, but not in person. The message had come via Carole-anne Palutski, which was a whole different thing. It was akin to no message at all. What Jenny had really said and what Carole-anne *said* Jenny had said was the difference between chalk and cheese.

That morning Jury had opened his door to find the dog Stone sitting there with a pink slip in his mouth like a second tongue.

This was Carole-anne's new way of delivering phone messages to Jury that she hoped would get lost, or drooled all over, or even eaten before

Jury had a chance to read them. Messages that got this treatment were from women that Carole-anne didn't know and therefore couldn't approve and wouldn't approve if she did know them, since Superintendent Jury wasn't to move, woman-wise, beyond the circle of his Islington digs.

The caramel-colored Labrador lived on the floor above between Jury and Carole-anne. Clearly the message had come last night or earlier this morning when he'd been out and Carole-anne was in, *in* meaning in his, Jury's, flat. Instead of writing it down and leaving it beside the phone as any normal person would have done, she had taken it up to her own flat, elaborated to the point of indecipherableness—Jury strained his eyes, cursing the tiny handwriting—and then had given it to the dog to deliver. Shortly after the dog's appearance, Carole-anne herself had come running down the stairs, a blob of brilliant blue and red-gold, hurrying off to work, *sorry, Super, got to run*—when he had tried to stop her about the message.

Irritated beyond belief, Jury had put the kettle on and then tried through squinty eyes and reading glasses to get some sense out of it:

Afraid please may come from links mix own fungus

and blank, blank, blank—impossible to read at all—then

Straightforward to rest.

and the rest of it a little black-ink melting pot. Wait'll he got Carole-anne alone.

He went back over it. *Afraid* he understood. Was the next word *please*? "Please come." No, "*police*," that was it. So it must be Lincs police-something. *Mix own.* Jury scratched his head. Max Owen! that must be it. But it still didn't make sense. *Fungus.* Fun . . . oh, for God's sake, "Fengate." Had Carole-anne been right there, he'd probably have throttled her.

Yet, the other messages she'd taken last night were clear as crystal and in block letters:

INSPECTOR SAM LASKO CALLED AND CLEANERS CALLED
ABOUT YOUR SWEATER THEY RUND.

Had Jury not been privy to the cleaner's having spilled dye on his sweater, he would have been at a loss over RUND. Stone watched as Jury tried to squint up the words in the Jenny-message. He knew the reason for what seemed like paragraphs of writing: recently he had complained that a message from Jenny had translated by Carole-anne into "ZILCH." So now she was writing everything she could think of in this tiny little misspelled hand. Fortunately, the kettle whistled before he went daft or blind.

Stone followed him into the kitchen where Jury dashed some loose tea into the teapot. He muttered, "'Straightforward, straightforward . . .'" He looked up. *Stratford!* My God. Who else but Carole-anne could manage that interpretation? "To Stratford to rest." Jury held up the pot and said to Stone: "Shall I be Mother?"

The dog appeared to nod.

Maybe Jury should give the message to Stone to interpret.

Though he was afraid he knew what "to rest" meant.

◆

Wiggins's voice brought him out of this reverie. "You should try some of Vera's remedies, sir. Really, I've felt quite free of symptoms the last week or two. Like having a holiday by the sea." He breathed deeply, as if inhaling the air on Brighton's pebbled beach.

Jury shook his head. He failed to see the effect of Nurse Lillywhite's nostrums, but he supposed the point was that Wiggins saw it. Perhaps that's all change meant: rearrangement. If you stopped being addicted to Bromo-Seltzer and black biscuits, you'd become addicted to apricot juice and seafern. Addictive personalities, that's what he and Wiggins were. Hadn't had a smoke now for a month (well, three weeks, well nineteen days—oh, who was he kidding; he knew it down to the insufferable hour!). Now, what was this new addiction? To lethargy, probably. He found it difficult to move.

The ringing of the phone made him jump.

"Fiona," said Wiggins as he replaced the receiver. "Says you're to come round to see the guv'nor. When he gets back from his club."

"And just when will that be?"

Wiggins shrugged.

∽

Fiona Clingmore sat behind her desk with the patience of Job, waiting, apparently, for whatever she had on her face to turn her into Madonna. What she had on her face looked like thick layers of cling film or one of those clear plastic masks. A face under ice, static and frozen.

"Hullo, Fiona. Cyril." Jury nodded toward the copper-colored cat Cyril, who sat in regal splendor, tail coiled about his paws, with equal patience, as if he too were embalmed in ice. Cyril, Jury thought, could beat all of them in the looks department. "What's that stuff?"

Fiona had begun to peel away the mask, starting at her forehead. She couldn't answer (beyond saying something like "*um buh mau allah*") with the mask still around her mouth; she held up a pale yellow and white jar with a label that read *Pearlift*. Finally free of this youth-giving anodyne, Fiona said, "It's a lift. If you take the regular course of treatments—that'd be two a week—it'll take years off. See?" She turned her face this way and that.

Fiona looked exactly the same. "Beautiful."

"It's a new discovery. It's got crushed oyster shell in it, which they say tightens the pores and firms you."

"I've always thought oysters looked surprisingly wrinkle-free."

Fiona sniffed as she plucked lipstick and eyeliner from her sponge bag. "You can laugh. You're a man. Disgusting the way so many men just get better-looking as they get older. Look at Sean Connery, for instance. But women, they just go downhill. Name me one woman—*one*—you can say looks better with age." She applied eyeliner as Cyril, who had sprung up to her desk, stalked the sponge bag.

"Mrs. Wassermann?"

Fiona put down the liner. "You mean that grandmum type that lives in your building? How old's she, then?"

"Seventy-five, around."

Fiona frowned. "Well, how old was she when you first saw her?"

"I don't know. Sixty? Sixty-five?" Jury shrugged.

"Well that doesn't count, for heaven's sake."

"Why not? She looks better. You said—"

"Oh, stop. Come on, I want to show you something."

Jury followed Fiona into Racer's office. Cyril followed Jury.

The thing that Jury's eye first lit on was a wire cage that resembled the sort the air carriers used for transporting animals. "What the hell's *that?*"

"You watch," said Fiona, winding up the mechanical coyote that Jury had brought back from Santa Fe and which (for some reason Jury couldn't imagine) was sitting on the desk blotter of Chief Superintendent Racer—or, as Wiggins liked to call him, "the guv'nor."

Fiona set the little coyote, tightly wound, on the floor. It zipped off, making straight for the cage.

It didn't take much intelligence to work out that Cyril was supposed to be in hot pursuit of the toy coyote.

Cyril yawned.

"Well, of course," said Fiona, "that cat's bored with it already."

Jury was over examining the cage. Inside was a small dish with something oily in it, tinned herring, perhaps. He reached his hand in and the cage fell down on his wrist. Another of Racer's Cyril-traps. Jury shook his head. "Then what? Racer calls British Airways and sends the cat to Siberia?"

"Can you believe he'd think Cyril's so stupid he'd fall for something like that? I don't know what the point is."

Jury was looking at the mechanical coyote. "What's he got on here, a magnet?"

Fiona nodded. "And hitched one to the cage, too. So the coyote—"

"Keep away from the sardines, Jury," said the voice of Chief Superintendent Racer, who at that moment was coming through the door. "If you want lunch, there's a caff down the street."

Seeing Racer, Cyril's tail began twitching. His head swiveled. Mobilizing his forces, thought Jury. Cyril turned and streaked out of the office.

"You wanted to see me?" Jury settled into the chair on the other side of the big desk, the mendicant's side.

Racer's smile was carved in ivory. "Not especially." The smile vanished. "What in hell's going on with this Danny Wu business? That restaurant's set up for traffic in drugs and you know it. You've been on this for months!"

"Years." Jury corrected him.

"When am I going to see some results?"

"I expect when you hand it over to the Drug Squad."

"That Chink restaurateur had a dead body turn up on his doorstep. *That's* a homicide, man!"

"Not necessarily related to Mr. Wu." Jury sighed. "It's pretty much a dead end."

"Trouble with you is you want it handed to you on a platter. You need a bit more tenacity!" Racer waved him out of the office. Out of his life would have been too much to hope for.

When Jury got back to his own office, Wiggins was turning from the phone and mouthing something, a name that Jury couldn't make out; his heart lurched. Hoping to hear Jenny's voice, he grabbed for the receiver.

"I've been trying to get hold of you, where've you been?" Sam Lasko sounded a little affronted.

"In Lincolnshire, that's where." Jury wiped his hand over the message slips—yes, there were two from Lasko. "I didn't see the message until today."

"I'd've thought you'd be contacting me, anyway."

"She rang me but I can't get her on the phone." He did not think of identifying the "her." Who else could they be talking about?

"This Lincs policeman—"

"Arthur Bannen?"

"Right. You know there's been another murder?"

"Yes. That's why I wanted to know if Jenny was in Stratford."

"Now, you mean?"

"Then. When the second murder took place."

Lasko paused. "As far as we know. She says she came back on the Tuesday."

It was the "as far as we know" that made Jury nervous. "On the fourth."

"Yes. CI Bannen, the Lincs cop. I have a feeling he's going to arrest her."

"I think she has the same feeling."

"Thought you hadn't talked to her," said Lasko.

"I haven't—oh, never mind."

There was some talk about police procedure before Lasko rang off.

Jury put down the receiver rather harder than was necessary, causing Wiggins to jump. It was not Jury's style. "Is it Lady Kennington, then, sir? Is something happening?"

"Something's going to." Jury washed his hands over his face.

"You'll be going to Stratford, then?"

Jury glared. "Friend or not, I can't just drop everything and run off to Stratford." He looked again at the pool of pink messages as if they were runes and wondered why he'd said that.

Wiggins looked alarmed. Was this the treatment Jury's friends could expect from now on?

Jury sat there for a moment, unhappy because Jenny hadn't asked for his help. But, then, couldn't that have been the message rendered in Carole-anne's tiny handwriting? No. "Afraid police may come from Lincs" was more informative than panic-stricken. Jury preferred Carole-anne's version, after all:

"Afraid. Please come."

6

Carole-anne Palutski stood, or rather leaned, in Jury's doorway, watching him press small bits of colored glass to a box partially covered with turquoise tiles, about the size of the sponge bag in Carole-anne's hand in which she stored beautifiers to gild the lily.

She asked, "Is that to hold me after I'm cremated?"

"Nothing could hold you, love, not even your ashes. No prison, no urn."

Carole-anne leaned over a bit to see his face, bent over the box. "Is that one of your compliments?"

"Are my compliments so different from other people's?" Jury blew on a bit of sapphire glass, the color of Carole-anne's eyes, and pushed it down into the wet-clay covering.

She was silent for a few moments, but then had to ask: "What are you doing?"

"Sticking these bits to this box."

An impatient sigh. "Well, I can *see* that, can't I?" She was wrapped up in a Chinese robe, turquoise silk emblazoned with a dragon, in which she'd been trailing around all morning.

"It's for a friend," said Jury.

"And you a police superintendent. Hard to believe." She yawned.

The yawn was fake. She wanted to appear completely indifferent to Jury's gift for his "friend." He pressed in a bit of amber. "Me, a police superintendent, haven't been having much luck policing. Of course, if we got our messages taken down right—"

Carole-anne kept shifting her position in the doorway, occasionally re-belting her silken robe when it threatened to separate in front. "Still on about that, are we?" She yawned.

"We are, yes." Why she didn't come in he could only assume was be-cause of the brouhaha over the message. Jury had, he supposed—and she insisted—got a trifle "shirty" over the whole thing. Carole-anne feared there might be a bit of shirtiness left over. "*'Fungus? Don't be daft. It's that house you was at, whyever would I say 'Fungus'?'*" She had un-tangled the message, which turned out to be as much Carole-anne's as it was Jenny's. That is to say, most of Carole-anne's crabbed writing had been what Carole-anne had told Jenny: *"So I says to her, 'Well, he hardly has time for a social life and wouldn't if I didn't make him go down the pub and etc.'"* God only knew what part of Jury's adventures the "and etc." would encompass. He had said to Carole-anne that if she kept it up, this bungling of messages taken from Jury's lady-friends, well, his social life would be "completely rund, Carole-anne, completely rund."

So Carole-anne just leaned against the doorframe like the Lady of Shalott. Often, he found her in here, lying on her stomach reading a mag-azine. He didn't mind. He rather liked it, as a matter of fact. Better than coming back to a cold grate (if he had a grate, which he didn't).

Following up on his supposed failure as a policeman, she said, "Maybe it's because you spend your time making stuff like that for your friend. Whoever *he* is."

Jury just loved the "he." "It's a she."

"Is it that JK?"

It was impossible for her, despite her façade of cool disinterest, to keep the note of anxiety out of her voice.

"No."

No information forthcoming, she sighed, changed her position so that now her arms were behind her back and her back was against the door-jamb. The robe separated around mid-thigh. Her face was upturned, as if looking through the ceiling at goings-on in heaven.

The pose (for he knew it was one) recalled the painted calendar girls of the forties and fifties—the succulent roundnesses of thigh, breast, and hip. Carole-anne's, though, were very real. And undated.

"I wish Stan was here." She heaved another sigh, looking ceilingward.

Stan Keeler was her antidote to Jury's "friend." He was the tenant who had met Carole-anne's stiff criteria for letting the flat above Jury: handsome, dark, intense, talented, and independent, the independence meaning that he was free of "friends," such as the one Jury was pushing colored stones into clay for.

"As long as he hasn't got his guitar."

This gave Carole-anne an excuse to be accusatory and let off a little of that steam that threatened to erupt over Jury's jeweled box. "What? Are you saying you don't like Stan's *playing*? Well, I expect you're just getting old."

Jury smiled at a bit of blue stone. "His playing is near-divine, as long as he's doing it in the Nine-One-Nine and not over my head. When Stan lets loose with a riff it's a little like being woken by the IRA with Uzis."

As if Jury had admitted to disliking both the riffs and Stan himself, Carole-anne said, accusingly, "You're the one that found him, after all!"

"He wasn't lost." Jury had met Stan Keeler several years before at the club where he played regularly, the Nine-One-Nine. He was a sensational guitarist. "And, as I recall, you're the one that let out the flat to him."

Carole-anne just bulldozed on. "Probably you don't even like Stone."

Stone was Stan Keeler's dog. "How could I not like Stone? He's got more sense than both of us put together."

Stan was more of an underground, a cult sensation. He wasn't modest about his talent; at the same time, Stan didn't appear to be bothered by Fame—whether he had it; whether he didn't. He was one of the most single-minded people Jury had ever known. Perhaps that was the reason he and Carole-anne were not having a "thing." At least he didn't think they were.

"So what are you going to do with that box when you finish?"

"Take it to Heathrow. She works there." She seemed visibly to slump. He really should stop teasing her. "You can come along if you like."

"Think I'll have a cuppa. Want one?" She didn't wait for his answer but walked across his sitting room back to his tiny kitchen. From there he heard china clatter and water run.

He had forgotten that Carole-anne was intensely afraid of air terminals. She never flew; she never went near them. Whether the danger was real or imaginary, he wasn't sure, but he thought, real. She had once told him a story about some people she had seen in an airport—a mother and child, both of them crying bitterly, and Carole-anne had concluded that the little boy was being separated from his mum. And the mum from the boy. It seemed like a forced separation, neither wanting it. The little boy had wiped the tears from his mum's face. It had made her sick for days, she'd said. Could hardly bring herself to get out of bed, she'd said.

In Jury's mind, there wasn't much doubt that the child was a girl, not a boy, and the girl had been Carole-anne. For she had never said anything about her family except for a few vague references to uncles and cousins. Not Mum and Da. Questions about them she evaded quite expertly, as if she'd had a lot of practice.

As beautiful and brash as Carole-anne was, for Jury she had become the picture of poignance. He had sometimes caught that look on the faces of witnesses. The moment when the guard comes down. Jury would wait for such moments (hard, of course, to let down the guard if the police were asking questions), for he felt he got some of the most honest answers then. For it was then that the person became real; it was as if they had slipped the reins or yoke that held them back or down.

Jury was thinking about all of this when he realized Carole-anne's hand was extending his mug of tea. "Thanks." Jury sipped it and said, "Listen, how about the Angel? It's nearly opening time. Time you get dressed it will be. Care to bend your elegant elbow with me?"

She seemed slightly breathless with the way the tide had turned in her favor. "But—I thought you was going to Heathrow."

Jury made an impatient gesture, brushing off Heathrow. "I can go there anytime. No rush."

To say that Carole-anne brightened was to put it mildly. She glowed. She absolutely glittered in the stream of sunlight coming through Jury's window. That copper-colored hair, that rose-tinted skin. Another sun. He remembered Santa Fe and smiled. "You belong in the Southwest, Carole-anne."

She frowned and retied her robe, her tea forgotten. "Torquay, like?"

Jury laughed. "No. New Mexico, Colorado. That Southwest. You remind me of the sun going down behind the Sandias."

Her frown deepened. "Is that one of your compliments, then?"

The conversation, Jury thought, had come full circle.

7

There would be no living with Trueblood now that Richard Jury had given the man the actual *assignment* of tutoring Plant in antiques. Melrose stood on the step outside the door of Trueblood's Antiques, waiting for him to answer the knock. There was a little clock-sign, one of those cardboard things you could change the hands of, informing customers exactly what time the proprietor would return. Melrose knew the proprietor hadn't really *gone* anywhere; he was in there getting ready for Melrose's lesson.

Trueblood loved it all; instructing Melrose was such an occasion for little jokes and jibes, put-downs and deceptions, such as palming off a Louis Quinze armchair as some bit of flotsam he'd picked up in the Portobello Road for a few quid. It was the most fun Trueblood had had since they'd written up Count Franco Giopinno's memoirs and posted the notebook to Vivian. And since the Week End Man competition had fallen through with the appearance of Miss Fludd at Watermeadows (clearly *not* a Week End Woman) Trueblood was presently entertaining himself with Melrose's lessons. That, and the *Ardry vs. Crisp* affair.

Lady Ardry was suing Ada Crisp for damages caused by one of her pavement chamber pots and her Jack Russell terrier. Agatha had been spending most of her time in Sidbury with her solicitors—a whole boatload full of them, to hear her talk. Agatha was claiming that Miss Crisp's bits-and-bobs of furniture sitting on the pavement were both an abomination to look at and dangerous to life and limb. Look what had happened to herself! She had got her foot stuck in one of the chamber pots, and Ada's Jack Russell had jumped her and nearly taken off the foot at the ankle. "Nearly tore it to shreds," was Agatha's recollection of the "accident."

While he waited, Melrose turned so that he could see Miss Crisp's secondhand furniture shop. Ordinarily, the pavement outside of her door
was filled with bits and pieces—flowered jugs and porcelain chamber pots,
gaily painted bedsteads and wooden chairs, everything old as the hills yet
finding a place in the sun as a result of Miss Crisp's ministrations. But today the pavement was empty. Deserted, almost; almost abject.

"*Your aunt,*" Trueblood had exclaimed a few days ago, "*is the most liti-
gious mortal I've ever seen!*" He was referring not only to the chamber pot
case, but to the suit against Jurvis the butcher five years before when
Agatha's Morris Minor had managed somehow to get its wheels up on the
pavement and knocked down the butcher's plaster-of-Paris pig. It was the
pig's fault, she had claimed, and had actually won the case because the
magistrate must have fallen asleep. He had not been foolish enough, however, to honor her injunction to keep the pig off the sidewalk, there being no cases to cite as precedent. "So the pig still *hogs* the pavement,"
Trueblood was fond of saying to her.

Anyway, she now had an opportunity to go after Miss Crisp, a pleasant,
timid little woman who was in a great state of nerves about all of this. She
could not believe (nor could Melrose) that the terrier had actually *attacked*
one of the villagers. In a small way, every dog and cat on Long Piddleton
had attacked Agatha, for animals always seem to sniff out people who dislike them. Agatha was suing to have the poor dog "put down." She was
being just as intolerable in this instance as she'd been in going after Jurvis
the butcher. Nearly caused the man a total breakdown; now Ada Crisp's
emotional state was even worse.

All of this went through Melrose's mind as he waited on Trueblood's
stoop.

Finally, the door was opened to him. Trueblood's enthusiastic greeting
was followed by "Done your homework?" *Whack!* went the hand on
Melrose's back, making him stumble into the shop.

"Oh, cut it out!" said Melrose, moving without haste to the rear of the
shop where Trueblood had set out an old student's desk, even filling up
the inkwell and supplying a quill pen.

The sun was strong for February and would have streamed through the bay window of the shop had it not been blocked by a massive break-front bookcase and a Georgian console with a gaudily carved and gilded eagle base. Interior lights from porcelain lamps, low-hanging chandeliers, and lighted wall sconces provided a misty and mysteriously lit world of credenzas, tea tables, bureaus and bookcases, fauteuils and davenports, richly carved and polished; huge beveled mirrors and gilt wood. Ada Crisp's secondhand furniture shop was directly across the street from Trueblood's Antiques, and to go from the one to the other was like seeing the Cockney wench transformed, midstreet, into the elegant lady of fashion.

In the back of the shop, the rear door was open on the alley where sat Trueblood's van, used for deliveries and for transporting stuff he bought at country auctions. Inside the open gate of the van, Melrose could see the scrolled arm of a rosewood sofa and the leg of a table. Trueblood hopped up and pulled the table to the edge.

"Look at this. Isn't it gorgeous? A *table à la Bourgogne.*"

Melrose studied the elaborate marquetry, stained wood on a fruit ground. It was a handsome table.

"Beautiful façade and with a surprise inside—" Here he opened the top. "A jack-in-the-box of drawers!"

Recalling what they had once found inside a *secretaire à abbattant*, Melrose said, "I don't much care for your furniture surprises."

Trueblood jumped down from the van and they went inside again.

"Did you call Max Owen, then?" Melrose was almost afraid to hear.

Trueblood sank down into his desk chair and waved an arm indicating Melrose should sit. "Not at that child's desk, thank you." Melrose sat down, already exhausted, in a wing chair. "Did you call him?"

"Yes. I told him an acquaintance of his had mentioned he wanted to find a *table à la Bourgogne.* That's what we were looking at just now."

Melrose frowned, "Who told you he wanted one?"

Trueblood leaned backward in his swivel chair, looking and sounding pained. "*No one* told me, old sweat. I had to have a reason to call him, didn't I? We chatted for some time. People in the trade can talk for hours—"

"I've noticed."

"—and during this conversation he asked me if I knew anything about the table, and what was its provenance, and a few pieces he himself owned. A *bonheur-du-jour* for one, and when I said, yes, indeed, I did, he asked me if I might have time to go up to Lincolnshire and have a look at his stuff. So I told him I had to go to Barcelona—"

Melrose frowned. "For what?"

"*Nothing.* I'm not going to Barcelona, I just told him that. But that I knew just the person for this appraisal job."

Melrose looked at him in alarm. "Listen: I hope you were careful of the background you gave me. I'm not Count-bloody-Dracula, Week End Italian."

Trueblood made a noise of disgust. "Of *course* not. Don't you trust me?"

"No."

"Never fear. I said you lived in London. You're an amateur, not a professional, so you're not necessarily known round Sotheby's and Christie's because you keep a very low profile, not being in it for the money but just for the enjoyment. That's in case he should mention your name when he's at the auction rooms. But there'd be no reason at all to check up on you, as he's already checked up on me. I said you will accept recompense only if you can demonstrate to Owen's satisfaction that the pieces he's concerned about are genuine or not." Trueblood sucked in his breath, thinking. "Being a gentleman of leisure, you have plenty of time to invest in this sort of research; it's a hobby of yours, and you go to the rooms not to buy but to watch others buying. *You* were the one who first discovered that the Elizabethan livery cupboard Christie's auctioned five years ago turned out to owe less to Elizabeth than to—"

"Hold it! I don't even know what kind of cupboard that is!"

Trueblood sighed. "There *wasn't* one, old sweat. But is Max Owen going to remember that? How can he remember something that never happened? I mean, that's the trick of it, isn't it?"

Melrose frowned over the logic of this.

Trueblood reached around to some heavy-looking books he had

stacked on his desk, pulled one out, flipped through it. Finding what he wanted, he turned the color plate toward Melrose. "This is the sort of cupboard." After Melrose had spent some moments studying it, Trueblood snapped the book shut, handed it to Melrose. "Homework."

Taking it, Melrose groaned. "I'd have to have months, years to digest what's in these books. Look how heavy they are. Don't you have anything for the layman?"

Ignoring these protests, Trueblood took a small paper from where he'd stashed it under his desk blotter. "It's not going to be all that hard for you; you can check Theo Wrenn Browne's shelves, the little shyster. Our friend Jury—clever cop, he is—left this list of pieces Max Owen wanted appraised. His wife pointed them out to Jury, and he jotted them down. There are only five pieces. You can certainly mug up on five pieces."

Melrose put up his hand. "I've got my own, thanks."

"That's not to say, of course, that by the time you get there—"

"There'll be twenty-five. Wonderful. Do you have pictures of all these things in the book?" Glumly, he looked at the list. He felt, actually, somewhat relieved there were only these five. But, as he himself had said, Owen could always spring a suspect Queen Anne sofa or a middling example of a Hepplewhite armchair on him.

"Probably don't have pictures of all five of them. Oh, and there's a rug, too. Ispahan." Trueblood pulled out another volume and leafed through it.

Melrose groaned. "I know less about rugs than about furniture."

"It's in here somewhere. Never mind, I'll dig it out soon enough." He snapped the book shut. "I'm parched. Come on, let's have a drink."

❧

In the Jack and Hammer, Joanna Lewes looked up from a short stack of manuscript pages. Joanna, who wrote her immensely popular novels with a Trollopelike efficiency, forced herself to write two hundred and fifty words every fifteen minutes. She was waiting, she had once said, for the Warholian fifteen minutes. She greeted them and went back to her editing.

Trueblood got the drinks while Melrose looked over her shoulder. "*London Love?* But you've already published that one, several years ago."

"I have," answered Joanna, sighing. "This is a revised text. I decided Matt and Valerie hadn't been having enough sex first time around."

Melrose sat down. "Joanna, if it's already published, why would your publisher do it again? I have always had the thrifty notion that the publisher only does that once."

"You're forgetting Robert Graves and John Fowles. *Good-bye to All That* was revised and republished. So was *The Magus.*"

"But if you thought it was rubbish once, wouldn't it be double-rubbish twice?"

She laughed. "Of course. Who cares? The publisher probably won't even remember doing *London Love* before, publishers being what they are." She slapped another page down on the stack. "One takes a perverse pleasure in watching fools be fools. Theo, for instance, is giving a drinks party. Didn't you love the invitation?"

Trueblood was back, setting down his own drinks: Old Peculier for Melrose; for himself a campari and lime. "Cream-laid paper. Engraved. Good lord. When the best way of issuing invitations is just to stand in front of the pub and holler."

Joanna evened up the stack of pages and rose. "Sorry. I've more writing to do. That last hour I spent is missing seven hundred and fifty words. Ta."

"Hells bells, there's Diane. I hope she's not headed here. I can't deal with Diane today."

"Looks like you'll have to, old trout."

Melrose groaned.

The arctic Miss Demorney, who was entering the pub now, was a person (they both agreed) wanting in any feeling that warmed the blood of the average mortal. To increase this icy impression, she liked to dress in white. Even the decor of her living room—white leather, white walls, white cat—augmented the glacial effect.

With the confidence of one who knew someone else would fetch and carry for her, Diane Demorney smiled at Dick Scroggs, who was already shaking ice off her martini glass. She furnished him with her own special brand of vodka and also had instructed him to keep her martini glass chilled. She still paid him full price for her drink. Diane might have been a lot of things, but she certainly wasn't cheap.

Trueblood, good-naturedly, swanned off to get her martini as Diane pulled out a chair, sat down, plugged a cigarette into her long white holder, and said, "I've only the time for one drink—"

Considering the potency of the one, she'd need plenty of time, thought Melrose.

"—as I'm going up to London. Ah, thank you," she said, as Trueblood placed her martini before her. The circumference of the glass was the approximate size of a skating rink. She smoked and allowed the olive to steep. "I don't expect either of you cares to motor up with me?"

"Hopes dashed to the ground, Diane," said Trueblood. "We're busy."

Melrose did wish Trueblood would stop answering for him, even though he had no wish to accompany Diane. He doubted she wanted company as much as she wanted a chauffeur. She hated driving herself, despite that absolutely wonderful Rolls. No one knew how Diane had come into her money—donated by the several ex-husbands, probably— still, she complained of feeling "pinched" from time to time. She was the sort of profligate spender who believed if one is good, two is better. So she bought a Bentley.

Now, she sipped her drink and then sat with her chin in her hand, saying, "Honestly, Melrose, that aunt of yours."

Must he be blamed for the relationship?

She continued: "Suing Ada Crisp, for God's sake. Has she no sense whatever?"

"Not really. But I'm glad you're on Ada's side."

Diane's smooth eyebrows arched. "I'm not on anybody's *side*. The point is, Ada has no money."

Trueblood said, "A benevolent way of looking at it."

Diane gave him a peculiar look. She was not used to the word. "Well, she hasn't a sou, not a bean, and I told Agatha that if she won her suit all she'd end up with is a lot of dusty old bedsteads and legless tables. Ada Crisp has nothing in that shop that's of value. Of course, Theo just *adores* the idea because he could buy up the property and expand. So he simply eggs Agatha on. He was the one put her in touch with the solicitors in Sidbury." She sat back and yawned, then said, "Well, it's all too strenuous for me, all of this activity." She tilted her head and exhaled a thin blue stream of smoke at the ceiling. "I wish there were something amusing going to happen."

"We could all go over to the Blue Parrot," said Trueblood.

"Oh, *that's* hardly *amusing*, Marshall."

Good lord, thought Melrose, if she didn't find the Blue Parrot's proprietor "amusing" she must be really hard up for laughs.

"And besides," she went on, "the Blue Parrot's absolutely *medieval*. It's so *rustic*."

Melrose had never heard the Middle Ages referred to as "rustic" before. "Diane, all of Long Piddleton is 'rustic.'"

"No, no, *no*," said Trueblood. "Quaint's the word."

Diane made a moue of distaste and turned to signal to Scroggs. When he finally looked up from the weekly gossip-sheet, she made a circular motion with her finger. She was standing drinks. Melrose sometimes wondered about Diane. Her generosity seemed at odds with the rest of her—coldly calculating, self-centered, feathers for brains. Diane *appeared* to be knowledgeable only because she had picked out one arcane or esoteric fact about nearly every subject under the sun. And only one. When Dick Scroggs brought the drinks she zipped open her suitcase of a bag and brought out her checkbook, shaking her glossy black head *No, no*, as Trueblood reached for his wallet. Diane disliked carrying money. She paid for stamps with a check.

This transaction over, she raised her glass, said "Cheers," and then sighed. "I only wish *something* amusing would happen." She frowned. "What about Vivian's Count—" She was trying to dredge up the name.

"Dracula," said Trueblood.

"His *name*," said Melrose, "is Franco Giopinno."

"Didn't I hear he might be visiting Vivian?"

"It is so rumored," said Trueblood, "but I can't imagine it."

She sipped her drink. "You know, I've often wondered about Dracula. . . . "

"Funny," said Trueblood. "I hardly think of the chap from one moment to the next."

"No, but can you imagine it? Only blood for nourishment?" She picked up her glass. "No pre-dinner drinks, no prawn cocktail for starters, a bucket of blood for your entree, and no sweet. How perfectly *awful.*"

"He's quite normal-looking, really," said Melrose. "Actually, he's handsome. Brooding sort of looks."

Trueblood was astonished. "You didn't tell me you'd seen him."

"It's been so long. I met him in Stratford-upon-Avon. He was with Vivian."

"I hope you were wearing your cross," said Trueblood.

"But hasn't she been engaged, so to speak, for donkey's years? Sounds bloody strange—no pun intended—to me," said Diane.

"Uh-huh. To tell the truth, I wouldn't be surprised if Vivian had him here to give him the boot. It'd be easier to do it here than to do it there, where he's surrounded by a lot of generic Italians," said Trueblood.

Diane gave him another peculiar look. "What do you mean? Oh, never mind." Diane was never one to explore areas of ignorance. "Is he rich?"

"Probably. He sounds rich."

Diane's porcelain brow furrowed in a passable imitation of someone thinking. "But I expect after he married, they'd have to live in—where does he live?"

"Venice," said Melrose.

"If you call it living," said Trueblood, firing up a bright pink Sobranie.

"He'd probably want to live in Venice and speak Italian—" Diane's perfect black eyebrows came together in a little frown.

"Venetians do go in for that sort of thing, yes," said Trueblood.

"It just might be too much trouble for our Vivian to go to." She took a sip of her martini. "Quite a bit of trouble for *anyone* to go to."

Anyone? thought Melrose. *Who might "anyone" be?*

❧

The bell over the door of the Wrenn's Nest Bookshop tinkled in an irritated little way as Melrose entered. The shop was itself almost insufferably quaint, with its exposed timber, low lintels—with silly "Mind Your Head" signs—and rickety staircase to the level above. Given all of Theo Wrenn Browne's sidelines—his lending library, the stuffed animals in a huge bin by the staircase, and now even T-shirts—the place was jam-packed. This (Browne had said) was the reason he needed more room, and the only room he could think of was Ada Crisp's secondhand shop.

Theo Wrenn Browne was presently engaged in one of his sidelines, the lending library. He was coming very close to putting Long Piddleton's one-room library straight out of business; since Browne had immediate access to all of the new books and bestsellers, he did nicely, even though he charged 10p a day. People were peculiar about books, Melrose decided, for when they wanted a new book, they really wanted it, expense be hanged.

Browne's borrower in this case was a small girl with flaxen hair and a sweet piping voice that would have melted the heart of the meanest of men, but not the heart of Theo Wrenn Browne, who was busy reprimanding her about the condition of her returned book. The little girl claimed that her brother Bub (even younger than she) was the guilty party. In any event, someone had cut up a page and Browne was going to make reparation or take away her privileges. And of course tell her mum.

Melrose had on several occasions come upon a scene such as this of Dickensian proportions, an exchange between Browne and some luckless kiddy. He wouldn't have dared try this if a parent had accompanied the child.

After a curt nod at Melrose, Browne went back to bedeviling the girl (whose name was, apparently, Sally): "This is the only copy I have of *Patrick*. And just *how* are we going to solve this little problem, hmm, young Sally?"

Melrose had always loathed this asking of questions that a child can't possibly answer, thereby doubling the anxiety.

"It was Bub did it, he don't know any better," answered Sally, who was pinching the skin of one hand with the other, as if an act of self-mutilation might make all of this go away.

Why the tears standing in her eyes didn't fall, Melrose couldn't imagine. Perhaps she had willed them not to, and thus avert further humiliation.

"Well, then perhaps we can have Bub come along and answer my question."

"No, he can't; he's only two."

Melrose said, "Sally—"

Though softly said, Sally backed away, for now she was flanked by two adults, a double-danger. "Sally, is this book one of your favorites?"

Not surprisingly, she was too bewildered even to answer that question. "I . . . don't know."

Theo Wrenn Browne was holding the book and Melrose removed it from his grip. He looked at the cover. *Patrick, the Painted Pig*. Patrick was a bright dripping blue, as if he'd turned over a paint can. Melrose began to turn the pages and make noises of approval. Thus Sally's energy now was taken up more with curiosity, which had reduced the fear—at least he hoped so.

Browne, clearly annoyed, stuck his pipe in his mouth with a mean little jab, took it out again. "What were you wanting, Mr. Plant? I don't think it's that pig book, now, is it?"

"Books on antiques, Mr. Browne. Sally, you might be interested to know that I have an acquaintance who painted himself blue and ran up and down the road and all around the houses in his neighborhood."

Sally's mouth flew open. Forgetting the pickle she was in, she came closer and said, "No, he never did."

"Oh, yes. His name is Ashley Cripps. Do you know him?"

Sally fingered a lock of her pale blond hair, pulling on it thoughtfully. "No. Why did he?"

Browne said, determinedly, "My books on antiques are right through that archway; I've a good selection."

"Thank you. Ashley Cripps just wanted to shock everyone."

"Which part did he paint?" asked Sally, close enough now to touch.

"All of him!"

Sally gasped.

"He didn't look nearly as handsome as Patrick here." Melrose snapped the book shut. "Very well, Mr. Browne, how much?"

"What? What do you mean? You mean that pig book?"

"I do." Melrose had taken out his wallet.

"But you don't want that . . . it's damaged."

"How much?"

When Browne came up with a price, Melrose slid the notes from his wallet, paid up, took the book, and handed it over to Sally, who was utterly speechless. Her mouth was open in a small O, as she looked from her book to Melrose and back again at *Patrick*. Then she half-giggled, clapping her hand to her mouth to hold it in. But it would not be held. "I'm paintin' Bub blue!" Giggling merrily, she ran out the door.

Theo Wrenn Browne, cheated of his daily dose of misery-making, pointed with a bony finger to the next room, as if he were sending Melrose to the gallows. "Back there, Mr. Plant. As I said, through the archway."

⁊ℛ

There were three shelves of books dealing with various subjects—glass, silver, rugs, porcelain, periods of furniture. Melrose sighed and took one down at random, opened it, got discouraged at the encyclopedic knowledge demanded of him, pushed it back. The next one, on Oriental rugs, he set on the floor next to a small stool. He shoved the next book back because of its sheer bulk and chose one on silver that was considerably slimmer. He put this one on the floor, also. Another book was a largish paperback titled *Helluva Deal!* which he put on his stack purely on the basis of the name. In the next book there were a lot of pictures, so he set that on top of the stack.

He sat down on the little milking stool beside his small pile of books and picked up *Helluva Deal!*, which appeared to have the most entertainment potential. He turned it over and looked at the smiling couple on the back—the Nuttings, Bebe and Bob—who had coauthored it. Melrose opened it at random to see a rather grainy reproduction of a picture of Bebe Nutting standing beside a cow. This, thought Melrose, was a refreshing change in an antiques guide, and he must remember to make Trueblood familiar with it. On the other side of the cow was its new owner, Mr. Hiram Stuck. Mr. Stuck had purchased this cow having been convinced by "someone" that the cow was a direct descendant "of that there Missus O'Leary. I got the papers on it." Melrose presumed Hiram Stuck meant the cow was the descendant of the O'Leary cow (rather than Mrs. O'Leary herself). As it turned out, Mr. Stuck was one of the several people Bebe and Bob had interviewed, all of whom had been taken in by one con artist or another working one scam or another.

The cow was the only actual *living* thing with a provenance—an alleged provenance—purported to be valuable. He certainly hoped the Owens wouldn't take him round the barnyard to value any livestock. The other objects in the book were conventional enough. Silver, Limoges, settees, urns, and so forth.

Melrose sat on the milking stool reading and being entertained for some moments. He then selected two other books from his stack—one on rugs, one a price guide—put them together with *Helluva Deal!* and went to the front of the store.

Theo Wrenn Browne was taping up a binding and talking on the telephone at the same time, in low tones. Quite pointedly, Browne turned away, lowered his voice even more, then rang off.

"Will that be all, then, Mr. Plant?" He took the three books from Melrose's hands.

"Yes, thanks."

Browne seemed to blow down his nose in a small fit of condescension. "Really, Mr. Plant, I don't think you'll get much help here." He looked down at the happy Nuttings.

"Oh, I don't know. You've read it, then?"

"Yes. Silly book, but some like that sort of thing." He sniffed.

"Uh-huh." Melrose dropped several notes on the counter, watching Browne tap a message of near–book length into his computer, then listened to the computer whir and whit. "I hope you don't mind my saying—"

Melrose knew he would.

"—but you're not doing that Sally Finch a favor by rewarding her for her bad behavior."

"But Sally didn't do it. It was Bub. Weren't you paying attention?"

Theo Wrenn Browne rewarded Melrose with a withering look as he bagged up the books.

8

Lincolnshire," said Melrose, refusing to lift his eyes from his book.

"Lincolnshire? Why on earth? You don't know anybody in Lincolnshire." Agatha reached for another scone.

Melrose smiled. Not at her. Her, he ignored. He was smiling over an account of an antiques free-for-all in Twinjump, Idaho, reported in *Helluva Deal!* On the floor beside his chair were two heavy volumes that Trueblood had forced on him in addition to the price guide which he'd been studying all of last night and the whole morning, hoping to stuff himself like an onion in preparation for his trip to Lincolnshire tomorrow. He thought he deserved something on the lighter side, and *Helluva Deal!* certainly met that requirement.

Dribble's (the price guide) he was finding extremely helpful. He'd been testing himself by pricing his own things. That Staffordshire shepherd and shepherdess there on his mantel *Dribble's* claimed were worth quite a lot. This surprised Melrose; they were such a boring couple to look at. His eye traveled now to a Chinese urn: according to *Dribble's*, a similar one went for £3,000. He felt far richer than he usually did, sitting here. With Agatha. Immediately, he felt poorer.

As she dug deeper in the marmalade jar for a spoonful to put on her scone, Agatha repeated, "I *said*, you don't know anybody in Lincolnshire."

Melrose sighed. She was always doing that—repeating things in the exact words as if not one word dare be ignored. She was so infinitely ignorable. "I want to see the fens, the tulips." He turned a page and found a picture of a massive chandelier that could have graced Versailles.

"In *Lincolnshire*? Tulips?"

"Lincolnshire, at least South Lincolnshire, is famous for its tulips and other flowers. Acres and acres of them, miles of them."

"There won't be tulips in February."

"No, but the fens will be marvelous this time of year. Bleak and dark. . . ."

"It sounds off-putting to me. You do have queer tastes." The spoon clattered round in the jar. Ruthven had taken the precaution of bringing the entire jar of Chivers on the tea tray because she was always complaining she hadn't enough. "Well, it's a place I've absolutely no desire to see."

Thank you, God. Melrose looked heavenward. He had been uncharacteristically precipitate in even telling her where he was going. Ordinarily, he wouldn't. But he'd simply wanted to change the subject from Ada Crisp and the Jack Russell terrier. He looked at his aunt's foot—ankle, rather—strapped up with tape. It rested on a needlepoint footstool.

She continued. "I can't leave now, anyway. Too busy with my solicitors."

A battery of them? wondered Melrose. How many were prepared to mount a case against a terrier? "For what barrister do your solicitors act as brief, then?" He closed *Helluva Deal!* and crossed his legs. He might be able to squeeze a moiety of amusement out of this solicitor-thing, after all.

"Really, Melrose. I hardly think it will come to trial. Theo agrees with me."

Melrose winced. If she invoked the name of Theo Wrenn Browne once more he'd have to call for the gin. "You've always loathed Browne. Why now is he suddenly crushed to your bosom?"

She waved this objection away. "We had our differences, yes—"

"Yes. That he was a 'dedicated jackarse' and you were 'a prying old windbag.' Those were your differences."

"You're making it up, as usual." She brushed scone-dust from her lap. "At any rate, Theo has advised an out-of-court settlement."

For the first time, Melrose was actually a little anxious for the fate of Ada Crisp. If that asp, Theo Wrenn Browne, was in on it, God knows where it would all lead. "And just what would that settlement consist of? Ada Crisp has no money. She would have to declare bankruptcy."

"There's her shop—"

"A*ha*! So that's it! One way or another, Mr. Browne is going to get her out of that shop!"

She split another scone. "Don't be ridiculous Melrose. Theo is merely a disinterested observer—"

"The only place where Theo Wrenn Browne would have been a 'disinterested observer' is at Tiny Tim's Christmas party. Or the sinking of the *Lusitania*. What *he* wants, has always wanted, is to get her out so he can expand his bookshop. Don't tell *me* he hasn't got anything riding on it." Melrose snapped open his book again and again closed it. He thought for a moment, then said, "Of course, you know, it just might go to trial"—if the magistrates were total nitwits—"it being, perhaps, a precedent-setting case." He smiled. "And if you lose, well, you'd have to pay costs. I hope you're prepared. Sounds expensive to me." He turned a page.

"Lose? *Lose?*" Agatha sat back, so shocked she ignored the scone she'd marmaladed up. "I assumed you were on *my* side in this."

"I'm on the side of Truth," he said, pompously. "And Justice." More pompously.

"Well, of course, that's what my side is!" She munched her scone.

"Agatha, hasn't your solicitor asked you *how* your foot happened to get in that pot in the first place?" Melrose had to exercise a good deal of self-control to keep from laughing himself sick.

"Naturally."

He raised his eyebrows. "Well?"

"What do you mean? You *saw* what happened. You were directly across the street, going in the Jack and Hammer, where, I might add, you spend entirely too much time—"

"What I saw was you landing a helluva kick"—he was picking up the Nuttings' bouncy language—"in the dog's side. *That's* what I saw."

"You saw me fall down—" She held out her arm, pointed a stubby finger at him. "So you want to blame the entire episode on me!"

Melrose held up his hands, palms outward. "Oh, far be it from me to do that. But I wouldn't be surprised if Ada Crisp might not take that view of things. Ada might take umbrage at your smashing up her property."

"I couldn't get my foot out. What was I to do? Walk around the rest of my life with my foot in a chamber pot?"

Melrose toyed with this image for a moment. Then he retrieved his book from the Sheraton table beside his chair and said, "Don't say I didn't warn you."

"For lord's sake," she said scraping the last of the marmalade from the jar, "it was nothing but an old chamber pot!"

"You *hope*." The book had fallen open to the middle section of illustrations. Here was the Meissen bowl the Spiker sisters of Twinjump had been setting on the floor for their mongrel dog to eat from and even after learning its value continued to put to that service. *("Ain't nothin' too good for our Alfie.")* Melrose felt like applauding the Spiker sisters. "You know, Trueblood had a look at that pot. Or the pieces, I should say. Said it reminded him of the Meissen bowl in his shop."

She sputtered. "Trueblood . . . he's a degenerate coxcomb!"

"Perhaps. But he's a degenerate coxcomb of an antiques expert, and that's something to think about when the prosecution gets going. Trueblood would make an excellent witness." His smile across the four feet of Kirman carpet (*Dribble's: £2,000*) was slight and unsympathetic. He was warming to the subject of *Ardry vs. Crisp* now. He reflected on the time that Richard Jury had scared the hell out of Theo Wrenn Browne when Browne had threatened Ada Crisp with a lawsuit years ago. Claimed the stuff she set on the walk outside her door was a hazard to life and limb. An obstruction of traffic. Ye gods, for years passersby had stepped gingerly round needlepoint footstools, ancient hobby horses—and, of course, the odd bins of china cups and plates—and never minded. It was just Ada's lot. Jury had scared Browne by telling him stories of the sad ends of landlords who had tried to evict sitting tenants. He had done it with a copy of *Bleak House* under his arm.

"Well?" said Agatha, holding a rock cake aloft.

Melrose raised his eyebrows. " 'Well' what?"

"What did he say? Trueblood?"

Despite her disdain of the man, to ignore his opinion in this case would prove costly. Melrose stared at a handsome hunt table he'd always liked. (*Dribble's: perhaps £500?*) and said, "Can't remember. Sorry."

He didn't want to put words in Trueblood's mouth. Trueblood was too good at doing that himself. And he knew Trueblood would go along with this happily. He'd been looking for a few new windmills to tilt at.

Having stripped the jar clean of its thick-cut marmalade and the china plate of its scones, Agatha sat back and made little adjustments to her person. Fiddled with the collar of her blouse, rearranged a chiffon scarf, rubbed at the semiprecious center of a ring.

Melrose watched her as she did this.

Brooch, scarf, ring. Army and Navy Stores: ten pounds, twenty pence. At most.

Part II

The Cold Ladies

9

He had got off the A17 on to one of the godforsaken B roads that was scarcely wider than a wrinkle on the face of the fens. It must have happened back there just beyond Market Deeping, where he'd taken the wrong road out and had wound up going round and round the tiny village of Cowbit. In his transit, he'd passed by a freshly painted cottage with the words written across its lintel in neat, black cursive: *The Red Last.* He'd stopped, idled there in his car for some moments, wondering what it meant. Probably been a pub once. Queer name. *The Red Last.*

Finally, a few more turnings took him back to the A17. What he saw before and around him was fen country, stretching south and east into Cambridgeshire and the Black Fens. The ground was stiff with ice on either side of the road and the land was crisscrossed by canals and drainage ditches. Since the Lincolnshire fens were sometimes referred to as "Little Holland," Melrose supposed that shortly these acres of cold brown fields would be a quilt of color. It must be glorious in the early spring with the bright reds, deep purples, yellows, shimmering in the sunlight across fields that looked like stained-glass windows.

Here was a directional sign, thank heavens: the way to Spalding was clear and simple. After seeing how fast Trueblood's van would go—eighty mph, not bad—he slowly put on the brakes because the welcome sign of a pub had just flown past an eighth of a mile back. He made a U-turn and drove back; he knew beforehand that directions would be needed to Fengate, and who better to supply them than a local pub. Having reached the car park, Melrose folded and pocketed his map. Crunching past the sign of the Case Has Altered, he once again ran over the details about the pieces Max Owen wanted valued. Melrose was also mindful of the fact that Owen would want them authenticated, would want to know their provenance.

As he did this his spirits flagged. But the promise of conviviality inside the pub—customers with their pints and bottles, the low hum of conversation, the pleasant bartender, the long mahogany bar—that perked him right up. Once inside, though, he found the conversation of the regulars wound down, then stopped. Why did people clam up this way? They clammed up because watching a stranger, any stranger, in their midst was far more interesting than the same old crack.

The bar was blue with smoke, the effluvia of many hours of cigarettes. He took his pint of Old Peculier and wandered over to a dartboard whose riddled concentric rings testified to its popularity. Melrose wondered if he was still any good at the game; he had been once, at age fifteen or sixteen. Quite the champ, actually. Or did he only imagine that? Was that another element in his fictional past? He bent his head and looked down at the thin layer of foam in his glass. The malaise that overcame him whenever he thought of those far-off days settled again. He felt sleepy, but he knew that too was a protective layer.

He drank his beer and thought of his approach to the Owens. Trueblood had talked him into delivering this *table à la Bourgogne* as even further window dressing. He looked down at his clothes. He had decided to look country and wore an out-at-elbow wool sweater and his Barbour coat. He thought this would be the costume of the true aesthete, not a suit with a waistcoat. And he also wore a cap much like that group of flat-caps up there at the bar having their friendly argument. Were they old fenmen? Spin-offs from the ones in the sixteenth century who had raised such a riot over attempts to drain the area?

He decided it would be a good idea to join the group at the bar and stand a round. That had always proved an efficient icebreaker. Though given a double murder in the area, there shouldn't be too much ice to break. He mentioned to the bartender to stand everyone a drink and said to the knot of rather rough-looking men and one woman, "Afternoon, gentlemen." Inclining his head, he added, "Ladies."

They murmured greetings, nodded.

"You be Londoner?" asked one of them, as a fresh drink was set before him.

"Good God, no!" He hoped he got it across, his detestation of London and Londoners. "I'm from Northants." That was a good solid part of the country—hardly worth envying a chap from Northamptonshire. He noticed, though, that their looks were a trifle severe and suspicious. These expressions relaxed into conviviality when the bartender set down the rest of the drinks.

The woman who wore a hat with plastic berries round the brim pulled down over her dishwater hair asked, "You be goin' to Spalding, then?"

"Not quite. A little village called Algarkirk." He was glad he had real business here, and didn't have to fabricate his destination. Like most prevaricators, Melrose was sure his country getup and affable beer-buying maneuver were as transparent as glass. "Got a delivery to make to a place called Fengate. Furniture. It's out there"—he nodded in the direction of the car park—"in my van." He wanted to get it across that he worked for a living hauling things about. But as the smoke from their several cigarettes curled upward to form a restive cloud below the ceiling, he found his announcement did nothing to stir them up.

"You be right on top o' it, then. This here's Algarkirk."

Why weren't they fascinated that Melrose was going right to the scene of the crime? Why weren't they telling him about their famous murder? Melrose raised his glass. "Cheers!"

There was more desultory conversation about the weather and the coming flower parade and the price of feed. Melrose decided to bring up the house he had seen near Cowbit. He told them about the name. "'The Red Last.' Odd that, isn't it? Was it once a pub, d'you think?"

One of the younger men, Malcolm by name, said, "Well, it's to do with shoes, ihn't?"

The others nodded. One said, "Aye, still, funny name for a pub. I ain't never heard of it . . . you, Ian?" He turned to the other younger man. He and Malcolm seemed to be mates. Ian shook his head.

"It's that thing they use," said Malcolm, proud of being the one whose intelligence matched that of the stranger, "you know, that wood thing that's the shape o' yer foot."

Some jocularity here about the various feet in attendance, until the one named Ian, probably tired of his friend's getting the attention, said, "Fengate House you're looking for? Ah, that be the place where that murder happened."

About time, thought Melrose, turning to the woman in the berry hat. "Murder?" he asked, wonderingly.

The woman put her hands around her throat and made ghoulish choking noises. "Found only wearin' a wrapper out on the fen." She lowered her voice. "Interfered with, they say."

One of the men, disgusted with the misreporting, said, "Warn't interfered with and warn't wearin' no wrapper, neither. They was one shot and one strangled, 'er and Dorcas."

"Good lord," said Melrose. "You mean you've had *two* murders here?"

They all nodded, pleased as punch that here was a beer-buying stranger they might be able to keep going until afternoon closing. "Aye, they was both of them from Fengate. There was poor Dorcas, and she used to work here too, am I not right, Dave?" One of the men addressed the bartender, who was probably the owner also. He smiled, nodded, went down the bar to fill another order. The old man picked up the account. "One was some woman who was guest there, she be the first to die—" Ah, the relish with which he said it! "Found her shot dead!"

The rest of them nodded solemnly.

"An' Dorcas, poor gurhl," said the woman, though it didn't sound like sorrow she was expressing. "Only twenty, was Dorcas. Whyever would someone want to kill poor Dorcas? Harmless, she was."

Fruitlessly, they argued over Dorcas's age. They each seemed to have a favorite number from nineteen to twenty-eight, until Dave came down the bar to join the talk and put paid to this disagreement by telling them Dorcas was twenty-two. They all deferred instantly to his age-assessment; Dave clearly had the respect of all of them on any subject from malt to murder.

When Melrose realized that he actually knew more about these deaths than the locals, he smiled and said he'd have to be on his way (but not forgetting to signal for one last round for his new friends). Then he asked Dave for directions to Fengate House, afraid if he asked the regulars it would start another argument.

Dave called across the room to a man who was passing the time leveling darts at the dartboard, "Jack! Someone here wants to know how to get to Fengate."

Melrose watched the tall man named Jack approach. When he passed the table where he'd apparently been sitting, he picked up the glass he'd left and drank the rest of it off. "You're nearly on top of it, it's just the other side of Algarkirk." He nodded his head in a westerly direction "Go on for under a mile and you're there."

"You're sure? I mean, that it's that easy? I'm poor on directions."

Jack laughed. "I should be sure. I live there. On the other side of Windy Fen out there. Here, I'll just draw it." He plucked a pencil stub from his pocket, grabbed a paper napkin from a holder, and in a flat fifteen seconds drew a road complete with trees and roundabout and a tiny house at the end, pillars and all. Then he resumed drinking and when the glass was nearly empty, dangled it in his long fingers.

Elegant fingers, thought Melrose, wondering if Price might be an artist or a pianist.

"You've some business at Fengate, do you?" His tone wasn't especially curious.

"I have, yes. A delivery for the Owens. Antique *table à la Bourgogne*." Melrose was, at this point, rather enjoying rolling that off his tongue.

"Never prove it by me; I'm thick as two planks when it comes to Max's stuff." He held out his hand, smiled at Melrose. "I'm Jack Price, incidentally."

Melrose extended his own hand. "Melrose Plant."

Price shook his hand, asked, "You a dealer, then? Or simply a transporter?"

"Neither. Occasionally, I'm called in to appraise a piece." That didn't sound quite right; he had made it appear that his might be the last word.

He cleared his throat, only too conscious of not being even the first word in determining value. "What I mean is—I'm not a professional, not at all. I have an amateur's interest in these things."

"What is it you've brought, again?"

"A *table à la Bourgogne*. Quite rare." He thought too late he should not be editorializing. However, if the table *weren't* rare, he imagined his error would be safe with Jack Price, whose interest in it was no more than polite.

"Sounds impressive. Sounds like something Max would kill for."

Melrose waited on this with a mild expression of curiosity. He thought it a rather careless comment to make about someone in a household connected with two murders.

"Max Owen is my uncle." His empty glass dangled from his hand.

When Dave appeared at Melrose's signal to collect the empty pint, Price thanked Melrose and handed over his glass. Then he offered Melrose a cigar, a thin panatella. Melrose thought that thin cigar between Price's fingers was the right touch for a figure in a Goya painting. It suited the rest of him so well: eyes of a brown so dark they were nearly black, longish dark hair that fell toward the side of his face when he bent the cigar over a match. In that light the irises sparked with pinpoints of red. Melrose wished he'd go on, say more. But he simply sat smoking his cigar, thanked Dave when his drink was set before him, thanked Melrose again.

Melrose said, "The table is something the Owens bought on approval. Since they wanted things at their house authenticated anyway, I offered to drive the van here."

"Max, not Grace."

"I beg your pardon?"

"Not Grace Owen. It's Max's passion, that stuff, not hers. She cares sod-all for it." Price dusted ash from his cigar into a metal tray. "I expect you must've heard about these murders we've had." He made it sound like a bout of bad weather. "It was in the papers, London ones, too. Max is fairly prominent in the antiques and art world."

"No, I don't recall reading about it." He inclined his head toward the group at the bar. "But they were just talking about it."

"Couple of weeks ago, it was. A weekend party. One of the guests was found dead—shot—lying out on the Wash, you know, the coast, which isn't very far from here. Local cops questioned all of us pretty thoroughly."

"They discovered who did it?" Melrose hoped he hit the right note of surprised interest.

"Not yet they haven't. The victim was Max's ex-wife."

Price was draining his glass pursuant to its being refilled once again. He held up two fingers, then set his glass on the bar, empty but for a swallow. Price had the manner of the long-standing drinker, one who could drink for hours and never show it. He tapped Melrose's nearly full glass. "You'll have another?"

"Better not, or they'll have to cart me in the house stretched over the table." Ex-wife. It was genuinely astonishing to Melrose that a man would have either the interest or the energy to marry more than once. For he himself, who had never been married, to discover one had made a mistake once would be a bitter experience. He simply could not think how anyone could repeat it. Horribly old-fashioned of him, he supposed.

Price volunteered that victim's name. "Verna Dunn. Frankly, I can understand Max's getting rid of her. Pretty insufferable."

Getting rid of her did not strike Melrose as the aptest way of putting it in the circumstances. He said, frowning, "The name's familiar." Only through Jury, it was.

"Uh-huh. An actress. That is, she used to be. Faded a bit these days, but still better-looking than a lot of younger women you see. She was never a very good actress; I've watched a couple of her films." He studied the end of his cigar. "It must have been goddamned provoking for Grace to have to entertain an ex-wife for the weekend. Especially *that* ex-wife." Jack Price made a sound that could have been an aborted laugh, could have been disgust.

Melrose made a mental note of that. And also of Jack Price's face when he said it. A flush had spread from his neck upward, which could, of course, be put down to more than three beers. He'd clearly been drinking before Melrose got here.

Jack Price started tapping his pockets for matches. His cigar had gone out. Melrose produced his lighter. Price smiled. "A trusty old Zippo. I've always liked them."

Once again Melrose noticed his hands. "Are you a painter, by any chance?"

"No. I'm a sculptor."

"Is that so? And is your studio there? At Fengate?"

"Um–hm." He turned the cigar in his mouth. "Got the old barn converted. It's quite nice. The Owens are generous people."

Well, if he was on to the positive side of his benefactors, Melrose doubted he'd hear much of value. "This has been enjoyable. But someone at Fengate is expecting this table and I'm later than I meant to be anyway. Care for a lift?"

Price shook his head. "Thanks, no. I always walk the footpath."

That, thought Melrose, was a fact worth noting.

10

The first person Melrose saw after he reached Fengate was an elderly man in rolled-up shirtsleeves and floppy wide-brimmed hat, with a shotgun broken over his arm. Another Momaday, perhaps? Behind him was a small wood, one of the few gatherings of desiduous trees he had seen in his whole long ride across the fens. Upon seeing the van, clearly marked TRUEBLOOD'S ANTIQUES in elegant black letters, this wildflower, whoever he was, appeared to be about to tell Melrose deliveries were in the rear. *("Take the van round back to where the kitchen it. Cook will give you something to eat.")* Then the gardener's glance moved from the van to its driver (who had alighted), and apparently thought better of sending him to the back door.

Well, thought Melrose, *quality shows. It's in the bones as well as the blood. . . .*

But not enough, apparently. The gardener descended upon him with that look a doorman wears when a tradesperson pulls up. Cheerily, Melrose called: "I've a delivery for Mr. Owen."

The man muttered something inscrutable and preceded Melrose along the paved path to the door (while beckoning for him to come on, come on). This done, he wandered away into another part of the house, leaving Melrose to inspect his soles for wayward mud. Was it simply a generic admonishment—*Wipe your feet*—to those in trade, who were always thought to have muddy shoes from walking through bogs and marshes and dung? Where was he to go? At the moment he stood in the foyer with a black and white patterned marble floor that contained what might have been an overflow of Max Owen's collection. In a number of niches sat bronze and marble busts, and the walls were covered with paintings, prints, and reproductions, a highly eclectic collection, he thought. A Matisse hung next to a Landseer, a painter Melrose could never understand. The Landseer was a depiction of a family scene incorporating the young Victoria, a gentleman Melrose assumed was her dear Albert, a lot of dogs and dead birds. One of the youngsters seemed to be about to pluck one up. Melrose shook his head. He supposed there were no limits as to what the Victorians chose to toss together. The painting hung above a credenza with a bloated front, its top holding a number of Dresden or Limoges figurines. He knew a little about porcelain, only because he had plenty of it at Ardry End.

A double-door to his right stood slightly open. He gave it a tentative push, stepped inside, and had to adjust his eyes to the relative darkness of the interior, largely the result of velvet curtains drawn almost, but not altogether, closed. Knives of light cut through the narrow openings.

The room was narrow but long, and a number of life-size, marble statues were positioned at points down its length. They were all women—or, rather, all female—for a couple of the figures were quite young girls. Near the door was one in a bonnet and a ruched bodice, the only one fully clothed to a Victorian nicety. Her hands stretched up in a gesture of feeding birds. Most of them were done in a classical vein, thinly draped, garlanded, and ageless. They were not set in alcoves, either, like the busts in the foyer. They stood in no particular relation to one another; if he were to walk the length of this gallery (which is what it appeared to be) he would have had, at some points, to navigate around them. He thought he detected on the one in the middle, nearest the slant of light, the wink of a gold or silver chain. When he went to inspect it more closely, he saw he was right. Someone had put a thin silver chain round her neck. Now he looked at the ones nearest him more closely; and saw they were similarly adorned with flowers or silver necklaces or bracelets on outstretched arms. The one nearest his end of the room wore a thin velvet band, ivory, round her neck. Melrose smiled, wanting to meet the fey person who had adorned them. Jury hadn't mentioned any Owen children.

The statues—eight or nine of them—were not alone in gracing this gallery. There were more paintings, perhaps better ones, in addition to a great deal of furniture, some delicate, some gaudy. Sideboards, armoires, credenzas, a Louis Quatorze commode, tables of Japanese lacquer, lavishly decorated in patterns of birds and flowers. A lovely Queen Anne settee was placed beside another bulbous credenza, perhaps the twin of the one in the foyer. There were a number of portraits, possibly of Owen forebears, more likely bought at auction. A beam of light struck one of these, a painting of two little girls in a garden who were fixing up some Japanese lanterns. Moving closer, Melrose made out the name of the artist. It was a John Singer Sargent, a copy, but a very fine one. Melrose had seen the original in the Tate Gallery.

The whole collection was surprising. Its eclecticism spoke more of the enthusiast than it did of the expert, so perhaps he wouldn't have as much trouble as he'd thought. There was a collection of glassware in a glass-fronted case. He thought he recognized a goblet similar to one Trueblood had shown him in the shop. The case wasn't locked so he opened it and took out the glass. It was handsomely engraved, depicting around its edge a sylvan scene of a girl and a boy and a few animals all chasing one another (as they were wont to do on old glass and urns). Then he heard a throat clear.

("Ahem!")

For a split second when he turned around he thought one of the statues had moved. No, a flesh and blood woman stood at the other end of the room. It was almost as if the little cough she'd given was to warn him that if he intended to steal that goblet, he'd better do it later, for she was watching.

"Mr. Plant? I'm terribly sorry to keep you waiting. I was on the telephone with the police. You know how they are. I'm Grace Owen. We had a murder here. Two murders, actually." Two seemed to discomfit her, as if she might be thought to be bragging.

She expected him to be startled, and seemed relieved when he wasn't. He told her he had been given this news already. "The regulars at the pub yonder"—Melrose inclined his head—"told me." He did not mention Jack Price, and did not know why he didn't. "I expect you know it? It's called the Case Has Altered."

"Oh, my, yes." She smiled and then stopped quickly, as if to smile in such circumstances was unfeeling. "Then you probably know it was my husband's ex-wife. And one of our staff, a young woman. That was only a few days ago."

Melrose nodded. She seemed so guileless, so—clear. Her voice, her expression. The clarity of crystal, like this goblet. He looked from her to the goblet, said, "Sorry," and returned it to its proper place on the shelf.

She smiled. "That's one of Max's favorites."

Hell's bells, thought Melrose. First time out and he was all at sea. Jury hadn't listed any goblet. Why hadn't he paid more attention when Trueblood was lecturing him on glassware? He wondered what other surprises he'd have in store for his unexpert eyes.

"Mr. Trueblood was very complimentary about the incredible range of your knowledge. And aren't you also a friend of that Scotland Yard policeman who was here?"

He swallowed. Of course, Jury had told her he knew a very good appraiser. There was nothing to do but acknowledge this. It just seemed to make his impersonation so damned untenable. Melrose kept a stupid smile plastered on his face and hoped she wouldn't revert to the origins or antiquity of the goblet.

"You'll need a wide range of knowledge. Max seems to like, well—" She spread her arms. "—everything."

He didn't know whether that made Max a man of generous spirit or an undiscerning one. Or perhaps it was just that he had an embarrassment of doubtful riches.

She was still standing a distance away from him, and in the gloom it was difficult to see her face clearly, but he could tell it was a pretty one.

"He calls this the 'Sculpture Hall,' which I think might be overstating its dignity." Here she draped her arm around the waist of the lady with the velvet choker, who looked uncannily like Grace Owen; she might have sat for this statue. Or stood. She went on: "The 'cold ladies,' I call them. Poor things." She patted the cold lady's shoulder. "This is Gwendolyn." She patted the statue's arm. "I've named them all. Their personalities are quite different. My husband thinks I'm crazy." This didn't seem to faze her one bit. "Incidentally, he's in London. I should have told you straightaway. But of course he knows you're coming, so he'll be back very soon, at least in time for dinner. He's quite eager to talk with you. Now, how long will you be staying? I only ask because my cook will nag me until she finds out. You're welcome, of course, for as long as you want." She was untying the velvet ribbon from Gwendolyn's neck.

"You mean—here?"

"Of course 'here.' That's understood." And she dropped the ribbon into the pocket of her gray dress. "It's *so* nice to have somebody new." She had moved over to the long window nearest her and was pulling the cord to close the curtains. "Max is afraid the light will fade his paintings and this old wallpaper; I believe it's William Morris." She went to the next window and closed it, and the next, proceeding down the room to the window nearest him. When she stood briefly in what light there was coming through the gathering dusk, the light fell on her face, across her cheekbones, her pale hair, her amber eyes. She seemed to have no trouble at all in simply speaking her thoughts. He was reminded of Miss Fludd.

Although he still had no clear picture of Max Owen, he had decided nonetheless that a man who would be parsimonious with light, when he had such a woman to stand in its rays, would probably cheat at cards.

"Let's go in another room, shall we? This hall is too cold." She closed the curtain, leaving only the bare inch of daylight to seep through. Only then, as she did so, did he notice that the statues, despite their position farther away or nearer, were turned in the same direction, blind-eyed, toward the light.

He felt a great sadness.

❦

The rug in the room to which she led him was Turkestan and probably worth a fortune. At least he thought it was a Turkestan. Rugs were incredibly confusing, not made less so by his reading. This one must have been twelve by twenty feet of deep, swirling colors. Probably it added as much warmth to the room as the crackling fireplace. He supposed it was a library: it was smaller, brighter, warmer. Warmth was supplied not only by the fire and the rug but by the many books that lined the walls.

In the center of the room was a grand piano, the top closed and covered with photos and snapshots in silver and wood frames. He looked carefully at the one in front. The young man in it, holding a bridle, and

with a horse blanket over his shoulder, looked so much like Grace Owen
it would be impossible to miss the resemblance. He had her open, amiable
expression. It must have been a relation of hers.

Grace Owen saw him studying the photo. "That's my son, Toby. He's
dead."

"I'm . . . so sorry." Jury hadn't told him this; perhaps Jury didn't know.

She nodded, looked at the picture herself for a moment, then asked
him if he would like tea or coffee . . . or perhaps a drink?

"Coffee would be fine."

Although there was a bellpull hanging beside the mirror over the fireplace, she did not use it, preferring instead to go herself. Melrose moved
from piano to window, which gave an uninterrupted view of the fens. No
trees this side. How lonely and bleak, he thought.

Grace returned, said, "Annie will bring the coffee. She's our cook.
Somber, isn't it?" She had joined him at the window. "The most brooding landscape I think I've ever seen. More than the North York moors,
even. The first time I drove one of these roads that goes up and *over* the
river, instead of just across it, I thought the world was turned upside
down. In some places, we're actually below sea-level. Once these fens *were*
the sea. They used to call the water the Bailiff. The Bailiff of Fens, come
to turn us out, bag and baggage, without warning." She smiled.

For a few moments they were silent, both looking out over this watery
land. Clouds were massing out there, prelude, perhaps, to a storm.

"Do you spend all of the year in London, then?"

Melrose was pulled back from this watery atmosphere; he had felt suddenly sleepy, a defense, he imagined, against the weight of his imposture.
He felt it might be unlucky to lie to Grace Owen. "I, ah, have a place in
Northants. In Long Piddleton." He did not add that the "place" was a
Georgian stronghold larger than Fengate and that it sat in over a hundred
acres of verdant woodland. "That's how I came to know Marshall Trueblood. That's where his shop is." He asked, somewhat anxiously, "You've
not been to his shop, have you?" He had a sudden silly vision of Mrs.
Withersby getting Grace aside and slyly pointing out Melrose. *"Now, you
best watch that'un, bit of a wide lad, him; he'll be trying t'trick you some day."*
Melrose shook this off. No, she said, she'd never been there. "Neither has

Max. Apparently, this dealer—Trueblood? Is that his name?—heard that Max was looking for an appraiser. I think perhaps it was our Scotland Yard detective who told him."

Melrose smiled at her appropriating Jury for their own. "I spend most of my time in Northants, not London." He thought it would be best to play himself as himself as much as possible. Fewer lies to remember.

"But this is not your work?"

Melrose reacted strangely to this comment. It was as if everything were encompassed in it—the circumstances that accounted for her presence here as well as his, in this house, and the house itself; the murders that had been committed close by, perhaps even the death of her son, even the landscape, the fens. As if Melrose had the power of some fiendish assessor to mold these happenings. He had turned up, like a devil on the doorstep. Or the Bailiff of the Fens, come without warning. He shook himself again; he could not understand this melodramatic turn of mind, or this guilty one. He reminded himself that he was trying to help out Jury. And Jenny.

"No," he answered. "It isn't my work, as you say. I'm a dilettante, an enthusiastic tracker-down of the false and phony. I'm not a professional by any manner of means. I don't even collect things myself." To fend off that speculative look she was giving him, he nodded toward the paintings on the far wall, the only wall not dedicated to books. "I must say I prefer the paintings in here to the ones in your entrance hall." *That* was certainly a safe enough judgment.

Grace smiled. "We all have our blind spots."

He hoped that was merely a generous assessment of her husband's lapse in taste and not of his, Melrose's.

The door opened just then and a woman in her sixties came in with a tray of coffee and biscuits. Her stout figure was wound with a white apron and, as some cooks look the part, she put Melrose in mind of fresh-baked bread and scones. Her hair was pulled back tightly into a bun. It was marsh-brown. Her eyes were darker, the color of peat. She carried herself stiffly, yet her hands were lively. Annie Suggins's hands got busy setting out the cups, clinking spoons into saucers, worrying off a coffee-cozy. All of her life must have gone into her hands. They were the hands of a fluttery sort of person who might be forever wringing them, or laying them aside her face in looks of astonishment, or jerking a fan about. But Annie did not otherwise strike Melrose as a fluttery person at all. To Grace's kind thanks, she nodded briefly, stiffly, and left.

As Grace set about pouring coffee, she said, "Annie's a wonderful cook. Rather conscious now of extra duties on her shoulders."

Melrose smiled. "Looks like one of those truly loyal servants."

Grace laughed. "To tell the truth, I doubt it. I think she's loyal to some Suggins-code that we can't penetrate. Cream?"

"No thank you."

"I mean, we all live by some weird notion of propriety. Even honor. Don't we? Sugar?"

No, he said again. There was that look on her face again. That smile. He thanked her as she handed over the coffee.

She took her own cup back to the window, drank her coffee as she looked out. For those few moments she appeared to be far away and he drank his own coffee in silence, wanting her mind to proceed along its own line. She then came back to the here and now, a much less demanding place to be, Melrose thought, judging from the difference in her expression.

"Sorry," she said. "Just woolgathering." She sat back down on the sofa, then leaned forward, and ran her hand over the rug under her feet. "This is one thing." She looked up at Melrose. "The rug, I mean. Max wants an opinion on it. The man from Christie's said it wasn't a genuine Turkestan. Just a reproduction. Or imitation."

Bending over to look at it, he was pleased that he had at least identified the style. "Oh? That seems unlikely." He put his spectacles on, hoping that would make him look smarter than he felt, rose and walked to the outside edge of the rug and flipped back a corner. "Thousands of knots here, and a very tight weave. The back's as clear as the front. It certainly appears genuine to me. And, also, you must consider the size. It's enormous, much too large to make reproducing worth one's while." Was that true? A pound of jellybabies might cost only a little more than half-a-pound; a case of wine would not be as much as twelve separate bottles. But did this two-for-one principle hold with Turkish carpets? Didn't the value increase incrementally, inch by precious inch? Well, he'd said it and he'd best stick by it.

Grace looked at the carpet doubtfully. "But the man from Christie's was supposed to be an expert. . . ." Then she blushed, perhaps thinking she'd insulted him.

Breezily, Melrose said, "Oh, experts can make mistakes too. *I've* certainly made enough in my time!" And then it occurred to him to wonder why Max Owen was getting these people in to do valuations. "Tell me, why is your husband doing this?"

"Max wants to sell some things. He prefers to do it at auction. But the Christie's man—" She shrugged.

"Sotheby's then?" Melrose hoped the "Sotheby's man" didn't agree with the "Christie's man." He would hate to go head to head with that lot, the premiere auction houses of the world. Oh, the hell with it. Most of any business was bluster. Blustering, dissembling—everyone did it until a person couldn't tell the Bayeux tapestries from granny's tatting. Melrose hoped she wouldn't ask for the provenance of that Russian amber necklace under glass—did it, in fact, descend from the Romanovs? The only jewelry he'd ever studied closely was whatever Agatha happened to have on, and that was only to see whether it had belonged to his mother. Indeed, he'd learned something about furniture from trying to ascertain what Agatha had nicked from Ardry End. Even tables and chairs had gone missing.

"I met your nephew. Mr. Price? I stopped in the pub to get directions. And a pint," he added, not wanting to appear holier-than–Mr. Price.

"Jack? The Case is one of his favorite haunts. Jack's my husband's nephew. He has a studio out back; well it's more of a converted barn, but he seems to like it, having a separate place. Sleeps there, too. Sometimes we don't see him for days. Sometimes, I think he sleeps rough, out on the fens."

"Are the police getting anywhere with these murders?"

Her luminous, gold leaf eyes regarded him over the rim of her cup. "If they have they're not sharing it with us. Poor Dorcas." Gently, Grace replaced her cup. It tinkled against the saucer because her hand was shaking. "Her body was discovered over on Windy Fen. 'Wyndham,' really, but we call it 'Windy.' It's National Trust property between here and the Case Has Altered. What I mean is, we take the pub for our north boundary—"

Melrose didn't want to get into a discussion of the fens and interrupted. "When did all of this happen?"

She thought for a moment. "Verna was—Verna Dunn, my husband's first wife—was killed two weeks ago. Her body was found late at night on the Wash. I honestly don't know what this Lincolnshire detective has turned up. Dorcas, that was just a few days ago—" The sound of an approaching car brought Grace to her feet. "—the night of the fourteenth. Here's Max!"

11

He was not prepared for Max Owen. Melrose had formed a picture of a fussy, somewhat arrogant dilettante, a proud man, perhaps. Anyone who set such a store by his belongings would be. But Max Owen wasn't. Melrose had been prepared to dislike him, probably because Owen and his collection were a hurdle he had to jump, a fallen tree across his path.

Now that Owen was standing in the doorway, the image dissolved. Melrose's irrational dislike of the man had mounted with every long-lived hour in Trueblood's shop trying to master the finer points of each serpentine chest, saber-legged chair, credenza, or Canterbury that Trueblood dragged to center stage. Once Melrose had actually fallen asleep listening to Trueblood drone on about a japanned chest *("Always be suspicious of japanning—")* only to be shaken awake and forced to repeat the more important points like a catechism. Melrose had complained that he couldn't possibly remember all of it and Trueblood had reminded him it was only five pieces he had really to know about. Not including the rug. The rest he could bluff.

"Like Diane. She's got bluffing down to a fine art."

"If there is anyone I do not wish to be like, it's Diane Demorney!"

Far from being intimidating, Max Owen was almost boyishly shy. It was this that constituted a large part of his charm, for he *was* charming. He was not especially handsome—his face too long, too thin, with eyes like muscat grapes. Where Melrose had imagined there would be a bespoke tailor in the background, he saw that Owen was an indifferent dresser: his subdued suit, dark gray worsted; his tie, a boring tartan. Melrose had expected a more flamboyant man—one who would wear a yellow waistcoat and was not to be trusted.

Grace said the coffee was cold, and Max said not to bother. But she would have bothered, of course, had not the cook, Annie, appeared right on his heels, with fresh hot coffee, leaving as quickly as she'd come.

Max sat down on the massive Victorian chesterfield, leaning back, legs thrust out before him, as if he were used to this sofa and often sat there. Melrose would have found it hard to get comfortable on such a piece of furniture, but then he imagined that Owen, like Trueblood, related to furnishings—"things"—far more sensitively than Melrose himself did. They could see comfort where he could not.

"Sorry not to be here to greet you. I've been all day at Carlton House. They're selling off the entire contents. You can imagine there were some good pieces." He looked at Melrose as he sipped his coffee; the look was encouraging, as if he expected something from Melrose.

Given his avocation, Melrose would be expected to have heard about this sale. "Marshall Trueblood told me about it. I would have gone with him had I not been coming here."

"I don't know your friend Trueblood. But I couldn't have picked him out anyway. A horde of people, really crowded."

"Trueblood was after a couple of carved boxes. Sixteenth century. I wonder if he got them." A small acquisition such as that probably would go unnoticed. He hoped he was being vague enough that Max Owen wouldn't question him.

Max frowned. "Don't remember seeing them in the catalogue. Anyway, I managed to walk off with the Carlton House writing table."

"Lord, do we have room?" Grace's laugh was rueful.

Melrose was glad she'd interceded since he was sure Owen was about to put a question to him about the writing table. He sat back down on the hard settee, hoping he would not thereby call attention to this ornately carved piece, as he had no idea about its origins. But he had to sit somewhere. He should have chosen the leather wing chair, which was straightforward Chippendale.

Grace spoke as she poured the coffee. "I was telling Mr. Plant about—"

Melrose smiled and accepted more coffee. "Melrose will do, thanks."

Max sat forward. "I understand you have a title. May I ask what?"

"Caverness, Earl of. But I prefer the family name."

"Why?"

Oh, hell. Was Owen going to be one of these quite literal types who had no use for nuance or intuition? "Titles are cumbersome."

"Wish I had one." Max sat back.

"Well, don't distinguish yourself in any way and perhaps you will."

They laughed, and Grace continued what she'd been about to say. "I was telling him about—what happened. Mr. Plant is a friend of Jennifer Kennington."

"Ah! She too had a title she disavowed. But she'd married one, so I expect it doesn't count for much. She didn't like it, either."

Melrose corrected Grace Owen again. "Acquaintance only. I met her once in Stratford." He told Grace he knew Jenny to avoid the consequences of some future slip that would make it clear he did know her.

"A coincidence." Was there something in Owen's expression, the trace of a smile, that said it couldn't possibly be coincidence?

Grace said, "And Dorcas. It was just three days ago," she added sadly.

Max did not reply, but looked out of the long window at the rising mist. It was by now early evening and getting dark. Fog blanketed the driveway and the flower beds and cut off the roots of trees, making the wood look impenetrable. "Poor girl," he said.

They were lost in a moment of silence and Melrose hoped they'd go on. He could certainly show a legitimate interest—a double murder was surely grounds for curiosity, no matter what your mission—but he felt it was too soon after his arrival to carry the brunt of the questioning himself.

But Max carried it on. "That place, Wyndham Fen—where Dorcas was found—that's what all of South Lincolnshire used to be like—real fen country."

"Max. You make it sound as if you mourned the loss of the fens more than the loss of Dorcas."

"I didn't know her well enough to mourn her, dear one." He held out his cup for fresh coffee.

This unadorned admission was rather refreshing, thought Melrose.

Why indeed would he "mourn" an employee with whom he'd probably had very little contact. "That's what they said in the pub; one old regular claimed we shouldn't call it the fens: 'It ain't fens no more.'"

Max laughed. "I'm sure. Sometimes I think we're as fragile as the landscape."

"This must be pretty horrible for you," said Melrose. "Police in your home and all the questioning."

"The whole thing is completely beyond me," said Grace. "What on earth was Verna doing late at night on the Wash? People don't walk out on those saltings for exercise." Grace looked thoughtful. "Two murders within two weeks."

Max put down his cup. "'Alleged' murders, you should say."

"Well, the alleged shot from the alleged gun caused quite an outpouring of alleged blood."

Melrose laughed, but without humor. He was too busy taking impressions. Grace Owen, for one, didn't appear to resent the ex-wife's presence at Fengate, alive *or* dead.

"Jennifer Kennington was the last person to see Verna alive." Calmly, she sipped her coffee.

No. The last person to see her alive would have been the killer, thought Melrose. "I find it hard to believe that Lady Kennington would be a suspect. She appeared to me to be so . . . gentle." They were miles from antique *bonheurs-du-jour* Turkestan rugs. But the Owens didn't seem to notice, submerged as they were in the strange business of murder at Fengate.

Grace nodded. "Yes, you're right. Except I think it's true that one can't tell what another's capable of in such circumstances. On the other hand, what on earth would her motive be? They didn't even know each other."

"You mean, as far as we *know* they didn't."

Melrose felt a cold spike of fear. They were seriously entertaining the notion that Jenny might have done this.

"Max would be a better candidate for chief suspect," Grace said, laughing. "Or I would, or even Jack. In fact *anyone* would make more sense than Jennifer Kennington." She sighed.

He would have loved to ask what motives she had in mind, but the question would wait.

"Grace—" Max put down his coffee cup. "You don't know what you're talking about." His tone was perfectly amiable. Then he turned to Melrose. "This detective from New Scotland Yard—he's a friend of Mr. Trueblood." He paused and searched through his pockets, finally drew out a card. "Superintendent Richard Jury, no less. Pretty high up, a superintendent." He looked at Melrose quizzically. "But you know him, don't you? Didn't he recommend you? Grace? Isn't that true?"

As Grace nodded, Melrose said, "I know him slightly, yes." He was feeling more and more uncomfortable, for he couldn't make out Max Owen. He couldn't make out whether he was being baited or whether Owen's questions were simply innocent. Melrose decided that he should be the one to turn the conversation to Owen's collection. "Where are the pieces you wanted me to have a look at?"

Grace broke in, tapping her toe against the carpet. "The rug. Mr. Plant says it's the real thing."

Quickly, Melrose said, "It's my *opinion* it's, as you say, the 'real thing.'" He turned a self-deprecating smile on Max Owen, who was clearly happy to believe that his guest's opinion was also the real thing.

"So Christie's and old Parker were wrong!"

"If they told you otherwise."

"Parker is a friend of Max," said Grace, "who loves to take issue with whatever Max acquires. He's knowledgeable, yes, but I suspect he's quite jealous, really."

Looking toward another room, Max Owen said, "Come on in here, Mr. Plant. There's another rug I'd like an opinion on." He was moving toward the door, and said over his shoulder, "Darling, bring the booze, will you?"

How wonderful! thought Melrose, trailing after Owen as Grace went to the sideboard and picked up a cut-glass decanter. *If it's rugs I have to classify, by all means, bring the booze.*

In the next room, Max and Melrose stood looking down at a rug of blues and reds and graceful swirls as Grace pulled glasses out of one of the many cabinets housing them. They would never be at a loss for a glass, the Owens.

"It's a Nain. You know, that very fine rug from Iran. But Parker says it isn't, says it's the wrong design. Supposed to be Ispahan."

Melrose put on a thoughtful expression. He only wished Grace weren't there, with her lovely lack of guile. He found it extremely difficult to put on his act in the face of her artlessness. He cleared his throat. "That depends on what one means by Ispahan, I suppose."

Max Owen looked puzzled. "Well, surely, people agree as to *what* that is!"

Melrose smiled, gave Owen a sad little headshake. "Mr. Owen, in this business there are very few things people agree upon."

Max smiled. "Since you seem to know rugs, you might give me your opinion of the ones upstairs."

Hell's bells, thought Melrose. Well, it was bound to happen, wasn't it, that Max Owen would go trolling beyond the boundary of Jury's list?

"I'm going to see Annie about dinner, then." She set cups on the tray, picked it up, walked out, calling over her shoulder, "Around eight? Will that give you time?"

Max said, "No, but eight's fine. I'm starved. Thirsty, too. Thanks." Grace handed them both a glass of whiskey, said she hoped the brand was all right with Mr. Plant. Any brand was all right with Mr. Plant at this point, threatened with a mess of upstairs rugs.

Max moved over to an open court cupboard (at least that's what Melrose thought it was, *Don't call it for God's sakes a "buffet,"* Trueblood had warned him). He picked up a deep blue ashtray of what looked to Melrose like Murano glass and brought it over to set between them on an old trunk. But Max Owen was so drowned in his antique sea, he forgot to light up, if that was his intention. "That *table à la Bourgogne* you brought I told Suggins to put upstairs in a small study I use. The pieces I'm wondering about are in here." Max handed Melrose a thick glass tumbler. "Such as that *secretaire.*"

If there was one thing Melrose knew it was *secretaires à abattant.* Or at least he thought he did, until his eyes fell on Max Owen's. This one was completely different from the one that had been in Trueblood's shop several years before. You couldn't have stuffed a body into this one, that was certain. It was black lacquer with gilt ornamentation, the front at a forty-five-degree angle which fell down to reveal a writing surface. He nodded; he frowned in turn in response to Max Owen's comments, understanding practically nothing of Max's antiquarian jargon, fashioned largely out of French. *Demi-lune; menuisier.* And it was amazing how the man could go on about marquetry and parquetry, soffits and jappaning. Why in the devil did he need any other opinion? Melrose stifled a yawn; he felt he could have communed with the *secretaire* on its own terms. By the time Max was finished, there wasn't an inch of gilding, a corner of ormolu, a tracery of acanthus leaves that Melrose wasn't intimately acquainted with.

Max lowered and raised the writing surface and asked, "What do you think?"

Melrose looked seriously thoughtful for several moments, chin resting in his hand, finger tapping his cheek, and said, "I think you're absolutely right."

Max Owen looked quite smug. "Even about the hidden drawer, the secret drawer? The Sotheby's fellow said he'd never encountered anything like that in the genuine article."

Had he missed the secret drawer? "You mean Tim Strangeways?" Melrose suddenly remembered that Strangeways was a name Trueblood had told him to invoke, if Max got onto some discussion about the people at Sotheby's. So Melrose's smile was even smugger than Max's. Strangeways had already been brought to heel.

Max laughed. "Good." Then he turned to another commodelike piece and started a little lecture on *bureaux-de-roi.*

Melrose's attention span was turning into that of a four-year-old. He simply couldn't keep his mind on this stuff for five minutes running. He decided not to open up a stall in Camden Passage. *Pay Attention!* he ordered himself.

". . . *de-roi.* This is an excellent specimen of the type."

Melrose was studiously examining the legs, running his hand up and down one, then he rose and pulled out one of the drawers, again running his hand along the joining, closed it, and sighed. "I'm not so sure." Well, he had to take issue at some point with the genuineness of one of these *objets d'art* so he might as well with this one, especially since it hadn't been on the list.

At this point, Max asked him to examine another, much smaller rug near the windows. *Hell, not another rug.* Melrose couldn't even remember what kind of Persian carpet was in his own drawing room, the one True-blood drooled over and said was priceless . . . a priceless—what? Now he was forced to inspect what Owen told him was an antique Fereghan. It was quite beautiful, a light blue background with a pattern of interlinked medallions.

"My friend Parker says the design isn't right for it to be a genuine Fereghan."

Melrose smiled. "Oh, I'm sure the medallion is genuine enough. But is your friend Parker?"

Max's laugh was a bellow; it seemed clear to Melrose that Owen and this Parker were highly competitive. And Max Owen wasn't looking for an expert; he was looking for somebody to tell him he was right. Melrose was happy to oblige.

Max had turned to the whiskey decanter, splashed more whiskey into his glass, held up the decanter in silent query to Melrose. Melrose shook his head.

Max replaced the stopper, asked, "Did you know her well?"

The question took Melrose completely by surprise. He feigned ignorance. "Know who?"

"Jennifer Kennington."

"No. As I said, I met her only the one time. In Stratford-upon-Avon. I think she lives there."

Max nodded. He was standing now, swirling the whiskey in his glass, his eyes seemingly fixed on the fog beyond the windows. "She needed investment money for some pub or restaurant she wanted to open. I'm the investor." He drank his whiskey, still looking out on darkness. "The few days in the country certainly turned out to be pretty unhappy for Jennifer, I'm afraid." He picked up a wooden chalice, examined it, replaced it.

From his expression, Melrose thought they'd been pretty unhappy for Max Owen, too.

ঞ৴

The Owens' friend Major Linus Parker joined them for dinner at the last minute. He preferred people call him, simply, "Parker." Melrose could sympathize with this ridding oneself of rank and title. Parker was a large man in his sixties whose house (which he had baptized "Toad Hall") lay off the public footpath, halfway between Fengate and the pub.

It was Parker who said, "It was almost comical, the police coming round. 'And where were you, sir, at the time of the murder?'" He said this in a deep voice, exaggerating the Lincolnshire accent. "I didn't think police actually *said* things like that. Sounded more like a parody of police."

"They apparently do," said Max Owen. "And did you give a thorough accounting of your movements?"

Parker said, "I was right here until eleven."

"After that, I mean."

"You've got me dead to rights; I was walking home."

Jack Price, who'd been silent for most of the meal, said, "And I went back to the studio."

"And Grace went to bed, and I went into my study. Not an alibi amongst us, too bad."

"I went to sleep immediately," said Grace.

"Ho-*ho*. Try telling that to our chief inspector!"

"Have done," said Grace. "Anyway, Max does have an alibi. You said sometime between eleven-thirty and midnight Suggins brought you a drink."

Max nodded. "Right. So it seems my future lies in the hands of our gardener, who likes a nip himself now and again."

"Which takes care of *his* testimony," said Parker.

Max said, "Mr. Plant's a friend of Lady Kennington."

"An acquaintance, rather," said Melrose.

"So you said." Max was looking at Melrose with a depth of glance that made him extremely uncomfortable and kept him turning the stem of his wineglass. "Jenny was with Verna, seems to have been the last person to see her alive. Or at least that's what I gather the Lincs police have deduced." He gazed at Melrose as if to see how he'd take it.

Melrose didn't take it at all; he made no comment.

"Verna's done quite well with a boutique in Pont Street. But not quite enough to back this play she wanted to star in. She was hoping I could help her there." Max shrugged. "I thought it would be an investment. Verna wasn't a bad actress."

There was a lively debate about this, whether Verna was, or wasn't.

Melrose frowned. It occurred to him they'd all been going on at some length about Verna Dunn, the ex-Mrs. Owen. Yet, no one was talking about the servant girl, Dorcas. "But what about the second murder? Your housemaid."

Both Grace and Max looked unhappy, slightly ashamed. He said, "Yes, you're right. You'd think we'd be more mindful of Dorcas. It's only been three days."

Price said, "It's because Verna was so flashy. Beautiful, or so most people thought. And somewhat famous."

"Yes, and Dorcas was so much the other . . . I mean, none of those things." Grace was looking down at her dessert plate. "Poor Dorcas." She picked up her fork.

Melrose bit into his gâteau and found it to be doused with cognac and a coating of dates and nuts; he took a moment to appreciate its moist richness. Then he said, "This young woman, Dorcas, I presume she had a gentleman-friend?"

"Dorcas?" Price sounded surprised. "I doubt it; she wasn't any too good-looking."

Melrose answered, I've never known that to absolutely stand in one's way." It occurred to him that Price knew a good deal about beauty, but probably not about people.

"You think a lover might have done it?" Parker asked.

Grace shrugged. "Don't police usually suspect one's nearest and dearest?"

"That's true," said Max Owen, who was concentrating on his dessert.

Parker, who had brought his whiskey glass to the table, drank off the remainder of the contents and looked around the table. "How could one suspect Lady Kennington of *that* murder?"

"I don't know, but I'm surprised that man Bannen let her go back to Stratford," said Price.

"Had to," said Max. "They couldn't keep her any longer. And she had no motive."

"But that," said Grace, "is true of all of us, isn't it?" She shoved back her chair. "We've none of us any discernible motive."

ᒿℓ

Melrose lay deep in a literal featherbed, his hands folded neatly over the duvet as he supposed he'd folded them as a child. His eyes rested on the pale ceiling, watching the shifting, watery light and lacy shadows reflected from the lamps outside around the drive. He turned his head and let his eyes play over the humped forms of furniture, relieved not to have to give out their provenance or state their value. Near his bed was an ancient rocking horse, picked up, no doubt, at one of Owen's country auctions. Its mane was tattered, its eyes dull from paint rubbed away. He had had such a horse, or thought he had. These drowsy reflections occupied his mind and kept him on the edge of sleep for some time. He thought about Dorcas Reese, Jenny, Verna Dunn. He stretched, lay with his hands behind his head. Now he knew that he wouldn't be able to sleep. Even the roots of his hair awakened with wide-eyed follicle-amazement.

He yanked away the pillow he'd just finished positioning under his head and tossed it on the floor. Now he would be awake the entire night unless he could think of something less hectic than murder. Counting sheep. Actually, that had worked once or twice. It was the awful boredom of the exercise that sunk you into oblivion . . . immediately he had a vision of Agatha's hand going back and forth to the cake plate. One fairy cake . . . two fairy cakes . . .

He was snoring before he'd gotten to ten.

12

Morning was at seven, happily for Browning, unhappily for Melrose. That was when he had snapped awake, muscles tense.

From what, Melrose couldn't imagine. A muscular dream? A pea under the mattress? No, the featherbed was actually too soft. Bleary-eyed he had risen, washed, dressed, and, still bleary-eyed, descended to the dining room. No one was there, but he did hear clattering in the kitchen and a tune half sung, half spoken in a low voice. Melrose stuck his head in the door.

Mrs. Suggins, the source of both the clatter and the tuneless tune, stopped singing and stirring as she looked around in surprise. She quickly wiped her hands on her apron and said, "Oh, sir, I'm just stirring the porridge and haven't started on the eggs yet. What would you have?"

"Nothing at all but a cup of tea. Ordinarily, I'm not up so early." *That* was the understatement of the year. He was never downstairs before nine-thirty. Melrose worshiped sleep as much as Trueblood worshiped things; all of that "knitting up the ravel'ed sleeve of care" went down a treat with him.

Of course she had a pot of tea ready and poured him out a mugful; she placed milk and sugar within his reach. "There you are." She smiled up at him. She was a short woman. Short and somehow the quintessence of Cook. Round-faced, round-bodied, like a couple of dumplings stuck together, she cheerily announced, "Breakfast when you like, sir."

Melrose thanked her. "What time do the Owens breakfast?"

"Between eight and nine is usual. Sometimes they eat together, sometimes not. Breakfast's a hard meal, keeping things hot, and they like different things too. And me with no help."

There wasn't any rancor in the tone; it was the sort of obligatory complaint one hears. (His own cook, Martha, occasionally muttered about lack of help.) Here was an opportunity Melrose hadn't foreseen. "I understand the young woman who helped you . . . met with an accident."

"Accident? Is that what they're calling it now?" Annie Suggins looked him over as if to say, *Oh, the fastidious rich.* She tapped her wooden spoon against the rim of the pot and went for plain speaking. "Murder, that's what it was. Awful thing, and her just a young girl." She clapped a lid on the pot, bent, and opened the door of the big oven.

A scent drifted out that made Melrose think twice about settling for tea only. He said, "Yes, an awful thing. Had she worked here very long?"

"Two years, about. Good worker, was Dorcas, even if she couldn't cook. She did the vegetables, you know, scraping and peeling, but times I let her cook them, they came out mush." Annie seemed to shudder, not with a vision of the murdered Dorcas, but one of overdone carrots. "A worse cook I've never seen." Annie Suggins was clearly a no-nonsense type of woman; she could still state plain facts even though Dorcas was dead.

Melrose sipped his tea and hoped she'd go on. Which she did after transferring the roasting pan from oven to table. When she lifted the lid to inspect the contents, he got the full, heavenly force of the aroma. Looked like a chicken or goose. He asked Annie.

"It's pheasant, a Scottish pheasant to be truthful."

(As if one were in danger of lying over pheasant.)

"—with apricots and dates."

Melrose took another whiff. "Lord, it's enough to make you forget about murder."

Annie laughed. "I hope not, sir. That'd be a tragedy. Though sometimes I think they've forgotten Dorcas was murdered, too."

Melrose agreed that Dorcas lay dead in the shadow of Verna Dunn. "Was she a local girl?"

A brief nod. "Spalding, if you call that local. Plain, decent family, though the father likes his whiskey." She stopped in the act of whacking at a small hill of dough and set her hands on her hips. "I don't think the lass had too happy a life, not her. I mean, I don't think she was treated bad, just that she was none too pretty, and that always tells against a girl." She remained in this stance, her expression mournful, and then started in on the dough again, slapping and pummeling it into a stain-smooth mound.

Melrose helped himself to more tea from the pot. He wandered about the kitchen as he drank, finding it quite splendid that she didn't think his presence a bit odd for a guest. What was an antiques appraiser doing (she might have wondered) in her kitchen? But, no, she appeared to take him as she found him and was happy to have him share her battle with the pastry dough, to which she was now doing something odd—fanning out a chunk of it, lifting it on her fist like a pizza-crust, and sending it circling around. "Burt!" She called over her shoulder. "You get out there and see to that hen!"

Burt was Suggins, her husband and the gardener. He slouched through a doorway, which Melrose took to be the one that would have been to the butler's pantry, had there been a butler. Burt Suggins tilted toward the door to the outside and, presumably, the henhouse. Melrose hated to think of the hen's fate as the door shuddered shut.

"That's Mr. Suggins what just went out," she said, as if the two of them had been watching an identity parade. "I expect he knows more about flowers than any gardener they ever had." She turned back to the cooker and the pot on the back burner, which was holding a pudding basin, covered with a cloth. Its simmering water puffed forth steam. She placed the steaming basin on the table and removed the cloth and set it aside. Then she stood with lips pursed and one hand on her cheek, considering the basin. He watched as she pulled over an assortment of tiny charms, picking up one, then another. He was curious. "What've you got there?"

"The bits and bobs you put in the Christmas pud."

"Christmas? In February?"

"Never you mind. Mrs. Owen loves her pudding. Sometimes I think that girl never grew up proper." She gave Melrose a patronizing look. *The rich seldom do.*

Melrose loved the motherly tone of "that girl." And it was true: Grace Owen did have a child's spontaneity. "It's very sad about her son."

Annie stopped counting the silver charms, looked off toward the door as if someone were coming through it. "Aye. Only twenty he was. As nice a lad as you'd ever hope to find." Businesslike once more, she went back to the pudding, stabbing the little charms into its surface. For all the excellence of her food, he thought Annie Suggins was on somewhat adversarial terms with the food she prepared. First was the beating of the batter, and now she was pushing the tiny charms into it as if she were driving rivets.

Melrose decided that Annie was such a plainspoken, uncomplicated woman that she would not be suspicious were he to revert to the subject of the *other* murder. She, herself, had brought it up. Verna Dunn. Given Annie's whirlwind movements from pastry table to fridge (getting out butter and milk), to kitchen door (calling for Suggins to be quick about the hen), to stove (clattering the pot off the burner), back to the "pud"—Melrose was surprised she could follow any conversational line at all.

He said, "It must have been appalling to find out their guest, Miss— Dunn? Was that her name? To find out she'd been murdered. Thank you—" he added, for she had poured him his third cup of tea. "Two murders. That's shattering."

It would take more than a couple of murders to shatter Annie Suggins. "Whatever she was doing out at night on the Wash, I can't imagine. And now they're saying it was the two of 'em might've drove there."

"'Two of them'?"

"Her and that Lady Kennington." Annie leaned over the table to say in a whispery voice, "Last one ever saw Verna Dunn alive, I don't wonder that policeman from Lincoln thought she must've had something to do with it. Wouldn't you? It's a serious business, a very serious business." She frowned, sighed, set her hands on her hips. "It's hard without the extra help. Dorcas worked at the pub, too, the Case. Our local pub."

"Two jobs. She must have been ambitious."

"Not her!" Annie laughed. "'Twasn't ambition got her going. Saving up for something, she said she was. The something must've had a man in it." She paused and seemed to be studying the pudding. "Anyway, she was right happy there for a while, not like she usually was, moody. Didn't last long, though," Annie said, ruminatively. "She was moping about the kitchen and saying as how she 'shouldn't have listened.' Dorcas was a right nosy little thing."

Melrose stopped the cup on the way to his mouth. "'Nosy'? What do you mean, Mrs. Suggins?"

Annie started looking in pots, clanging long spoons against their edges, bustling. "Now, I hate to speak ill of the girl, but I had to tell her more'n once to mind her own business. A couple of times, I caught her listening at doors. Well! Put a stop to that, I did!"

"'I shouldn't have listened'? Is that what she said?"

"Indeed. And 'I shouldn't 'ave done it.' That's what she said: 'I ought not to 'ave done it. I shouldn't 'ave listened.'"

Melrose frowned. "What do you think she meant?"

"Honestly, I've no idea, me. Dorcas had more'n one secret, I'm sure." Annie sighed. "For a while I thought maybe she'd got a crush on Mr. Price. He goes to that pub nearly every evenin' when he'd ought to be in bed. Gets up at dawn, he does. Goes slopping about the fens looking for buried trees the way others might go looking for buried treasure. Hmph!"

That Dorcas Reese might have had a crush on Price wasn't too surprising. It turned Melrose's attention to Price's bachelorhood and his dependence on the Owens. He seemed perfectly satisfied with his present arrangements; Max Owen was a fairly good stand-in for an eighteenth-century patron.

"It's beyond me," she said, pouring the batter into another pudding basin. "How these poor women met their deaths. It's got to be some sick sort of person." She shook her head and set the basin into a pot of hot water. Suggins had come in with a half-dozen eggs. "Would you rather have a boiled egg, sir? The Owens are fond of scrambled."

"That will be fine with me." He paused. He had not got an impression of "comings and goings" from the people around the dinner table last night. He'd been under the impression they had all remained in the living room, except for Price. But even if they had, there wouldn't have been time to get to the Wash, surely. It would have to have been *after* they'd separated for the night. "Major Parker was here, I understand, that evening."

The mention of Parker! She could not praise him enough. Surprisingly, it was his cooking that sent her into a near paroxysm of praise. "You've not tasted a beef Wellington until you've had the Major's, let me tell you." She seemed intent on comparing trifles—hers, his, God's. He saw that the kitchen clock had moved them closer to breakfast. The aroma of streaky bacon sputtering over the flame of the cooker told him it was none too soon. He was famished.

"Now *me,* I was in here late, getting the mincemeat ready for the pies. I make pies the night before, usually. So while I was in the kitchen, it's Suggins went to take Mr. Owen some whiskey. Mr. Owen was chatting with him about another delivery of antiques. So *Burt* has an alibi, but I don't!" Annie thought this alibi-business rather jolly; she laughed until tears formed on her lashes. Then she raised the corner of her apron and wiped her eyes. "I am sorry, sir, I shouldn't make light of it. But it's been a very hard situation, as I'm sure you can appreciate."

"Yes, I can," Melrose said, sympathetically, but seriously doubting its "hardness" on Annie. What he had supposed was that Jenny alone—in addition to Jack Price, at some point—couldn't account for her time. But that wasn't the case. It sounded as if the only ones who couldn't have got to the Wash and back was Max Owen. Parker had left a bit after eleven, Grace had gone to bed. Price was in his studio. None of the three could prove it. "You know, Annie, it's beginning to look as if *nobody* could account for his or her time." He laughed.

"What was peculiar was Burt found Miss Dunn's car parked at the bottom of the drive, and that was a distance from the house. Now, they heard a car start up and drive off around ten, I think. And Burt, naturally, he supposed she came back, when he saw the car after midnight." She sighed. "It's all so peculiar." As if to vent her dismay, Annie made a vicious little jab at the pud with another silver charm.

⚓

The bacon and eggs lost nothing in transit from kitchen to sideboard, where Melrose was scooping up generous portions of both. He had gone upstairs to put on his old Harris tweed (which screamed of "country") and when he returned to the dining room, Grace Owen was sitting at the table with a cup of tea and a thin slice of toast, reading a local paper.

From the sideboard with its line-up of silver dishes and delicacies, Melrose said, "Good lord, but how you can resist these mushrooms? These eggs?"

"You'd be resisting too if you were a middle-aged woman who's had years of Annie's breakfasts. I simply have to flip a coin: will it be breakfast? lunch? dinner? for I can't afford to eat all three."

Melrose opened the paper. "I see you're still page-one news." He saw a picture of Wyndham Fen and a white police van.

Grace munched her toast, tapped the photo of the van, said, "Peter told me they'd set up a van, an 'incidents room' or something, police called it."

"Peter?"

"Peter Emery. Oh, of course, you've not met him. Peter is Linus Parker's groundskeeper. Or was. He lives in a cottage on Linus's property. Linus has a great deal of property around here. The cottage is a little ways off the footpath on the way to the Case. Have you stopped there?"

"The pub, you mean? Yesterday, to get directions. The girl Dorcas worked there, I hear. I was up quite early this morning and had a cup of tea with Annie Suggins."

"I know." Grace smiled at him over the rim of her cup. "Annie thinks you're quite wonderful. 'A real gentleman, he is; niver talks down to a person.'"

Melrose laughed. "Mrs. Suggins does a good bit of talking herself."

"About what?"

Melrose flinched at the change in tone, a tiny shifting of gears, an urgency to know. "About these murders, of course," he said, as if it were the most reasonable thing in the world for Annie˙ to talk about them. "Wouldn't you expect the staff to take advantage of an opportunity to entertain a stranger with the story?"

She sighed and said she supposed so and turned a page of the paper.

"You said this Peter Emery used to be Parker's keeper?"

She nodded. "It's very sad. He's blind. He had a terrible accident about six years ago. And he's still a young man. Well, forty-five or -six. I'd call that youngish."

"Blind? That's rotten."

"Yes. It's very painful to see a man who lived in the outdoors more or less confined to indoors." She poured Melrose some more coffee and herself another cup of tea. "Linus Parker's given him a very nice little cottage a bit off the footpath. Linus's own house sits farther on. Anyway, Peter said Chief Inspector Bannen came round. Not much Peter could tell him, obviously."

Melrose ingested this piece of information along with his mushrooms and thought about Dorcas Reese. Nothing was all that obvious to him.

13

"Muckross Abbey school," said Max Owen, nodding toward the piano-fronted desk in the corner. Breakfast was finished and Melrose and Max were in the library. "The Bonham's man thinks it's quite a good example of its type."

Bonham's man? God, wasn't it enough to have to deal with the Christie's man and the Sotheby's man?

The desk was elaborately decorated with inlays of ivory, paintings of ruins, and carved ivy crawling up the legs. Melrose had never seen a piece of furniture like it, but then, he'd never heard of Muckross Abbey either. He gave the only response he could: nodded and said, "Umm." One arm crossed in front of his chest, elbow resting on that hand and chin in the other, he hoped his expression was sage. "Umm," he said again, nodding. "Muckross Abbey school, yes, definitely." It sounded more like a Sherlock Holmes story—"The Adventure of Muckross Abbey"—than it did a school of furniture.

It wasn't on Trueblood's list. Damn. He was afraid this would go on happening. In this room, from whose west-facing end window Melrose could see the companion-window of the long gallery, there were at least a dozen pieces that cried out to be admired. Not by Melrose, though, no, thank you very much. His hand was now at his forehead, rubbing.

"Something wrong?"

"Oh, no. Just another damned headache. Bloody nuisance."

"I'm sorry. Want some aspirin?"

Melrose shook his head. No, not aspirin, perhaps one of Diane Demorney's fatal martinis. He was giving himself a little time to study an intimidating-looking piece, which he thought might be the quarter-million-quid-worth of bureau-bookcase Trueblood had talked about. At least, he hoped so; it would be a piece he knew something about. Imagine having such incredibly expensive things sitting about. There was something to be said for the Spartan existence. *Whoa!* his other self said, digging in the heels of the high-horse he appeared to be up on. *Who are you to be questioning the Owens for their possessions? You don't exactly live in a bed-sit, do you?*

Dropping his hand, he strolled over to the bureau-bookcase and hunkered down (in imitation of a man who knew what he was looking for) and ran his finger along the seam where the top and bottom came together. "Now *this* is an extremely good example of its kind."

"It certainly is." Max came to stand beside him. "What would you guess its worth is?"

Melrose didn't answer immediately, but instead walked round the bureau, stopping now and then to mutter something and nod. "Bottom seems to be done in the same period, so I'd say it's the original, wouldn't you?" When Max nodded, Melrose said, "Well, if I had it I'd pay—oh, perhaps two hundred fifty, two seventy-five."

Max beamed. "Right on the nose. Two hundred and fifty-eight thousand."

Melrose managed a self-deprecating little murmer. Things were so much easier when one knew in advance. He said, "If you've had it awhile, by now the value's probably risen by another fifty." He stood looking at the bureau-bookcase as if stupefied with admiration when he was actually trying to work Max around to the night of Verna Dunn's murder. But he couldn't think of an approach. It wasn't the same as talking to their cook. To refresh his memory, he drew his little leather notebook out—everyone had a leather notebook to consult, surely—and ran his eyes down his price-list. But Max was on to something else.

"Look at this, would you?"

Melrose did. A small bronze statue that meant nothing to him. Bronzes, had Trueblood said anything about bronzes? "Unusual," he said, frowning in honest puzzlement.

"Remember that Adams sale? Of course, you must've been there. Bonham's did a great job, didn't they?"

"Stupendous."

"What did you get?" Max asked. "Anything interesting?"

Melrose opened his mouth to say—what? Fortunately, Max went right on talking. "These plaquettes are wonderful. And not too dear, either. It puts Renaissance bronze at least within the reach of people who aren't rich."

Yes, Mrs. Withersby had mentioned wanting several. "It is nice to find something not completely off the charts."

"Trouble is, they're the very devil to date. The after-casts must have been legion."

"The after-casts." Melrose rather liked the word. "Yes, the after-casts. Always does create a problem."

Melrose hadn't realized Max had moved on to another of his trophies until the voice came from the other end of the room. "This one is Grace's favorite."

If it's anybody's favorite it should damned well be on the list. Hell— Melrose took a deep breath—it wasn't. But people's "favorites" were tricky because the real value usually got lost somewhere in the sentimental morass. So that the piece was loved not for value but for some reason particular to the person who prized it. Melrose could tell from the sheepish expression on Max Owen's face that this particular piece was going to be difficult to assess. It looked like a reading table, except that it had two facing adjustable stands. "A reading table?"

"A double music stand, that's my guess." Max reveled a bit in his assessment.

It looked like a straightforward piece of furniture and Melrose had no idea how much it was worth. He said conventional things: "Fine patination. Looks original." That had a fifty-fifty chance of working out. Max nodded, so Melrose was in the right fifty. He frowned. Thoughtfully. "Elegant. Candlesticks are quite handsome." Melrose touched one of the two projecting candlesticks, once used for reading. A small, square box was set in the middle of the tripod. "What would that be?" He should express a little ignorance. Not hard, in his case.

"There's a little drawer in it that held rosin. That's how I deduced the music stand." Max moved on to a rather chunky bureau, nothing special, surely. Too plain to be in this collection, Melrose would have thought. But Max Owen apparently thought otherwise, treating it like the runt of the litter, something no one else could love. "Mulberry wood. You can tell here on the side where new wood was put in, not a very good imitation."

Melrose, who'd been pretending to make notes, now pocketed his pen and notebook. "You have a rare feeling for these pieces," he said, taking a closer look at the inlays.

Max thought for a moment. "It's because they have a history; I mean, I've followed some of them for years. I know their provenance." He moved to the painted writing table. "Take this *bonheur-du-jour*, for instance. First time I ever saw it was twenty years ago in the window of a dark little shop along the Old Kent Road. I think I was on my way to a funeral, can't remember whose." He looked puzzled. "On my way to— Brighton, maybe." They were standing near the needlepoint settee and Max said, "Sit down, why don't you?" with the air of one who's about to embark on a long story. "A nice old chap. Obviously not in the trade just for the money, but, come to think of it, a lot of dealers I know don't seem to be in it simply for the money."

Melrose sincerely doubted it.

Max went on. "I wonder if most of them don't have a talent for the past, you know?" Max patted his jacket pocket, brought out a pack of Silver Cuts, and offered them to Melrose.

It was someone to share a sin with. Melrose was glad somebody else still smoked, as he pulled his old Zippo from his pocket. Trueblood had scouted it out, saying it suited an eccentric antiques appraiser better than Melrose's gold lighter. He liked the way it clacked back, the rasp of the tiny wheel on the flint, the clack again as he closed the cover.

Max dragged over the blue Murano ashtray again and set it between them, then settled back on the settee, one ankle over the other knee, his hand rubbing at his silk sock. "This old fellow could see how enthusiastic I was about the desk, and I'm certain the price he quoted was lower than what he'd've asked someone else. But it was still too much for me. I hadn't a sou back then, or at least not enough to buy high-priced antiques. But we spent some time talking about this"—and he nodded toward the *bonheur-du-jour*— "and he showed me photos, snaps taken in the palace in

Madrid. I don't know how old the pictures were, but the desk was originally in the palace of Philip the Second of Spain. He had documents that showed this. Anyway, it was right after that I made my first real profit in the market and I went back to his shop, but it was sold. I asked him who'd bought it and he said he should keep that information confidential, but that I could buy him a pint and if he got drunk enough, he'd tell me." Max smiled, remembering. "He told me the name of a woman in Stow-on-the-Wold, a decorator. So I went there . . . when I was supposed to be going to—" He frowned. "Somebody's baby's christening. Was it Sis's—?" He shook his head. "I looked up this decorator's shop and there was the table, exactly the same, none the worse for wear. But she wouldn't sell it, said she'd bought it as the focal point for a client's bedroom—a bedroom! My God!"

Melrose listened to this tale of the *bonheur-du-jour* with a certain enjoyment and even a certain awe. What he found so compelling was that Max could hardly remember at all a christening, a wedding, a funeral at the same time he recalled every detail about the *bonheur-du-jour*, everything that had happened to it in the seventeen or eighteen years before he'd become its owner. It was as if this charming piece of furniture stirred in Max Owen all of the affection, or all of the poignance one ordinarily attached to beloved family heirlooms, or to photographs of one's family or even—and perhaps this was the point—to one's family itself. He didn't doubt but what there would be similar tales told about this needlework settee, about the heavy old mulberry-wood chest, the fabulous Court Chest, the papier-mâché and painted metal tables, the Renaissance bronzes. So if Melrose had supposed Max Owen to be one of the idle and acquisitive rich, he knew now that he was wrong.

Melrose got up to look at the Court Chest again. "You don't honestly intend to turn these things over to Sotheby's auction block, do you?"

Max's expression, the candid eyes and slow smile, was as beguiling as a child's. He seemed to be studying the end of his cigarette, and then he chuckled as if it were all a great joke. "No way."

Melrose smiled at the Americanism. "Then why did you need them appraised?" Melrose hoped he wasn't talking himself out of this job.

"I expect I didn't want an appraisal. I wanted an audience. No, not exactly an audience, just some smart fellow to talk to."

When he turned that smile on Melrose, Melrose felt a pang of guilt, as if he had intruded upon a scene of passion, a secret tryst.

Max went on. "The only one around here is Parker. Of course, there's Grace, but I've probably bored that dear woman to death with my accounts. Although she's willing to listen endlessly. She likes those Romanesque statues. I got those at auction; why I'm not sure. That was in my early days. Grace calls them 'the cold ladies.' Isn't that marvelous?" Then Max paused, flushing a little. "I must strike you as tremendously shallow, talking about bureaus and writing tables when there've just been two murders."

Speaking of that! Melrose wanted to say. But he was sympathetic. "Well, your 'stuff,' as you call it, might be your 'still point.' Your 'center.'" For there was no question that the man seemed to be enthralled by these possessions, no more and no less than are children who invest objects with magical powers. The dish runs away with the spoon; the Red Queen canters; the chessmen shout their disapproval of beleaguered Alice. "Magic," he muttered.

Max looked at him questioningly.

"Oh . . . I was only thinking of our relationship to our things when we were young, when we were children."

"Obsessive," Max said. "Maybe so; maybe we think they share in our problems and delights. Or maybe they're like children themselves." He lit another cigarette with Melrose's Zippo, flicking the lid open and closed and open again. "We don't have any children." He said this as if he were explaining something to himself. "Grace had a son." And as if this were a fact he hadn't quite come to terms with, he frowned and kept opening and closing the Zippo lid. "She was young—nineteen, twenty—when she was married the first time, and Toby was born a couple of years later. He died when he was twenty." Max leaned back with a kind of shudder. "Only twenty, and he had a riding accident, fell off his horse—" He motioned with his head to some vague point before them in a distant landscape. "Out there. It wouldn't've been serious for most riders, but Toby was a hemophiliac and he bled internally, you see, afterward." Max shook his head. "Grace hated to see him riding at all. But what can you do? Can't put a boy in cotton wool and never let him do anything. He liked riding, even though he had a hard time with horses. He'd hunted ever since he was young, when they'd lived in Leicester. It isn't really very far from here. Grace said he could never sit a horse properly. Still . . ." Max shrugged, somewhat helpless to convey his sorrow, or Grace's. Then he was silent.

"I'm sorry," Melrose said, helpless himself.

Max sat back. "You know, I think that's why she likes the gallery so much. She can look out of all of those windows to the copse. Maybe she sees him, I don't know. Out there in the mist." He rose, the cigarette dangling from his mouth, as if he'd forgotten its presence, and leaned down to look at the *bonheur-du-jour*, at its painted top. With his thumbnail he scraped at something. Then he straightened, remembered the cigarette, snuffed it in the ashtray. "It was my horse, you see. I'd got it for him for his nineteenth birthday. Bought it from Parker, who kept a couple of horses back then. So it was the one I'd given him."

"But he apparently had trouble with any horse—not just the one you'd given him."

"Yes." With his hands shoved hard into his pockets, Max said, "Still, I can't help but wonder if she holds me somewhat responsible. Instead of some impenetrable Fate. Me."

Melrose said, "She doesn't strike me as a blaming kind of person."

"No." Max turned and smiled at him. "You're right, she isn't." The smile lingered, and thoughts of Grace vanished at the thought of death. "Poor girl."

It had been Grace's comment over the death of Dorcas Reese.

Then Max was up and telling Melrose to come with him to the long gallery. *Oh, hell*, Melrose thought. *Not valuing the paintings, I hope.*

But it wasn't that. Max simply wanted to talk about them, to have them looked at by a fresh pair of eyes. Melrose followed as he moved from a small Picasso sketch, through some quite beautiful landscapes, past a Landseer of a roomful of dogs, on down past several portraits, one of which they lingered over. It was a charming study of two little girls in a garden, lighting Japanese lanterns, that he'd noticed yesterday.

"John Singer Sargent," said Max, "not the original, of course. That's in the Tate. Still, it is a superior copy. He hasn't lost the light."

Cones of delicate yellow shone upward from the light-suffused paper lanterns onto the two little girls' faces. Melrose said, "I'm used to seeing only formal portraits of Sargent. Not this sort of study."

"*Carnation, Lily, Lily, Rose*, it's called." Then Max recited:

> *Have you seen where Flora goes,*
> *Carnation, Lily, Lily, Rose.*

"I like that. Which one is Flora, do you guess?"

Melrose smiled. "Or 'Lily'? Or 'Rose'?"

His eyes still on the painting, Max said, "Grace wasn't jealous of my first wife. I had the feeling that detective from Lincoln thought Grace would have naturally hated her. Grace didn't dislike her; I think she even enjoyed her company."

Was it safe to ask? Melrose tried to be casual. "And the others?"

Max looked over at him. "Parker? Jack?"

Melrose shrugged. "I just thought . . ." He let his voice trail off.

But Max apparently didn't find the question odd. "They both knew Verna, of course. She lived here for several years."

"But did they like her?"

Max laughed. "Good lord, no. Neither one of them. Verna was a strange and pernicious woman. Verna was easy to hate, once you caught on to her."

"Well," said Melrose, "somebody certainly caught on."

14

Peter Emery's cottage looked like something out of a fairy tale: the whitewashed stone, the cobbled walk from the white gate to a door painted a bird's-egg blue, the neat window boxes of bulbs one or two of which were already sending out green shoots. Upended near the door was an old flat-bottomed boat that looked as if it might be getting a new coat of paint to judge from the paint can near it. Several fishing rods were leaning against the wall beside it. Melrose knocked on the door, which was opened by a girl of perhaps ten or eleven, with flamboyant ginger hair, a pearly skin, and eyes the cider color of the sky just before sunup. A fairy-tale child.

Not exactly. "We don't want none, neither of us." The door was firmly shut in his face.

Melrose stood staring at the blue door. He looked behind him and around him in some attempt to discover whatever would cause solicitors, pollsters, canvassers, beggars, or Hare Krishna-ites to beat a path to the door in such numbers the occupants would feel harassed by pleas to buy or sign or give. He knocked again. He refused to be put off by this fiery-headed imp of Satan. The face reappeared at the window, eyes peering out over the bulbs, and then withdrew.

Melrose tapped his foot. It seemed an ungodly long time until the door opened again.

"I *said*—"

"—that you didn't want none, neither of you. I am not soliciting, so call off your dog." The dog looked from between her legs. It was small and its stiff-haired gray coat looked like armor. Its lips stretched back in what might have been a snarl, or simply a Bogart dry-as-gin grin, for it made no noise. Melrose could see a mouthful of teeth. The girl was apparently thinking his words over and looked as if she might be about to shut the door again. He put his hand against it and his foot between it and the sill. She might have been spunkier, but he was bigger. "Do you *mind*?" He hated giving way to sarcasm.

The dog started circling round in a frenzy, then made a rush at Melrose, teeth still very much in evidence but still silent. Melrose braced his foot against the animal and his hand against the door. "Listen, now—I'm a friend of the Owens, you know them, the ones who live at Fengate. Mrs. Owen told me to visit. I was just out walking—" When she finally released her hold on the door, he nearly went sprawling into the dim little hall. He straightened up and looked down into those cider-colored eyes, flecked with brown and gold and anger. "I don't see why on earth you're so put out by me. *I* haven't done anything."

"You probably will. You're the police."

"Absolutely not! I only came here to talk for a bit with your father." Poor man.

"He can't talk to you. He's blind."

"I'm exceedingly sorry to hear that, but I've never known blindness to interfere with conversation."

"And he's not my father, he's my uncle."

From the inward rooms came a deep voice. "Zel, who is it now?"

"Nobody," she yelled back.

Melrose raised his own voice. "I'd like to contest that."

The owner of the masculine voice appeared in the doorway. He had to stoop to clear the lintel, as he was very tall. Tall and muscular and handsome, an advertisement for the outdoor life. The fishing rods and boat must be his.

"I told him you was busy."

"Find your manners, gurl!"

Melrose was sure he'd turn to a pillar of salt before Zel ever found her manners. Over the years of occasionally having to deal with the young (anyone under eighteen), Melrose had come to realize that he couldn't do it. Then he remembered Sally, and felt a moment of triumph until he also remembered he had had to save her from the grim sentence imposed by Theo Wrenn Browne, in addition to actually buying the book in question. With Jury, it was usually the other way round: kiddies usually gave *him* things. Jury could make a meal of one jelly-baby handed him by a half-pint person; whereas, Melrose had to promise them the whole sweet shop in order to get information. Jury's effortless manner of extracting facts annoyed Melrose no end. Often as not, it was some kiddy Melrose (he liked to think) had softened up, and then along came Jury to reap the rewards, Jury with his uncanny knack for worming his way into their little hearts and minds. Melrose usually didn't get beyond the *"we-don't-want-none"* stage.

It was the kitchen doorway Peter Emery had come through; Melrose glimpsed an Aga cooker, white as snow, in the room behind him. He would not have known straightaway that Emery was blind, for the man shifted the direction of his unseeing eyes to the source of the voice speaking, and even downward to the dog, who was now yapping. He told Zel to go and make some coffee. "The best coffee in Lincolnshire, Zel does." Zel bloomed in the sun of her uncle's approval. "And some of those biscuits you made. Zel's a first-rate cook, and I do like good cooking. Maybe it's because she's forever hanging around at Major Parker's house." Peter added, "If you'd rather tea, I think the kettle's about to boil."

"Coffee's fine," said Melrose, as the kettle did indeed shriek out its readiness. It was as if Peter Emery had not only fine-tuned his other senses, but had replaced the sight he'd lost with second sight.

Zel went off obediently, almost merrily, to make the coffee. And after Melrose's preamble to conversation, that he was a guest of the Owens come to look over Max Owen's collection, they settled down for real talk, most of it Peter's. Melrose was perfectly satisfied to listen; listening was the reason he'd come.

Peter had lived in Lincolnshire most of his life, but had spent many years in Scotland where his uncle had been factor on a great estate in

Perthshire at the foot of Glenolyn. Hundreds of acres this estate had comprised, with walked up grouse shooting and black game and stalking. And, of course, fishing in rivers clear as glass. It was his uncle who'd taught him to fish and hunt. Before "this" happened he'd been one of the best shots in the country. He made an impatient, stabbing gesture at his eyes. "Damned annoyance." He went on. "Most people say the land round here's dull, that the fens is dull, for it's all this great flatness. It always amazes me, how people only have one notion of beauty. They have to be in the bloody Alps to appreciate mountains. How can they miss this mysteriousness, like when the fog comes down of a sudden so thick it looks solid as a wall?"

Reminiscence was probably something Peter Emery seldom had an audience for. So Melrose was quiet and let him talk. "My daddy went through more'n one flood. I can remember one, I was maybe five or six, fen bank over on Bungy Fen broke. No matter how hard they worked to keep the dike from crumbling, it did, and pretty soon the whole of the land was a dozen feet under water. Far as the eye could see there was water, a vast sea of it. Our crop, my daddy's barley crop, went a' floating off and took the old scarecrow with it. The scarecrow from out the field, swimming right along—oh, there was a sight! We had the punt, except it got caught up too, so my daddy, he put us into a big tin washtub and I thought that was grand. Punt finally went aground, so we got it back; that's it"—he inclined his head—"out there. I kept it all these years. I'll tell you this—" He sat forward and said with a near-ferocious intensity, "You can't let the elements stop you. Nature can be tough, so you've got to be tougher."

Melrose was intrigued by all of this. He was fascinated by this intrepid man, still young and active, who could refer to his blindness as an "annoyance." There was a subtle sense of hubris about Emery, a suggestion of challenging God and nature. Melrose could picture, in his mind's eye, Emery storming blindly across the heath in a scene out of Shakespearean tragedy.

He was called back from this theatrical fantasy by Zel, who came in to serve the coffee. It was indeed excellent, and the accompanying shortbread, melting now in his mouth, turned him from Shakespeare to Proust. "Delicious!" Melrose exclaimed. "Best I've ever eaten." This was the truth. Zel said he couldn't have the recipe, for it was a secret.

Having made a good impression with coffee and shortbread, she apparently set out to make a better one—the quartermaster who ran this outfit—by getting out a broom and rag and starting to dust the bookcases.

Peter went on, talking about his father's farm and how he had never liked farming much, but he had liked the shooting. Melrose didn't share in his affection for frosty dawns and sitting pheasant, and lord knows not for lying on his stomach for hours in the old punt waiting for tough-fleshed birds to whisk out of water and fly upward against the sky.

Melrose hesitated to bring up the murders while the little girl Zel was within earshot, so he asked her if he might not have another piece of shortbread. She left to get it.

"If you know the Owens—"

"I do, of course," said Peter. "Grand people."

Melrose asked, "Then did you know the—did you know this Dunn woman?"

"Indeed, I did," he said roughly as he got up to mess with the fire, which was already drawing so well the flames stood up like spikes. With perfect assurance, his arm reached out for the poker, his hand found it and raised a log that then crumbled and spat. Peter replaced the poker, returned to his chair, and said nothing further.

It was difficult to build on nothing, that is, if you weren't a policeman, but Melrose tried. With an artificial laugh, he said, "Sounds like you didn't care for her very much."

"Aye. You're right there."

"But you weren't the only one."

"Oh, of that I'm certain. A lot of trouble that woman—"

They both stopped talking when Zel came in with the shortbread.

"If the Queen's biscuit cook gets wind of this shortbread, you'll have to give up the secret."

Zel took the compliment with a blush and then set about her business. Or businesses, if one were to believe her round of activities was the usual round. It was as if she wanted it marked that her days were not spent in idle chatter before the fire. Melrose could scarcely keep up with her: Zel dusting, Zel sweeping invisible debris out the cottage door—the stuff Melrose was supposed to know he'd dragged in on his person—Zel adjusting things on shelves, Zel telling the dog Bob she'd get his dinner in a moment (and instructing him as to proper nourishment).

It was exhausting in a wonderful sort of way. Her various duties performed, Zel planted herself between their two chairs and leaned heavily on the arm of Melrose's. She was ready for relaxation, which meant, for her, tearing up bits of the local newspaper. These she rolled into tiny balls and tucked them into her jumper pocket. This activity went on for another ten minutes while Melrose and Peter talked about hunting and shooting and old-fashioned punting. Fifteen minutes had certainly exhausted Melrose's knowledge of the subjects.

Melrose did not feel he could justify lingering at the Emery cottage in his capacity of antiques expert before Peter Emery grew suspicious, so he thought he might as well leave the matter of Dorcas Reese for a later time. He said he must be off, that he had work to do at Fengate. "The Owens will be wondering where I've got to."

Emery started to get up, but Zel shoved him down again, an action Melrose attributed to her wanting to be Melrose's escort, and not to any concern for her uncle's well-being. Zel ran toward the door with Bob at her heels. They both stood just outside of the path, Zel looking up. In the west the sky looked bruised.

"Rain," said Zel. "You're going to get wet." She rocked on her heels and held her hands behind her back, one hand gently slapping the palm of the other, an older person's posture for thinking weighty thoughts. "Where're you going?"

"No place in particular." His destination was the dike in Wyndham Fen where Dorcas Reese's body had been found. "Want to come along?"

"No. I'm not walking on that footpath." Resolutely, she folded her arms over her chest and glared at him as if prepared for an argument. Still, she did not seem terribly eager to get rid of him. They were moving slowly along the cobbled path and from here one could see the wood, just the edge of it, that graced the Fengate property. "You can't tell what's out there." She scratched at her elbows. Bob was staring up at Melrose as usual with that silent snarl on his face. "It runs all the way from before the Owens back there and across Windy Fen." She paused and tried to sound indifferent. "That's where Dorcas got killed."

"Did you know her?"

Zel reached into her pocket for one of the tiny balls, which she inspected as she shrugged the question away. "I used to see her. I wonder if you heard about Black Shuck. Did you?" She spit the newspaper ball at Bob, who yawned and shook his queer gray coat.

"Black Shuck? No, I can't say I've come across whatever that is."

"Black Shuck's a ghost dog. He stalks people and kills them. Probably eats them too." Another spitball in Bob's direction. Bob was off his haunches and giving Melrose his silent snarl as if he, Melrose, were the ghost dog.

He knew Zel was waiting for him to come up with something that would release her from the dread fantasy of Black Shuck. Like all adults (except, perhaps, Richard Jury), he came up empty-handed.

She said, "It's somebody walked on that path that did it." Suddenly, the subject was changed. "Can you touch your toes?" She started going up-down, up-down.

"Of course I can."

"But with your hands flat?" Down she went again, straight-armed, palms out, her long hair cascading over her head and fanning out. It looked less reddish-gold than hair on fire.

"Probably, but why would I want to? Now, listen—"

But she didn't. She was too intent on placing the flat of her hands against the ground. Never had Melrose seen such electric energy; she might just as well be plugged into a socket. Bob watched her, beating his tail on the stone walk like a baton keeping time with her movement. "Are you married?"

"No. I haven't had the good luck to be."

"Are you going to get married?"

"Whenever you're ready."

She stopped dead and made a face. "I'm not old enough. I'm going on ten. Uncle Peter almost was, but she fell in a river."

Somehow, that way of reporting the tragedy made Melrose want to laugh. "That's terrible, awful."

"She was really beautiful, too." She bounced a spitball on her palm. "It was up in Scotland."

"I'm sorry." Melrose sighed. "This is jolly, but I must get on. It's going on two. Well, good-bye and it was lovely meeting you." He said this to her downturned head. "I must be leaving now."

Less than a dozen steps down the cobbled path, he heard her voice. "That Dorcas was always going over to Mr. Parker's. He lives away over there."

That did interest him, as she knew it would. She had discovered a way to keep him stopping here indefinitely; she would let out just enough information to keep him hooked. He walked back the several paces. "Why would she do that? What for?"

Deaf and dumb, she set about doing waist-whittling exercises that Bob could not mimic, as he had no waist. Hands on hips, she twisted back and forth. Bob turned in circles.

Melrose supplied a possible answer to his question: "Perhaps she was working for him?" Though given her two jobs—at Fengate and the pub—it was hard to see how. "Cooking, possibly?"

Zel's fiery hair flew about her face as she turned quickly from one side to the other. Decisively, she said: "No. She. Wasn't."

"Look here, you can't be so certain of this. How do you know that she didn't go there occasionally to cook a meal for him? She helped Mrs. Suggins, after all. And Major Parker lives alone; he'd probably be glad for the company." Melrose thought suddenly of Ruthven and his wife, Martha, and tried to picture Ardry End without them. He couldn't.

"Well, maybe he'd want the company, but not the cooking." Zel stilled herself long enough to add: "Dorcas wasn't a good cook. She was only vegetable cook, and she wasn't even good at that. She got things mushy."

Zel made a face. "*I'm* a better cook than Dorcas ever was; Mr. Parker says so. He's the best cook around. He hardly ever goes out to meals because he doesn't like the way other people cook. Except for Mrs. Suggins."

The dog Bob, who had been listening to them with a disturbing intensity, once again drew back his mouth, exposing his yellow teeth for Melrose's delight. "What does your dog think I am, a dentist? All the same"—Melrose went on, as Bob streaked off in pursuit of a hare—"you can't really know what she was doing at Major Parker's."

"I know *that*, don't I? Mr. Parker wouldn't pay anybody to cook for him. The Owens, that's different. He thinks their cook's the best, next to him."

Melrose was delighted to discover that Annie Suggins had been right about this facet of Parker's personality.

Zel went back to her exercises, saying, "I bet you can't cook, except eggs."

"Of course I can cook. I was once *sous*-chef at Simpson's-in-the-Strand. Now, why—?"

"No, you weren't!" Her response rang in the frosty air. "*I'm* going to be a chef."

"A chef! What a much more noble aspiration that is than teacher or doctor. I'll certainly come to your kitchen for dinner, then."

"If you're invited. Mr. Parker makes plum ice cream."

That would go a long way toward making Parker the most popular adult in Lincolnshire. "Well, I can make Christmas pudding. With silver charms in it."

That stopped her turning. "You?"

Melrose proceeded to describe that morning's performance, only with him in the starring role instead of Annie Suggins.

Zel was impressed. But not for long. She started hopping. "Mr. Parker makes it, too. And plum ice cream."

"You said that. So . . . you were spying on Dorcas."

She stopped and looked at him. *Hopeless, hopeless.* "I wasn't *spying*. I was *seeing*."

"Ah! You were 'seeing.' Then what happened?"

"Nothing. She could've come out and gone to the pub. That's where everybody goes that takes the footpath. It goes nearly to the back door of the pub."

"Did you just see this once?"

"No. Lots of times."

That could mean anywhere from two to two hundred.

"Mr. Parker's rich. You can do anything if you're rich."

"No, you can't." Melrose contradicted her.

"How do you know?"

"Because I'm rich."

That stopped her. "Can you buy cars and hogs and houses if you want?"

"Yes. I'm not especially set on the hogs, although my groundskeeper might argue the point."

She gasped. "*You* have a keeper? Like Uncle Peter?"

"No, nothing like your uncle, believe me. Mine just roams around and shoots things."

"Is he a good shot?"

"No. And it's just as well."

"Uncle Peter used to be the best shot around. He could shoot out a snake's eye."

"An admirable accomplishment." Melrose stopped to dislodge a pebble from his shoe sole.

Zel said, "Wyatt Earp could. Did you ever hear of him?"

"Off and on. It's a shame your uncle lost his sight. It's as bad as could happen to a man, I expect."

He assumed her silence meant compliance with this judgment. No.

"Yes, there is. You could be captured and tortured until you talked."

"Oh? Is this the fate you envision for yourself, then?"

"No-oh!"

There it was again, that drawn out *o* like a lasso round his neck. Melrose loved the way she could drag two syllables from a single one. But he thought the response too certain to pass for denial. "We should be glad we don't have information someone else wants." He glanced at her.

Her mouth was as set as concrete. "*I* don't know anything to be tortured about, but I don't know about *you*."

"You needn't sound hopeful."

"What's the worst torture you can think of?"

Children were so bloodthirsty. "Having to watch Bob floss his teeth." Melrose canvassed the surrounding landscape. "Where is he? I don't want him jumping into my path with his ivory grin." Although it would be a hard landscape for Bob, or anyone, to hide in.

Zel moved off down the path, steering her perpendicular course, a sidewise skipping movement. Her brilliant hair leapt and settled with each movement.

Melrose shook his head in wonder at the way children could abandon themselves to motion, certainly in a way forbidden to adults. In the short while he had known her, Zel seemed to have shed whole lives— cook, nurse, caretaker, crabbed adult—to arrive at her ten-year-old self-hood.

Thoughtfully, he said, "'Zel.' 'Zel' is a most unusual name."

She didn't comment; she kept on skipping.

"Is it a nickname?"

"No."

"Is it a family name?"

"No!"

"Is it from the Bible, then?"

"No!" she called back. She was some distance away, by an old stone wall that had once been the limit of someone's land. Her answer rang frostily in the air.

The fens stretched away beneath a sky that looked so close to the ground he fancied he could see the earth's curvature. The footpath shot on, arrow-straight until it was lost in the distance. He thought he could make out a broken line of roofs and chimney stacks of which the Case Has Altered might have been one.

"Windy Fen's just beyond," cried Zel, pointing to a part of the landscape whose outline was undifferentiated trees and thickets. And further off ran a road—the A17, he thought—the one on which he himself had traveled and on which distant cars passed.

Zel was back, huffing from her bout of exercise. "I can't go any farther; you'll have to get along without me. I don't want to meet up with the bogey-dog."

Melrose checked his watch. "It's only a little after three o'clock. Does he come out before dark? Anyway, he's probably up in the Highlands by now." He paused. "Look, are you sure you don't want me to walk back a little of the way with you?"

"You'd only get lost. Then I'd have to find you." To prove how nonchalant she was, she ran off speedily, moving so quickly her bright hair streamed behind her like the tail of a comet. Three times she stopped to look back and wave.

Her small body seemed to melt into the land. He felt bereft. For some inexplicable reason he felt that he and this child shared some secret history, some common past, as if he'd known her for a long time.

*

Wyndham Fen was acres of waterland in the care of the National Trust. Once it had been drained to plant wheat and corn; then, the whole area had been reflooded. Lincolnshire, Cambridgeshire, the Isle of Ely were once an enormous mere. Mere, bog, and reed-bed. The wide washes of the Great Ouse, the Nene, and the Welland testified to that. When the Romans came, they would have needed boats to move through this countryside.

He found the boardwalk erected so that the visitor could walk over the dikes and observe. It was windy and the tall reeds rattled like sabers. Disturbed, a mass of birds that he couldn't put a name to flew upward in a blue blur. Marsh violets moved gently in the water where he imagined Dorcas Reese had lain—such a pathetic and insignificant little person that people had to think before they could call up her face.

Melrose looked off in the direction of the public footpath, judging the distance. Anyone at all might have known of Dorcas's habitual attendance at the Case Has Altered. Had she been going to meet someone here? He looked off toward the small building that he supposed was the Visitors'

Center and which lay some hundred feet away. She might have waited there, taking shelter from the rain.

It was so silent that Melrose could hear something plash in the water. An owl hooted. Over the top of a stunted willow, there was a quick stir of wings as a line of mallard beat upward. He watched them against the sky and then silence rushed back to claim the fen again.

15

The man who stood in the living room gazing out of the long window in an attitude of deep contemplation turned at Melrose's entrance. The meditative expression evaporated and was replaced by one even less committal. He cleared his throat, brought a closed fist up to his mouth and said, "You must be the Owens' houseguest. The antiques appraiser?"

Melrose wished people would stop calling him that, and simply call him by name, but he smiled and reached out his hand. "My name's Melrose Plant."

"I'm Bannen. Lincoln CID."

He gave the impression of being the mildest of men, a façade that Melrose supposed exerted a certain charm over witnesses. But the mild manner didn't fool Melrose, not after his long acquaintance with Scotland Yard CID. Jury could also appear mild, sometimes to the point where his selfhood almost vanished, offering whatever witness he was questioning a mirror image of himself. This Chief Inspector Bannen, Melrose bet, was that kind of copper. If to countermand any impression of cleverness, Bannen rather clumsily raised his hand and rubbed at his neck. It was a farmer's gesture, one that went with the pause to adjust the cap, to wipe the sweat from a forehead.

Bannen's thin mouth seemed to stray upward in a half-smile. Only half for Melrose. "I expect you know about this business, Mr. Plant. Awfully unpleasant it is." He shoved his hands deep in his trouser pockets.

Melrose agreed with him, finding it strange—and somehow discomfiting—that Bannen was alone in here. It was as if having a high-ranking CID man standing in one's living room were the most natural thing in the world. "You'll probably have it all sorted out in no time," said Melrose. *How banal.* But he felt uncomfortable just standing there.

"I do hope so."

"I'm slightly acquainted with one of the people involved. Jennifer Kennington." Melrose wanted to get that on record and not give the man a chance to think Melrose was hiding something. "Hard to imagine she'd have anything to do with all this."

"Ah." Bannen nodded. It was perfectly clear that the chief inspector already knew about Melrose's acquaintance with Jenny Kennington; whether he set any store by it, however, was not at all evident. "And were you acquainted with either of the victims, Mr. Plant?"

"No. No, I wasn't. Do you—do you think the two murders are connected, then?" Another banal question.

"Yes, I'd say so." He sighed. "The death of Verna Dunn made quite a splash in the tabloids. She's very newsworthy, I take it, having once been an actress. I expect she was fairly well known. And prominent in London society." He rubbed his thumbnail across his forehead, as if he could rid himself of the frown that had creased it.

Melrose waited for him to go on, but he didn't. As much to relieve a tense situation as to get information, he said, "But it's difficult to discover a motive in all of this. I mean, no one seems to have one." When Bannen simply watched him with his mild but disconcerting gray eyes, Melrose went on, now from sheer nerves. "No one in this house, at least. They seemed all to have been on such good terms."

Bannen smiled. "But then of course you don't know them, do you? I mean, except for Jennifer Kennington."

Melrose shook his head. He didn't much like the pause before Jennifer's name. He knew something was seriously wrong, but he felt helpless to protest.

ೋ

The two rooms—living room and gallery—jutted out, with their side windows at an angle to one another, so that anyone standing at one could see into the near end of the other room. It had been in the living room that Bannen had stood waiting—for what? Melrose had the odd feeling when he now walked into the gallery that the detective and Grace Owen could have been looking out of their respective windows, staring at one another. It was the angle of her head that told him Grace was looking not directly ahead, but to her right, into the living room.

She had not heard him come in, so intent was she on whatever she was looking at. She had opened the curtain of this side window only, and an oblong of light lay across her skirt and the statue behind her. The rest of the room was as usual in deep shadow and now came this clear pale banner of light, cold and brittle. The gallery, always colder than the other rooms, seemed frigid. His hands were like ice.

He meant to speak, opened his mouth to speak to her, but did not. Instead, he stepped even farther back into the unlit corner where Max's painting of Sargent's two little girls hung in strange anonymity. He thought of Zel.

With the cold, the silence deepened. The only sound was the ticking of the longcase clock. At another time, he might have found it comforting, like a heartbeat. Now it sounded merely relentless, a message that time was running out.

Melrose thought he heard a door close—the front door, he decided, judging from the heavy thunk of the door's feudal bearings. Grace Owen leaned forward a little and held the curtain with one hand, probably to see better who had left the house. Through that part of the window which he could see, he made out the figure of the CID man. He was moving about at the mouth of the copse, leaving and entering Melrose's line of vision. Bannen had turned and seemed to be staring straight in through the window. Grace took a step back, and, absurdly, Melrose himself tried to melt farther into the shadowy corner. But the inspector probably could not see Grace, for the clear thin light had faded. Bannen was simply standing, turning his head.

Then in the distance Melrose thought he heard a car approaching, and from the sound of the gears shifting, it was Max Owen's pricey sports car. Grace must have been watching the car, yet made no move to go out and greet her husband.

Melrose left the room and climbed the stairs to his own room to find pen and paper with which to write a note to Jury. No, he should phone.

His face was hot with what he assumed must be shame at his voyeurism. With his strong sense of privacy he could not think what impelled him to watch from the shadows of the gallery. The writing table in his room was directly in front of the window, a window above and to the right of the gallery window. He saw that Max Owen had not come directly into the house, but had stopped outside, been stopped, he assumed, by Bannen. They stood talking. Rather, Bannen talked. Max simply listened. The conference did not last more than a few minutes before Bannen turned and walked across the gravel to his car.

Max watched the policeman head down the drive.

What had happened? Max Owen had left the circular drive, and Melrose found that he was looking out on the vacant day, bleached of color, everyone gone.

16

Pete Apted, QC, shied an apple core toward his wastebasket and watched it arc, glance off the metal rim, and tumble to the floor.

"You're not in trouble again, are you, Superintendent?" Pete Apted smiled. He was referring to that sad episode several years back when Jury had been a suspect in a murder case. The case hadn't gone to trial. Jury had discovered most of the truth; Apted had discovered the rest. Jury wished he hadn't. Ever since then, the thought of Pete Apted had made him flinch.

But not now. Now, the thought of Pete Apted, QC, made him hopeful. Apted was one of the most respected barristers in London. He would certainly have been a member of Parliament had he chosen to be.

"No, I'm not in trouble. A friend of mine might be."

"Who's the brief in this case? Ordinarily, I—"

"There isn't one, yet. I thought perhaps you could recommend one."

Apted's chair squeaked as he shifted, took his hands from behind his head, took his feet off his desk. The desk wasn't large, nor were the other furnishings at all luxurious. The room had a pleasantly tatty quality. The long curtains were in need of cleaning and the grim portraits could have stood a dusting. Jury especially remembered these men in silks looking down at him as if they could hardly wait to prosecute.

"Good lord, Superintendent, you must know more solicitors than I do."

"No. But the point is . . . I wanted to make certain you were free—"

"I'm never free." Apted played a riff with his thumb down a stack of briefs.

Jury's smile was constrained. "Besides that, I mean."

Apted's smile was warmer. He creaked back in the swivel chair and resumed his former position. "Okay, what's it about?"

"Do you remember the lady—actually she really is a lady—Lady Kennington—who retained you to help me?"

Apted looked away briefly, returned his look to Jury, said, "Kennington. Jane . . . no, Jennifer. Jane was the name of the other lady—" And then Apted looked away again quickly and cleared his throat. "Sorry."

Apted, Jury thought, was a remorseless man, but not an insensitive one. He knew that for Jury, that affair had been extremely painful. "Never mind. Anyway, it's Jenny Kennington who's in trouble. A double murder in Lincolnshire—"

"I read about one—the actress Verna Dunn. I saw her once. Is the other murder connected?"

"Yes. I mean, I think they're connected."

Pete Apted rooted in the brown bag on his desk and came up with another apple. "You're not supposed to 'think.'" He bit into the apple, said, "This is the law you're talking about." He swallowed, turned the apple for another big bite. "We go by appearances, one and all." The crisp sounds of chewing filled the room.

"Well, the appearance here is that Jennifer Kennington's guilty."

"I'm not talking about that kind of appearance; I'm talking about the one that I'm remorselessly led to after sifting through the so-called facts."

"I don't know what you mean. Anyway, this is a shift in your way of thinking. I seem to recall being told—by you—'If it looks like a duck, and walks like a duck—'"

"'It must be a duck,'" Apted finished for him.

"Well, in this case it certainly looks like a duck. Jenny—Lady Kennington—was the one with the most opportunity. And possibly motive." He told Pete Apted about the movements of the several guests after the dinner on the night of the first of February. Jury had to admit he had never been convinced that Jenny and Verna Dunn were strangers to one another.

Pete Apted stopped munching, tossed the core along with the comment: "Yeah, I'd say this is probably Walking Duck material. Where's the gun?"

"Max Owen's. But it sat in a mudroom off the kitchen where anybody could have got hold of it."

"Let me guess: the Lincs police have narrowed the 'anybody' down to one. Jennifer Kennington?"

"It looks that way, yes."

Apted grunted, said, "Could she use a shotgun?"

"Rifle. I wouldn't think so, but this Lincs policeman, Bannen, thinks she can."

Apted frowned, thought for a moment. "The second murder?"

"Two weeks later, on the fourteenth, one of the servants, a girl named Dorcas Reese, was strangled. Garroted."

Apted shook his head. "That's not ordinarily a woman's method. What about motive there?"

"Nil."

"Opportunity?"

"Also, nil. She was in Stratford-upon-Avon at the time."

Apted pushed his chair back. "Or says she was. Not much of a distance to cover, though." He looked at Jury. "Two murders? Off the record—do you believe she did it?"

Dryly, Jury said, "If she had, do you think I'd tell you? You once said you can't represent someone you know to be guilty. But, for the record, no, she didn't. Of course she didn't."

Apted's eyebrows shot up. " 'Of course'? Where's the 'of course' in this business? You know better than that."

"I also know Jenny Kennington."

"You also knew Jane Holdsworth."

Jury sat back, feeling he'd just been punched. "Thanks for reminding me."

Apted chewed at the corner of his mouth. "Sorry. But you of all people should know that no one's innocence is a dead cert."

"I don't agree."

"Your privilege."

"You'll take the case, then?"

"I didn't say that. But I'll talk to her." Jury felt a wave of relief, the first he'd felt in the last twenty-four hours. Apted when on: "And get her a fucking solicitor, will you? Now, tell me what you know."

"Everything?"

"No, just tell me half of it and let me guess the rest." Apted dragged a legal pad toward him.

Jury told him. It took a good half hour, ending with the telephone call from Plant yesterday evening—the reluctant telephone call.

"I think my days as an antiques appraiser are finished. I'm going back to Northants."

Ever since Plant had called him and told him that Jenny might indeed have a motive they hadn't heard about, he'd been fearing Bannen might charge her. He was brought out of this fruitless replay of his conversations with Melrose Plant by Pete Apted's voice. He missed the first few words. He'd damned well better pay attention. Apted didn't like to have to repeat things.

"—this Lincs policeman let her go back to Stratford-upon-Avon some forty-eight hours after the Dunn woman's murder. Which is where she was when the second murder occurred." He looked up. "She says she was in Stratford-upon-Avon?"

"Yes."

"Stratford is around eighty miles—"

"Seventy-three. No more than two hours, certainly."

Apted nodded, asked, "Why did police let her go back to Stratford the first time?"

"Not enough evidence to hold her, much less arrest her. At that time, no motive."

"The motive was subsequently discovered."

Jury nodded. "I don't know precisely what it is, but apparently they'd known one another for years."

"So she lied."

Jury winced at this chilly appraisal. "I expect she was frightened. After all—"

"Before the murder?"

"What?"

"You're saying Jennifer Kennington was frightened *before* the Dunn woman was murdered."

Jury frowned. "I don't—"

"Yes, you do." Apted studied the ceiling as if watching a scene being enacted at Fengate. "Lady Kennington walks into the drawing room where the Owens and guests are gathered for cocktails. Does she say, 'My goodness, Ms. Dunn, I haven't seen you for years!' Or even, given the old relationship, 'Hullo, you bitch.' No, instead, she pretends she's never met her. So you're saying she must have been afraid before the murder."

"Probably not."

"'Probably not' is right. So 'fear' doesn't account for her silence. Her silence *could* be accounted for if she planned to kill the Dunn woman. As this—" Apted drew the pad toward him. "—Chief Inspector Bannen clearly knows."

Jury said nothing.

Neither did Apted for a moment as he ran his pencil between his teeth as if it were an ear of corn. Then he tossed it on the desk and said, "Still, a past dispute, assuming there was one, no matter how acrimonious"— he shook his head—"seems a bit iffy as a motive." He picked up the pencil again and flicked it like a small baton over and around his fingers. "Who's this confederate of yours at the Owens' who's been feeding you information?"

"Melrose Plant. He's good at—" Jury tried to describe what Plant had been doing without making it seem underhanded.

"Infiltrating, anonymously, other people's lives. Does he want a job now this one's over?"

"Plant?" Jury smiled. "I doubt it."

"Charly Moss could use a good footpad."

"Who's Charly Moss?"

"Lady Kennington's solicitor, or will be." Apted wrote the name on a pad, tore the paper off, and handed it to Jury.

Jury relaxed for the first time since he'd walked in. "To brief you, you mean? You'll take this on?"

"Did I say that? What were Kennington and Dunn arguing about?"

"No one appears to know. They were already outside when they started."

"So? Why were they outside? You said it was after dinner, near ten P.M. Did they have to leave the company of the others in order to start bickering?"

"No one knows that, either. They both wanted a breath of fresh air, Jenny said. Once they got outside, they argued. A little while later, fifteen or twenty minutes later, the people inside heard a car leaving."

Apted frowned. "Why didn't she come in immediately?"

"I don't know. She said she wanted a walk. To clear her head."

Apted just looked at him for a few seconds. "Did she take a pig to look for truffles?"

"All right, I realize it sounds like strange behavior—"

Apted nailed him with a look.

Jury went on: "I've been wondering about the wife, Grace. This didn't have to be premeditated, after all. Perhaps it could be explained by a fit of passion. Not caring if anyone saw you or not."

Apted made a sound that showed how much he believed that. "Subsequent events show that whoever did it very much cares if he or she is discovered. A rendezvous on the bloody Wash, for God's sake?" He snorted. "Is Grace Owen given to fits of passion?"

"I've no idea. She strikes me as a rather serene woman. Childlike in some way."

Apted got up, shoved his hands deep into his trouser pockets. He turned now to the window and stood silently looking out.

The morning's gossamer drizzle had stopped and washed away the gray film of the day, now the sunlight, even though weak, coated the mullioned pane with silver, so that Pete Apted stood in a web of silvery netting. Jury was again surprised by how young the man looked. This room, Apted's office, had amused Jury the other time he had been in it, for it looked so much the chamber of a much older, conservative, crotchety lawyer. Oil paintings on the walls to right and left showed stern old men in silks, lawyers or judges, all of whom would have thought Apted a renegade, a revisionist. Jury recalled once broaching the subject of Justice and

Apted had looked as if the word were from some law-lexicon he himself had never heard of.

Everything in the room—curtains, chairs, the leather sofa—was fine and old and dusty, and made one think that Pete Apted had simply borrowed the place for a while from one of his elders whose pictures hung on the walls. Jury waited for him to speak, and when he didn't, Jury said, "What about Dorcas Reese, though?"

Apted shook himself, as if he'd been dozing. "The second victim. I almost forget her."

"Everyone seems to." Jury told him what he knew about Dorcas, and what Annie Suggins had told Melrose. "She wasn't a very bright girl. The cook says she was a terrible snoop, looking in drawers she shouldn't have been, listening outside doors. She said to the cook—Annie Suggins—or if not said directly to her, said where Annie heard it, 'I shouldn't have done it. I shouldn't have listened.' Not the precise words, but . . ."

Apted sat down in his chair and stared at his desk blotter for a few moments. He looked up. "So the motive in that case you assume to be Dorcas Reese's overhearing something that made her dangerous. Something pertaining to the murder of Verna Dunn?"

"I can't think of any other motive, assuming the same person who killed Verna Dunn also killed Dorcas Reese. Dorcas otherwise doesn't sound like a threat. She's so colorless people forget her."

"Oh, I don't know. These 'colorless' types have a way of asserting themselves if the occasion allows for it. There's always blackmail. Hasn't anyone considered that as a motive?"

"I expect Bannen has. There's no evidence of blackmail."

Apted shrugged. "Maybe she hadn't collected yet. I'll tell you one thing, though: if there's no more evidence than you've given me, it sounds like the Lincs police don't have a very strong case. The gun, for instance. They went out for air. Where was Lady Kennington carrying the rifle? In her cigarette case?" Apted frowned, leaned his chin on his tented fingers. "The car leaves; the car returns; Lady Kennington returns. Ergo, Lady Kennington returns in the car. What kind of reasoning is that?" Apted sat back, started rolling his tie up from the bottom. "This gets to look less and less like a duck, Superintendent."

17

Lord knows what had routed him out of bed the following morning at not enough past six to even consider leaving the warm and downy confines of his bed. Perhaps it was a moral awakening, for Melrose had no intention of its becoming a bodily one. He closed his eyes.

And in so doing, saw again, heard again the news that Chief Inspector Bannen had come to tell them the Lincs police were about to arrest Jenny Kennington. The motive seemed fairly clear now.

"You didn't know, any of you, that they were related? That they were cousins?" Bannen had said to the astonishment of Max Owen. What it had taken so long to surface was the longstanding animosity Jennifer Kennington had felt for Verna Dunn. It would account for a motive.

"What really told against her," Max Owen had said, *"was keeping it a secret, was lying about it."*

That wasn't all. The findings of the medical examiner had turned up the rather surprising news that Dorcas Reese was not pregnant.

"Was not pregnant? Whoever said she was?" said Max.

Dorcas, it appeared, had told a friend of hers and also an aunt, a woman who cleaned for Linus Parker and who had told the police that Dorcas had told her, but had not told her the name of the father. According to the aunt, she had seemed quite sanguine about her condition—satisfied, even. There was no doubt in her mind that she would be married within the month. Dorcas had said all of this. Madeline Reese (Dorcas's aunt) had not told this to police before because she hadn't wanted to add to Dorcas's parents' already too-heavy burden. And what possible good would it have done, anyway?

Chief Inspector Bannen was (he had said) of two minds about this "disclosure." Possibly, she had told this tale to get the man to marry her. He wondered if Dorcas might have confided in someone in the Owen household. No, unless Dorcas had told Annie Suggins. When questioned, the cook had said she couldn't imagine Dorcas being "sanguine" about a pregnancy. That would take a woman of great maturity and with more self-command than Dorcas had ever had.

In mulling all of this over, Melrose knew he would never go back to sleep. It had been especially difficult to tell Jury about Jenny; yet, Jury seemed to have seen it coming, although not the form it would take.

Melrose gave up any thought now of going back to sleep. He got up and got dressed. But when he got downstairs, he heard none of that friendly tuneless humming of the previous morning coming from the kitchen. It was cold; gray shadows pooled in the corners, and the windows gave out on a dawning day so fresh, the whole landscape might have been born at that moment. He found the tea, made himself a cup, and went out.

✃

He wasn't the only one up and about. A hundred feet off the path, all standing in a ground mist that made it appear they were floating there, ghostly excrescences of old fenmen, were a tall man that he thought was Jack Price, two other men, farmer or laborer types, and two enormous horses. Melrose was glad he'd had the foresight to wear wellingtons, so that now he could make his way across the peaty land to join them. What on earth were they doing out here, plowing at this ungodly hour? Melrose watched Jack Price gesturing in his talk with one of the farmers, behind them a team of horses that looked big enough to plow Hell under. He trudged over to where Jack Price stood.

"Morning," said Melrose. God only knew if it *was* morning, still darkish at six-forty-five. Probably analogous to midday to those farmers out there. Melrose shivered. What a life. Probably ate their evening meal at four P.M.

Jack Price, in his standard gear of flat cap, rubber coat, and rubber boots, nodded to him, said around the dead cigar clamped in his teeth,

"He nearly broke the plow." Here he indicated one of the men with hands around the bits in the horses' mouths. "Bog oak. Ever seen one?"

"Not seen and don't know. What is it?"

"Just a tree." Jack tossed away the stub of his spent cigar. "Especially big one, might be lying down there eighty, ninety feet. Got buried under peat and that preserved it. Could be upwards of four thousand years old. These trees must've blown over some time in the past. This is probably just a piece of one. Wonderful firewood they make. Ah—"

Melrose saw that with a mighty tug, plowhorses and men had got the tree, or part of a tree, aboveground. "Good lord, it must have the girth of a sequoia."

"I love this wood. It's soft now, has to dry. But I like it for my work, the bigger pieces. Bog oak trunks were lying about like fallen ten pins after they drained the fens. In the eighteen hundreds they found antlers of extinct red deer and skeletons of grampus. Water back then, the flooding, would drown the land for weeks at a time. Parker likes to talk about how his grandfather kept his boots by his bed because the floor could like as not be inches under water. A lot of this country still lies below sea level." Jack stopped to take another cigar out of his pocket, bite off the end, light it with a flame-thrower of a lighter. "Dick, over there"—he inclined his head in the direction of the men—"he loves to say, 'If nature'd meant these here fens t'be dry land, she'd o'made 'em dry in the first place.' It's the 'damned Dutchmen' who have to bear the brunt of the blame, of course. Getting in here and building all of these dikes to rush the water out to sea. To hear Dick talk, you'd think it was only last week the draining took place. In a way, I envy him. It would be nice if the past were that close and accessible."

"Depends on the kind of past one's had, I expect." They were standing near a small, dilapidated bridge, stretching six or eight feet across a narrow canal. The bridge seemed to serve little purpose, for one could have made a short leap across the water. Perhaps the bridge was simply built for aesthetic reasons, beneath willows that trailed leaves over the rotting wood, beside rush, water dock, and loosestrife, which seemed favored by butterflies. Several fluttered above it.

The bridge looked romantic. Indeed, the entire scene around looked romantic. Perhaps it was the antiquarian nature of their task that made it seem so. The horses lunging away, pulling the oak a bit farther from its watery bed; Jack Price in his boots and cap and with his cheroot; the sinewy old farmer, and his young big-muscled son; the steaming dray horses' breath, white in the early morning air. It was as if some canvas by Constable had come alive and moved. Melrose watched the chalky water moving in the dike and asked Jack what river it fed into.

"Welland, most likely. That reed bed's turned to swamp over there. Used to be open water. After the reed swamp takes over, you get woods. Or carr. There's enough flora and fauna in this one place alone to keep researchers going for a long time.

"Do they all flow into the Wash, the rivers?"

"Yes, I expect so."

Melrose asked, carefully, "Aren't you awfully curious about what Verna Dunn was doing at the Wash?"

Jack smiled. "I try not to wonder too much about Verna, the artful little bitch. But, yes, I find it very peculiar. She was hardly the type to take herself off to some place like that to commune with nature or think brave thoughts. Can't imagine why, except—"

He paused, and Melrose was about to prompt him when Jack excused himself and moved closer to the bog oak operation. He spoke for a minute or two with the two men, gesturing toward the horses. Melrose wondered if the horses were quarterhorses or dray horses. When it came to horses, Melrose didn't know much of anything, never having been a horseman, despite his upbringing. This always seemed to annoy people who were hellbent on getting him to a hunt. The very idea made him shudder.

When Jack Price walked back to stand beside him and relighted his cigar, Melrose said, "We were talking about the body on the Wash. You were saying you couldn't think of any reason, except—"

"I was thinking that Verna loved games; I mean, she might have agreed to go to such an unlikely place for a lark. She was like that; she was mercurial, unpredictable. And the person who got her to go there might simply have wanted to dissociate her from Fengate. Because one of us, obviously, might be the guilty party."

"True." But that still didn't explain, for Melrose, the murderous venue of the Wash. "How long have you lived with the Owens?"

Jack removed his cigar and checked the end to see if it was still lighted. "Long time. It's hard for me to call him 'Uncle' Max because there's only about fifteen or sixteen years difference in our ages. He took me in after my mother—Max's sister—died. I was a teenager. My father was never much good—a drunk, mostly. I didn't even see him for the ten years after that before he died. I've lived with Max ever since." He smiled and puffed on the stogie. "My arrangement would be the envy of any artist trying to scrape by with a regular job. Not only do I have a studio, but I have my privacy. I could stay out there and work and brood for days and no one would invade it, my privacy. If I'm working, they assume I don't wish to be disturbed and Suggins puts a tray by the door. It's as good as an artists' colony—no, it's better. It's bloody wonderful. I get my meals cooked by Annie and served in a candle-lit dining room with several bottles of wine. To top it off, the Owens are simply great people. Max always was, but now there's Grace. Imagine a new wife taking on a grown nephew as part of the marriage deal."

"A rare deal, I agree. You were part of the 'deal,' as you put it, when Max was married to Verna Dunn. I get the impression she was no Grace."

Jack Price laughed: "Your impression is quite correct. Verna was nothing but trouble. That Max could put up with her as long as he did simply testifies to his resilience—his kindness, really."

Melrose was afraid his questions were imprudent for one who was on the scene as an antiques appraiser, but he went on asking them anyway. "I get the impression the Dunn woman was rather, well, profligate. Did she ever try anything with you?"

Price laughed again. "Of course. I think the only man around she might have missed is old Suggins."

Melrose wanted to ask, point blank, if Jack Price had accepted Verna Dunn's favors, but he didn't, not only because the question was not one for a stranger to put, but because the answer probably wouldn't have helped. In the dim, damp air, a tempest of birds rose from the willows and reed beds and the sun was bright enough to glaze the reeds and reflect on the smooth water of the dike. Except for them and the horses straining against the heavy, buried wood, there was nothing inhabiting the flat land for as far as Melrose could see. It was as if theirs were the last activity on earth.

Melrose took another tack, mentioning a fact that was by now general knowledge at Fengate. "Strange about this girl Dorcas's so-called pregnancy, isn't it?"

Jack Price shifted, as if uncomfortable. "Surprised me, certainly. Although some people might not think so." He tipped his head in the direction of the footpath and beyond. "Regulars at the Case might have me auditioning for the role of father. That little barmaid certainly would."

"Well, then, would they have had you auditioning for another part, too? The killer's?"

"Oh, of course. Probably had that buzz up anyway. Dorcas presumably had a 'crush' on me. Presumably, she'd a man in her life, a mysterious man. I'm as good a prospect as any, I expect. Excuse me. Doesn't look like they're making much progress." Price walked again over to the men and horses.

It was like uprooting some ancient tomb at an archaeological dig.

"Do you shoot?" Melrose asked.

Price looked somewhat astounded. Laughing, he said, "Not really; I don't care much for it. However, if you're asking can I load, aim, fire a gun, the answer is yes. But did I load, aim, fire at Verna? Answer is no."

"Oh, but I wasn't really—"

"Yes, you were. Really."

Melrose knew he'd asked one question too many. So he attempted to demonstrate he was hardly a threat by adding, "Sorry. Didn't mean to be nosy. Anyway, I'm going back to North—back to London today. I've been as much help as I can be here, and there's an auction coming up at Christie's I'm interested in."

Jack was silent for a moment looking off toward the two men and the oak trunk. Then he said, "Jenny's a friend of yours, you say?"

Melrose was surprised that the conversation would take this turn, especially as Jack's voice had taken on a note of intimacy Melrose hadn't heard before. "Not a friend, exactly. More of an acquaintance. Why?"

"It doesn't look too good for her, does it?"

Melrose was again surprised by the distinct note of gloom in the voice. "No, it doesn't."

Jack plucked the stub of the cigar from his mouth and tossed it into the wet grass at his feet. "Sorry you have to leave so soon." Then he walked off toward the bog oak, leaving Melrose to wonder just how good a friend Jack Price might have been.

◊◊◊

Melrose did not know whether Max Owen's friend Parker could be of help, or would even want to talk to him, but as Zel had said that Dorcas Reese had stopped there, and more than once, Melrose thought he might as well find out what he could before returning to Northants.

After the call last night to Jury, he had taken his final and spurious notes regarding Owen's furniture and told Max and Grace that he would be leaving today. That before he left, he wished to take up Major Parker on his kind invitation to lunch. *Lucky man*, Max Owen had quipped. Despite his clear discomfort over Bannen's visit, he'd managed a smile and told Melrose that he was going to lunch with arguably the best cook in South Lincolnshire. They all took it as a compliment (especially their cook, Mrs. Suggins) that Parker came to dine with them.

◊◊◊

His shirtsleeves rolled up, his forearms whitened with a flour-film, Parker's "cook" persona looked ready to walk on stage. Parker apparently thought the world would see nothing at all unusual in the master of this enormous pile of stone in kitchen-kit. But there was nothing stagy in this greeting; it was sincerely warm, so heartfelt Plant was a little ashamed that his motive in coming here wasn't simply luncheon.

Parker led Melrose through the high, wide, cold hall, through a room three times the size of Grace's "gallery," but quite unlike it in furnishings. From what Melrose could see in their long walk to a place to sit down in, the pieces in these rooms, although possibly very valuable (he should know, he was an appraiser) had little to do with one another. They didn't mesh. In one of the drawing rooms (there were several such rooms) a Spanish sideboard of a wood so dark it looked burnt fought for place next to an Italianate settee.

As if he were reading Melrose's mind, Parker said, "Shows you, doesn't it, how awful furniture can look if it's just tossed together. Max, now, has a genius for arrangement. But I'm sure you noticed that."

"Absolutely," said Melrose, thinking that if Parker saw Max's stuff as "arranged," no wonder Parker's own pieces looked tossed together. His eye was held by what might possibly have been a Botticelli original, but which managed to look suspect because it was so carelessly placed beside a wondrous Dutch painting, luminously dark.

Finally they came to rest in a small, snug room with a blazing fire and a table holding glasses and two decanters. "Whiskey all right? I've got some sherry but I don't much hold with these effete directors of tongue-taste that say whiskey messes up the tastebuds. Whiskey never messed up anything as far as I'm concerned." He set about pouring into two squat glasses.

"A few lives, perhaps. Thanks." Melrose took the glass.

"Yes, there's that. Cheers, anyway."

Melrose took out his cigarette case, held it up. "Do you mind?"

Parker laughed. "I feel like a pariah when I take out the smokes. Give me one, will you? Mine are in the kitchen next to the *tagine*. If you're wondering what this is, it's stew—but Moroccan stew." He took a cigarette and accepted a light. "I'm not showing off, mind you. I just love the foreign sounds of these dishes. I mean, *tagine* sounds a hell of a lot better tasting than 'beef stew,' wouldn't you say?" As he waved his arm back toward the kitchen, flour dusted the air. He took out his handkerchief and brushed it over the other arm. "I'm a messy cook. Hope you're hungry; I'm starved. Eat too much and drink too much of this"—he raised the glass—"but there's not much left to enjoy at my age."

Melrose smiled and settled deeper into his chair. Parker had gone somewhat soft, perhaps, in the jaw and belly, but was by no means fat or even "corpulent." He had more than six feet to spread any excess over,

and comfortably did so. He was not a handsome man, but an exception-
ally attractive one—at least, Melrose imagined women must think so.
Why? For there was not a feature of his appearance that one could call ex-
ceptional: eyes too small, hair too sparse and balding in back, nose a little
too broad, and an undistinguished mustache over a rather thin mouth.
And yet one probably wouldn't notice any of this unless one were attempting, as Melrose was, to discover Parker's appeal.

He was at the moment talking about this house, or this land. "I'm a
farmer, you know; rather, I *was* a farmer. Stopped because it was just too
damned hard and as I'm comfortably fixed, well, you wouldn't call me
much more than a 'gentleman farmer' anyway. The fields lie fallow now.
This big pile of bricks has been in my family forever. Plumbing's in an up-
roar most of the time, heat's about as effective as if boy guides supplied it
by rubbing sticks together. It's an absurd place for a dozen to live in, much
less one. Yet, you couldn't pry me loose."

Parker scratched his forehead, then scraped the soft and thinning hair
across it in a boyish gesture. He gave the impression that he'd been waiting for ages for just such a person as Melrose Plant to come along so that
he could get down to the business of living. And Melrose thought this
must be the source of his magnetism—that he gave the impression the
company he had to hand was the only company that suited him down to
the ground. He did not waste time in small talk; he plunged right into the
way he felt about life. Unlike many who gave the impression of divided
attention—whose minds, you knew, were elsewhere—Parker's attention
was wholly concentrated on the person he was with; he projected a sense
of immediacy. He was not afraid to reveal things about himself, which invited whoever he was with to do the same. This was the source of the
comfort Parker unknowingly and unselfconsciously offered. One felt at
home. Parker was the sort of person one confided in without intending
to, perhaps even without knowing one was doing it. Melrose therefore
wondered how many confidences the man had shared and how many secrets he knew.

"You've known Max Owen for a long time, haven't you?"

"Yes. So I also knew his first wife."

Parker's somewhat inscrutable smile implied that he knew what Melrose had really come to talk about. Melrose moved in his chair, as if trying to shake free of the suspicion that everyone could see straight through him. "I must admit I wonder about her, the dead woman. It's very queer, isn't it?"

"To tell the truth, I'm not surprised somebody finally did in Verna, a manipulative bitch by anybody's standards. Beauties usually are, aren't they? Moneyed and beautiful is doubly bad—spoiled and with the means to indulge it."

"I thought she'd come here to ask for money. From Max Owen."

"For the play, you mean? Yes, well perhaps she did, but I doubt it. Verna just enjoyed making mischief." Parker tossed back the rest of his glass and poured himself another finger of whiskey.

Melrose declined a refill and wondered if Parker himself had been manipulated. He ventured: "For everyone or only Max?"

For a moment Parker simply looked down at his glass, then answered obliquely. "She was a good deal of trouble, that woman. As far as I'm concerned, anyone of us might have been moved to do it; I was only surprised by the one who finally did."

"Lady Kennington? But that, of course, hasn't really been proved." He said this a little too passionately for a disinterested party.

"She's a friend of yours, Max says."

"Not really. More of an acquaintance. I met her once in Stratford-upon-Avon."

Parker grunted. "Nice woman." He paused. "Unusually so, I'd say. A sympathetic person. The Spanish have a better word—*simpatico*. It suggests 'kinship.' He paused again, drank off his whiskey, said, "Come on, let's eat our stew. It's very good."

It was indeed. Seldom had Melrose eaten food so delicious. "I heard about your cooking. You've got a great fan."

"Oh? Who?"

"That little girl, the groundskeeper's niece. Zel."

Parker laughed. "Ah, she's an experience, I can tell you."

"She says you're the best cook in Lincolnshire. Your specialty is plum ice cream."

"Which says more about her taste than about my cooking." Parker re-filled their wineglasses and returned the bottle to a cylindrical stone cooler. "Zel comes over here quite a lot. She helps me cook and she is, for one so young, remarkably good at it. Says she wants to be a chef."

Melrose smiled. "That says a lot for your influence."

Parker colored slightly, but seemed pleased. "Zel is the sort of child who makes one a bit sorry he hasn't any. This wine is quite good." He poured.

Melrose noticed the label. "It should be. You drink a Grand Cru with lunch every day?"

"Oh, no. Sometimes I suffer through a Premier Cru. When the lunch isn't all that good."

"This lunch certainly is 'all that good.'" Melrose broke a flaky roll, but-tered it, and said, "It's too bad about Zel's uncle. What happened?"

"Shooting accident. Did you see that old punt boat of his? He liked to take that out in the early mornings, out for partridge or plover. Some damned idiot trying to shoot in all of that fog accidentally shot Peter. Didn't even know he'd done it, so Peter lay there half the day until some anglers found him. Damned fools with guns. They're a menace. I keep telling Max's gardener to stop shooting at anything that moves." Parker sighed. "Pretty awful thing to happen to a man whose whole life is the outdoors. Peter's just unlucky, I think. Everything bad that could happen, happened. He might have told you he worked for years as a young man on this hunting estate in Perthshire. When his uncle stopped, he took over the estate—huge estate. I expect he's one of the youngest factors there ever was, a plummy job. There was a young lady, Scottish lass he was go-ing to marry, but she drowned when she slipped from a footbridge. Peter was blamed, although he said he wasn't within a mile of the place, poor fellow."

"That's pretty rotten."

"Worse, the girl's father claimed Peter had pushed her because he didn't want to marry her. You see, the coroner discovered the girl was sev-eral months pregnant. Old Mordecai was a fire-breathing fundamentalist Presbyterian—"

"You sound as if you know all of these people."

Parker looked surprised. "Do I? Well, I expect somehow I do after listening to Peter talk about it over the years. The father triggered an investigation, but there seemed little to investigate. Still, he was arrested and tried for manslaughter. Poor devil couldn't put together much of a defense—how could he? And he didn't deny he was the father. I think the thing that told most against him was that he was quite the ladies' man— by his own admission—well, he's still a very handsome fellow, but after he met Maggie, he changed his ways. The prosecution nonetheless managed to stir up feeling that Peter went about seducing and then leaving sweet young things. He was convicted. But the sentence was light, only two years, and he got out after serving one.

"After he came to Lincolnshire, I first hired him to do odd jobs, realized how good he was, then kept him on and let him have the cottage."

"What about Zel? Where are her parents?"

"According to Peter, the mother was a tart, the father—his own brother—a shiftless drifter. Neither one of them wanted a child. So Peter took her in. I've no idea where they are now."

"That must be pretty hard on her."

"Yes. It might account for her extremely lively imagination."

Melrose smiled. "Zel thinks the public footpath out there is cursed. She's inclined to blame Black Shuck."

Parker laughed. "Oh, yes, I've heard about him. It."

Melrose said, "Quite the lad, he or it is. That reminds me. Zel said the Reese girl—woman, I mean—often took the public footpath."

"Stick with 'girl.' Not very grown up was Dorcas. More soufflé?"

Melrose held out his plate. "Twist my arm." Parker served him and he said, "You knew her, didn't you?"

"Of course. Saw her in the pub any night I happened to go there."

"Did she do any work for you?" Melrose couldn't think how to put a question of Dorcas's visits. "Helping you with the cooking, perhaps?"

Parker looked up as surprised as if Melrose had valued all of his collection as worthless. "Cook? Dorcas? Not likely." He laughed.

But Melrose had picked up another note behind the laughter. Not quite comfortable with this line of questioning, Parker wasn't. "No one seems to have *known* the girl, really. Excepting perhaps for Mrs. Suggins."

"It's not surprising."

"Mrs. Suggins said she was rather, ah, too inquisitive—"

Parker smiled. "Bit of a snoop, Dorcas was. Perhaps when you haven't a life of your own, you want to borrow others."

"She must have had some life of her own. She told one or two people she was pregnant, after all."

"Ah, yes. Forgot about that. Maybe that's why she was killed. Some fellow that didn't want to marry her—Dorcas was the type who'd marry or be damned." Parker topped off their wineglasses. "Or there's the possibility she knew she wasn't and just went about saying it. To show, as I said, she had a life."

"It's quite possible, yes. Only, if she wanted people to know it, why wouldn't she have told people who'd be likely to spread it about? The aunt sounds more like a person who'd keep a secret."

"Madeline? Any secret would be safe with her. But, then, the girl was murdered and I suppose secrets do come out."

"Not enough to clear things up, though." Melrose sat back, feeling drowsy from the weight of the food and the wine. "I was thinking more of something else: that she might have overheard something, or seen something that made her dangerous."

Parker was silent, thinking this over. "Hmm! That's a thought, certainly. Knew something about the death of Verna Dunn, you mean?"

"Possibly."

Parker picked up his wineglass, swirled the wine a bit, thought some more. "Dorcas was the type of servant who could be right at your elbow and you'd not know it. The girl was infinitely unknowable. She simply didn't stick." He drank his wine.

There it was again, this queer feeling that poor Dorcas *was* so "unknowable" she faded right into the background of watery land and opaque pearl sky. She fit it so well, this flatness, so difficult to measure and, by some accounts, so dire.

◈

Heading toward Northampton, Melrose could not fathom how he'd wound up in the Deepings and Cowbit on his journey to Algarkirk.

He put it down to a total lack of any sense of direction. Or probably he'd gone into one of his fugue states that followed some interminable conversation with his aunt. Just outside of Loughborough, he ran into road works and pulled up behind a stream of cars that looked as if they'd been there for days. Melrose sat and thrummed his fingers on the steering wheel, wishing the Rolls people had had the foresight to include a CD player in these old Silver Shadows. A bit of Lou Reed would shake up these yobs in their neon orange vests, who appeared to be taking a tea break. At least the one standing over by the side had a Styrofoam cup in his hand. Staring at Melrose as if planning where to put the next stick of dynamite. Resentment of the Ruling Class, that was it.

The beefy fellow walked over to the Silver Shadow, said to Melrose, "Nice car, verra nice, like one meself, I would, only it's too pricey for me."

"Well, you'll be getting this one pretty soon when all of us die from exposure, sitting around watching you chaps."

The man laughed, thought that was rich. "Never mind, at least you don't have to take the bleedin' detour. Had to route traffic off onto one of the B roads and they weren't 'alf mad 'cause of that, I can tell you. But we'll be finishing up in two days time, or should be."

"How long's this lot been going on, then?"

"'Bout two weeks, I expect. No, less than that, as we started on the Wednesday, I remember it was the fifth because me mum's birthday came on that day and I missed the cake. She wasn't 'alf mad, me being the only son—"

Drone, drone, thought Melrose, closing his eyes as the roadworks fellow went on about his mum. *Birthday!* Melrose snapped awake. Oh, God, Agatha's birthday was either today, or perhaps yesterday. Or tomorrow. Sometime around now. How old was she, anyway? A hundred and twenty? Of course, he'd got nothing for her and checked his watch, wondering if he could make it to Northampton before the shops closed.

"Okay, mate, be on your way in a minute. Nice talkin' to you." The roadworks fellow slapped the side of the car as a small truck leading the traffic in the other lane came close. Well, he decided, getting past the ditch-digging or whatever they were doing, he'd make it to Northampton after all.

A smile split his face as he thought of the perfect present. He gunned the car and blasted off, waving dementedly back to his new pal.

18

Jury sat in the Stratford-upon-Avon police station, waiting for Sam Lasko to reappear. The way Lasko's secretary described the inspector's comings and goings made him sound a little like the genie-out-of-a-lamp. Jury was her Aladdin, a little kid without an ounce of imagination who came here occasionally to call in his wish-markers. Since this visit was his third, it better be his last (Jury could almost hear her say).

"I'll wait, thanks," he had said fifteen minutes before. She had given a little *suit yourself* shrug of the shoulders and returned to her brisk typing.

She was middle-aged, possibly more than "middle," tall and thin and wearing a putty-colored jumper over a cloyingly pink blouse the color of bubble gum. Everything about her looked pulled tight—her hair in a punishingly tight chignon, her straight, flat mouth, her thin nose. She put Jury in mind of a schoolmistress who fastens on the lives of her charges, looming in disapproval over the clumsy translations of Ovid. The name on the little black plaque on her desk read *C. Just*. Miss Just. Jury liked that. During the fifteen minutes of his presence, she had looked up from the rattling typing and said that she had no idea as to when Inspector Lasko would return, and wouldn't he prefer to come back? In the question there had not been a trace of concern for the comfort of the visitor, merely the testiness of one who feels her work interrupted by the looming shadow of Scotland Yard. It was clear to Jury the first time he'd seen Miss C. Just that she suffered poorly policemen whose rank outstripped that of her boss.

Sam Lasko finally appeared, his lamp left behind somewhere, looking his usual woeful self. The look had nothing to do with the way things were going in his life; he'd cultivated it over the years to disarm the public in general, and to throw suspects off their guard in particular. And to get favors out of people like Jury. Could anyone refuse such a miserable man as D.I. Lasko? Jury hadn't been able to resist Lasko's hangdog look once, and he'd found himself involved in a triple-murder in Stratford some years back.

"This gentleman's been waiting to see you," said Miss Just.

As if he'd come to report a cat up a tree. To her chagrin, Lasko actually put on a broad smile and cuffed Jury several times on the shoulder as they went into Lasko's office.

"I expect you're here about your lady friend?" Lasko sat down heavily in a swivel chair that needed oiling. He started creaking it back and forward like a rocker.

"What about this 'imminent' arrest, Sammy?"

Lasko rubbed at a spot on the toe of his shoe, his foot against the edge of his desk. "That's what I heard."

"Don't make it sound like a rumor. Is it true? Or just good PR for the Lincolnshire police? Do you know this DCI?" Jury asked.

"Not before this business, no. I've heard about him. He's even more relentless than me." Sam made another pass at his shoe.

Jury smiled. "Wow." Then he got serious. "Even if Jenny did have a motive for killing Verna Dunn—and I'm still not convinced she did— how can he ignore absence of motive in the case of Dorcas Reese? Moreover, how can he ignore the possibility there are two killers or that it's a total stranger?"

Lasko spread his arms. "Both connected with Fengate? Anyway, don't ask me, I'm just the baby-sitter." He wiped his eyes, beginning to water from some allergy. "Fucking pollution. Look, Bannen wouldn't make an arrest unless he was sure he had a case. Because she'd have some flash git of a lawyer getting her out before you could say—" Lasko sneezed, then blew his nose.

"It's total nonsense. The woman was shot with a rifle; how did she get it there?"

Lasko shrugged, opened and closed drawers. "Got it into the car somehow beforehand? Planted it at the scene? Her prints were on it."

"Everybody's fingerprints were on the damned gun, including the cook's. So were Verna Dunn's." Jury said it again: "Total nonsense."

"Is it? How do you know?"

"You just know a person, that's all."

"Yeah, that's probably what the wife of the Yorkshire Ripper said."

"Come on, Sammy." He watched as Sam's other hand started shuffling through files.

"Look, as long as you're here—"

"No," said Jury, rising.

∂∫

The door of the Ryland Street house opened just as Jury was raising his hand to the brass knocker. Jenny took a step backward. "Richard!"

"Hullo, Jenny." He saw that she was wearing the brown coat and Liberty scarf she'd worn the first time he'd ever seen her. Ten years. How could so much time have passed with so little to show for it? "Going out? I'll go along with you." Jenny was elusive. She always had been.

"Only for a walk by the river." She smiled and started to close the door behind her. Then she said, "Wait a minute; I need something." She went in, ran up the stairs, then was back.

As they walked along the pavement toward the church and the public park, he wondered if she knew about this imminent arrest and decided she didn't. He told her about having seen Pete Apted; her reaction to this was apprehensive.

"If I need Pete Apted, I must *really* be in trouble. Who's paying him, for heaven's sake?"

Jury looked at the church façade and smiled. "*Pro bono*, as they say."

"Oh, *certainly*." Her laugh was rueful.

They passed the church and came to the river, where they stood side by side. Jenny pulled a plastic bag from her pocket and started throwing out bread crumbs to the ducks. The ducks farther out caught on to this and steered toward shore.

It occurred to Jury that Sammy's question was as valid as Apted's had been. How could he be so sure she hadn't done this? Yet, so was his reply that one just knows about some people. What he knew about her was that she was generous, kind, loyal, and self-effacing. Yet about her past he knew very little, and it surprised him to realize it. She had been married to James Kennington, who had died before Jury met her, and she had been in the process of leaving their big house, Stonington, selling it to raise some capital.

That was all he knew. There was something about Jenny, a whole side that she kept to herself, and it made him uncomfortable. He could not explain this discomfort. Even now she maintained an unnatural calm given the danger she was in. She fed the ducks and swans with a serene disdain for what might be going on around her. It was such a tranquil scene; murder and Lincolnshire seemed far away. She appeared unmoved by her danger, perhaps (he told himself) because she knew herself to be innocent. Nothing then would happen to her.

A bossy swan shoveled his way between a bank of ducks and snatched up a large knob of bread. Jury said, "You're in some danger, you know that."

"Yes," she simply said. Now the greedy swan collided with another and started chattering. Jenny shook the bag, loosening up any stray bits, threw them over the water, and shoved the bag back in her pocket. She dusted her hands and said, "May I have a cigarette?"

Automatically, Jury's hand went to his pocket. Ruefully, he smiled. "I quit."

"Of course. I forgot." She returned her gaze to the river. "I wish I could." After a moment's silence, she said, "You want to know what happened, I expect. And you want to know about me and Verna Dunn. What did that Lincolnshire policeman tell you?" Her hands were buried in her big coat pockets, the wind off the water fluttered the edges of the Liberty scarf.

"I'd rather hear your version than Bannen's. According to him, you'd known her for years."

"Yes. I'll get to that. That night, though, we had an argument after dinner. I wanted to know how she'd have the gall to go to Fengate. She said Max was backing a new play, some sort of 'vehicle' in which she'd planned a comeback. Well, that might or might not have been true, but I know it wasn't her reason for turning up that weekend. She wanted to make trouble. That's all. Just trouble." Jenny shook her head. "I told her to leave him alone. Leave the man alone or I'd tell him what kind of person she really was. That had no effect. After all, she'd been married to him; she knew him better than I did. This was after dinner, Saturday night. The others were having their coffee. I couldn't stand her any longer—all I wanted to do was get away from her, and I didn't want to go back to the house because she'd be there, too. So I simply left her standing there out in front of the house and started walking the public footpath. I walked it for some time, thinking I'd go to the pub and have a drink. Then I heard a church bell sound the hour a long way off and checked my watch and saw it was eleven o'clock. The pub would be closed. So I started back." Sadly, she looked at the ground. "That's the lot."

"You didn't hear a car start up? It would have been around ten-twenty or so?"

"Verna's car?" Jenny shook her head. "I was on my way to the pub, I told you. I'd have been over halfway there, too far away to hear a car."

"The Owens thought the two of you had gone off in it."

"That's ridiculous. In the midst of a dinner-party two of the guests go larking around in a car?"

"I expect the Owens assumed whatever the argument was about took precedence over good manners. So tell me about Verna Dunn."

Jenny studied the cold night sky, and said, "I was related to her; we were cousins. . . ." She looked away, started in again. "We lived together for a time, Verna and her mother with me and my father. Her mother wasn't a bad person, just a little dim. Of course, she couldn't believe what I told her about Verna. Nor could my father. It was just too outlandish to believe. Even as a child she seethed with jealousy. She hated me, but I somehow came to believe it wasn't personal. Verna was relentless in her pursuit of other people's possessions: dolls, pets, money, husbands. She went after all of them. She seemed to be more of a force than a person; she hated most people—perhaps all people, but anyone standing in her way if she wanted something, such as my father's full attention; toward such a person she was remorseless.

"Listen to this—" Here Jenny drew a small leather book with a gold metal clasp from her pocket. It appeared to be one of those diaries with flimsy pages that girls are fond of keeping. She read: "'Sarah is gone from the barn. I can't stand it, it won't do any good for me to look anymore, only I keep on looking because if I stop I know I'll never see her. I know Verna let her out and did something—'" Jenny stopped and said, "Sarah was my pony." She turned to a later part and read: "'I can't find Tom.' Tom was my cat. And there were my doll, my favorite dress, my gold bracelet. I never found them. I never knew what happened to them. No one, not my father and certainly not her mother, believed Verna could have done this. Every time the look on Verna's face was one of pure triumph. It was near unbearable. You see, I never knew what happened to them. Had she killed the animals? Had she just taken them somewhere and left them? Had she given them to people, saying they were strays? Well, it's hard to do that with a pony." Jenny's smile was rueful. "The trouble was that Verna was so clever about hiding this compulsion to ruin things for people. That's the way it often is with disturbed people; they're so *plausible*. After she'd cheated at some game or other and I told, she would weep copious tears, she'd be the picture of heartbreak—"

Jury said, "That's all dreadful, Jenny. But I can't imagine a prosecutor would take a child's diary seriously as evidence."

He was surprised by the shrillness of her voice, for Jenny was ordinarily a soft-spoken woman. "You don't think it *stopped* after childhood, do you? That these were just pranks and she finally grew up? When I was twenty-five she broke up my engagement. I really loved him. And I don't know what happened. All I know is that one day he simply wasn't there. Years later, after I married James, I thought I was shut of her. And then she started calling, calling James and making up stories about what hard luck she'd had and getting his sympathy. It was of course far more subtle than I make it sound." Jenny pulled her scarf away from her hair and held it at both ends. She looked at it as if she wished it were a garrote. "I told James not to talk to her and *never* to let her come to Stonington. I'm not sure he absolutely believed me—who would? You don't."

"Jenny, that's not true."

Her smile was bitter and disbelieving, but she continued. "So when I saw her at Fengate, it had been the first time in fifteen years."

"And yet you didn't let anyone know she was your cousin." No wonder Bannen thought he had a case.

Jenny tied the scarf round her neck and pushed hair out of her eyes. Rain, more a mist than rain, had come with the wind. "No. I'm not sure why. But, you see, neither did *she*. Why didn't she say, 'Jenny, my God, after all these years'? I knew she must have planned something. With Max Owen in mind, probably."

"But she'd divorced him."

"For Verna, nothing was ever final." She pulled her coat collar tighter. "Except death." She paused. "Within a year Max Owen turned round and married his present wife. The point being that Max was then happy. To Verna that would have presented a challenge. She couldn't have him be happy with Grace after being miserable with Verna herself. You know, I doubt Max ever caught onto her. She was masterly at making the other person think his misery was caused by himself, never by her. Nice people like Max tend to take responsibility for misfortune. He'd have had a problem sorting out their life together. He'd have taken most of the blame."

"I still can't understand why Grace Owen invited her."

"I don't know. It wouldn't be difficult, if I put my mind to it, to work out the approach Verna would have used."

"How well do you know Grace?"

"I'd been to Fengate once or twice over the years after Max married Grace, never when he was married to Verna. My husband was a friend of Max, and we went there once just before James died. Max met Grace in Yorkshire when Sotheby's acted as agent for that glamorous auction at Castle Howard. Max was still married to Verna and Grace's husband had died a few years before. The Owens divorced about a year after the Castle Howard auction. And within another year, Max and Grace married. I expect you know she had a son."

"Yes. He died in a riding accident, something like that, didn't he? Pretty awful." He did not add that the source of his information about much of this was Melrose Plant.

"Toby was a hemophiliac."

"That must have been a terrible strain for the Owens. A kid who can't participate in sports, a mother who has to keep constant vigil because death waits round every corner."

"Or Verna Dunn."

Jury frowned. "Meaning?"

"She used to be an occasional visitor at Fengate. That's what she told me, probably to provoke me. I just wonder if this so-called accident happened during one of her visits. No one witnessed it, as far as I know. I wanted to ask Grace, but I couldn't bring myself to do it. I was afraid of the answer."

Jury frowned, thinking about Grace Owen. In the silence that followed, he watched the river where the ducks slept now in the rushes, bobbing on ripples the wind stirred up. The ghostly white swans, farther off, coasted. He wondered if they stayed in this part of the Avon the year round. He remembered Bannen talking about the swallows, how their exodus always made him feel strangely hopeless. Jury had been struck by this small confession, for Bannen impressed him as being an intensely private sort of person, even for a police officer. Jury looked at the swans now bathed in moonlight and shared Bannen's feelings.

"One thing that might work in your favor, ironically, is Dorcas Reese. Not only did you have no motive, you weren't even around when it happened."

She was silent. She seemed about to say something, and stopped. Then she said, "They'll just say it's not very far between Stratford and Algarkirk. Still, what reason would anyone have for killing the girl?"

"She might have presented a danger. According to—" He didn't want to bring Plant into it; it would merely confuse things. "According to Annie, the cook, Dorcas was somewhat nosy. Perhaps she overheard something? Hard to tell."

"Then I'd have as much reason as anyone, wouldn't I?"

"Any of the people Bannen questioned—" Jury gave it up. He didn't make a hell of a good comforter. He was sure Job would agree.

Jenny looked down at the ground, pushed a pebble with her foot. "Don't think I don't appreciate what you're doing for me." She took his hand, said nothing else.

Her failure to mention Jack Price wasn't lost on him. But he wouldn't ask, at least not now. He could feel her eyes on him but didn't meet her gaze for fear of ruining what little resolve he had. He would have to tell her what Lasko had said. It was difficult; it would mean her giving up the luxury of doubt. If in her mind there was still room for that. Bringing in someone like Apted made the whole thing a certainty.

She shook her head. He could see panic written all over his face. "I simply wanted to make sure Apted would be available if, as in my case, things go that far. Just a precaution." How banal. She didn't believe it for a minute, that it was precautionary.

"It's all against me, isn't it?"

Her face was white as the moon. He wanted to say, No, of course the facts aren't all against you, but he couldn't. Because he was afraid they were. It was true that Verna Dunn appeared to be universally disliked, but that almost canceled out motives for the others at Fengate, for there was nothing specific that had surfaced. "Pete Apted never loses, remember that."

Her brief laugh was tear-choked. "There's always a first time."

Then a long silence with neither of them moving.

She hadn't—not in so many words—actually said she was innocent.

And he hadn't asked.

19

In his own house, seated in his own chair, and by his own fireplace, Melrose sat quietly turning the pages of a picture book about the fen country; here was a fine photograph of a fogbound mere. He supposed this absurd nostalgia he felt for the fens, for the good company and the good talk, was partially owing to the impoverishment of both in his present circumstances. He sighed deeply and allowed his spine to creep farther down in the wing chair, and looked at the picture of the Black Fens of Cambridgeshire, a seemingly endless expanse of soft, black soil. He could feel its silkiness running through his fingers, as he heard Agatha's voice running through his mind, catching only a word here, a word there. He had become quite expert at holding a sieve to her mouth.

". . . minded," she said, then took a sip of Fortnum and Mason's special blend tea.

"I beg your pardon? I didn't catch that." Most of it had gone through the sieve.

"You should be more civic-minded, I said; you should shoulder more of your social responsibilities."

He stared at her. "There's no society around here that one could possibly feel responsible for." He set aside the book on the Black Fens and scooped up *Helluva Deal!*, an absolutely wonderful little book, in spite of (or perhaps because of?) the Nuttings being totally clueless when it came to prose style. But that hardly mattered since they provided so much entertainment in describing country auctions in small-town America. He was now reading the section devoted to "scams" in the antiques market—at least small-town

American scams. He especially enjoyed reading about the Pointer cousins who had discovered a fortune in first editions up in an attic. It wasn't, however, their attic and in order to get possession of this large box of books they had offered to clean out their neighbor's attic. "Clean out" in every sense of the words. The treasure in books belonged to a little old lady who hadn't a sou, who was living at bare subsistence level. The ebullient Nuttings (he an auctioneer, she a dealer) couldn't get enough of these tawdry episodes. Neither could Melrose. He especially loved Peregrine "Piggy" Arbuckle, whose set-up included a little boy and a so-called doctor. It pleased him to find that Piggy was a Brit now living (and plying his trade) in the States.

Agatha took up an argument Melrose hadn't known he was engaged in. "You know perfectly well that Ada Crisp shouldn't be allowed to continue at that shop, that the pavement is a death-trap, what with all of those dribs and drabs of second- and thirdhand junk sitting about, not to mention that nasty little dog—what are you doing? Can't you put that book down for a moment?"

Melrose sighed. "Piggy Arbuckle had a good thing going."

"What?" Her brow furrowed as neatly as the black soil of the fen in Melrose's photograph.

Agatha shut her eyes as if she were suffering from a migraine. "Oh, *do* stop being idiotic, Melrose."

He reclaimed the Fens and opened the book to a photograph showing a field of tulips and another of daffodils that would inspire Wordsworth to write a sequel. *"I wandered lonely as another cloud, That floats o'er fields and hills again . . ."*

"Don't try to change the subject."

Subject? Had there been one?

"We were talking about your being a witness."

"Witness?" As if he didn't know. "Surely, you're not serious about that?" Of course she was. She talked of nothing else these days.

Her eyes clamped tight shut in annoyance, as if Melrose's person were too bright and blinding. She said, "Don't try and diminish the accident or the attack by that nasty dog. You were right across the street, coming out of the pub."

"Drunk as a lord." Melrose corrected himself: "As a commoner, I mean. How could you possibly expect me to remember what I saw?"

"Melrose! You shall be subpoenaed if you don't cooperate."

"I'll be a hostile witness, then." He smiled.

"You will be nothing of the sort!" With her usual assumption that both God and the Law were on her side, she added, "You'll be under oath. So will Trueblood be. Both of you were standing in front of the Jack and Hammer watching and no doubt making imbecile comments—"

"Trueblood? You're planning on calling him, too?" Melrose was astonished. She wouldn't call on Marshall Trueblood for help even if she were sinking into a bog like the one in his fen book. "Well, I fear you're to be disappointed. Trueblood *didn't* see anything. His back was to you." Melrose was almost sorry, for the thought of Agatha's case depending on them made him laugh. Talk about *folie à deux*! "John Grisham would love it."

"John who?" She held a rock cake aloft. It looked like a lumpy spacecraft.

"You know. That lawyer-chap in the States who writes legal thrillers."

"Oh, him." Agatha waved the lawyer-chap away.

"'Oh, him' has made millions." Melrose took a sip of cold tea. Agatha had drunk up all the hot. "Who has Ada rounded up for her defense?"

Indifferent to Ada's defense, Agatha shrugged and selected a triangle of anchovy toast. "I've no idea, nor do I care. Probably have to get someone to take it *pro bono*."

Melrose slid even farther down in his chair, turning this foot-in-the-chamber-pot over in his mind. He could surely get some mileage out of this. "Who else is your chap going to call? What's his name?"

"Simon Bryce-Pink. He's quite good, everyone says so—"

"Everyone" probably meaning Theo Wrenn Browne. "Besides me, who else has he got on his short list?"

Narrowly, she looked at him. "I don't think I should tell you. I can't trust you."

"Oh? Then why on earth are you having me as your star witness?"

"I didn't say 'star.' Theo is to have that distinction."

Melrose knew that she'd got together with the slippery Theo Wrenn Browne and between them they had maximized the extent of the injury.

Probably found a bent doctor to verify it. And there were always the psychological damages when they got through with the physical ones. She had come to Ardry End today with her zimmer frame, which she had shed quick enough in making her way to Melrose's tea table. The aluminum walker had four little wheels on it, so the poor invalid could move more swiftly. Wasn't it something of an oxymoron to couple wheels and a zimmer frame?

"Poor Ada. Just when is this case scheduled to be tried?"

"Not for weeks. There's quite a backlog of cases." She looked at him. "And why 'poor Ada'? I should think you'd save your sympathy for your own family. Well, when she loses, she'll have to pay costs."

"You're so certain she'll lose?"

Agatha looked at him as if he were witless. "Of course. Why not?"

Melrose was about to answer the question, rhetorical or not, when Ruthven appeared (thank heaven!) to summon him to the telephone.

"Who is it, Ruthven?" Melrose asked, as he walked to the door.

"It's . . . the butcher, My Lord." Ruthven's smile was sly.

"Jurvis? Why on earth is he calling me?"

Ruthven's answer was lost in the wake of Agatha's shout: "See that Jurvis defats that lamb! Martha never does a proper job."

With Agatha's voice finally sinking behind him like a depth-charge, Melrose yanked up the receiver and said, "Hullo, Mr. Jurvis. What can I do for you?"

"It's Mr. Jury, actually."

"Richard!"

"I'd like you to come to London tomorrow."

"Well, I could do, though you'd be tearing me away from my aunt, you understand. But why?"

"You can go to the solicitor's with me."

"Solicitor?"

"Pete Apted's brief. His name's—where's that scrap of paper?"—rustles, crackles coming down the wire—"Moss is his name. Charly Moss."

Melrose asked, rather tentatively, "Have you talked to, ah, Lady Kennington, then?" He still found it difficult to mention her. She stood like a shadow between them.

"Why so formal? Yes, I saw Jenny. I'm glad I did before Lasko got there."

"You mean she's really been arrested?"

" 'Fraid so. We were expecting it, anyway." Jury sighed.

Melrose's legs felt rubbery; he dragged over a chair. "What was the charge?"

"Murder."

"Hell," breathed Melrose. "In both cases?" When Jury said yes, he asked, "What could he possibly have found to link her with Dorcas Reese?"

"I don't know. Unless Dorcas knew something, and the implication is that she did. I'm surprised Bannen waited this long to charge her. It makes me wonder if he was waiting for something more—some bit of physical evidence, some report or other, and now he's got it. I saw Pete Apted, remember him?"

"Hell, yes."

"He who demolished my illusions," said Jury, trying to make his tone jokey.

"He didn't demolish your illusions; he confirmed your suspicions."

Jury was silent. Then he said, "I expect you're right. Anyway, he's taking her case. That's why I'm—we're—seeing this solicitor. If Apted uses him as instructing solicitor, he must be good. I saw Apted yesterday morning, early. He's in his office at seven eating apples. Just as intense as ever, just as uncompromising. So can you meet me tomorrow in Lincoln's Inn, say, at ten?" Jury gave him the address, without waiting for an answer. "Sorry to drag you away from Agatha."

"I'll never forgive you. See you tomorrow, ten o'clock."

20

Jury kept his eyes on the road, straight as a runway and running parallel to a wide drainage ditch. On the other side, across the blank fields of dry stubble, there must have been a dike or weir densely populated by water-fowl. As he watched, a skein of geese took flight, the stillness on all sides making their beating wings audible.

To show just how relaxed he was, Wiggins yawned and stretched one arm. The other hand was manning the steering wheel. "I think it's that generally speaking I'm a bit more settled in myself; I take things *comme ci, comme ça*–like, and don't let them bother me," he said, and looked out of his window. "Except this landscape," he added, darkly. The flight of geese had disappeared, taking with them life and movement. "The only sign of life we've had for miles was those geese. It's eerie; it's empty. Doesn't surprise me people get murdered here." He shivered.

Jury, who Wiggins had noticed was not in the best of moods, merely grunted.

Wiggins went on. "The setting for this murder seems awful peculiar to me. The Wash isn't exactly a place where I'd expect two people to ren-dezvous, much less someone like Verna Dunn. Why does everyone seem to think Lady Kennington was the one who drove to the Wash with her?"

"Everyone doesn't," said Jury.

Wiggins went on: "Strange. The way Lady Kennington tells it, after this quarrel with Verna Dunn, she walks the footpath to the pub, but halfway there she realizes it's so near to the pub's closing time she just turns and walks back the way she came. He or she'd be depending upon

Lady Kennington's absence from the house until the whole thing was finished. It all sounds very unlikely to me."

Jury said, "I don't think the killer was depending on Jenny Kennington doing anything; that she went for a walk on the footpath was pure coincidence. It's too bad Jenny didn't get to the pub; there would be people to corroborate her story."

"But why'd the killer pick the Wash?"

"Perhaps so that her body wouldn't have been discovered for a while. Desolate place. Bannen thinks it's to do with the tides and the shifting sands. Cover the body, at least; take it out to sea, at best. Only thing is— Be careful, there's a horse and cart ahead."

Wiggins sighed. "Yes, I *can* see, sir."

For the next few miles, they drove in silence past dark furrowed fields. Against a skyline that looked as hard and gray as a band of steel, the isolated house or barn sprang up like a mirage. Jury's eyelids felt like lead. It was true that he'd had very little sleep in the last few days; nonetheless, this gray singularity of land struck him as hypnotic. In that far field, an abandoned plowshare could as easily have been an artifact, some ancient instrument heaved up from mere or bog. He was inclined to agree with Wiggins; it wasn't a place he'd care to live in. It lay too heavily upon the soul. It would take a greater subtlety of mind than his to appreciate it, the nuances of light and shadow, wind and weather. He laid his head back against the leather seat and wished he had a cigarette.

"We passed one of those new Happy Eater motel-like places outside of Spalding," said Wiggins, alerting Jury to a possible break for tea. "Another should be coming up soon. One of them got the 'cleanest toilet' award."

"That's a treat," said Jury who had turned his head to gaze out of the passenger window.

It didn't surprise Jury when Wiggins's fast-food-prediction turned out to be correct. In another mile appeared the bright orange sign of a Happy Eater. Enthusiastically, Wiggins told him, "Now the Happy Eaters do a really good plate of beans on toast. See, there's one just coming up—"

"An oxymoron, Wiggins. It's impossible to do something 'good' with beans on toast."

Undaunted, Wiggins stuck to his guns. "I could fancy some, anyway."
He slowed the car, though not substantially, merely dropping the speed to
some point around fifty mph. He did this so that Jury could tell him to
pull over. "I could use a cuppa, how about you?" When Jury nodded,
Wiggins made for the exit.

Jury had to admit that the Happy Eater was the most garishly clean
place he had ever seen outside an intensive care unit. It certainly could
have deserved "cleanest toilet" award hands down. Painted to within an
inch of its life in bright orange, daffodil yellow, and emerald green, it was
a toast to all of childhood's colors. Indeed, it appeared to cater for kiddies,
as one section of the room was cordoned off and furnished with down-
sized chairs and a table and baskets of blocks and games. Two children
were playing in it now, bonging one another with brilliant blue blocks of
wood, a pastime that would no doubt escalate into acrimonious battle and
police—meaning Jury—would have to break it up.

After the pretty waitress had appeared at their table with their tea and
beans on toast and gone crisply off again, Jury said, "What about Jack
Price? I didn't see him when I was at Fengate. According to Plant, he said
he left the living room around ten-thirty. The drive to the Wash wouldn't
have taken more than quarter of an hour, twenty minutes. Time for him
to get there and back. Indeed, any one of them could have got there.
Price, after ten-thirty; Parker, after eleven; the Owens also after eleven."

"Not him, though, sir, not Max Owen. This gardener, Suggins, said he
took some whiskey up to him, didn't he?"

"Um." Jury fell silent, drank his lukewarm tea, watched the kiddies
with the building blocks. Then he said, "Let's stop off first at the pub and
then I want to see that footpath. Plant mentioned this chap, Emery, who
works for Major Parker." Jury looked at his watch. "I'm meeting with the
solicitor in the morning, so we'll have to get back to London tonight."

Wiggins looked mildly unhappy. "Night blindness" (whatever that was)
was one of the many entries on his roster of ills. Jury's better judgment
demanded he not inquire into this scourge, but the temptation was always
too much for him. "What the hell's that? 'Night blindness'?"

"Surely, I've mentioned it, sir. It's what happens to my vision after a long time having headlights of other cars shining in my eyes. My vision becomes impaired." With that haughty comment, he went back to his beans on toast.

Why argue? thought Jury. "Then I'll drive."

Wiggins gave him a speculative look. "You've been looking kind of peaked. Night driving is more tiring than people know."

Jury knew that Wiggins was always up for a motel. He loved motels. "If worse comes to worse, Wiggins, we'll stop somewhere along the way."

Happily, Wiggins filled him in on the state of the mattresses in the Raglan chain ("lumpy"), the quality of the air ("awful close and humid") in the Trust House Fortes, the sad state of the breakfasts in most B&B's ("burnt toast, thimbles of juice").

"We're looking for a bed, Wiggins, not an experience."

❧

The sullen barmaid in the Case Has Altered confirmed that they didn't do rooms, didn't cater for overnighters, and that they ought to try back in Spalding. The girl had short-cut brown hair and dull eyes the color of peat. Still, there was a sort of prettiness in her heart-shaped face and tilted nose.

Jury ordered lager; Wiggins, a Diet Pepsi.

"How long have you worked here?"

She shrugged. "Off 'n on, couple a months. I'm in charge when they're gone." Vigorously, she started wiping down the bar. Having been left in charge, she was going to exert her limited authority and flaunt what sexuality she could muster. It wasn't much, despite the short red skirt, the black jumper. She left off rubbing the bar down to reach inside the neck of the jumper and reposition a strap.

"Then you knew Dorcas Reese?"

She didn't answer immediately. When she got the gray lump of rag going again, she said, "What if I did?"

"Because *if* you did, you might be able to help us, love." Jury shoved his ID up to her face, an act she might have thought hostile, had it not been accompanied by his disarming smile. "Dorcas worked here part-time, didn't she? Like you." It seemed to quiver in air, the implication that the fate of one could be the fate of the other.

The girl swallowed hard, got even paler. "I'll get your drinks."

As she moved away to the beerpulls, Jury looked at her flamboyant tights. A motif of black vines and leaves coiled up her thighs, disappearing under her very short red skirt. In a moment, she was back with the drinks. She certainly wasn't slow. She set the drinks before them, said rather haughtily that she'd got to get other orders too, and rolled off again to the end of the bar, where sat the two men who'd been trying to get her attention by banging their pints on the bar. She called to the one named Ian to shove it.

"A bit snippy, wouldn't you say, sir?"

"Never mind. I expect she wants us to know this is her manor." Jury drank his lager and looked at an old newspaper clipping thumbtacked to the wall. It was dated January 1945 and showed photos of the Ouse and Welland rivers, their banks overflowing and land under water as far as the camera-eye could see. There was a picture of the tiny town of Market Deeping, its streets turned to rivers. As he read the captions, he caught himself smiling and wondered what he was finding in this report to smile about, given that this flooding of the fields must have spelled difficulty if not disaster for the land's inhabitants. Perhaps he was relieved to see that Nature, once again, had refused to roll over for man.

She was back. Stubbornly, she folded her arms across her breasts and studied the bitten nails of one hand.

Jury still smiled as he asked, "What's your name, love?"

Truculently, she answered: "Julie. Rough." When she saw Sergeant Wiggins getting out his notebook, she added, "R-O-U-G-H. It's not the way it's pronounced. That's 'R-O-W,' like 'Row, row your boat.' My first name's actually Juliette, you know, like in 'Romeo and.'"

Here was a name that certainly did not fit an imagined face. There was no hint of the tragic about Julie Rough.

"Age?" asked Wiggins.

You could tell she was considering her answer. "I turn twenty-one Christmas. I'm twenty, if you must know."

Jury bet eighteen, tops. He asked, "So tell us what you know about Dorcas Reese, Julie."

She shrugged. "Seein' her around . . . you know, the shops and all. Mebbe have a coffee, tea in the Berry Patch. That's a caff in Kirton."

At the end of the bar sat a tableau of what could only be regulars—an old man flanked by two younger ones, but so fascinated by the strangers that they all seemed to stare and breathe as one. Jury asked Julie who they were.

"Them? Oh, that's just old Tomas and Ian and Malcolm. Always here, them three."

Jury told Wiggins to have a talk with the customers, starting with Ian or Malcolm. Wiggins moved off down the bar. The only other customers were a gray-haired woman reading what looked like a racing form, and a fellow throwing darts.

"Did Dorcas talk about herself at all?"

"Now and again, I s'pose. She worked over at Fengate. But you know that."

"Tell me what you know about it."

"I know she didn't much like all that choppin' and peelin' she was set to do. But she was ever so keen on the lady."

"The cook?"

"Nah." Julie made a face. "Mrs. Owen. She called her 'Grace' but I expect not to her face."

"What about the others? Max Owen and Jack Price?"

"No, she never talked about Mr. Owen. He was hardly ever around to speak to. And Jack Price, he's a regular here, nice enough bloke. Comes in all the time, stops here the way other people do at home." She looked toward the shadowed rear of the room. "Sits back there, 'e does, hardly makes a sound. But he's quite nice. Gentleman-like."

"Did the two of you, you and Dorcas perhaps exchange confidences?"

"Opinions, more like."

Jury thought this to be a nice distinction. "Opinions about the people at Fengate?"

"Yeah. Except I didn't know them only to see, like. I been over there a few times when Dorcas and me was goin' out, maybe to the pictures or there's a disco in Kirton."

Julie and Dorcas were clearly closer friends than she'd allowed, but he let that go. "Did you ever happen to meet this Dunn woman, the one who was murdered?"

Julie's natural bent toward the salacious overcame any misgivings she had about involving herself. "I never did, but Dorcas did, said she thought 'twas ever so peculiar, Mr. Owen having his first wife there. I mean right in front of Grace. That's Verna, the one you say got herself murdered." Having been coerced into cooperating with police, she seemed only too eager to keep Jury listening. She lowered her voice: "There was talk, see. About Dorcas. It was goin' round she was—you know—had a bun in the oven."

"Pregnant, you mean." He lowered his own voice to match hers. The regulars at the other end of the bar were clearly fascinated by Wiggins, who had his notebook out, but seemed to be doing more of the talking than they. Prescribing, probably.

Julie flushed. For one who apparently wanted to be considered to know her way around, if not actually libertine or wanton, she got embarrassed easily.

"Did Dorcas herself tell you?"

She nodded, absently wiping the cloth over the bar.

"Ever say anything at all that would connect any particular man to this pregnancy?" When she frowned, Jury said, "It's important, so think, Julie."

"Thinking" was apparently a rather novel act for Julie, and an intensely physical one. She folded her arms and scratched her elbows, squinting up at the ceiling; she drew her mouth back revealing teeth as small as a child's, then pursed the mouth, repeating this process several times. She might have been indulging in some of Fiona's facial exercises. Her neck seemed to strain upward as if there were a rarefied air up there necessary for cerebral activity. Jury had to give her this: that unlike most people, Julie took thinking damned seriously. Then, chewing at her bottom lip, she said, "There was a bloke she must've been goin' with, secretive she was about him. Never told me the name, though. Well, that surprised me, it did. Anyway, she was goin' to London, she said."

"London? Did the boyfriend live there?"

"No, no. I think he was from round here. Dorcas was acting pretty la-de-dah about it."

"No name, no description?"

Julie shook her head. Finished with the three at the end of the bar, Wiggins came back, asked for some more Diet Pepsi as his throat was scratchy. He nodded toward the three men. "It's all that smoke blowing right in my face. . . ." Sadly, he shook his head. Julie refilled his glass.

"How much did she make here?" Jury asked Julie, wishing Wiggins would stop breaking his rhythm.

"Same as me, I wouldn't wonder. Four quid an hour. It's only part-time. 'Course, Dorcas had the other job at Fengate. So that'd give 'er another forty or fifty quid, on top of the regular job. Then she got her room and meals there and that counts for a lot, especially the way Dorcas liked to eat. I'm not one to talk, me . . ." Julie giggled and pulled her jumper down, whether to expose more of her figure or hide it, Jury couldn't say. "We were both slimming."

Jury smiled. "Was Dorcas as popular as you with the men?"

Julie giggled. "Now, how'd you know I am? But Dorcas? No, not at all. She just was too plain-as-a-pudding. Hardly anyone'd look at her. That's why I was so surprised about this bloke she had. Whoever he was." Julie giggled again and then leaned across the bar and crooked her finger at Jury to draw him nearer. In a low voice she said, "Now, keep this under your hat, will you?"

Dryly, Wiggins said, "Mum's the word, miss."

"—but she was going to London to get a you-know-what."

Jury guessed correctly that the you-know-what was an abortion.

Julie righted herself, adjusted her jumper once again, having delivered the coup de grâce. "She wouldn't ever want it done around here, it'd be all over the place."

"Like London, abortions can be expensive. She might have been earning double, but she'd have to have saved up a tidy sum for a doctor. Was she a saver? Did she put money by?"

Julie laughed. "Not her, never. I heard her say several times she could hardly get by from one payday to the next. Said she was glad they were different days or she'd be skint five days outta the week." Then Julie's dull brown eyes brightened. "*I* know what you're thinking. You're thinking: Where'd she get the money? From him, maybe?"

Jury smiled. "You're a mind reader, Julie. Now, do you have any ideas about him?"

Julie didn't hesitate. "I know one thing; I *don't* think it's who some do. That Mr. Price." She shook her head, emphatically. "Whatever would he do with someone like Dorcas?"

"That's what people around here think?"

"It's only because she fancied him at one time. He'd walk her back to Fengate, and why not? They both lived there. That don't mean they was . . . you know. He was nice to her; he's nice to me too but that don't mean he's looking for you-know-what."

"What? Police are terribly literal, miss," said Wiggins.

Julie rolled her eyes, shook her head in a wondering way. These policemen clearly lived in the sexual Dark Ages. "Dorcas might of 'ad her faults, but she was generous. You can't say better than that about a per—"

Julie looked beyond Jury toward the door of the pub, which had opened and shut, admitting icy air and a tall, thinnish man, together with a tall woman. The two stood speaking for a moment and then separated, the woman taking a seat at the bar. She looked vaguely familiar; Jury couldn't think why. Julie had started wiping the counter vigorously, as she looked up from under her lashes at Jury and gave a tiny nod in the direction of the man, who had taken a seat at a table. She whispered, thin-lipped, "That's him, Jack Price. Let me just get his pint for him. Always has the same thing, pint o' Ridleys."

Jury finished off his pint and rose, saying he'd take Price's drink over to him. He thanked her for all of her help, produced a card, and told her that if she remembered anything else to call. When she'd drawn the pint, she handed it to Jury and he and Wiggins moved away from the bar, while Julie went to wait on the woman.

The man who'd been the object of Julie's speculation looked up at Jury and Wiggins, his expression registering an unasked question. Or what Jury could see of his expression, coming as it did through a haze of smoke.

"Mr. Price? I'm Richard Jury, this is Sergeant Wiggins. We're with Scotland Yard CID."

Price nodded, said nothing, and looked only mildly surprised when Jury produced his identification, but even more when Jury set his drink on the table. "Do you mind—?" Jury pulled a chair around and sat down. So as to make his note-taking less obtrusive, Wiggins seated himself at a short distance from the table, farther back in the shadows. This turned his naturally pale face even more starkly white.

"No," said Price, his sardonic smile suggesting that, since they were already in chairs, he hadn't much opportunity to object. "Thanks for the drink. I must say I'm surprised the Lincolnshire police would ask for help from Scotland Yard. The man in charge—Bannen?—dosen't strike me as the type to ask for help."

"He isn't and he hasn't. He's just letting me look round. You're certainly not compelled to tell me anything."

Price started to reply, but started coughing. "Actually, it's not the smoking causing this, it's the damned trees, the stuff that comes off the alders." He slid the packet of Players toward Jury. "Smoke?"

"No thanks. I've stopped. Wiggins never started."

In a gentlemanly gesture, Price stubbed out his own cigarette. "This must be a kind of hell, smelling the stuff."

"Go right ahead. I have to learn to live with it."

As if setting the shadows alight, Wiggins moved in. Literally, as well as metaphorically. He dragged his chair closer to the table and said, "It's the spoor, sir. It can get in anywhere. It seeps; it's airborne. Now, the catkins off the alders don't bother me for some reason. I've got an allergy to just about everything else, though." Wiggins drew a small envelope from his inside pocket and shook out a few white pills. "Right here's what you need; works every time for me. It's a new thing called 'Allergone.' Couple of these, you'll be fine."

Jury rolled his eyes. Wiggins came prepared with nostrums the way others came prepared with a murder bag. He waited for Wiggins to get through prescribing before he introduced the main subject of conversation. "You knew that Lady Kennington and Verna Dunn weren't strangers to one another?"

Jack Price worked a little pile of ash into a pyramid. "I knew, yes."

"And didn't tell Chief Inspector Bannen. Why is that?"

"Because Jenny didn't, that's why. I mean didn't tell him." Price continued to sculpt his ash-pyramid. "If she didn't want anyone to know—" He shrugged.

Jack Price, at this moment, appeared to know more about Jenny than Jury did. "Didn't the whole thing strike you as distinctly *odd*? Here are two women who are related—not friends, certainly, but cousins—and they keep it a secret?"

"It struck me as odd, yes. For Jenny, it did. Jenny's a very candid person. But for Verna? That sort of charade was typical of Verna. The woman loved secrets, mystery. . . ."

"What about Max Owen?"

"What about him?"

Impatiently, Jury said, "Surely he knew the two women were related."

Price shook his head. "No, I don't believe he did. Jenny steered very clear of Verna. I don't think she'd seen Verna Dunn in ten or fifteen years. She read about her in the Arts section of the *Sunday Times*, knew Verna had married—and then divorced—Max, but that was years ago. She was completely taken aback to find Verna here that weekend."

"How do you know?"

Price looked puzzled. "I don't—"

"Lady Kennington must have done a masterly job of hiding her feelings. No surprise registered. Nothing was said. She displayed *lack* of surprise, from what I hear, as if she'd never seen the woman before. So how do you know?"

Price said, simply, "Oh. She told me."

Jury knew he was irrationally angered by all of this. "And when was that? That she told you?"

"We were having drinks, cocktails, before dinner. We were off from the others, chatting."

"I can't understand anyone's withholding information like that from police. Not her, not you."

"I've already said that since she didn't acknowledge Verna, I certainly wasn't going to give the show away. I told you that I have a great deal of affection for Jenny—"

"No, actually, you didn't. You knew her well?"

Price shrugged. "Depends what you mean. In a friendly way, certainly. I've seen her half-a-dozen times, I expect. I knew her husband, James."

Some moments ticked by until Jury broke this uncomfortable silence (uncomfortable for him alone, he was sure) by bringing up Dorcas Reese. "Did you perhaps know *her* better than you said?"

"Superintendent, you seem to be taking this rather personally, if you don't mind my saying—"

Jury could barely keep from saying *"I do."* He said instead, "Only as a policeman. You people are obstructing our investigation, you know."

Wiggins turned a page of his notebook and looked at Jury. He wasn't used to hearing such pronouncements from the superintendent. Much too cool, was the superintendent, too clever to "stoop" to such procedural maneuvering, though he was right. That sort of thing put witnesses off.

Price asked, "Did I know Dorcas 'better'? Are you going to allow yourself to be taken in by all of this twaddle? A bunch of yobs sitting round in a pub or little old ladies round their teapot, talking a lot of nonsense? I walked Dorcas back to Fengate sometimes. After all, we both lived there."

"Dorcas told several people she was pregnant. Did she tell you?"

"Dorcas did not confide in me; anyway, according to the Lincs police, she wasn't."

"Why would she say she was?"

"I have no idea. I assure you, I was not the suspect father."

"Julie says she fancied you. But Julie doesn't, let me add, believe you're the man responsible."

"Bless her heart." He raised his glass in Julie's direction. "Look, I dislike saying unkind things about a girl who's dead, but Dorcas wasn't exactly a knockout."

"So everyone seems to agree." Jury thought for a moment about this, then said, "You usually take the public footpath, do you?"

Price nodded. "Always. Makes a nice walk before and after. It gives me a couple of miles' walk, the only exercise I'm likely to get, every day. The thing is, though, that a lot of people take the path, even Max and Grace.

It's a pleasant walk. So if you're asking whether I took it the night Dorcas was murdered, the answer's yes."

"Your only connection with Dorcas was seeing her at Fengate and here in the pub, then?"

"And I scarcely saw her at all at the house."

Softly, yet in a tone like lead, he said, "You knew Jennifer Kennington had a motive."

"To kill Verna?" Price snorted with laughter. "Didn't everyone? She was a bitch, a vicious, conniving woman, and we're better off without her, Superintendent."

"But general dislike doesn't usually add up to a specific motive. And there's the question of opportunity, too. Lady Kennington had both motive and opportunity, apparently."

"Perhaps." Price continued calmly to smoke. "But if that's so, well . . . maybe she did it. What do they say?" He dribbled ash onto the pyramid and it broke apart. "If it walks like a duck—"

"Don't say it." Jury got up. "Thanks. Perhaps I'll see you later."

Price gave Jury a mock-salute. "I'll keep myself available, Mr. Jury."

Jury returned the salute, but his expression was grim. As he and Wiggins started toward the door, Jury said, "I want you to go to Fengate, Wiggins. See what you can find out, probably the servants would be a good starting point. Take the car; I'll meet you there."

"Seeing it isn't our case, sir—" Wiggins's tone registered discomfort with what was clearly not proper police procedure.

"Don't worry. They're extremely cooperative people. They certainly have been with me. Take the car. I'll meet you there in an hour or two."

"What about you, sir? Where are you going?"

"I'm going to take a walk," said Jury.

21

It was that ambiguous hour in the afternoon before dark, before dusk even, when the fens seemed to smoke beneath a layer of marsh gas. In the west the sky was an icy transparency, the early-risen moon was colorless as mist.

Out from under the roof of the Case Has Altered and the branches of old birch and one young oak showing its first green leaves, Jury stepped onto the public footpath. At this point it was muddy and lined on either side with buckthorn and sallow; it stretched before him across straight-furrowed fields to the left and the waterlogged pasture to his right. Across the field light itself was like water filling the furrowed grass. He wondered how near a river was—the Welland, the Ouse—and if its banks still over-flowed. He wondered further if these flooded pastures showed him what the ancient marshlands had been like. No clouds, no wind. A vast empti-ness. Except for Jury's footsteps, there was a complete absence of move-ment, as if he were the only sign of life in a becalmed universe. He might have been in a boat drifting without sails or rudder, without breezes. Then suddenly a tempest of birds blew upward from distant scrub or wa-ter. He felt as if he were setting off on a journey whose destination was not a shoreline glimmering with lights, but the edge of a continent shrouded in fog. Jury could not shake free from the notion of a painful foreshadowing of unhappy events. Looking up at the blank white sky and the limitless fields beyond, he felt all of this strongly.

The path was straight as a die and he wondered if it had once been a drove used by fenmen who cropped the sedge. He had been trudging for perhaps a quarter of a mile before he saw what could have been Wyndham Fen off to the left. In all of this flatness, it looked as landscapes do in dreams, appearing suddenly and inexplicably.

He was wondering about Jack Price. And what he was wondering was whether his relationship with Jenny was more than either one of them—Jenny or Jack—had acknowledged. It told against her, he thought, more than anything else, that she had failed to disclose to the Lincolnshire police (failed to tell *him*, even) the nature of her relationship to Verna Dunn and about having known Jack Price. She would not keep such secrets from Pete Apted, that was certain. The evidence against her was circumstantial, true, but circumstantial had been known to convict defendants before.

He left this part of the public footpath and veered off to walk the roundabout way to the Visitors' Center. From there he took the boardwalk to the dike nearest the building where the body of Dorcas Reese had been found. Jury had seen it before, but still he stood in an almost reverent silence, prompted not only by the end of Dorcas Reese, but also by the place itself. What a poignant setting for murder, he thought, looking down at the quiet water, the marsh violets and yellow bladderwort that blossomed above the water, the rush grass and marsh fern. He heard the reeds clicking at a little distance and saw a heron flapping upward, disturbed, perhaps by himself. Jury walked back along the boardwalk.

Like some ossified, prehistoric beast, stranded after the flood waters receded, the rusty white police caravan—the temporary incident room—sat at a little distance from the Visitors' Center. Its small squares of window glowed with a greenish light. He headed for it, through the reeds and grasses, past a willow holt where a gull swayed atop a willow pole and whistled away at his approach. Somewhere an owl cried. The water of the dikes lay dark gray and motionless as lead. None of it was congruent with the bright yellow crime scene tape that stretched around this part of the fen. There were of course no visitors today. He imagined anyone coming would have been turned back by police up nearer the A17.

The greenish glow was coming from several computer screens, left on, ready for action. Inside, the van was blue with smoke. Bannen liked cigars. He was sitting alone punching up data on his screen.

"Ah. I had an idea I'd see you again, soon."

It was a smile that Jury couldn't read, not before, and not now. Bannen would have made a superior poker player; he always seemed to have something in the hole.

Here, Jury bet Bannen had plenty. Perhaps not; perhaps it was just a Bannen bluff. Jury nodded, smiled slightly, pulled over one of the folding chairs. "Sam Lasko tells me you're about to make an arrest."

"That's not precisely what I told him, however—" Bannen took the cigar from his mouth, scrutinized the end, relit it, looked at Jury.

"'Not precisely?' I wonder what that means." Jury got the impression from Bannen's direct gaze that he could have wondered till he was blue in the face and he wouldn't find out. He leaned his chair back on two legs, tried not to sound agitated, and said, "You'll have to forgive my prying"—he should not engage in childish sarcasm with this Lincs policeman, he knew—"but she's a friend."

"Yes, you told me. It now sounds as if she's a very good friend." The word seemed to relegate any judgment of Jury's to a dustheap of poor deduction.

"Very good. But friend or no friend, you have sod-all to hold her."

Bannen sighed. "Well, we'll just have to leave that up to the Crown Prosecution Service." Bannen moved his hand across several files and papers on his desk as if his magician's fingers would turn them all into visible proof of what he had to hold Jenny Kennington. "Mr. Jury." He cleared his throat. "Her motive was very strong; her opportunity—her 'window of opportunity' as it is currently described—excellent. She had access to the rifle that was used. To top it all, she lied. About several things. As I'm sure you've by now discovered. I hope you've found her a good lawyer."

Jury wondered about the "several" lies. He knew of only one. "Tell me: Why would Lady Kennington kill the Dunn woman now? Fifteen or so years after she'd last seen her. Fifteen years after the injury was done—injuries, I should say. Verna Dunn apparently inflicted a good many, and not only on Jenny Kennington."

Bannen's voice was mild. "Who says it was for an injury done fifteen years ago?"

The legs of Jury's chair hit the floor, hard. "What recent damage had she done?"

Bannen wasn't about to answer Jury's questions. He shrugged. "If there were nothing, no motivation, then why didn't Jennifer Kennington admit that she knew her all of those years ago? That they were, indeed, related?"

"That isn't so important—"

"It isn't? I wonder what Oedipus would say to that."

"Why didn't Jack Price say he'd known Lady Kennington? I'm merely pointing out there could be perfectly innocent reasons for not announcing that you knew someone in the past."

"Hmm. But then Jack Price didn't kill Verna Dunn." Bannen smiled a quick, false smile. "There seem to be a number of people Lady Kennington didn't want to acknowledge knowing."

Jury ignored the circular reasoning Bannen had used with relation to Jack Price. Bannen knew he was doing it. "Two. Not 'a number.'"

Bannen shook his head, implying disbelief that the superintendent could really be as thick as two planks. He ran his hand back over his thinning hair. "If Jennifer Kennington had gone back into the house and, say, bolted up to her room because she was angry or whatever, I'd say that was understandable behavior. Instead, she leaves the Dunn woman standing in the wood and, leaving her host and his guests, sets off for the local, some distance away. Then, after walking for ten or fifteen minutes, realizes that the Case would have already called for last orders and would be closing. She turns and retraces her steps to Fengate." Bannen sat back in his swivel chair. "Now, does that sound like plausible behavior—for an innocent person, I mean?"

"Then why haven't you charged her?"

Bannen rocked in his chair a bit, undisturbed by the question. "I'm showing remarkable restraint. I'm making allowances."

Jury shook his head. "I doubt it." Jury inclined his head to one side, gesturing in the direction of the boardwalk and canals. "What about Dorcas Reese? Are you saying Jenny did that too?"

Bannen's smile was maddeningly enigmatic. "Yes."

Jury felt a real chill. He had expected uncertainty here. "But why? What possible motive—"

Bannen sighed. "Dorcas Reese presented a danger to her."

"Listen to me: yesterday I talked to Jenny Kennington. In Stratford. She said something strange: that she wondered if Verna Dunn was nearby when Grace Owen's son met with his accident."

Bannen frowned at his computer screen, as if it had failed to bring up an explanation of this sudden switching of subjects. "If you're suggesting that Grace Owen held Verna Dunn responsible for her son's death"— Bannen rolled the cigar in his mouth—"why on earth would she choose an occasion to shoot her when others, strangers, were present? It would surely be more sensible to go to London, to go to Verna Dunn's house, than wait for her to come to Fengate. That just doesn't make sense."

"Of course, it doesn't. Not if the murder was premeditated. Grace Owen might only have just found out that weekend. How many occasions were there, after all, when she was in the presence of the ex-Mrs. Owen?"

There was a silence. Then Bannen said, "Lady Kennington's comment about the son was merely speculation."

"It would certainly be simple enough to find out." Jury rose. "I have a feeling you know more about this than I do."

Bannen laughed. "I certainly hope so, Mr. Jury. Because you know—to use your own words—sod-all."

Part III

The
Red Last

22

Jury looked for some moments at the house a short distance away on a rise of ground. "Toad Hall" Plant had said Parker called it. A whimsical man. Jury wondered if Linus Parker felt an affinity for animal-things, child-things. And how he'd react to an unannounced and unofficial visit from Scotland Yard. Given what Melrose Plant had said, probably with grace.

It was no member of the staff who opened the door, that was clear. In spite of the white apron that fell nearly to the ground (Parker, he knew, loved to cook), this tall man with the mustache and thinning hair would never be taken for anything other than one of the upper class. Something in the bearing, in the barely perceptible cocksureness of the way he held his head.

"Mr. Parker? Major Parker?"

Parker nodded and with a smile slightly ironic, said, "Believe me, 'Mr.' will do, and plain 'Parker' is better. That's what people call me. You the Scotland Yard chap?"

Jury stopped in the act of getting out his small wallet that held his ID. Surprised, he said, "How did you—"

"Know? Ah, news travels like lightning in these parts. Come on in." Parker stepped back from the door and gestured for Jury to pass through it. Parker removed his apron, tossed it over a bronze bust, and then took Jury's coat. With more care he deposited the coat over the arm of a rather ostentatious chair, Louis Quinze, perhaps, which was the only Louis Jury could remember. "This way, Mr.—ah, I wasn't told your name, however."

"Richard Jury. I'm with the CID."

They arrived in a large yet cozy room, its hominess owing no doubt to a big, wild fire raging in an enormous fireplace. The fire and the crammed-in furniture. Jury had never seen such an eclectic mix—Art Nouveau jostling Chinese lacquer; worthy American-looking pine and oak in tables and trestles; several periods of one Louis or another—it was quite overwhelming, more so than Fengate, overflowing with objets d'art, many of which looked to be of museum quality, but none of which seemed to go together. Yet all were well cared for—no table, no silver or copper unpolished. Paintings, mostly unhung, were scattered about, leaning against mahogany sideboards and blanket chests; two weathervanes, horse and stag, tilted against the far wall; urns and cast-iron animals sat about; commodes inlaid with mother-of-pearl sat beside a marquetry table; a jade head and an ivory horse graced the mantel of the fireplace together with a number of small bronze pieces.

Jury and Parker sat on facing faded velvet love seats with a cobbler's bench that served as coffee table between them. A cut-glass tumbler with a finger of whiskey in it sat there beside the book, which was open and face down.

Jury said, "I interrupted you. I hope you don't mind."

Parker laughed. "A welcome interruption, I assure you. Been getting maudlin, drinking and reading Swinburne. D'you like Swinburne?" Not waiting for an answer, he scooped up the book and read: ". . . *That no life lives forever, / That dead men rise up never, / That even the weariest river / Winds somewhere safe to sea.*" He snapped the book shut as if he'd just made a cosmic point. "One of my favorites. I take comfort in it." He held up his glass. "Comfort in poetry and a good stiff drink."

Jury said, "Doesn't sound very comforting. 'The weariest river . . .'"

"Oh, but the point is it flows to sea, it connects with something."

Jury settled back on a sofa that was far more comfortable than it looked and felt that he was in the company of an old friend. How strange. They sat for a moment in silence as Jury let his gaze wander about the room.

Parker said, "Looks a little like a junk shop, doesn't it? I live rough."

Jury said, "If you can call being surrounded by jade and ivory and these paintings 'living rough,' I suppose you do."

Parker relit his pipe and fanned out the match. "Max Owen can't breath in this room. Pretends to have an asthma attack every time he gets in here. But I expect it's just jealousy." Parker looked about him. "Max has a better eye for arrangement than I do."

So does the cat Cyril, Jury wanted to say, but smiled instead.

"It was my char."

Jury didn't know what he was talking about. "Pardon?"

"Madeline, the woman who comes to char for me, she walked into the Case when you were there. It's how I knew who you were. She's every bit as good as a newspaper. What can I do for you? Or, better yet"—Parker rose and walked to a rosewood sideboard—"what can I get for you?" He unstoppered one of several hundred pounds' worth of cut- or pressed-glass decanters. "Whiskey? Cognac?"

"Whiskey, thanks." Before the cut-glass tumbler was in his hand, Jury could taste it. The glass seemed to have trapped the amber light. Old whiskey from old glass. Jury took a drink. It went down his throat like burning silk, the heat of it relaxing his muscles, expanding his veins. Ah. Was alcoholism the next stop? He'd given up cigarettes (and was trying to keep his eye from roving toward that japanned box on the coffee table, just right for a pack); would whiskey be the next to go in his small repertoire of bad habits? "This is the smoothest whiskey I have ever drunk."

"Umm. Good stuff, I agree. Forgotten which one it is."

"I'd sooner forget my financée's face."

Parker laughed and tossed his drink back in one gulp, quick and neat. He repositioned the pipe stem between his teeth, puffed a bit.

Jury regarded the pipe, watched the puffs of smoke winding a ribbony path upward. He asked, "Were you a cigarette smoker once and switched to a pipe?"

Parker frowned a bit, as if thinking this over, thinking back. "Not really."

Not *really*? Good lord, could one *perhaps* in one's youth have smoked them and then forgotten?

"I take it you were?" Parker smiled through the sensuous smoke.

"Pack a day." Actually, more like two. Pack-and-a-half, at least.

"Um. Don't you miss it?"

Jury stared, blinked. He shrugged. "I can pretty much take it or leave it, I can." He rocked his hand. "*Comme ci, comme ça,* that's me."

Parker smiled, looking as if he didn't believe a word of this, then said, "You know Mr. Plant don't you? He lunched with me."

Jury smiled. "Don't I know it? He's still talking about it." Too late, he recalled his knowledge of Mr. Plant was supposed to be "slight."

But Parker was too taken with the compliment to notice. "Tell him he's welcome any time. Nice chap." He was silent for a moment, and then prompted, "I assume you want to ask me about these two women?"

"Oh. Sorry." Jury sat up, replaced his glass. Sadly.

The astute Parker rose, replenished both of their glasses. Jury sat back again, sipped. "Yes. You knew Verna Dunn pretty well?"

"I did. And didn't like her much."

"That seems to be a majority opinion. She was Mrs. Owen when you knew her?"

Parker nodded. "Verna was an actress. All the time. She was adept at masking her true self. If indeed there was a 'true' self. I'm inclined to believe she was a series of sham selves."

"Any idea why they were arguing, or what about? Did they show any signs of anger during dinner?" Jury wondered, not for the first time, if Max Owen had really been the cause. That was the trouble with lying once; you might be suspected of lying twice.

He must have winced because Parker asked, "Anything wrong, Superintendent?"

"No, no. About that argument—?"

Parker shook his head. "Hardly spoke to one another at dinner. Though that, I expect, could mean something in itself. I wasn't, of course, looking for any such sign, so there might have been something I altogether missed."

"If you missed it, so did everyone else, apparently. What topic could have been so explosive it would cause Jennifer Kennington to shoot Verna Dunn?"

"Oh, but did she?"

"I should have said 'allegedly.' I'm too used to the Lincs' police version."

"Where in heaven's name was the gun—a shotgun, too. Or was it a rifle? Either way, bit hard to hide in a handbag, wouldn't it be?" Parker was up again, topping off their glasses.

"I expect one could argue the gun—a rifle—had already been placed in the car or left at the Wash to be retrieved. But it's a weak point in their story—the police version, I mean."

Parker repositioned himself on the small sofa, made a few jabs at his pipe with a pipe cleaner. "I'd say there's more than *one* weak point there. The story as I understand it is that Jennifer Kennington and Verna Dunn got into Verna's car and drove to the Wash, to the inland part of it, specifically what's apparently called 'Fosdyke's Wash'—a name that no one was acquainted with until its present notoriety—and here Lady Kennington shot Verna Dunn, got back in the car, drove back to Fengate, and parked the car down the drive far enough that no one heard it. *Then* Lady Kennington appeared at Fengate sometime after eleven with what police regard as a very strange and spurious story about having walked to the Case—or nearly to it—and then walked back again."

Jury nodded. "That's Chief Inspector Bannen's line, yes."

"I'd say it's a good deal easier to believe *her* story than your DCI Bannen's."

Jury laughed. "He's not *my* DCI Bannen." Jury swirled the whiskey in his glass, holding it up slightly so that it caught the saffron light of the fire. "But he's damned smart. He's self-effacing enough that one could easily forget that. Remember, you left Fengate at eleven or eleven-five. So why didn't you pass her?"

Parker stopped in the act of tamping down the bowl of his pipe. "Yes. That is true."

"There is really no other route, is there? No other way she might have gone?"

Parker frowned. "Oh, there might be some rubbishy old trail from here to there. But why would she take it?"

"In any event, she said she took the footpath."

Parker sat back. "One of us must be lying." When Jury merely nodded, Parker asked, "Is that why you're here?"

Jury gave an abrupt laugh. "No. I don't see that you'd have had much opportunity. Unless you . . . oh, went home and immediately picked up your own car and raced to the Wash."

"It's possible, isn't it? Isn't there some question as to time of death?"

"Yes, there is. But there's also no evidence of more than one set of tire treads. And then there's motive. Granted, Verna Dunn seems to have been universally disliked, but there's no evidence of motive in the case of any-one else. Max, Grace—those are the most likely insofar as motive is con-cerned. But there opportunity really takes a hike. At least, in the case of Max Owen it does."

"What about Dorcas Reese? How does she fit into all of this?"

"That's even more of a puzzle. She wasn't shot; she was strangled. Gar-roted. Lady Kennington claims to have been in Stratford-upon-Avon, but police were quick to point out that it would be possible to drive from Stratford and back in a few hours."

"Surely, that's cutting the cloth to make it fit, isn't it?"

"It seems so. But no one can come up with anything better." Jury put down his glass. "I was, I suppose, hoping you might have remembered something helpful. . . . She's a good friend of mine, Jenny is. Well, I've got to be getting along." Jury rose and so did Parker. "I thought I'd talk to your—groundskeeper, is he? Peter Emery?"

Parker nodded, walked with Jury to the door. "You know Peter's blind? Has been for several years. It was a shooting accident. Terrible thing, as Peter was in love with the outdoors. He lives with a young niece. . . ." Parker stopped. "I wonder, would you mind taking something along to them—that is, if you're going there now?"

"Be happy to. I'll have to ask you directions, though. I know the cot-tage is also off the footpath."

"Better than that, I'll let you have an ordnance map. Back in a tic." He hurried off.

Jury smiled, wondering if the kitchen weren't Major Parker's real do-main. Jury looked around again at the pieces out here, crowding the en-trance hall. And it was quite a large hall, at that. Wonderful staircase, the sort one might fantasize beautiful women in ball gowns descending.

"Here we are." Parker returned, a map in one hand, a white cardboard container in the other. "Plum ice cream. I promised to take it round to-day, but I've got very involved with this dinner I'm experimenting on. And here's your map. I've marked the way. It's quite simple."

"Plum ice cream. Sounds good." Jury put out his hand. "But not as good as that whiskey."

♋

Plant had told him about Peter Emery's blindness. *"Still gets around, though. His memory serves him to find his way through the woods; he's been with Parker for at least a decade, so he manages."*

Jury left the footpath for the sodden and spongy grass, crossing over it to the cottage path. It was, as Parker had said, quite easy, once you have a map. Most things were.

Plant had warned him about the little girl Zel and her fiefdom. Thus, when she yanked the door open, Jury was prepared to have it shut in his face. But it wasn't. Plant, exaggerating again, he thought. She looked up at Jury, and said, "Oh. Hello."

Jury answered her hello and inclined his head toward Bob, who struck Jury as pretty much like any other dog he'd ever seen—tongue out, panting, tail wagging. He wondered how Plant came up with these wild stories he told.

Jury introduced himself, held out the carton of ice cream. "I'm just the delivery chap."

The little girl's eyes widened. "It's my ice cream?"

"Plum."

That he would be entrusted to dispatch something this valuable clearly raised him in her estimation.

It must be her uncle, Peter Emery, who'd come to the doorway of the little parlor and overheard this transaction. Jury introduced himself, said he'd just come from speaking with Major Parker. He wasn't officially on this case and Emery shouldn't feel obliged to talk to him at all. It was Zel who answered.

"We like company." She turned in a quick circle, her red-gold hair flying, and raced for the kitchen with her ice cream.

Peter Emery laughed. "True enough. Come on in and sit awhile."

When Jury was arranged in a comfortable chair, and Zel returned and arranged beside it, Jury said, "I understand you once were factor on an estate up in Perthshire. Gorgeous country."

Emery needed only this barely stated urging. "Aye, it is that: I remember—"

He spoke for some moments, uninterrupted. Jury thought it was natural for a man who couldn't see to covet memories of those places and things from a time in which he could. Peter Emery was a grand storyteller, too; the timbre of his voice could have enthralled an audience by merely reading a ' in schedule.

During her uncle's recitation, Zel had been moving covertly, with a little sideways maneuver of her feet—toes, heels, toes, heels, that corny music hall routine—moving closer and closer to Jury's chair until she could place both hands on its arm and, gaining purchase to push off the feet again: toes, heels, toes, heels, until her uncle had to tell her, Zel, you mind now, and she stopped dead. Willingly. Right beside Jury, who smiled at her, but vaguely, as his attention was still fixed upon her uncle Peter. So having got some of Jury's attention, she set out to get the rest of it by walking her fingers up and down the chair arm as if she were practicing scales, the fingers recklessly close to Jury's own hand. Her head was down, following the progress of feet or fingers as if they were the source of endless fascination.

Jury had managed to work Peter Emery's conversation from Scotland to the murders and Emery was saying what a "turrible, turrible tragedy" it all was.

"You liked her?"

"Oh, she was all right, I suppose."

"No, she wasn't, Uncle Peter. You said so."

Emery blushed and smiled. "The mouths of babes. All right, I tell a lie, then. No, Zel's right; I didn't like her. A person doesn't want to speak ill of the dead."

"No one I've talked to seems to mind speaking ill of Verna Dunn," said Jury, smiling.

Zel chimed in: "*I* don't!"

Peter said, "Verna Owen she was then. He's not been married to Grace for very long, six, seven years maybe. Lovely, Grace Owen is. But Verna, I can see why he got rid of her—"

"Did he? Did Max Owen initiate the divorce?"

Peter Emery snorted. "It wouldn't have been her, that's sure. Not with all of Max's money. She shoved people about. I mean, moved them like she was playing a game. For her, it was. Life was a game."

"You've been here for ten years, did you say?"

Zel piped up, "Eleven and a half. Eleven and four months." She seemed to think her exactness over this must surely please a Scotland Yard detective.

"Did you know Verna Owen very well? I mean, had you much personally to do with her?"

"Some. Enough to dislike her."

"She wasn't a very popular woman, apparently."

"With good reason."

"Such as?" inquired Jury.

"She was a ruiner. You know—" Then apparently recalling his niece was present he said, "Zel, you was to fetch us some tea."

"No, I wasn't," she answered, a stickler for facts. Her back was to Jury's chair arm now, and she was bending her head as far back as she could, looking at Jury from her upside-down eyes. And then she must have thought tea might get her points: to Jury (and Jury alone) she said, "You want tea?"

"I certainly do," he said, his smile winning. "Don't we get any of that plum ice cream?"

Zel looked uncertain, looked from her uncle to Jury, who kept his expression unhelpfully sober. "It isn't really ready yet. It has to sit." She paused, thinking. "It has to blend."

"Really? Major Parker seemed to think it was pretty well blended. Imminently edible. At this moment. Right now."

"Zel!" Her uncle was not really angry, only slightly embarrassed. "What kind of hospitality's that, now?"

She crackled to life and ran toward the kitchen.

Her uncle raised his voice even more to her vanishing back. "And don't you be hanging about the door, there, gurl. You just get that ice cream and tea."

A cacophony of glass and metal, dishes and cups and kettles, sounded as if to assure her uncle that Zel was busy and had no time to be hanging about doorways.

When she was out of earshot, Peter Emery said, "I don't want t'go setting a bad example, or her learning from me to hate people, you know? Zel's so impressionable."

Jury smiled. He seriously doubted it. Well, Peter Emery wouldn't be the first grown-up who didn't know his charge. "A 'ruiner' you called her?"

"Aye, she was. She just liked t'muck up people's lives, just fer the hell of it. She was that kind."

"And did she try to muck up yours?"

Peter turned his face to the pale heat of the dying fire. "Tried to, that's sure."

When he didn't embellish upon this, Jury asked, "Was it sexual?"

Obliquely, Peter answered. "Several times she came here. At first it was—it seemed—innocent enough, her wanting to know something about Mr. Parker's land, saying she was thinking of asking him to sell her some acres. A bunch of nonsense. But then she got pretty, well, friendly—"

"Tried to seduce you, you mean."

Jury thought it was a natural conclusion to reach, especially in light of Emery's obvious embarrassment. He must be a bit of a prude. But that was probably better than counting one's conquests. Any woman might make a play for him. Emery was not only handsome; there was an aura of sexuality that clung to him like smoke.

Emery said, "This Lady Kennington who stayed there, she seemed a nice woman. Why would she . . ." Peter shrugged, cleared his throat, as if the thought were difficult to put in words. "Why would she shoot her?" He leaned forward. "And why go to the Wash? Everybody at the pub was talking about it. Why would Lady Kennington kill her?" he asked again.

"It's quite possible she didn't."

Emery shook his head. "'Tis a rumor with teeth in it. That policeman from Lincoln was here. Looking for guns, he was, rifles. I think he must've collected every .22 caliber from here to Spalding. I used to be a good shot, myself." Peter sighed and edged down in his chair. "I don't mean to flatter myself that I'm—you know—irresistible to women. But Verna Dunn . . . awful embarrassing, that was. Her being Owen's wife and all. A woman acting that way, what good can you say of her?"

"Mr. Emery, what—"

"Peter." He leaned forward and whispered, "You wouldn't have a smoke about you, would you? The lass hides them from me. I was doing two packs a day."

Jury shook his head, and, realizing Emery couldn't see that, said, "Sorry, I don't. But God knows I can commiserate; I haven't had one in a month. Sometimes I think the lack will kill me long before the smoke would've."

They laughed, and while they were enjoying this ebullient mood, Jury returned to the matter of guns. "Would anyone else have access to your guns, Peter?"

"Same thing that Lincs copper asked. Answer is, yes, probably. We don't keep this cottage locked tight as a drum. The thing is, though, I expect he might've wound up with too many possibles rather than too few. That lab the police have would find it hard going to narrow anything down."

Not if it's a rifle, Jury thought. "You mean whether the gun had recently been fired?"

"That's right. I don't know how many the coppers took in for testing— well, they must've found a shell casing or something where she got shot. But probably every rifle they looked at had been fired recently. Old Suggins, he gets in his cups and starts clearing out squirrels— Tea ready, Zel?"

Zel had come in with the tea tray.

Peter went on. "I don't think the police are going to be able to narrow much down when it comes to the people concerned, either."

"What do you mean?"

"I mean just about everybody round can use a shotgun or hunting rifle. Even the ladies. I gave Grace Owen lessons when first she came here, even. Major Parker, obviously. Max, he can handle one though he's not all that good." He paused, accepted a cup from Zel, sipped his tea. Peter shook his head. "Good tea, gurl," he said to Zel. "Did you bring any biscuits?"

Zel heaved a sigh. "I'll get them."

When she'd run off, Peter leaned toward Jury. "I'll tell you what I think. I think that detective inspector's got it wrong, got it backwards. If anyone could set something like this up, it was Verna Dunn. Just her style. And she could shoot, mind you. She was a good shot, better than Max or Parker. I can just see her hiding a rifle somewhere round there and luring whoever out there."

Jury thought it was, at least, a fresh notion. "And the 'whoever'?"

Emery shook his head. "Verna—"

Zel was back with a plate of biscuits, which she passed to Jury. And a little glass dish—a very little dish—holding about two teaspoons of ice cream.

Jury took it. "Dessert for a mouse, is it?"

Zel looked put out. "I only brought enough to taste. You probably won't like it." Anxiously, she watched him sample it. When Jury said it was good, but he'd rather have chocolate, Zel looked enormously relieved. "I told you so." She set the dish back on the tray and handed him a mug of tea. Her uncle told her to go along and find Bob, and with many a dark look, she left.

"I was a fair shot myself, years back. Until this." He gestured toward his eyes. "People just aren't careful enough with guns; it's no wonder it's so hard to get a license."

"Yes. What happened?"

" 'Twas years ago—seven, eight—and I had the punt out, into one of those narrow channels other side of Windy Fen, probably too close to Windy Fen—" He opened a small drawer in the table beside the sofa, searched it with his fingers, withdrew his hand, sighed. "Kept some fags in there, but Zel must've found 'em. Anyway, that shooting morning, oh, it was grand, one of those misty dawns, the sky silvery, and everything hushed-like, and I was going to one of my favorite places for partridge. Gliding through that river fog was like moving through a haunted world, and all your senses are heightened. Willows and hedges like wraiths and shadows, everything unreal. It's hard to describe, a morning like that." Peter shook his head, as if finding himself wanting. "Anyway, I settled down in the punt, lying there listening to birdwhistle and wind stirring, scraping through the reeds. I lay there watching a butterfly, a Dark Green Fritillary it was, and they're rare; it was sitting on a long bit of grass, swaying. And then off to my right, I heard someone call, and then there must have been two hundred birds—mallards and teal and widgeon—flaring; I stood up in the punt—stupid thing to do—brought my gun around to shoot, at the same time I heard the crack of at least two other shots, and I felt something hot as a razor slice my head, and that was all, everything went black." He kept his face turned toward the fire. "Funny, but what I remember most clearly isn't the birds but that butterfly, swaying on that marsh grass." He leaned back in his chair, his long legs stretched out. "The one who did it never knew because I didn't make any noise and my boat was so well-screened. . . ." Peter shrugged. "I expect I should be glad the only thing the bullet took with it was the optical nerve and not my brain." He smiled with astonishing cheerfulness, as if he'd had all the luck.

Jury set his teacup on the table. "I don't think you need to feel glad. I wouldn't have half your spirit." Jury stood up. "Thanks for the tea. I'll see you again, perhaps."

❧

I'm sorry I can't be of more help," said Max Owen. He'd just returned from London and he and Jury were having a drink in the living room. "It's true that it was Grace who invited Verna. Grace seems to like her—liked her, I mean. I know Jennifer Kennington's a good friend of yours. She's a fine person; it all seems so utterly unbelievable. All of it." He looked down into his whiskey, swirled the contents, shook his head.

Jury nodded. "As far as I'm concerned, it's very decent of you to bother talking to me at all. You and your wife must be sick of coppers running amok all over your house."

Max laughed. "A slight exaggeration. Can you picture Chief Inspector Bannen 'running amok'? I can't."

"Nor I. You've known Jenny for some years, is that right?"

Max studied a small black-lacquered box he'd drawn from his pocket. Part of his auction-spoils today. "It was really her husband, James, that I knew. Jennifer I've only run into, oh, five or six times over the years. The longest I was ever around her was years ago when I went out hunting with James. Jennifer came too on that one occasion. They lived in Hertford-shire, a place called Stonington. Do you know it?" Max was looking now at a small ivory carving he'd taken out of his other pocket. More spoils.

"Yes," said Jury. "I know it. You said Jenny went out too, hunting. You mean she can use a shotgun? Or a rifle?"

"Oh, yes; quite adept." Max looked up, suddenly, grimaced. "Sorry I put it that way. Mr. Bannen asked me the same question. I did *not* say 'adept.'" He sighed. "For all the good it did." Max rose, drank off his whiskey. "I've got to go up and scrub some of this London filth off." He dropped the ivory piece back in his pocket, left the box on the table, and looked around, as if he just now missed her. "Has Grace gone to the kitchen? Listen, stay for dinner, won't you?"

"It's very kind of you, but I've got to get back to London. I've an ap-pointment tomorrow morning. I should say *we've* got to get back. I mean my sergeant. Do you happen to know where he is?"

"I think you'll find him in the kitchen, too."

Jury smiled. "Why am I not surprised?"

⊄⋂⋅

He didn't see her until he was nearly through the room. It was the change from dark to light near the window that caught his eye, and he looked into the shadows to see if one of the Cold Ladies had moved.

"Grace?" The first name was out before he could shift to *Mrs. Owen*, and he realized it seemed much more natural. He took a step away from the kitchen door. "Grace?"

She was standing before the window, having just pulled back the cur-tains, and rubbing her arms as if she'd left a chill. The room was cold; Jury thought it must always be cold, the kind of cold that deepens with dark-ness. There was a sadness in this, that Grace Owen preferred this room over others, this particular window.

From which she turned, now, and he had the fleeting impression that she was expecting him to ask her questions. All she said was "Oh, hello."

Jury moved over to the window to stand beside her. The deep blue dusk gathered in the wood and then, as easily as turning a page, night fell and he saw the moon floating high in the sky. Its light grazed the water nymph in the driveway's fountain. After a few moments of silence, Jury asked, "Was it out there that Toby's accident happened?"

"Yes." She didn't turn. "It was out there."

"I've been wondering. Was Verna Dunn here when it happened?"

She appeared to be giving some thought to her answer. "Yes. She was here." And now there was a longer pause before she asked, "Why?"

The question had such a weight to it that Jury felt at a loss to answer. "She seems—seemed—to bring bad luck with her."

"Ah." Grace said this in a way that implied something had finally been explained to her. "But I don't think luck had anything to do with her."

"How well did you know her, then?"

She paused, rubbed her upper arms again. "As well as I ever wanted to."

⁊℘

So much, thought Jury, moving toward the kitchen, for Max Owen's remark that his wife "seemed to like" Verna Dunn.

Wiggins was sitting at the big kitchen table, the staff table, flanked by the Sugginses, who were enjoying his company. When Jury came to the door, they had suspended eating in order to laugh heartily at whatever Wiggins was talking about. He was saying, ". . . so I says to her, 'Nurse, if you do that once more, I'm afraid I shall have to charge you with breaking and entering.'" He waved his fork as his two dinner companions laughed uproariously. Suggins slapped the table several times with the palm of his hand, jumping the dishes—

Jury smiled and shook his head. Sergeant Alfred Wiggins, raconteur. He stood just inside the kitchen door, almost hating to break up the party. He thought that for Wiggins, eternity should be spent round a table just like this one. Then he moved into the room and greeted Suggins and his wife, Annie.

Wiggins rose quickly, pulling away the snowy napkin tucked under his chin. "Sir!" He all but saluted.

"Never mind, at ease, as you were, parade rest, Sergeant. I just wanted to let you know we'll be leaving for London"—he nodded toward some pots steaming on the cooker—"when you've finished."

Annie Suggins said, her napkin pressed to her bosom, "We generally have our own supper after the others, but tonight, seeing as how Sergeant Wiggins here was so famished . . . not had a bite all day."

So soon does one forget the Happy Eater's beans on toast, Jury thought, looking at the untroubled Wiggins. Jury kept a straight face. "A policeman's life is full of grief, Mrs. Suggins."

"Me and Mr. Suggins, we both decided to take our supper now, too."

Wiggins was already sitting back down, stuffing himself with what looked like golden Yorkshire pudding.

"But wouldn't you like a cup of tea, sir?" Annie was already pouring from the fat pot on the table.

For once, Jury was willing to believe that a cup of tea would fix anything. "Thanks, I believe I will. I wonder if I could have a word with you, Mrs. Suggins?" Far from appearing distraught that Scotland Yard might have business with her, Annie looked pleasantly surprised. "And you, Sergeant Wiggins, perhaps you could have a word with Mr. Suggins?"

"About what? . . . Oh, yes, of course. Just what I was doing when you came in."

"Uh-huh." Tea in hand, Jury followed Annie to a chair by the fire. Kitchen fireplaces offered a special kind of comfort. He had always felt they made people want to take their shoes off, unbutton, let their hair down. "Annie, help me out here, will you? So far, I've got nowhere with the little information I've collected."

Arms folded firmly over her bosom, Annie rocked and turned her mind to Jury's problem. "One does hear things, sir. That was Dorcas's trouble, the silly girl: *She* heard too much, to my way of thinking."

Jury frowned. "Such as what?"

"I can't say 'what' exactly. It's just that she was that nosy I told her it'd get her into trouble one fine day. Many's the time I seen Dorcas with her ear against a door."

THE RED LAST • 213

"Did she have anything to do with Lady Kennington or Verna Dunn?"

"She did, certainly. It was her that took up their morning tea and fetched anything they might want. Not having any upstairs help"—here Annie's scandalized expression told Jury just what she thought of *that* arrangement—"Dorcas had to double as a maid-like. Not that there was any real work in it, and I know that Miss Dunn would have given Dorcas quite a tidy sum when she left. She was generous, I'll say that for her."

Jury smiled, sipped his tea. "What *won't* you say for her? You knew her when she was Mrs. Owen, didn't you?"

"Indeed I did. I've been cook for him since he was a young man. Him and Mr. Price."

There was something in the way she said it that made Jury ask, "What about Mr. Price?"

"Oh, nothing about *him*, sir. No, Mr. Owen and Mr. Price get along like brothers, always have. No, it was *her*."

Jury had the feeling Annie thought he should be able to sort this out, but he felt merely baffled. "Her? Verna Dunn, you mean, caused trouble there?"

Annie sighed, got up to poke the fire, then sighed herself back into her chair. "I'd say so, yes, though I'm not a person to pass along gossip, and I wouldn't want to say anything Mr. Owen might take umbrage about. At that time, he was only really using this house on the weekends. Spent most of his time in London. Mr. Jack was here *all* of the time; he loves it for his work." She paused, smoothed her apron over her lap.

"And so was Verna Owen. Is that what you mean?"

"I wouldn't be telling a lie if I said so, no, sir."

"You think they were . . . having a relationship?" The brief nod of her head answered the question, and Jury thought about that for a moment. "Mr. Price apparently knew Lady Kennington, too."

"Years back, I remember seeing her here. Just the one time. She certainly is a lady, in every sense of the word." Annie sighed and shook her head. "I can tell you that if Miss Dunn suspected *her* and Mr. Jack was . . . well, she wouldn't like it, that's sure."

"I wasn't suggesting—" But he supposed he was. It was like all the rest of it that he didn't know about Jenny. He didn't want any confirmation from Annie Suggins.

There was laughter from the table. Suggins was slapping his knee.

"No, I didn't know," he said, as if Annie had asked. It was only her countenance that looked the question. He recovered as quickly as he could, feeling horribly vulnerable and hating the feeling.

Suggins hovered with a fresh pot of tea. Jury shook his head. "Did you tell this to the Lincolnshire police?"

Annie sniffed. "No, I did not. I was told quite smartly it wasn't my opinions that was wanted, only what I knew for a fact." Curtly, she nodded, as if she'd fulfilled her role with the Lincs police quite as they wanted. "I'm not by nature a gossip; I told you because you asked for my help."

Much of what she'd said, though, actually was "fact." She'd seen Jenny Kennington here years ago and in the company of Jack Price. Jury placed his cup, undrunk, on the hearthstones. The fireplace had not offered the needed sanctuary. "Thanks, Annie. I appreciate it."

Annie leaned forward and, in a companionable gesture, placed her hand on his arm. "I didn't like the way the police was going on to Burt, there—" She leaned her head in the direction of the table, where Wiggins appeared to be conducting some very unofficial business with another biscuit in hand. "That rifle that Burt's used all along for squirrels and rabbits, like they thought maybe Burt himself shot her, which is too silly to bear thinking about. Well, I'm not about to help them out any more'n needs be. I don't mind tellin' you, I took umbrage, I really did." She sat back, rocked fiercely. "Far as I'm concerned, what they asked, I answered, and no more. Asked and answered, that was how it went."

Asked and answered.

✐

Between the beef and the biscuits, find out any more, Wiggins?"

"Afraid not, sir. Well, you said before that as we're not officially on this case, I wasn't to be my usual relentless self." Wiggins was warming up the engine between yawns.

It was the first time in the last hour Jury had felt like laughing. "What about the rifle? Who else used it?"

"Nearly everybody, over the years."

"I'm talking about recently."

"Suggins had to allow as how he couldn't be sure. I didn't say, 'Of course you couldn't, seeing you're tippling most of the time.' But that's what it adds up to, isn't it? The rifle's always there in the mudroom that anyone can get to. Suggins would never know who'd been in and out. You can get to that mudroom from either inside or outside. Anyone could've reached in and taken it, then returned it. What about fingerprints?"

"Hard on a gun stock. Although there are absolutely no rules about latent fingerprints. Probably, they came away with something, but I doubt it was conclusive. Unless—" Jury slipped down in the passenger seat. God, he was tired. "—Bannen knows but isn't telling me." They started down the drive. Jury closed his eyes and kept them closed for several miles.

He opened them as one surprised out of sleep. They had left the Case Has Altered behind and were coming up on the bright orange sign of a Happy Eater. Jury said, "It occurs to me: maybe there's a lot Chief Inspector Bannen isn't telling me because he wants me to tell *him* something. I don't know why it hasn't occurred to me before that he's using me."

"Oh, I don't think he'd do that, sir."

"That's what you're supposed to think, Wiggins. No, we're not stopping."

Like a second sun, the bright orange sign faded from view.

23

Richard Jury and Melrose Plant, having been shown into the solicitor's office by a plump little receptionist, stopped dead.

Their surprise must have shown on their faces, for Charly Moss uttered an expletive they couldn't quite catch. Then, "*Why* doesn't he tell people?"

"You're a woman," said Jury.

She had risen from her office chair and now stood, arms stretched out as if doing a fitting at a dressmaker's. "It would seem so, yes. Sometimes I think he does it just for the fun of it."

"Pete Apted, you mean?"

Jury and Plant took the two hard chairs she gestured toward.

"Pete Apted, yes." Quickly, she picked up a near-to-overflowing glass ashtray, and banged it against the metal wastebasket, hard, as if it were resisting being emptied. When she set it back on her desk, Jury saw black ashes still clinging to its center, ashes from last week, last month, perhaps last year, hardened on the glass. (Take a bootscraper to get that lot off, thought Jury.) Then she reached for her pack of cigarettes, looked at them from under lowered eyelashes—neither a coy nor a coquettish glance, but a shamefaced one. She offered the cigarettes around, saying, "I don't suppose . . . ?" The invitation to share in Silk Cuts plunder trailed off weakly. Hopeless that anyone else in the whole world smoked these days.

Melrose Plant came to her rescue and took one. "You suppose wrongly." He pulled out his lighter and reached across the table. "Only the sissies have stopped."

"He means me, Sissy Number One."

Plant's smile was, well, *dapper*. That was the only way to describe it—it went with silk cravats and spats. Right now he was inhaling smoke as if it were a vintage wine.

"Women solicitors aren't uncommon these days."

"Ones named 'Charly' are. I mean, if you're set for a man, you sort of have to readjust your expectations. And sometimes I honestly believe there are people who don't trust me—clients, I mean—don't trust me as a brief because I'm a woman and because of *this*." She waggled the cigarette. "It's come to be as bad as a bottle of whiskey and a dirty shot glass on the desk."

"I'd trust the judgment of anyone Pete Apted recommended," said Jury. Her smile was ingenuous. Jury thought that she didn't have the sort of looks that would hit you all at once, on impact, looks that bowled you over. Her hair was drawn back (with tendrils escaping) and hooked with a tortoiseshell barrette. It was an unexciting brown, until light hit it, as did this morning sun's streaking suddenly through the window. As her eyes that appeared light brown turned to copper as bright as pennies in another shaft of light. Most of her lipstick was nibbled away, leaving the outline. It matched the burnt-orange silk blouse. She wore a hunter green tweed suit. The colors of fall. An autumn woman. He thought that the more one saw of her, the more one would come to think her extremely pretty.

"Then tell me," she said, "what this is all about."

Perhaps he'd been invited along to light Charly Moss's cigarette, thought Melrose Plant, who wasn't listening very attentively to Jury's recitation of the facts. He knew it all. His instructions from Jury were to sit quietly until Jury signed him to speak.

"Like my dog Mindy, you mean? And what do I bark out when you tell me to speak?"

"Oh, you'll know."

He sat there watching Charly Moss take notes—she was taking them rapidly, slapping back sheets of the yellow pad as if tossing the paper out of her way.

Jury stopped talking.

She stopped writing. She said, "Hmph!" Then she left her chair to turn and look out of the window behind the desk, in much the same posture

Apted had assumed. Her arms were folded across her chest, her back to them. "Hmph!" she said again. She turned back and leaned against the window, frowning. Her head rested against a sunny pane and Jury could see the red in her brown hair.

Charly asked, "How well do you know her, Mr. Jury?"

Jury did not like the question. That *frisson* of fear raced through him again. He didn't (he knew) know Jenny as well as people would be likely to suppose. "Pretty well," was all he could think to say.

She was back in her chair now, leaning across her desk. "Well enough she'd confide in you?"

"Yes—"

No. That was what her look said. "But she didn't, Mr. Jury."

Jury's face flushed.

"Do you think she'd tell me the truth?"

"If you don't think she told *me* it, then how can I say?" He hated this defensive posture.

"Perhaps she did tell you the truth. But she delayed it, certainly. It would be impossible for me to work up a defense if Jennifer Kennington were holding back, that's all." Then she turned her attention to Melrose. "You were in her house in Stratford with the local police? Detective Inspector"—she consulted her notes—"Lasko?"

Guiltily, Melrose said, "Me? Well, yes, and the one policeman, that was all." As if only "one" policeman would make the whole visit informal.

Charly tipped her legal pad toward her and wrote again. "With a search warrant?"

Melrose slid down in his chair. Why was *he* feeling guilty? He wasn't the Stratford-upon-Avon police. Yet, why hadn't that occurred to him the day Lasko got him to go along to Ryland Street? He said to the solicitor: "Well . . . uh . . . I expect I can't say?" Yes, he could. He remembered Lasko's words to the cat.

Her look was severe. "That's illegal, Mr. Plant. You do know it's illegal, don't you?"

Defensively, he said, "Hell's bells, it wasn't my idea." Huffily, he added, "I was there only because I was *asked* to look for Lady Kennington. By

Superintendent Jury, here. No one knew where she was, including Stratford police."

She looked from Plant to Jury and back again, as if they were in ca-
hoots. Back to Plant. "Was anything found? Anything taken?" She returned her gaze to the legal pad and wrote furiously.

"*I* certainly took nothing."

"Detective Chief Inspector Lasko?"

Melrose had been so busy that day looking for signs of where Jenny
might have gone, he wasn't paying strict attention to Lasko. He simply remembered him clumping about upstairs. Had he taken anything? Melrose
shrugged, smiling foolishly.

"Because anything taken from that house won't be admitted as evidence."

Good God, what about the silence he was supposed to be sitting in? He
wasn't supposed to say anything until Jury told him to. And here was Jury
himself with raised eyebrows, apparently wondering why he hadn't been
told about his and Lasko's visit to Ryland Street. "I'm being grilled," said
Melrose, assuming this would elicit from this lady solicitor blushes and
apologies.

"Get used to it" was what she said. "Obviously, I'll have to get in touch
with Chief Inspector Lasko. Now, this other woman, Dorcas Reese." She
looked up over their heads, staring at the air or the wall for so long, Melrose turned to see if someone had come stealthily into the room, gliding
silently across the rug. The rug (which Melrose decided was not Tibetan,
not Karistan, and worth two hundred, three, maybe, tops) was the only
thing in the office that might have been called a bit of a luxury. The desk
looked like police-issue gray, the filing cabinets, ditto. Everything was bat-
tered and used, right down to the dark smudges on the edge of the desk,
her side. Cigarette burns. This redeemed her slightly. She too was human.

No, she wasn't. Right now her burnished copper eyes were narrowed
at both of them. "The barmaid, this Julie Rough, told you the Reese girl
had 'a bun in the oven'—?"

Jury shook his head. "The M.E. said she wasn't pregnant." He inclined
his head toward Melrose. "Mr. Plant was there when DCI Bannen
brought that news."

Charly Moss turned her sharp eyes on Melrose.

"Well, good lord, *I'm* not the alleged father. It's just a bit of information I picked up from the Owens. Mr. Bannen was not interrogating me." *Unlike some others*, he hoped the message to her read.

Charly Moss leaned toward them over crossed arms. "If she honestly believed she was pregnant, the same questions would apply about her feelings, her attitude. How was she? How did she act?" Charly chewed at her bottom lip, erasing more lipstick.

Jury shook his head. "Normally, from what I hear, with pleasure or excitement, at least for a while. I think it would have meant she quite definitely had a man on a short lead. At the same time, I was told Dorcas was considering an abortion, but seemed *willingly* considering it."

Charly looked down at her pad, brushing a stray wisp of brown hair behind her ear. "A great deal of attention has been focused on Verna Dunn, but very little on Dorcas Reese. It's as if she's merely a supporting player. It's quite possible she was killed by a different hand, let's say, for instance, the father of the baby, who might not have cared for the 'short lead.' Say he didn't want it, or didn't want it known. A man already married or prominent or both. Or anyone who didn't want this baby. A vengeful wife, perhaps? But I find it interesting the murder of Dorcas Reese takes a back seat to the Dunn woman's murder. Class? Who cares about a maid? Or something else?"

Jury opened his mouth to answer, but she hadn't really been asking.

"Grace Owen says she went to bed at eleven. No way of knowing whether that's true. Still, she'd have had to take a car if she did indeed go to the Wash; her husband, someone, would have heard a car leave. And there was only the one car, one set of tread marks."

"A car could have been left, say, in Fosdyke village, and the rest of the way taken on foot."

Charly Moss was frowning. "Unless she was shot elsewhere and the body transported—no, the Lincs police, the medical examiner, could have told that from the postmortem." Charly shook her head. "Where is Jennifer Kennington now? In Stratford? Has she actually been arrested yet?"

"I don't know."

Charly looked at her watch as if it would notify her of the passage of those moments. "She'd be in Stratford-upon-Avon otherwise?"

"Yes. Look"—Jury slid forward in his chair—"based on what we've told you. What do you think?"

He liked the fact that Charly Moss did not answer questions immediately; she needed to think things through. Now she said, "I'd say that the case against her is circumstantial, pretty speculative. There's no hard evidence. The rifle is problematic, certainly. Anyone could have taken it, brought it back. Yet. The man in charge, this Lincoln chief inspector—"

"Bannen."

She nodded. "Mr. Bannen might have a number of unplayed cards. He's not obliged to let you see them; he's not even obliged to talk to you. But you know that. Give me his number and hers. Does she know you're retaining me?"

"She knows about Pete Apted, yes. I mean, she knows I've talked to him. But not you."

Charly tapped her pencil against her teeth. "Isn't this up to her? She might not want me as instructing solicitor."

"I think she will."

"She's luckier than most, having a detective superintendent on her side." Charly looked at Melrose. "And an antiques appraiser, of course." She beat a little drum-roll with pencil and pen.

Melrose's smile was slightly artificial. He inclined his head, nodding.

She said, "Speaking of retaining—this will cost her a bundle. I hope someone has enough money."

With that, Jury turned to Melrose, gestured elaborately.

You'll know, Jury had said.

"I have enough."

જ઼ૡ

"So that was it. You just wanted me along to make assurances that I'd mortgage off Ardry End." The damp February wind was channeled by the Inns of Court and drove a spike of cold across their faces.

"Nope," said Jury. "I wanted to make sure you knew what you're paying for." He smiled.

"And there was never any doubt I'd pay?"

"Of course not. Do you think I would ever doubt your generosity?" Jury's smile widened.

Melrose sighed and turned up the velvet collar of his chesterfield. "I'm going back to Brown's. What about it? Do you want some breakfast?" He checked his watch. "It's only eleven."

"Why not? I mean, if you have enough money."

"Oh, ha."

Melrose hailed a taxi.

※

Brown's Hotel was one of the finer London hotels, identifiable by a discreet bronze plaque on its brick front. Inside, it was just as quietly stated and decorous, rather self-consciously so. It did not shout LOOK AT ME! but it certainly murmured it. The flocked wallpaper, the rich velvets, the heavily curtained high windows in the room where the hotel served its popular afternoon tea.

Plant and Jury were in the dining room, uncrowded at this late hour, eating their eggs and bacon in comfortable silence. Jury's butter knife scraped across his crisp toast. Melrose was cutting his toast up into fingers.

Jury frowned. "What're you doing?"

"Making soldiers."

"Good lord."

Melrose didn't care. His three-minute egg had been topped, and when he had finished cutting up the oblongs, he dipped one in.

"A grown man," said Jury, shaking his head.

"I always eat my eggs and toast this way."

"Maturity generally has us grown-ups halving our toast."

"Maturity curdles in my aunt's company. One feels one is right back with Nurse at the nursery tea."

"Well, I wouldn't know. I hadn't much experience of nursery teas as a kid." He had finished his own bacon and was looking at Plant's. "You going to eat that bacon?"

Melrose shoved the plate toward him. "Help yourself."

"Nurse Jury wants some more." Jury's fork stabbed the last of the bacon. "Thanks."

Melrose looked around the room and saw that several other candidates for lung disease were lighting up cigarettes. "We're in the smoking section. Doesn't that bother you?"

"No." Jury was piling blackcurrant jelly on his last piece of toast. "I asked for it."

Melrose's cigarettes were out and he was fishing for his lighter. "That's extremely generous of you. Requesting it for my sake."

"It's not generosity. It's superiority." Jury flashed a smile with jelly on it. "What'd you think of her?"

"Our hard-headed lady lawyer?"

"Chauvinist." Jury permitted himself to lean into the smoke gently rising from Plant's cigarette.

Melrose smiled. "Sorry. I thought she knew what she was doing. She's smart." He smoked.

Jury finished the bacon. "Bannen knows something relating to Dorcas Reese's death. Relating, I mean, to Jenny. He gave me the impression he was pretty certain Jenny had also killed Dorcas Reese."

Melrose sat back, startled. "That's bad news."

"Yes."

"But the good news is, nobody concerned has an alibi, except for Max Owen, perhaps. Plenty of time for any of them to get to the Wash and back." Melrose poked his finger through a smoke ring and watched the smoke, pale blue in the noon light, disperse. "Verna Dunn was last seen with Jenny Kennington a little after ten P.M. The car was heard starting up between quarter after and ten-thirty—"

Jury said, "Could it have been another car? Say, Max Owen's, that night? And later, someone drove Verna's car to the point where her body was found?"

Melrose snorted. "Shouldn't one go with the obvious explanation?"

"All right, I'm floundering."

"That's okay. You deserve the occasional flounder."

"Thanks." Jury looked at his watch. "Hell, I guess I have to get back to Victoria Street. What are you going to do? Back to Long Pidd?"

"I expect so. What's the next step in all of this?"

"The next step, I'm afraid, is that Chief Inspector Bannen will arrest Jenny."

Melrose said, "Getting back to Price, though. You say he was an old friend of Jenny's?"

"I'm afraid that tells more against Jenny than against Price. Another lie. Anyway, he has no motive."

"Not one we know of. We've only recently realized Grace Owen had a motive. That is, if she thought Verna Dunn had harmed her son."

Jury said, "I keep running these events through my mind: the fight, the car, the footpath, the Wash, the body . . . They don't compute. Something's wrong. Out of place." He shook his head.

The dining room was emptying out, the last couple but for Plant and Jury rising and carrying their cigarettes curled in their fingers like diamonds. Jury sighed and longed for just one Silk Cut. He said, "Don't you think that someone who really cared for you would confide in you?"

Melrose pushed his bread plate toward Jury with the tip of his finger. "Have a soldier."

24

Jury had managed to set aside the Lincolnshire gloom, only to be over-taken, this afternoon, by the Victoria Street gloom. The breakfast with Plant had helped to raise his spirits a little. Not for long.

Not when he'd just got off the phone with Sam Lasko who'd been decent enough to let him know that not five minutes ago, they'd brought Jenny Kennington into the station.

"Waiting for Bannen to get back and tell me when his people are coming to escort her to Lincoln," Lasko said.

"Back from where?"

"Scotland." He tried to cheer Jury up by telling him he didn't really think Bannen had all that much of a case. "Or he wouldn't be lollygagging around by Loch Ness, would he?"

Jury couldn't help but smile at this image. He stopped smiling. "All that much of or not, it's enough of a case to take her into custody." Jury told Lasko about Charly Moss while he doodled tiny cats. "Of course, that search of her house doesn't make Stratford police look good." Jury pulled over a pad, started doodling Lasko's eyeglasses.

"What search?"

"You know. That unwarranted search you and Plant made of her house."

Lasko was silent, thinking. Then he said, "I wasn't searching the *property*, Jury. I was searching for *her*. *Nothing* was removed from the premises."

Jury smiled. "Oh? Plant says you were rummaging around upstairs. Expect to find her under the bed?"

"Very funny. I was looking for clues as to her whereabouts."

"Suit yourself. 'Bye, Sammy." Jury hung up, smiling over his doodles, decided he shouldn't quit police work to go to art school. He sighed, tore up the paper. Slapped open an old file.

"It's good you've got her lawyered up, sir. A good move."

"Got her *what?*"

"Lawyered up. It's how they say it in the States."

"Sounds like something they would. Me, I'm completely Racered-up. Soho, again."

Wiggins was irate. "He hasn't got you back on that, has he? That Dan Wu business? You know that's a case for Drugs, not us."

"Well, Mr. Wu has recently branched out into dumping bodies in the Thames. Pardon me, *allegedly* dumping bodies in the Thames." Jury slapped the file shut, tidied up the photographs, and dropped them in another file. He sat there staring at the gray rain-streaked window. Where had the sun gone? Where the sun always goes, he imagined.

Wiggins said, "You did everything you could, sir."

"No, I didn't. I'm missing something. And Bannen knows what the something is."

25

I've told Theo Wrenn Browne that if he persists in this harebrained scheme to close down Ada's shop, he can look forward to a life of persecution that will make the Spanish Inquisition look like a weekend in Brighton." Marshall Trueblood pursed his lips and reconsidered. "I'll tell him he'll wind up in some dank little cellar by the sea selling old copies of *Playboy* and French postcards, wearing vests with holes in them and brown cardigans."

"I get the picture," said Melrose. They were sitting in the window embrasure of the Jack and Hammer. "Except isn't it really Agatha's scheme? She's the one bringing the complaint before the magistrate."

"Browne's behind it all; she's merely his puppet. It's him wants to get hold of that secondhand furniture shop so he can expand his bookshop. Let's have another." Trueblood rose and gathered in their pints.

A shadow fell across the window-table and Melrose looked round to see his aunt outside the pub, tap tap tapping her ringed finger against the leaded glass pane. Blocked by the tight fit of the leaded seams (or a sympathetic God), whatever she was saying out there on the pavement couldn't penetrate, became sounds even more impenetrable by the mechanical Jack above her, out on the end of the beam, bonging—or pretending to—the hour. Melrose enjoyed her fruitless talk and started in mouthing words of his own. He found it restful, lips moving without the companion-sounds issuing from the larynx. Talk without the responsibility for it, which was just his aunt's line of country. It was rather like clicking the "mute" button on the telly's remote and watching the butterfly movements of lips without having to hear the idiotic dialogue. She walked away, crossed the street.

"I see the bandage is off," Melrose said to Trueblood, back with refills. "Does that mean the ankle isn't even broken? I thought there were X-rays. For God's sake, has she found a doctor who can't read an X-ray? Where's her case, then? I still can't understand why this Pink fellow would entertain such a case for a moment. The man must be mad." It irritated Melrose nearly to death that such a blatantly spurious case could even be argued.

"Pink-Bryce or Bryce-Pink," said Trueblood, plucking an emerald green Sobranie from the black box. He offered the box to Melrose, who declined and took out his own case. Expertly, Trueblood struck up a kitchen match by rubbing it against his thumbnail. He had lately taught himself this trick and was fond of doing it. He inhaled deeply and exhaled a series of little smoke rings. "You know, you're disturbingly idealistic. You appear to believe that the Law and the Truth have some tenuous connection."

"Admittedly, I do." He saw Agatha now across the street talking to Theo Wrenn Browne. "Cooking things up," he was sure; getting their infernal stories straight.

"Now, that's where you're wrong, old sweat. A trial has nothing to do with Truth and everything to do with Argument. Had Socrates been a barrister, he'd have won every single case:

" 'You, therefore think, Alcibiades, that because the tires of Euthyphro's Jaguar convertible exactly match the tread marks on the victim's back, that the Jaguar ran him down?'

" 'I do, Socrates.'

" 'And that the defendant—the driver of the Jaguar convertible—had been guilty of robbing the victim, raping his wife, destroying his reputation, and blowing up his yacht?'

" 'That, Socrates, has been proved.'

" 'And that therefore these acts constitute motive on the part of the driver of the Jaguar convertible—?' "

"For heaven's sakes," said Melrose, "you don't have to keep saying 'convertible.' "

"Yes, I do. Socrates was nothing if not absolutely precise: *'And you think that these acts,'* blah-blah-blah-*what I said before*—*'constitute motive?'*

" *'It would appear so, Socrates.'*

" *'And you further think that the results of the DNA testing which exactly matches the blood on the topcoat of the driver of the Jaguar convertible with the blood of the victim*—*you think that this constitutes indisputable proof of the guilt of the driver*—*'* "

"—*'of the Jaguar convertible*—*'* This is beginning to sound like 'The Twelve Days of Christmas.'"

Trueblood held up his hand, asking for silence. He continued:

" *'So, Alcibiades, you think that the tire tread marks, the DNA*—*'*

"That's the trouble with Socrates, he's always summing up. Every other statement is a summing up as if Alcibiades couldn't remember the argument from one second to another."

Trueblood sighed. "Be quiet, will you? '—*the tread marks, the DNA, the windscreen*—*'* "

Melrose stopped making wet circles with his glass. "Windscreen? Where did this 'windscreen' come from?"

Impatiently, Trueblood said, "I'm not giving you Socrates' entire argument or we'd be here all day."

"I feel like we've been here all day as it is."

" *'—treads DNA windscreen*—*'* " Trueblood repeated with bulletlike velocity, " *'—you seem to think that these results place the driver of the Jaguar convertible and the victim at that particular corner of Greek Street at the same time?'* "

" *'Greek Street?'* How did Greek Street get into this narrative—oh, never mind."

" *'I can't see how it would be otherwise, Socrates,'* said Alcibiades.

" *'Ah, Alcibiades, you are deceived.'*

" *'In what way, Socrates?'*

" *'Alcibiades, you think that the physical evidence together with the proximity of defendant and the driver of the Jaguar convertible*—*for these reasons you think that the latter is guilty?'*

" *'I do, Socrates.'*

" *'Think again.'* "

Melrose's head came up quick as a whippet's. "What? *'Think again'?* *That's* an argument?" He watched Trueblood fire up another kitchen match.

Around his shocking pink Sobranie, Trueblood said, "Well, you seemed to be getting so impatient, I thought I'd stop." He tossed the match in the metal ashtray. "Anyway, I'm not Socrates." He blew some more smoke rings.

Melrose gritted his teeth. He felt like hitting him. Or hitting something, anything. For a moment he fumed and then remembered that fuming did nothing to Marshall Trueblood. He asked, "But what about Ada Crisp? Who's her lawyer?"

"Not got one, far as I know. I don't think the poor woman can afford one."

"Hell's bells, *I'll* find her one."

"That's decent of you, Melrose. But Ada wouldn't let you pay for it. For such a timid little woman, Ada has a spine of steel. She won't bend her principles."

"That's not principle; that's legal suicide. Agatha and Pinkeye will demolish her. You saw what Agatha did to Jurvis the Butcher a few years ago! And the Crisp case is every bit as silly."

"You're right, of course." Then Trueblood fell into a brown study, slowly turning the black Sobranie box over and over on its end. After a bit he smiled, and after the smile, he laughed.

"What's so funny?"

Trueblood said, "I realized that, as you said, the prosecution's case is perfectly silly. Trouble with us is, we've been talking about Truth and Argument, we've also been assuming Law and Reason are necessarily bed partners. Actually, it's all entrapment."

Melrose frowned. "What do you mean?"

"*I'll* defend Ada Crisp."

"*What?* Are you crazy?"

Trueblood looked at Melrose through narrowed eyes. "You think, Melrose, that I couldn't do it?"

"Damned straight, I do!" Melrose pounded his glass on the table.

For a moment, Trueblood studied the coal end of his cigarette. "You think I couldn't do it because my past schemes have not met with the greatest success?"

"Hear, hear!" cried Melrose, almost happily.

"Because I haven't yet, say, sorted out Vivian and Count Dracula? Or haven't yet discovered how many Week End People we have? Because you don't see me as very quick? Quick enough to think on my feet? Is that what you think, Melrose?"

"That's *ex-act-ly* what I think!"

Through the upward spiraling smoke, Trueblood smiled. "Think again."

26

The Ides of March were no kinder to Melrose than they had been to Caesar.

It was weeks later, and the rain, unstinting, which should have kept his aunt by her own fireside, had instead driven her to Melrose's.

Agatha's assault upon the legal system was about to result in a trial in four days' time, which was going to overlap with the trial of Jenny Kennington at Lincoln's Crown Court. He had been served a subpoena by Agatha's solicitor's office. Absurd as the case was, he supposed he'd have to comply. Well, he didn't have to appear in court for several days, so he could at least go to Lincoln tomorrow. Damn her and her chamber pot, anyway!

At least, it might supply some small measure of entertainment. Marshall Trueblood had indeed offered to defend Ada Crisp, and Melrose was surprised that Ada Crisp had accepted, making the inscrutable comment that it was always best "to keep these things in the family." He did not know which of them was the crazier, but he supposed he'd find out in four days' time.

Yet, Trueblood-for-the-defense had had at least one salutary effect: Theo Wrenn Browne was noticeably worried. He apparently thought that an amateur would not be acting as counsel unless that amateur knew something Theo Wren Browne didn't. He'd been exhausting himself trying to discover what this evidence was that Trueblood had turned up. As far as Melrose knew, Trueblood had "turned up" exactly nothing. Still, Melrose had to admit Marshall Trueblood had thrown himself into his job. He was forever in the Northampton library and had gone twice to

London to the British Museum and the London library. He'd even taken Melrose's copy of *Helluva Deal!* and hadn't given it back.

Bryce-Pink, Agatha's solicitor, was to argue the case (there being no Pete Apteds to deal with local civil matters) before that sleepy old magistrate Major Eustace-Hobson, the same magistrate who'd listened (during his waking moments) to the case of Lady Ardry vs. Jurvis the Butcher in the matter of the plaster pig.

⚭

So," Marshall Trueblood said, "I can't use the pig as precedent, since your aunt actually won that case. Unbelievably. For it's much the same thing, isn't it? The plaster pig allegedly attacked her on the pavement, and in this case it's the chamber pot. I can't think of two things more alike."

It amazed Melrose that Trueblood was so deep into law he could make statements like this without laughing. But on the other hand that was what too much law did to one. "What I fail to understand," Melrose said, "is why Pinkeye would agree to represent Agatha. It's not as if she had money."

"No, but she's probably convinced him she'll be coming into a fortune. Yours."

"Well, she won't. Anyway, I have to die for that to happen."

"She's probably convinced him you will."

This conversation had taken place earlier that day, when he and Trueblood had gone for a walk. A stroll, rather. Trueblood claimed a stroll was more contemplative. You don't stop talking long enough to contemplate anything, Melrose had said. They had taken in the post office, the pond with its ducks, the churchyard, and had been standing then in front of Betty Ball's bakery, examining the window of delicious-looking scones and cakes and buns.

"I will say, though, it's quite admirable all this reading up on the law and going to the British Museum and so forth."

"*Law?* Good lord, I haven't been reading law, old sweat. No sense in confusing the issue. Agatha said she'd been doing her shopping the day of the alleged accident." Trueblood tapped the window. "Hot cross buns."

"Then what have you been studying up on?"

"Antiques."

"What? But you *know* about antiques!"

"Not everything, old chap. Though I'm sure it appears so at times."

Melrose asked, "When are you going to give me back my book? I'd like it back, please. *Helluva Deal!* What good can it do you? The Nuttings only hang out with scam-artists."

"That's right. It will go so well with the Law. I quite enjoy being on the defense, for that means Pinkeye has to tell me everything he's got, but I need tell him nothing, not one morsel. It's the rule of discovery. I fancy a hot cross bun, how about you?"

"It's just as well, since you've nothing to disclose."

"Don't be so sure. Let's have a coffee."

27

"You can expect to be called as a witness for the prosecution," said Pete Apted, reaching in a paper bag and bringing out an apple.

"Prosecution? But I'm your witness, a defense witness."

Apted bit into the apple with a loud crack. "Apparently, the prosecution thinks you're theirs. At least some of you. The part that Jennifer Kennington told her story to. Her relationship with Verna Dunn."

"Bannen knows it."

"But not the details. Anyway, it's as much the manner of the telling as the matter. Highly emotional. You could gather from what she said that she hated the victim's guts."

"How would that be admissible? I mean, it would have me drawing conclusions about her state of mind."

"Umm . . . maybe."

A voice behind Jury said, "This is why we wanted to see you." The voice belonged to Charly Moss, who had delegated herself a leather armchair set back and almost out of sight. She had said nothing until now other than a warm "hello" to Jury. Perhaps that's what she supplied, warmth. He wondered at her being able to play a lesser role, a supporting player. Apted was certainly star material. Charly Moss didn't appear to mind.

Apted was in shirtsleeves and braces. He'd polished the apple he was now eating on his sleeve. "I'm going to get personal." He was leaning against the heavy velvet window curtain, which had exploded its cache of dust when he'd done so.

"Go ahead."

"You and Jennifer Kennington."

"We're not lovers. I assume that's what you mean."

"You assume right."

"Friends. Very good friends."

Apted studied him. "A little less than love, but more than lust? That what you mean?"

"I doubt it," said Jury wryly.

Apted smiled. It was a slow and rather disturbing smile. "Charly," he said, nodding past Jury.

Charly Moss said, "Detective Inspector Lasko claims that you were desperate to find her when she ostensibly 'disappeared' for several days."

Jury turned in his chair to look at her. "He's right, but 'desperate' is Lasko's word. I'm not sure I'd say—"

Charly held up her hand, cutting him off. "He would. His testimony is 'He must've called me half-a-dozen times to see if I'd had any luck finding her. He was distraught, he was.'"

Jury frowned. "Even so, I can't see what difference it makes. Whatever my feelings for Jenny Kennington, I just don't see the relevance. If I were her lover, even, does that mean I'd lie?"

Apted shook his head in feigned disbelief. "And you a detective superintendent. Expect the prosecution to say 'yes' to that."

Jury was feeling defensive. "What I want to know is, why can't you get this case dismissed in magistrate's court on a bloody technicality? Police didn't have a search warrant." He felt low, saying this, given that "police" in this instance amounted to Sammy Lasko.

"Any evidence resulting from an illegal search is inadmissible, as you know. As you also know, but apparently wish you didn't, it's not enough to get us a dismissal. I don't think that would help us much except as yet another example of police mishandling."

Jury frowned. "What else have they done?"

"Nothing. One can but hope. But let me go on with some devil's advocacy. Look at these facts: After dinner the night of February first, Jennifer Kennington and Verna Dunn leave the others in the living room to go outside and have a cigarette. A few minutes later, the people inside hear raised voices. Another ten minutes pass and they hear a car start up and drive off and assume it's the two women gone for a ride. Nearly an hour after that, around eleven-fifteen, Jennifer Kennington returns from her walk, a walk that she decided to take because, according to her, she was so angry she needed to cool off. Needed a drink, too. She left Verna Dunn standing in the drive near the wood, smoking a cigarette. When she's nearly to the Case Has Altered, she realizes that it's just short of eleven and that the pub will already have called last orders. The pub and the Owens house are just under a mile apart; the public footpath is a convenient way to reach it, if one doesn't mind a longish walk.

"The Owens have assumed that Verna Dunn and Jennifer Kennington went somewhere together, and Jennifer Kennington appears to be as surprised as they are to hear that Verna Dunn never returned to the house. Now the Owens assume that just *Verna Dunn* got in her car and drove away, possibly even to London. She's a capricious woman, does what suits her at the moment."

Jury interrupted: "I know all this."

"Of course. I just wanted to make sure *I* did. Let me go on: second murder. In this case the victim, name of Dorcas Reese, was seen leaving the Case Has Altered alone the night of fourteen February just after it closed and was seen to take the public footpath, which was her usual route back to Fengate. Somewhere between the hours of eleven and twelve-thirty, as far as the medical examiner can put it, she was garroted. Since we know it would have taken her, say, fifteen minutes to reach the Visitors' Center, we can whittle that down to between eleven-fifteen and twelve-thirty.

"Theory number one: the two women took Verna Dunn's car, drove to the Wash or, at least, that's where the body ended up. Jennifer Kennington shot her, then returned with car to Fengate, told her trumped-up story about taking a walk.

"Theory number two: Dorcas Reese, being a Nosy Parker, discovers something, overhears something, or finds something that makes her potentially dangerous to the murderer of Verna Dunn. If you accept theory number one, that person must be Jennifer Kennington. She returns to Lincolnshire, having contacted Dorcas, and told Dorcas to meet her in Wyndham Fen, and kills her. This presumably is what the prosecution will argue. The question of the transporting of the rifle to the Wash I'm sure they'll have an answer for; the question of the killer shooting one victim, garroting another, I'm sure they'll also have an answer for."

There was a silence during which Jury could hear behind him the whisper of silk. Charly Moss had shifted in her chair. He had almost forgotten she was there. "I'm waiting for theory number three, the one that doesn't star Jenny Kennington as the killer."

Pete Apted dropped the velvet curtain tieback he'd been fooling with and went back to his desk, where he didn't sit down, but stared at the several files and stack of papers. "The theories I just ran through are the more popular ones with the Lincolnshire constabulary. I expect Mr. Bannen has pretty much dusted off one or the other, with numerous variations." He scratched behind his ear, shook his head. "You can hardly blame him. The most damaging bit is that Jennifer Kennington kept quiet about her relationship with Dunn. Then had a noisy fight with her, and then left the scene at the same time that Dunn disappeared. And was gone for close to an hour."

"It's what happened."

Pete Apted was flicking through the papers and files on his desk, and answered, with an abstracted, almost absentminded air, "No, it isn't."

Jury sat up, astonished. "What?" He looked around, looked over to Charly as if she might offer support. But she said nothing.

As if he hadn't heard Jury, Apted went on: "What I can't understand is why, since she obviously had to account for her movements, she didn't simply say, 'I was tired, I went up to my room without going in to the others—rather rude, I know, but I felt unwell.' Something like that. It beats me." He shook his head, kept flipping through papers. "I don't see— Charly, read that part of your interview again."

Charly Moss thumbed up the top pages of the pad in her lap and read: "'I was so outraged by her attitude, I—I just walked away and left her smoking a cigarette.' Then I said, 'Outraged about what? That's never been clear.' I'll just read the rest of this, questions and answers.

"JK: 'The investment. Max was investing in a pub I was to buy. She said she'd convinced him that such a venture would be a losing one.'

"Me: 'But why would she do that?'

"JK: 'To make things difficult, to hurt me. Verna's always been like that. She doesn't have to have a reason other than that.'

"Me: 'Go on. You walked away . . .'

"JK: 'I, uh, I . . . found myself on the footpath and decided to walk to the Case Has Altered. It's a pub near Fengate; I—'

"Me: 'The Case Has Altered is nearly a mile along that footpath. Didn't that seem a bit far to go for a drink? When you could have simply gone back into the house?'

"JK: 'No, no!' Shaking her head, 'I didn't want to talk to anybody and certainly didn't want to see Max Owen. I was afraid I'd say something.'

"Me: 'Yes, but if you wanted a drink, as you say, there was a decanter of whiskey right by your bed.'"

Apted asked, "How'd you know that, Charly?"

"Because I'm blessed with second sight. Also, because I saw her room when I went to the Owens' house. The room, incidentally, is in a part of the house that would have allowed her to bypass the living room. If she hadn't wanted to rejoin the group there, she could easily have avoided it." She returned to her notes: "'. . . whiskey right by your bed. Wouldn't that have been less tiring than walking a mile to the pub? Especially since it wasn't open?'"

Apted held up his hand to stop the reading and said to Jury, "Does that sound reasonable to you? You've just had bad news; you want to be alone for a good cry; you also want a slug of booze. Solution: go to your room, drink yourself blind from the decanter, cry in your pillow. Right?"

"And so what Jenny was *really* doing," said Jury, barely able to control his anger, "was getting into Verna's Porsche with her, driving to the Wash, shooting her, then driving back to Fengate. That might make sense to you, but it doesn't to me. It's crazy. The bloody *Wash* . . ." Jury recalled Bannen's description of the tides. "You'd have to be a local, wouldn't you, to be familiar with the tides? Had it been a spring tide, the body would almost certainly have washed out to sea. How would Jenny have known that?"

Apted shrugged. "I don't see why she couldn't've. High tide, that's fairly common knowledge. You can depend on the prosecution's saying that. High tide, spring tide, or even neap tide: prosecution can say that the murderer might have counted on any high tide—not simply the spring tide—washing the body out to sea. So either the tide or the sands would cover the body and delay discovery."

"If you're convinced she's guilty, why are you taking this on?"

"Did I say I thought she was guilty? I don't remember saying that. All I've done is, one, toss out a couple of theories the Lincolnshire police are toying with, and, two, said I didn't believe Jennifer Kennington took a walk to the pub."

Jury sat back, his anger receding. Still, he felt he was being played with, felt he might as well be in a courtroom. "All right. Then where was she?"

Apted was still standing at his desk rather than sitting, and he pulled down the knot in his tie and rolled his head as if his neck ached. He massaged the muscles, said, "You appear to be missing the obvious."

Jury felt again the rush of ice in his veins, as if the air in the room had suddenly plunged to zero. "Price's studio?"

"Of course. Jack Price went back to his studio a little after ten. Just as Kennington was setting off on her so-called walk." Apted shrugged, arms extended, hands palm-out, in an exaggerated pose.

Jury blustered. "But . . . there's no reason she shouldn't have gone there. She knew Price, had known him, I mean." Jury thought of what Annie Suggins had said. "She knew Max Owen and so it's logical she would have known Price, too."

"Absolutely right. But then why should she try to hide it? Especially in such circumstances? Why keep it secret?" Finally, Apted turned his swivel chair and sat down. "Why keep any of this secret? Her relation to Verna Dunn, her having known Price?"

Jury said nothing.

Apted said, "It's unfortunate you have to find out about your lady's past in this way, but—"

Barely controlling his anger, Jury said, "She's not 'my lady,' Mr. Apted." He got to his feet.

"Suit yourself. Except, well, don't make a habit of this." He smiled, a genuinely friendly smile, but stopped short when he saw the expression on Jury's face. Then he shrugged. "Did I say something wrong?"

*

*D*id he say something wrong?"

Charly Moss and Jury were walking down the steps of Apted's office, Jury still feeling the smart of the barrister's words.

"Yes. He thinks I'm stupid, dumbly following at the heels of whatever femme fatale crosses my path. A sort of Moose Malloy." Jury's smile was grim.

"The big lug in the Raymond Chandler novel?"

"That's the chap. You like detective novels?" They started walking.

"The good ones. Most of them aren't. P. D. James, hers are wonderful. And the one whose protagonist is a female solicitor."

Jury grunted. "I'm not sure I should have Jenny lawyered up."

Charly's smile was broad. "Gee, thanks."

Jury smiled in response. "Nothing personal."

It was one of those rare near-spring days that wash over the city, cleansing it and softening the sharp edges of buildings, the air like a scrim behind which the distant Thames turned the color of pearl. Jury looked up at the sky, a milky blue, and said, "He was talking about a case I was working on three years ago. For one brief, shining moment I was a suspect since I'd been close to the lady in question and had, apparently, been the last one to see her alive."

They had walked from Lincoln's Inn to the Bell Yard and into Fleet Street. It was there that Charly took in a quick, sharp breath and stopped. "You mean she was murdered?"

"She—" He was surprised by the force of the feelings he thought he had laid to rest. The memory of Jane Holdsworth caught him surprisingly unaware, even though he'd just before felt like smashing Pete Apted for bringing it up. Yet, he recognized some alchemy, some change that had occurred in the interceding years since she'd died. Sorrow had become less sorrow, had become more resentment. He felt tricked. But he had surely felt that from the start: tricked, cheated? Perhaps only now did he feel it undisguised and undiluted by contrary feelings of loss and remorse. . . . *Give it a rest, will you?*

"Okay," said Charly, looking up at him from under a hand that shielded her face from a sudden glare of light.

Jury came out of his fugue, realized he'd spoken aloud. He laughed. "Not you, I didn't mean you. I was talking to myself. Thinking out loud. Pete Apted makes me nervous as hell. I'll probably be a lousy witness. He's too damned clever."

Charly laughed. "You can't be too damned clever in this business." She looked up at him. "Was he too clever three years ago?"

The question was oblique, the sort where an answer doesn't give much away. "Yes."

They continued their slow stroll in silence, Charly suggesting they cross over to Dr. Johnson's house. Standing outside, she looked around. "Imagine what all of this was like in the eighteenth century. Imagine having your morning coffee, or whiskey, for that matter, with Johnson and Boswell and Oliver Goldsmith. Imagine." She shook her head in a sort of wonder, and they walked slowly back to Fleet Street. "Not so many years ago, the newspapers were housed here. Now it's all computers. They can't use the old buildings."

They stood on a corner, waiting for a light to change. Jury said, "You've said nothing yourself about Jenny Kennington. Did you think she was lying, too?" He wished he could keep the anxious note out of his voice.

"Concealing would be the way I'd put it. Yes. I do think she's concealing something."

Jury smiled thinly. "Isn't that the same, really?"

She shook her head. "I don't think so."

Jury watched a wave of office-leavers flood a bus stop in the Strand. They always looked sad, almost frantic to him. "All right. But any way you put it, Jenny's holding back."

Briefly, Charly nodded. "You didn't feel it?"

The light changed and they started across the Strand, dodging traffic that paid little attention to lights. Once on the other side, Charly picked it up again. "Pete and I both felt it."

Jury said, "I wouldn't think Apted would place much faith in intuition."

"I think he calls it something else, 'gut-level rationale' or something equally inventive. But that's what it is: intuition. He's a highly intuitive man." Charly turned and started walking not backwards, but at an angle so that she could see Jury's face, her feet doing an odd little crisscross movement—sideways—and her handbag clutched behind her back.

Jury smiled. He knew who Charly reminded him of now: Zel. Zel grown up would look this way.

She said, "You want to believe you don't like him much, don't you?"

Jury stopped dead, looked up at the sky. "That's a strange way of putting it; actually, I don't like him at all."

"*That* isn't true." She smiled. "You're a lot like him, you know. Although he doesn't have your superficial charm." She looked dead serious.

"Thank you for *that*." He stopped suddenly when he saw they were getting close to Leicester Square. "Good lord! We've walked this far?"

"A distance, anyway." Jury's mind had registered, but vaguely, the statue of Nelson, the National Gallery, St. Martin-in-the-Fields. Yet, there had been no sense of time passing. He had been able to move through a familiar landscape and block something of it out, and because of that, he was able to set aside his anxiety, however briefly. In this there was an astonished sense of relief.

"Look: you wouldn't want to go for a meal, would you? I know it's early, but—"

Charly interrupted. "I'm terribly hungry; I skipped lunch. We're nearly in Soho and I love Chinese."

Jury laughed. "And I know absolutely the perfect restaurant. Been there many times." As he took her arm to steer them through the rush-hour traffic, Charly said, "But it should be on me. You're by way of being a client."

"Wouldn't think of it."

"Oh, don't worry. You'll pay for it in the end. Or your friend Mr. Plant will."

"Deal. He can afford it."

28

If ever there was a place not bound to take your mind off your problems, it had to be the Blue Parrot.

Melrose sat at the bar, waiting for Trevor Sly to return so he could have another beer, and wondered why it appeared so insular, so untouched by time and the changing seasons. The Jack and Hammer, now, it always registered them: the cold clamminess of winter, the soft air of spring, the autumn haze.

The Blue Parrot, on the other hand, was never anything but a desert waste. The only clue to the seasonal change came when Trevor Sly hung bells on the papier-mâché camel and strung a few lights on the palm tree.

Melrose wondered, as he looked at the big birdcage by the door, why it had taken Trevor Sly so long to bring in a parrot. Fake, of course, with multicolored feathers—it irritated Melrose that it wasn't blue, but he was damned if he'd ask—and riding on a painted perch. Melrose stayed clear of it; it was voice-activated and sat by the door so that every customer who entered got treated to *Ahoy!* followed by some scrofulous comment Melrose couldn't make out. He wondered if Sly himself had taught the parrot its alphabet.

Speaking of customers—

Where were they? The place was blank as a dune even though the banner across the mirror announced a HAPPY HOUR 4–6 FREE BAR SNACKS. Melrose was the only customer in the place, and Mine Host was now coming through the beaded curtain with a plate of the free bar snacks.

Trevor Sly was an uncommonly tall, thin man with arms as long as pulled taffy and stiltlike legs. And when he started in with his humming sort of voice and sycophantish head-dippings, Melrose wondered if Sly might be about to coil.

Actually, he did when he arranged himself on the tall stool he liked to sit on and twined his legs round it. First, though, he placed the suspect-looking tidbits on the bar. Melrose looked them over. Cheese? Potato? Fish paste? At any rate, Trevor did try to ingratiate himself to his customers, which was more than could be said for Dick Scroggs.

Sly claimed his custom came not before dinnertime, but after it. "Mostly at night, you know. We attract a fairly wild bistro-type crowd, the young ones, you know."

Melrose didn't. The "young ones" he'd seen could hold a party in a dustbin; they had no need to search out a pub in the middle of the Mojave and be insulted by a parrot.

Melrose pushed his glass forward for another Cairo Flame (was he mad?) and told Trevor Sly to set himself up, too, at which the man slid off his stool like a waterfall and thanked Melrose with many a humble hand-washing. He then served himself an inch of fifty-year-old single malt whiskey and collected Melrose's ten-pound-note.

After Sly resettled himself, Melrose looked around and said, "No one about much," as if he were genuinely surprised.

"Never is on Tuesdays," said Trevor.

He always had some inexplicable reason for the lack of custom.

"Still, I have to do the bar snacks, as that's what I've advertised. And you never know, someone might come. I just started my Happy Hour and news travels slow around here, as you know."

Slow? He must not know Agatha. "But you do have a few regulars from near here. They're the people at Watermeadows, isn't that so?" *The people* meaning Miss Fludd. Miss Fludd was the real reason Melrose had come here.

"Oh, yes," said Trevor Sly. He did not embroider.

Melrose sighed and drank his Cairo Flame. Must he have another to pry information out of the man? "Finished your drink, Mr. Sly? I say we have another!" Melrose thought that sounded hearty enough.

Sly simpered and uncoiled himself and set up the drinks again. Why was it, Melrose wondered, that the man had to shut up like an oyster when there was something he really wanted to know? On the subject of the Fludds of Watermeadows, Sly was perversely mum. Lord knows it wasn't out of discretion, which Trevor Sly lacked in abundance.

"I recall that Miss Fludd was here one day when Marshall Trueblood and I stopped in. I expect, with Watermeadows being so near" (which it wasn't—it was just near*er* to Sly's than to anywhere else) "that she must be one of your regulars."

Trevor Sly served him his drink and then took down the pricey whiskey, pouring out another inch. He collected another tenner from Melrose, recoiled himself on the stool, and cast his eye ceilingward, speculating on the truth of what Melrose had said. "I suppose you could say that, um."

Melrose laughed, artificially. "Actually, Watermeadows is my neighbor. It's next to Ardry End, you know." If *next to* could sensibly describe two houses with so much land between they were a good half mile apart. "So Miss Fludd—the Fludds—are by way of being my neighbor. I haven't met all of them, though. Only her. And she seems a nice enough person. Wouldn't you say?"

"Oh, indeed, Mr. Plant, indeed. Quite a nice person."

Silence fell like lead.

Melrose racked his brain for some way of getting Sly to talk. He ought not to have bought him that second whiskey so soon. Yet, Melrose doubted Sly was keeping mum deliberately. The best explanation was the man didn't know anything. He should have brought Trueblood along. Trueblood would have wrung it out of him. The trouble was, Trueblood was so all fired up with the Law these days—more strictly speaking, with his interpretation of same—that it was hard to get his attention about anything.

The Fludds (however many of them there were) had turned out to be cousins of Lady Summerston, who owned Watermeadows but hadn't been in residence for some years. Miss Fludd was the only Fludd he'd met. He had been so smitten he'd even forgotten to find out her first name.

"It's a shame," said Melrose, "that Miss Fludd has that difficulty with her leg."

"Sad, init? She wears a brace."

As if Melrose were blind. "I can see that. I wonder how it happened."

"Yes. I wonder myself."

"Can't be polio. I mean, polio was stamped out ages ago. Now, if we were all living back four decades ago, why, polio's the first thing I'd think of."

Sly's mouth formed in a little moue. "And you'd be right, sir, I expect. Yes, I do expect you'd be right."

Tired of this mirror-talk, Melrose stopped speculating and stared at the sediment in his glass. Steel shavings, probably. And he'd now drunk two of them. That's what being smitten will do to a fellow. He sighed. What disturbed him was that he couldn't work out *why* he was smitten. She was pretty, but no prettier than, say, Polly Praed. Not as pretty as Ellen Taylor. And not a patch on Vivian. Or Jenny Kennington—

Oh, God. He should have been putting all of these frivolous thoughts to one side and thinking about Jenny. Poor Jenny! Melrose drew from his jacket pocket the little spiral notebook he'd taken to carrying (which looked like the one Jury used) and opened it.

"Headache, Mr. Plant?"

"What? Oh, no. Mr. Sly, if you don't mind, I shall take my drink to one of the tables and try to work on something I've been thinking about. I don't mean to be rude—"

Trevor Sly flapped a long-fingered hand at him and said, "Not at all, not at all. You just go right on." He picked up the plate of untasted bar snacks. "I'll just pop these in the microwave for a few seconds to reheat 'em."

Melrose took his notebook over to one of the tables in the shadows— the Blue Parrot being drenched in them—and thumbed backward through the few notes he'd made. *Table à la Bourgogne. Ispahan. Verna Dunn.* More items on his list. *J. Price.* Notes on J. Price. He flicked back and forth, surprised the notebook was nearly full. *The Red Last.* That house in Cowbit with the odd name . . .

"Hullo."

His head snapped up. His mouth dropped open. And his cracked voice echoed the greeting as he started to rise from his chair.

"Oh, please don't let me disturb you. He"—her head made a gesture toward Trevor Sly—"told me I'd better not bother you, that you were trying to concentrate, that you were working on a case," said Miss Fludd.

Melrose smiled but when he looked in Sly's direction his thoughts were murderous.

"—but I just wanted to say 'hello' and hope maybe we might have another talk sometime."

"*This* time. I mean, uh, right now. Please have a seat. Sit down."

If she noticed this odd mode of address, combined pleas and commands, she gave no sign. How in the name of God could he have missed seeing or at least hearing her come in? The leg brace she wore dragged against the floor planks quite audibly. He was beside her, pulling out a chair, taking her drink and setting it gently on the table as if it, as well as she, might break if he wasn't careful. She was wearing the same dark coat, a bit short in the sleeve, barely covering the wrist bone. Her hair this time was drawn back loosely and held with a narrow band of black ribbon into which a few blossoms had been shoved. Cornflowers and daisies.

He sat down. "I like your hair," he blurted.

She reached back to touch the flowers. "I thought, well, it's nearly April, and I should do something." Then she pulled a cornflower from the hair-bouquet, reached across the table, and pulled the stem through the buttonhole of his jacket. This gesture appeared to her to be completely natural, expected. "That's a beautiful jacket. It's some sort of silk wool, isn't it?"

Melrose pulled back the side as if he'd find a label with the name of the owner or the blend of the material there. He shrugged. "Don't know."

"It is. I know material. That's of a very high quality."

"It is?"

She nodded and drank her beer. He hoped it wasn't Cairo Flame.

She said, "I've been hoping you'd come back. I really enjoyed our talk. I don't often get an opportunity to really talk—"

"Beggin' your pardon, both of your pardons—" Trevor Sly slumped over them washing his hands and smiling his quarter-moon smile. "But I see you don't have a drink, Mr. Plant, and you, miss, you've nearly finished yours—"

"Two more!" barked Melrose. Damn the man. "Did you come here from London?"

"Yes. I was living in London, in Limehouse. When Aunt Nora offered Watermeadows for the year, I loved the idea. Space to roam around in, country air, all that."

"'Aunt Nora?'"

"Lady Summerston. Eleanor. She's my great-aunt. Well, by marriage."

Suddenly, Melrose sat back, as shocked as if Sly had thrown the beer in his face that he was now setting on the table. Then he walked off. Slithered, more like. "But then you must be some relation of—" Melrose really didn't want to say *Hannah Lean*. It had all been simply too sad. For Jury, not for him. He looked at his glass, moved it in damp circles.

Waiting for him to finish, she leaned toward him slightly. "Related to who—?" It was her turn to recognize the significance that Watermeadows would have to the people who lived around here. The *who* . . . ended on a long indrawn breath. "Ah. Hannah. That's who you mean isn't it? Hannah Lean? Aunt Nora's granddaughter." Sadly, she shook her head.

Melrose saw that she too was studying her drink, or whatever was deep and beyond it.

"I heard . . . some story . . . about her husband. I never knew him." She looked expectantly at Melrose, as if he might be able to tell her the story.

Which he did. That part she didn't already know.

"How awful."

They drank their drinks and looked in different directions at indifferent space. Her view would have been the barren land beyond the window; his was the poster of the film *Lawrence of Arabia*. And beside it *A Passage to India*. It had been four or five years, but he still felt awful when he thought about Hannah Lean. And Jury.

"Do you like it? Watermeadows, I mean." He wondered how she felt about living at the site of such a tragedy. He expected the question to elicit an immediate response. Instead, she sat silently looking at her glass of bitter. For a long time, she did this. Long enough for Melrose to become a little uncomfortable in the silence. He hoped he wasn't prey to the anxiety occasioned by silence, as so many were, and therefore filled the air with empty talk.

Yet she seemed quite unaware of this, when she finally said, "I don't know. It's certainly beautiful, the most beautiful place I think I've seen. Those gardens and that lake. The willow trees, the statuary. It's Italianate, I think, a lot of it. I'm not much good at gardening—" She patted the brace just below her knee. "—it's all of that kneeling, that getting up and down, but I am good at pruning. I take care of the trellises and some of the rosebushes.

"I've lived all of my life in London, with my uncle. We have this narrow little house in Limehouse. A 'mean' little house, some would say. 'Mean,' that is, before the gentrification of Limehouse when 'mean' became 'chic.' The old moldy warehouses, now luxury flats. My uncle could have sold his house for an astonishing price. He used to laugh about it. He likes to count the foreign cars. The 'gin and Jag set' he calls the gentrifiers." She laughed. "Anyway, he wasn't about to sell up, and then Aunt Nora offered us Watermeadows. Uncle Ned jumped at it, but I think it was for me, not for him. He wanted to get me out of London. Fresh air and flowers."

She leaned forward, cupped her chin in her hands. "I'm glad he only rented it, though. I love that London house. There's nothing at all to distinguish it from a million other terraced houses, but I love it. It has an attic you have to have the skills of a rock climber to get up to. It's got these mingy little stairs. But there's a window up there looks right out over the Thames. The room's very dark and the window's round; it reminds me of a *camera obscura*, for it seems more like a screen than a window, and the panorama more like something viewed through a periscope or a mirror-reflection. It's so dark my eyes never really adjust to the light. Through that window I could see the Isle of Dogs. People complain about how things have been ruined by all of this new development. But the outlines are still there, the footprints." Abruptly, she stopped speaking, and then said, "I don't know what this means." But she seemed to be questioning herself, rather than Melrose.

She went on: "What I saw out of the attic window looked more like a representation of the Thames—a moving picture, a series of snapshots—

than it did the Thames itself. As if I could remain aloof from reality." She shrugged. "I don't know. Yes, I like Watermeadows, but I expect nothing's quite as good as the house you left behind. Don't you feel that way about Ardry End?"

For some reason, Melrose was surprised she knew the name. "Yes, I expect so. You know we're neighbors?"

"Yes. That beautiful manor house. I'm sure I've walked on your land. It's hard to tell where one leaves off and—"

"Be careful!" Melrose threw up his hands in mock horror. "Wear those neon stripes that joggers do and keep a good lookout. I have a grounds-keeper. At least that's what Momaday calls himself. He thinks himself a dab hand at shooting. Walks around with a shotgun broken—I hope—over his arm. Occasionally, I hear shots. Distant shots. I worry."

She laughed. "I'll watch out for him. Do you walk a lot, too?"

"Absolutely." Melrose was prompt with his lie. Which he modified a little with a bit of truth. "To the Jack and Hammer, that's a pleasant walk." It wasn't really; it was boring. He added, "For my daily saturnalia. Actually, I lead a comparatively quiet and generally worthless life."

"How pleasant. But what's this investigation Trevor Sly says you're doing? You can't be a detective, can you?"

"Do not put too much credence in anything Mr. Sly tells you. No, I'm not a detective. That's a friend of mine, name of Jury, who's the detective. He's with New Scotland Yard. A superintendent."

"Really! And does he come here, to Northampton?"

"Watermeadows is really in Long Piddleton. Yes, he comes here. He was here on the Simon Lean business. And years ago, when we had a string of murders. It all started with a pub called Man with a Load of Mischief."

"I've seen it. It sits up on that hill overlooking the village. But it's closed."

Melrose told her that story. She didn't move; she barely breathed. Riveted. She said, "He sounds brilliant." She was speaking of Richard Jury.

"Oh, he is—" Melrose began, enthusiastically. Then thought, Hold it! Let's not shift what little limelight there is! He sucked in breath, thinking, and said, "—at least he was. That sort of life takes its toll. It ages one pretty early on, I think." He took out his cigarettes. "You can't keep your mind working at fever pitch and not pay the price. And going at the pace Jury goes at, well, you begin to look pretty haggard, too."

"I saw his picture."

The chair Melrose had been rocking back on two legs clumped down. "Where? When?"

"*Telegraph*. I just now remembered as you were talking. He didn't look at all haggard to me. He looked quite handsome."

"Jury's very photogenic. But what was it about?" Jury wasn't the primary—hell, he wasn't even the secondary investigating officer in the Lincolnshire business. For him, it was all unofficial.

She squinted, trying to recollect. "It was . . . something about a Soho restaurateur. But I expect you know about it."

Melrose hadn't a clue. Why the devil was Jury leading this double life, when he, Melrose, sat around in pubs, un-impressing people? "Oh, something of it. Not much. But I can tell you this—" He leaned forward across the table, pushing the camel matchbook holder to one side. "Did you read anything about the double-murder in Lincolnshire? Near Spalding?"

"Oh. Yes. The woman was an actress, or something. And the other was a servant, wasn't she? You had something to do with *that*?"

It had been in all of the papers; he was not divulging any information that had not been made public, except for his own role as "appraiser." He told her the story, and, as he did so, drew a small picture, a diagram of house and pub on a page of his notebook. He continued on another page with the location of the Wash, trying to describe to her the events of that night.

She went silent for some moments, her head leaning on her hand, still looking at the notebook pages.

"Is something wrong?" Melrose asked, when the extended silence began to eat at him.

"No. I'm only thinking." She sat back then and looked up at the ceiling.

Stared up. The magnetic pull of someone's staring at something was irresistible. Melrose had to look too, even knowing there was nothing there but a ceiling fan. "Do you have some idea, or something?" The big fan turned slowly and creakingly. The white globe in the middle was shadowed with the corpses of dead moths.

"This murdered woman left the grounds of the house and drove to the Wash." Her face screwed up in a frown. "Isn't that an odd place to go?"

"Distinctly odd."

"Why do the Lincolnshire police think that place was chosen?"

"To delay discovery of the body. People don't go there; it's not a beauty spot trod by tourists. For one thing, it's rather dangerous because of the mines still left from the Second World War. But also, it's a good spot because of tides and shifting sands. The body might well be covered."

She looked at the diagram again. "What do you think? Could she have done it?"

It was his turn to be silent, now. He felt he should have been able immediately to dismiss such a question as too ridiculous. But he couldn't. Chief Inspector Bannen certainly didn't find it ridiculous. "To be honest—I don't know." He was looking toward the bar and saw the big clock with its palm tree hands. He was amazed that it was nearly seven. He turned to her. "Look here, would you like to have dinner?"

Her smile lit up her face. "Oh, that's very nice of you, but I've already cooked dinner and it's rather special. It's a friend's birthday." She started gathering her coat and scarf together.

"At least," said Melrose, "let me offer you a ride." Why did he feel slightly miffed he wasn't being invited to this party? Nor had there been mention of the sex of this "friend." He rose and started around the table as she struggled out of the chair, but held back from actually putting out an arm for her to lean on. Instead he took the coat from her, helped her on with it.

"I'm saying no to that, too. See, I've got to walk. One reason I come here is for the walk."

It was hard to feel slighted. But he did.

"May I take this page?" She picked up the notebook. "It's a puzzle I'd like to think more about."

"Of course." Melrose tore off the page, handed it to her.

She turned the page over. "There's notes on the back; do you need them?"

"No, they're not much use to me now."

She frowned slightly, reading: "'The Red Last.' What's 'The Red Last'?"

"A pub in Lincolnshire. I mean it was a pub once, must've been. Now it looks like a private home. Just one of those weird inn names we like so much. Nobody seems to know what it means. Something to do with shoes, probably. The 'last' of a shoe."

She stared into the gloom for a moment. "Or 'end.'"

"What?"

"'End,' you know, 'final,' as one might say 'women first, men last,' or 'the white first, the red last.'" She was looking at the piece of paper.

Melrose was astonished. "My lord. Of course. Why didn't I think of that?"

She shrugged. "We get set on a certain answer and it's nearly impossible to dislodge it, I think. If someone asks you to give the opposite of 'left,' you'd say 'right.' But the answer could as easily be 'taken.' 'Left,' 'taken.'"

"Well, that's certainly a turn-up." It reminded him of something, but he couldn't think what. They walked to the door and outside and she bade him good-bye. Melrose stood leaning against the doorjamb, watching her make her slow progress along the unmade road. And then he stood straight, realizing he still didn't know her name. He called to her. She turned. "Do you mind if I call you Nancy?"

She seemed to be thinking about this. "No, I don't mind. My name's Flora, though."

29

"Chief Inspector Bannen, would you kindly tell the court what you found when you arrived at the scene—" Here, Oliver Stant turned to a segment of a blowup of the Wash and another of that section where Verna Dunn's body was found.

The air outside Lincoln Castle where the court convened had the softness of a near-spring day, which contrasted with the building's bleak and cold interior. The place took its emotional coloring from the tensions, frustrations, sadness of the beleaguered whose business was conducted there. Melrose had begun to feel a sadness emanating from the corridors as soon as he'd walked in.

Bannen nodded. "We found the body of a woman lying in the saltings in that part of the Wash called 'Fosdyke Wash.' It's the area nearest the village of Fosdyke. The 'Wash'—as it's commonly known—is a shallow bay on the Lincolnshire and Norfolk coastline. Technically, a 'wash' is the area between water and bank which permits an inrushing of water, and in this way prevents flooding, or tries to. The body was found on the sand, lying facedown in a small pool of water. She'd been shot in the chest."

"The weapon was—?"

"A rifle, twenty-two caliber."

"And you deduced the victim, Verna Dunn, had got there—?"

"By car, her own car, a Porsche. We found tread marks up beyond the seawall, back some distance. The killer left the body there and then, presumably, drove the car back to Fengate. At least"—Bannen hastened to add before Apted was fully on his feet—"that same car was seen back at the bottom of the drive around twelve-thirty. It had been moved, according to the gardener, moved, that is, from its original position."

"And would it have been possible to make this trip, murder the victim, return to Fengate within, say, fifty minutes?"

"Yes."

"An unlikely place to choose for murder, wouldn't you say?"

"Yes. That's what makes me wonder—"

Oliver Stant was quick to cut this line off. "Could one explanation be that—?"

Pete Apted got to his feet: "We'd prefer to hear any explanation come from the witness alone, Your Honor, rather than from the prosecution."

His Lordship agreed.

Stant put the statement as a question. "Why might this place have been chosen?"

"I'd say because of the tides and the shifting sands. The tide would certainly have carried the body out to sea, or the sands prevented its ever being discovered. Neither happened."

"Now, the defendant has claimed that after leaving Verna Dunn outside in the drive, she took the public footpath which runs past Fengate to a pub called the Case Has Altered."

Bannen nodded. Anticipating the next question, he said: "The pub is somewhat under a mile from Fengate, about seventh-eighths of a mile."

"The defendant claimed that, in order to 'walk off her anger,' she took the footpath, intending to stop in at the pub. Would you consider that reasonable?"

Bannen permitted himself a ghost of a smile. "It's not totally unreasonable. The hour was late, though, and the pub would have been closing before she got to it."

"You say the Case Has Altered is approximately a mile—"

"A little less, seven-eighths," said Bannen with a trace of impatience. Hadn't he been exact?

Oliver Stant nodded. "Now, could you tell us how far the Wash is from Fengate?"

"Perhaps three miles."

The prosecutor continued: "Mr. Bannen, had Jennifer Kennington ever walked this public footpath before?"

"Oh, yes. Twice, I believe she said, with the Owens. The second time had been that very afternoon. After lunch, she—Lady Kennington, that is—told me. The Owens confirmed this."

"So the defendant knew how far it was and how much time it would take to get there?"

"Presumably. As to time, that is. Walking at a not-too-energetic pace, twenty minutes, or so. It's impossible to gauge with any precision how long it would take a certain person to walk it."

Melrose listened as Bannen recounted the events of that night, a methodical retelling of the actions undertaken by police. An ideal witness. Calm, methodical, unimpressed by his surroundings or himself. Melrose had an idea that the only thing that did impress Bannen was the moment when he came upon the truth of a matter. Something told Melrose that the chief inspector, in this case, wasn't certain he had stumbled upon it yet. Melrose turned his attention to Jenny, seated in the dock. He felt an absence, her absence. She was there but not there. As if she had come and gone, said hello and good-bye all in an instant.

"—so that time it took to walk to the pub and back would have been only a little less than the amount of time it would take to drive to the Wash and return to Fengate. And, in between, to shoot the victim."

"Yes."

"Mr. Bannen, what particular circumstances led you to charge Jennifer Kennington with this crime?" Here, Oliver Stant turned, rather dramatically, to look at Jenny.

"Well, of course the evidence isn't conclusive—"

Apted rose quickly. "Isn't material, don't you mean?"

This time the judge was sincerely aggrieved and Oliver Stant made the most of Apted's interruption. Bannen, however, smiled and answered the charge. "*In*conclusive evidence is almost necessarily not material. It's circumstantial. I didn't think I needed to say that the circumstantial evidence is inconclusive. That's a bit redundant."

Melrose's heart sank. Bannen was as cool a customer as Apted.

"Continue, please," said Stant.

"Jennifer Kennington had opportunity, had motive—the only one with motive, insofar as we know—and was the last person we know of to see Verna Dunn alive, and witnesses—the Owens—can tell us they were having quite a heated quarrel. I felt this sufficient evidence to charge the defendant with Verna Dunn's murder."

"Now, Chief Inspector: since Mr. Apted has raised this point, perhaps we can address it: the matter of 'circumstantial' evidence and its dependability. What is it that circumstantial evidence neglects to provide? What does it fail to bring forth?"

"It doesn't provide for an eyewitness."

"Roughly, what percentage of your murder cases *do* involve an eyewitness?"

Bannen gave this some thought and said, "Seventy percent perhaps."

This wasn't the answer Stant wanted, or expected. Here was a classic example of what might happen if you didn't know the answer to a question you'd asked. "But, of course, not all seventy percent of those cases are comparable to the case to hand?"

"That's correct, as most murders are not planned out. You've got your armed robberies in which the perpetrators planned the robbery, but not the murder of some bystander; you've got your crimes of passion; you've got your domestic violence cases. All of these make up most of the murders I have to deal with. They're witnessed, or if not that, the perpetrator is still on the scene—husband, say, who's just finished off the argument with his wife by means of a bullet or a knife. He's there, sobbing his heart out. But the premeditated, planned killing is, by comparison, relatively rare. I'm omitting, obviously, terrorism and political murder."

"Let me rephrase this, if you don't mind, just so that we all understand: this particular murder is not characteristic of that large percentage of murder cases you've been involved in."

"That's right."

Stant then asked a number of incidental questions to prepare the ground for Jenny's having withheld the fact of her early painful relationship with Verna Dunn. This was perhaps as incriminating as the establishment of opportunity and motive (neither of which was entirely certain).

In the course of this questioning, Jenny's telling Jury about the relationship came up. "Didn't you feel that Superintendent Jury was withholding evidence?"

"No. Mr. Jury wasn't officially on this case. He was under no—"

Quickly, Stant interrupted, not wanting Bannen's lack of professional jealousy (which Stant was hoping for) to make a point with the jury. "Yes, of course. In time, though, you did discover the relationship between the defendant and the deceased, Verna Dunn?"

"Well, it wasn't at all difficult. A simple inquiry into Lady Kennington's background turned up the fact they were cousins."

Here a rash of whispers broke out in the courtroom. The judge demanded silence.

"Were you surprised to discover this, Chief Inspector?"

"Why, naturally. She'd made no mention of it. To anyone, apparently, except later, to Mr. Jury."

"Then Max Owen, when he was married to Verna Dunn, didn't know of her relationship to Jennifer Kennington—"

Apted was on his feet again. "Objection, Your Honor. There is no way the witness can know what Max Owen knew."

The judge agreed.

Stant said, "I'm trying to get at the fact that the defendant made no mention of the relationship, nor even of knowing Ms. Dunn, even though this was the first occasion for their meeting in a dozen years."

Although Apted gave the impression of lazily rising, he was up in a second. "Is there a question buried in this somewhere?"

The judge instructed Oliver Stant to get to it.

"Wasn't there a long history of enmity—?" Again he was interrupted by Apted's calling "Hearsay."

The point, however, was made: Jenny had kept the relationship, acrimonious at least, a deep secret.

"This enmity you took to make up a large part of her motive? Fired perhaps by the argument that night—"

From his seat, Apted said, "I prefer that the conclusion be reached by the chief inspector himself, Your Honor, rather than the prosecution."

The judge turned to Oliver Stant. "Mr. Stant, if you wish to ask a question, ask it. If you wish to hear the witness's conclusion, don't give it yourself. That at least I should think a rather obvious point." The judge shook his head and returned to his note-taking. Wayward boys. No sense at all.

"Would you kindly tell the court what you concluded from the defendant's secretiveness?"

"I took all of this to mean that the defendant had a motive."

"A motive for murder?"

Bannen did not answer immediately. When he did, Stant was less than happy. "For something, certainly."

To cover his disappointment in the weakening of his point, Stant said, "It's quite all right for you to reach a conclusion by yourself, Chief Inspector." He smiled widely to indicate that was the only reason for the answer.

Bannen wanted to say something: "But I—"

"Chief Inspector, we greatly appreciate the honesty and fairness of your testimony. That will be all, and thank you very much."

Pleased with his recovery of the point about motive, Stant sat down, laced his hands behind his head.

Let me ask you this, Chief Inspector," said Pete Apted. "In the two weeks following the first murder, Jennifer Kennington was in Stratford. Isn't that so?"

"Yes, it is."

"Why was it that you didn't simply arrest her following the Verna Dunn murder? Why did you permit her to go home?"

"We couldn't detain her for more than twenty-four hours."

"But you did indeed detain her for forty-eight hours, didn't you?"

"Yes. We got the magistrate's permission to do that."

"Then why not for longer than that? Another twenty-four hours."

"We couldn't get permission for that."

"Why?"

Bannen hesitated. He had no choice but to say it: "Lack of evidence."

"You had nothing with which to charge her, isn't that right?"

"Subsequently, we—"

"Thank you, Chief Inspector."

ぐ℘

Grace Owen was asked few questions by Oliver Stant, who relied on her only to confirm his previous point about Jenny Kennington's "secretiveness." Grace had not, she said, had any notion of their relationship. Oliver Stant handed her over to Pete Apted.

Apted rose and smiled. "Mrs. Owen, you were in the living room with the others on the night of February first?"

"Yes. I was."

"You've told us that you and your guests left the table and went into the living room at about ten. In what order did your guests leave, after that?"

"Well, of course, the first ones were Jennifer Kennington and Verna Dunn. Then, at about ten-fifteen or twenty, Jack—Jack Price—who went out to his studio; after him, Major Parker at eleven."

"Mr. Price went to his studio, you say?"

"Yes. It's really a converted barn; it's his living quarters, really. He needs a lot of room for—"

Apted did not precisely choke off her words with his upheld hand, but the gesture did stop what might have been more than he wanted to hear. "Thank you. And Major Parker left at eleven. Did anyone else leave?"

She shook her head. "No."

"You've said that the defendant and Verna Dunn, neither by words nor actions before or during dinner, suggested that they were having a dispute. By the same token did they do or say anything that would tell you of their former association?"

"No, no. Nothing."

"You were then extremely surprised when you learned of it?"

"Very surprised, yes."

"Mrs. Owen, didn't you resent your husband's first wife being present?"

"No. Actually, I was the one who suggested he invite Verna."

"*You* were?" Apted said it as if he hadn't heard of this invitation. "But—why?" He shrugged and looked round the room as if he were baffled.

"Because I thought it would be convenient for Max—for my husband—as he had business dealings with her and things to talk about. Verna lives—lived—in London, and Max has to go so often to London on business . . ." Her voice trailed away as if she had started a statement she didn't know how to finish.

"What sort of business dealings did he have with Verna Dunn?"

She hesitated. "Verna was interested in a new play in which she was to appear. The producers needed financial backers. Max was interested in putting money in it. An investment." Her tempo picked up; her fingers gripped the railing of the box. "You should understand that my husband and Verna Dunn had an amicable divorce."

It sounded to Melrose as if the taste of pennies must have flooded her mouth with this remark.

Pete Apted's smile suggested he shared Melrose's belief. "Is there such a thing?"

Stant was on his feet before the question was out. "Is this question being put to the witness or to the world at large, Your Honor?"

The judge looked down over the tops of his narrow glasses. "Frankly, I fail to see where this is leading, Mr. Apted."

"If you'll bear with me a moment longer," said Apted. "Mr. Price was the next to leave, is that right?"

Grace said, "Yes. He said he was going to bed."

"I believe you testified that you saw him taking the path at the rear that leads to this studio." When she said yes to this, Apted asked, "But there are no windows in the living room that face out over the rear garden. So, how did you see him?"

She hesitated, looked surprised. "It must have been out of the upstairs window, then, in my room."

"So you yourself *also* left, did you not?"

"But—well, yes. But it was only for a moment. And I didn't really *leave*, not in that sense—"

Apted said cheerily, "In what sense, then, did you 'leave'?"

"I only meant—I didn't leave the house. I dashed upstairs to find a wrap. It was chilly in the living room."

"I see. Tell me, Mrs. Owen, when did they discuss this play?"

"Wha—?"

"Your husband and Verna Dunn."

She looked perfectly blank.

"When did they have these talks?"

"I beg your pardon?"

"You said you invited the deceased because it would enable your husband to talk with her so that he wouldn't have to go up to London, although he made frequent trips there. I just wondered when all of this talk took place."

"I—"

Melrose saw that she was clearly flustered and he wondered why.

"Yes, Mrs. Owen?" Apted prompted, smiling.

"I don't know."

"There'd have been little opportunity for them to talk, as they were, either one or the other of them, entirely in your company, or others'. If that was the only reason for asking her to Fengate, why did no opportunity arise?"

Again, Grace said nothing, and into this silence Apted asked, "Could you have had another reason for inviting Verna Dunn?"

Grace looked completely bewildered. Her confused denial made no difference; the question itself was enough to plant doubt in the jurors' minds about the investigation.

"Mrs. Owen, I'd like to go back some years to another incident and I apologize in advance for bringing up this painful subject—"

She flinched. She already knew what the subject was.

"—of your son's death. Would you be kind enough to tell the court what happened at Fengate on that particular day?"

Oliver Stant was on his feet. "Objection: I see no relevance—"

"Your Honor, it *is* relevant insofar as concerns motive." The judge allowed him a little leeway, and Apted turned again to Grace.

Obviously, she did not want to talk about Toby. Melrose felt a great sympathy for her as she haltingly described the accident that had occurred. "Toby—that's my son—liked to ride, and he was riding on a bridle path not far from our home. He'd promised me not to try anything foolish—hazardous, I mean—like galloping the horse on uncertain ground—the thing was, Toby was a hemophiliac, and he had to be very careful. Well . . . he wasn't careful enough that day; the horse stumbled and threw him. It wasn't the sort of accident that would be serious for others, but for Toby—" She looked down at the hands gripping the ledge of the witness box. She didn't finish the sentence.

"How old was he at the time of this accident?"

"Twenty," she said in a voice that was barely audible.

"I'm very sorry." Apted sounded as if he truly were. "Could you tell us who else was present in the house besides you when this happened?"

"My husband and Jack Price, and . . . I don't mean, you know, that they actually saw what happened—and Mr. Parker and—"

"Yes, go on."

"Verna Dunn."

Her movement when she said the name was scarcely more than a flinch, a flicker of eyelids, a trembling of the mouth—tiny signals of distress. Such was the power of sorrow that the years following the event had done nothing to loosen its grip.

"Thank you, Mrs. Owen." Pete Apted excused her, turned away. Leaving her high and dry in the witness box. As if she'd had to relive that whole dreadful experience, Grace Owen stood rooted to the spot. Tears tracked down her face. When she didn't move, the judge asked the clerk of the court to help her.

It was a moving close to this day's testimony.

30

Jury spent barely fifteen minutes on the witness stand that morning, re-counting what Jenny Kennington had told him in Stratford-upon-Avon. For him it was fifteen minutes too long.

Oliver Stant was winding up. "The defendant lied about her relationship with Verna Dunn."

"I wouldn't say that, exactly. Perhaps it was the sin of omission." That sounded weak.

The smile on Stant's face showed he agreed. He did not even bother to take it up. "But the defendant's hatred of her cousin was quite clear?"

Jury paused a beat. "Yes. But—"

Oliver Stant did not want to hear any qualifications; he cut into Jury's disclaimers. "Thank you, Superintendent Jury. I have no more questions."

❧

Jury and Charly were sitting in a dark booth at the back of a pub crowded with the same people who'd been crowding the Castle nearby. It was as if they'd all removed themselves to the Lion and Snake by mutual consent, in packs, like wolves. The air was thick with the fumes from cigarettes, pipes, cigars—the no-smoking section was a joke—and Jury wondered how long it would be before he no longer wanted to claw the Marlboros and Silk Cuts out of the mouths of the people smoking them.

"I didn't know Jennifer Kennington had hired Pete to defend you," said Charly, smoking instead of eating the ploughman's lunch she'd ordered. It was a point Oliver Stant had disinterred to show that Jury's defense of Jennifer Kennington was much colored by love, sex, or obligation.

"There wasn't anything to it, my so-called 'case' I mean. Jenny was actually repaying a favor. Years ago I recovered something for her she'd had stolen. Now, *I'm* repaying *her* favor." He smiled. "Will the two of us go through life repaying favors?"

Charly looked at him for a long time. "You could do, I expect. Seems a waste of a good relationship, though." She glanced at her watch. "It's nearly two. Better get back."

"You didn't eat your lunch, not any of it."

"Trials take my appetite."

Pete Apted walked into the pub and Charly waved him over, furiously. "My God, Pete—that ballistics expert's testimony took up nearly the entire *morning* and did a lot of damage—"

"Hatter? No, he didn't." Apted looked at their plates. "Anything edible here?"

"Pete! Not only was his evidence damning, but he himself was simply—I don't know how to say it—'unimpeachable.' I was watching the jury; they were fascinated, they were *awed*."

"Of course they were; it's all that stuff about being able to tell which bullet came from which gun. That kind of stuff even fascinates me."

Charly groaned. "I asked you: where's *your* expert witness, then? You haven't even lined one up to refute his testimony."

Pete Apted shrugged, pulled an apple from his pocket. "I'll just use Hatter."

Charly stared at him. "He's the *prosecution's* witness. Have you forgotten?"

"If I don't get what I want on cross, then I'll drag in somebody. You going to eat that?"

❧

Matthew Hatter was the picture of probity as he said, yes, he understood that he was still under oath. His testimony that morning had been especially damning to the defense because there was no doubt in Hatter's mind as to which rifle had been used. The bullet had answered that question for him: the rifle found in the Fengate mudroom, the one that Suggins sometimes used, and Max, the one accessible to anyone.

"But, of course, you can't settle on *who* had fired this fatal shot." It wasn't even a question, the way Apted put it.

"No." The thing about Hatter was that he didn't appear to care for whatever havoc his findings wrought. He was a prosecution witness, but that didn't mean he was especially interested in prosecuting, per se. He was, however, interested in his own reputation, so he would not look happily upon his findings being disputed.

"The thing that led you to pick this particular gun is the bullet that tore through Verna Dunn, the bullet allegedly fired from the rifle in evidence, is that right?"

Hatter permitted himself the tiniest smile. "Not 'allegedly' Mr. Apted. This bullet *did* come from this gun."

"I chose the word deliberately, Mr. Hatter." Apted went on: "Now, you have told this court that you ran tests to determine whether this bullet found at the crime scene was indeed fired from this rifle."

"That is correct. I showed the court the enlarged photos, the comparison of the bullets. Weapons leave distinctly different impressions. So by comparing the bullet found at the scene and a bullet fired from that gun in our lab—this should remove any doubt that the two come from the same gun."

"'Should'?"

Hatter nodded briefly.

"You said in your earlier testimony a bullet begins to change the moment it's fired."

Hatter said, serene in his knowledge of bullets: "It does. Microscopic bits are deposited in the barrel of the gun."

Apted continued: "And continues to change. Wouldn't it be extremely difficult if the bullet being tested had been deformed upon impact?"

"Yes. But what I was speaking of was that everything the bullet passes through, because of the distortion of the nose, can be seen. The passage through fiber, flesh, bone, organs, or contact with soil, stone, whatever—that can be traced. We found, for instance, fibers—"

Pete Apted cut him off. Bad enough he was managing to testify twice supporting the prosecution's case. "Yes, I understand that. But I'm more interested in all of these changes that take place. Bullets have been known to go to pieces."

"Yes, but one could still determine a number of things merely from the fragments. Anyway, the bullet in question was in fair condition."

"Fair? In other words the comparison would not have been ideal."

"Not ideal, no. Few things are in this business." Hatter offered the court a crimped little smile.

"Kind of touch-and-go, you mean?"

Hatter flinched. "I would not describe the work of our lab as touch-and-go, no, sir."

"I'm sorry. I certainly meant in no way to call your work into question. I'm merely puzzled by your absolute certainty that this bullet came from this gun. I'm not as convinced as you appear to be that the bullet is a fingerprint, has its own DNA."

A withering smile from the expert to the amateur. "I am certain, sir. No two barrels have the same striations, for one thing."

"Yes, but in your testimony you established that it was impossible to tell that a particular round is fired from a particular rifle."

"Well, yes, but that's only the begin—"

Apted cut him off, saying (in imitation of a man totally bemused by what he's heard), "So this is what we've got to work with, Mr. Hatter: one, bullets change when they leave microscopic bits of themselves in the barrel of the gun from which they're fired; two, whatever they pass through—even something as nonresistant as fabric—alters the bullet; three, even *more* alterations to this bullet occur when it passes through muscle, organ, flesh of the victim. Yet you can test a bullet that's undergone all of these changes with a perfectly fresh bullet from the suspect gun and say the match is one hundred percent, the bullet from that particular rifle—the *only* gun the defendant had access to—that this rifle was the murder weapon."

Hatter's knuckles whitened on the witness box. "If there is any doubt at all, it's the merest shadow—"

Hatter looked as if he could cut out his own tongue.

Apted smiled: "The merest 'shadow of a doubt' I believe you were about to say?"

Hatter just stood there, looking cold as an ice-floe. "Let's put it this way: I have a ninety-five percent certainty that the bullet retrieved at the scene came from the gun introduced as evidence."

Apted just shook his head, as if pityingly. "There's always that damned pesky five percent, isn't there? No more questions, Your Honor."

◊&

Your reason for subjecting Verna Dunn's Porsche to various tests, and also the clothes worn by the defendant and the victim, was to determine where the car had been and if Jennifer Kennington had been in it. Is that correct, Mr. Fleming?"

Art Fleming was another forensic witness. He headed up the Forensics Department.

"Fibers were found in Verna Dunn's car that came from the defendant's dress. A green wool dress she wore the night of February first."

"That's correct."

"What chance is there you might be wrong?"

"Oh, one in a million, if that." Fleming was confident, but not arrogant. He was merely stating the facts.

"That's fairly certain, I'd say. How did you reach your conclusions, though? Could it not have been another person who also wore a green wool dress?"

Fleming shook his head once, decisively. "No. Not only are fibers identifiable, colors are also. Every manufacturer has his own dyes and these color-formulae are secret. They'd have to be, wouldn't they? No two manufacturers produce garments of exactly the same color. To the naked eye, a cursory examination might make them appear to be the same, but they aren't. I guarantee it." Fleming smiled. "You can take it to the bank, as they say."

◊&

Mr. Fleming," began Pete Apted, "you say there's little question that the car, the victim's Porsche, had been on that site, near the seawall. Samples of mud, dirt, and sand lodged under the front bumper demonstrate this."

"Yes, that's right."

"And traces of the same mud, sand, and dirt were found on the inside on the mat below the steering wheel, the driver's side."

"Yes."

"Yet you found no such specimens on the shoes of the defendant?"

"No."

"Then your reason for subjecting the car itself and defendant's and victim's apparel to various tests was to determine where the car had been and whether either or both the victim and the defendant had been on the Wash?"

"Yes."

"Is there anything in the way the mud and sand and dirt of the Wash in general differs from any other wash—Cowbit Wash, for example?"

"We didn't of course collect samples from those places but off the top of my head I'd say no—a qualification: there's been some building going on near Cowbit Wash, I think. That could change the way the soil is constituted; other materials could contaminate it. But, in the case of the Wash itself, no."

"Now, in the case of the footpath: you did take soil samples from several different places on this public footpath?"

"Oh, yes, definitely. Five different places, some hundred different samples."

"And you found traces of soil consistent with one or more of those samples on the defendant's shoes."

"Yes, definitely. Several traces of the loam we found halfway along the path and a bit of the soil fifty feet along the path from the house."

"You would say, then, unequivocally, that there was no proof the defendant had, number one, been in that car during or after it had been driven to the Wash, and, number two, there *was* evidence she *had* walked the public footpath?"

Fleming seemed to be sorting through this thicket of reasoning, but had to agree: "Yes to both of those conclusions."

⚬⚮⚬

M r. Fleming, just one or two questions."

Oliver Stant was on his feet again, with what looked like perfect confidence in how his questions would be answered. "First, with regard to the defendant's having been in the Porsche: the *lack* of residue really proves nothing, isn't that true? There are a number of explanations for this; one might be that the defendant removed her shoes, covered the shoes, cleaned the shoes—or otherwise removed the possibility of tracking sand or mud into the car. The lack of such residue is merely exculpatory evidence, isn't it?"

"Absolutely, yes."

Stant nodded. "A second question: is there any way to tell *when* the person wearing those shoes might have picked up these particles of loam from the footpath?"

"No, unless something else had been going on that would fix a particular time."

"For example?"

"Well, I mentioned building materials. You know, sawdust, other building materials that might be carried on air to mix with the soil of the footpath."

"But nothing like that, nothing that might change the constituents of the soil, was going on?"

Fleming shook his head. "Not to my knowledge, no."

"So the defendant might have picked up this loam on her shoes at any time? The day before? Two days before?"

"Yes."

"Given that, there would be no way of knowing, from the evidence of the soil found clinging to the shoes, that she was on that path between ten-thirty and eleven-thirty on the night of first February?"

"No."

"Thank you."

ce/s

Pete Apted rose, smiling: "Mr. Fleming, wouldn't the same thing apply to Jennifer Kennington's having been in Verna Dunn's car? I mean, presence of fibers and hairs doesn't tell you *when* the defendant was in the car, even if they tell you that she *was* in it. You've testified that you found green fibers from Jennifer Kennington's dress, the one she was wearing on the night of the murder, February first. Now, when it comes to the transfer of fiber and hair, there are numerous ways to do it, correct?"

"Yes, of course."

"What you appear to be assuming is that, given this green fiber on the front seat, the defendant had sat there?"

Fleming shook his head. "I'm not assuming anything. I'm telling you what we found."

"Good. So if these two women were in physical contact—say, standing close together, or brushing against one another, the fiber could have been transferred to the victim that way, and the *victim* could have got it on the front seat of the car?"

"Quite possibly, yes."

"So that if we can't say that the defendant was actually in the Porsche, the 'when' she was in it becomes a moot point, doesn't it?"

Fleming smiled slightly. "You could say so, yes."

Apted smiled back. "I do. You can take it to the bank."

ce/s

In the Lion and Snake, Melrose said, with a show of impatience. "But the logistics of Jenny's being with Jack Price in his studio that night are so difficult—if she didn't drive to the Wash *with* Verna, how the devil did she get there?" He had just set their drinks—his, Charly's, and Jury's—on the column-table. They never seemed able to get a seat in here.

"In her own car," Jury said shortly. "It was parked at the far end of the drive too."

"There was only one set of tire marks."

"Follow the same reasoning we used for Grace Owen: she could have left it near Fosdyke, walked the rest of the way. It's not that far. Anyway,

Price could have provided an alibi only up until the time she appeared again, a little after eleven."

"Nevertheless, why wouldn't he have come forward?"

"My guess is because she didn't want it known she was with him. I'm curious as to why Pete Apted hasn't called Jack Price as a witness, though." Jury said this to Charly.

She had been silent since they'd come in here, nor did she answer at once. Jury prompted her. "Charly?"

She sighed. "Oliver Stant would have a field day. Doesn't it occur to you—" She paused.

"Doesn't what?"

"This isn't what we believe, understand."

Jury nodded. "Fine. Just tell us what you don't believe."

"The prosecution could easily raise the question—were they in it together?" She held up her hands when Melrose and Jury were about to protest. "The two of them. The two cars. Each could have driven one back to Fengate."

"And *his* motive?"

She shook her head. "Don't know. But I'm sure Verna had a good deal to do with Jack Price in the past. Possibly even in the present." After Melrose lit her cigarette, she said, "Pete won't allow Jenny to testify because she'd make a terrible witness. She's been caught out in lies several times; she hasn't been registering much emotion; she's secretive—Oliver Stant would make a meal of her. *Did* she go to his studio that night? We still can't be sure."

"Since when was sex a motive for murder?" asked Melrose.

Charly dipped her head to look into his downturned face. "You *are* kidding?"

31

He's not the sanguine sort of cop people take him for." Jury was talking about DCI Bannen. They were dining, Plant and Jury, at a local restaurant on roast beef and browned potatoes and drinking a Brazilian wine sturdy enough to stand up to beef and Yorkshire pudding. Melrose planned on mince pie for dessert.

Jury lay down his knife and fork, tines spearing a bite of rare beef. He had thought he wouldn't be able to eat. But hunger had consumed him. "As much as we dislike it, old friend, face it: the evidence points to her and her story's terribly weak."

"But the prosecution's case is even weaker, when it comes to the murder of Dorcas Reese. Yes, she *could* conceivably have driven back to Lincolnshire, but that's really forcing the issue." Melrose stopped in the act of refilling their glasses. "It would have been more convincing, though, to say she'd gone to Price's studio, never mind the 'why.' It's going to be no secret that she knew him. And why *shouldn't* she have known him? Why was she keeping that a secret as well? Why are these people so secretive? Jenny, Verna, Price?"

"Too many secrets, that's the trouble, or one of them." Jury pushed back from the table, pined for a cigarette, and said, "What worries me is that she's keeping things from Pete Apted." He shook his head and felt weary again. "Such as what were they fighting about."

"Then you don't believe it was Max Owen?"

Jury shook his head.

"Why not?"

"Because Max Owen's not a fool. He'd be able to see through Verna Dunn's manipulations. She tried it on him enough times, I expect."

The old waiter came to ask them if they'd quite finished. They had, they said, and the waiter collected their plates and shambled off.

Melrose thought for a moment. "What about Parker?"

"What about him?"

"He left Fengate at eleven, didn't he? I'm still wondering why he didn't pass her. I'm surprised Oliver Stant hasn't called him." He was distracted by a young woman with black hair who reminded him of Miss Fludd. "Unless they'd planned to meet . . . no, that doesn't make sense. She'd just met him."

"So she *says*," Jury said, wryly. "It's a little hard to tell whom Jenny does and doesn't know." He had a table of cigarette-smokers under close scrutiny. He shook his head. "The trouble is, she's been found out in too many lies."

"This business about the Wash: It's possible, you know. The more I think about it . . . Verna Dunn leaves the wood right after Jenny does, gets in her car, drives the four miles or so to the Wash. That would only have happened, surely, if she'd been meeting someone—"

"Well, obviously, it wouldn't have been Jenny, then." Jury watched a good-looking woman bring a silver lighter up to her cigarette. "I don't think anybody's out of it. I wonder abut Grace Owen," Jury said after they sat in silence for a while. "If what Jenny implied was true, that Verna Dunn could have had something to do with Grace's son's death. God, talk about motive . . ."

"Grace was with Max and Parker, though."

"Not all the time. Not after eleven o'clock. I'm suspicious of this 'headache' that had her sleeping through Jenny's return."

"How would she have got there, to the Wash? There'd have to have been another car."

Jury went on. "Burt Suggins saw the Porsche at the bottom of the drive sometime after midnight, so assuming Grace wasn't in bed, there'd have been ample time. Maybe she took her own car, left it in Fosdyke."

"And about the tides. I can believe one might choose to kill another on the Wash because the body would be carried out to sea. What I *can't* understand is making a pig's breakfast of the tides. There *are* tables, after all. And the shifting sands: true enough, they do shift, but this is very iffy."

"I agree." Jury thought for a moment. "Suggins's testimony will pretty much let Max Owen off the hook, if not Grace." Jury sighed; he wanted coffee. His brain felt addled from thinking about this case. He changed the subject. "So tell me about her."

"'Her'?" Melrose screwed up his face in a near-cartoon version of puzzlement.

"You know who. Miss Fludd."

"I told you, she's related to Lady Summerston. Distant, you know, like a hundredth-cousin-by-marriage."

Jury looked at him for an uncomfortably long time. Melrose looked away. "Lady Summerston has given her the use of . . . the place for an indefinite time." He didn't want to name it.

Watermeadows. No one really had to say the name to him. That episode seven years ago was always just under the surface of Jury's mind. It took very little to start a wave of memory. *Watermeadows.* The place itself impressed him by its sadness, the gorgeous, overgrown grounds, as if beauty were so ample they could afford to bury it or toss it to the winds; the great silent mirrored room he had been told to wait in, probably a *salon* when such things were fashionable. Furnished only with a long silk and gilt sofa, a small table holding a vase of flowers. Watermeadows was a place one encounters in dreams. Uninhabited, a place from which everyone has fled. Jury wondered if such dream-houses weren't symbols of the self. He could almost hear the wind blowing through that wide, unfurnished room. Blowing through him.

He sighed, lifted the fresh glass of white wine—another bottle Plant had ordered. It tasted of winter. He thought of Nell Healy. Hannah Lean, Nell Healy, Jane Holdsworth. Jenny Kennington. "What is it with me and women?"

Happy to be off himself and women, still, Melrose was surprised. Jury didn't often speak in these terms.

"Am I doomed? Is every relationship doomed?"

"Not you. Perhaps the women are," said Melrose, sadly.

Jury laughed abruptly. "You're no better, that's certain. You ignore them even with them falling all over you."

"What? *Me?* Falling all over *me?* You're crazy. The only one ever interested in me was Penny Farraday, and she was fourteen, a*nd* she lost interest after I told her I wasn't an earl any longer."

"Uh-huh." Jury laughed.

"Meaning what? Just name one. Go on, name me a woman you've seen 'falling all over' me."

"You *are* kidding."

Rather violently, Melrose shook his head. "No, I'm not. You can't think of anyone—"

"Polly Praed, Vivian Rivington, Ellen Taylor. Even Lucy St. John, remember her?"

Melrose made a rubbery sound with his lips, a mock-laugh, disbelieving. "Oh, hold on! You said Vivian. That's *Vivian Rivington.* You have never in your life seen Vivian falling all over me."

"I don't mean literally. But haven't you noticed that they *all* act in the same way around you? Sticks out like a sore thumb."

"What? Act how?"

"As if they can't stand you."

Melrose looked stupidly up at the ancient waiter who placed his pie before him and a dish of brandy sauce between them. "*This* is supposed to make me feel loved? *This* is supposed to be good?"

The elderly waiter backed off a step, aggrieved. "I'm terribly sorry, sir, but we've never had any complaints about our mincemeat pie."

Melrose reddened, apologized profusely. When the old man had gone off, Melrose whispered savagely, "This is your evidence?"

Tucking into his dessert, Jury said, "Suit yourself."

"'Suit myself?' What's that supposed to mean?"

Jury shrugged, cut into his pie. "Brandy sauce, good."

Realizing Jury wouldn't say anything more, Melrose shrugged too. "Tomorrow, I have to leave, you know."

Jury frowned. "Leave Lincoln? Why?"

"I've been subpoenaed, that's why."

"Oh—*please!*"

"Subpoenaed, right. I'm to testify in the matter of the dog and the chamber pot. I saw with my own eyes the horrific attack on my dear old aunt's ankle by the slobbering dog."

"My God, he's only two inches long. What damage could he do?"

"None, of course." Melrose shrugged. "Don't ask me why Agatha thinks she has a Chinaman's chance of winning. Anyway, Trueblood seems very pleased with himself."

"Trueblood's always pleased with himself. Why this time?"

"I thought I told you: he's handling Ada Crisp's defense."

Jury quickly returned the bite of brandy-sauced pie to his plate. He would have choked on it, laughing. "It's better than Jurvis and the pig. I still can't believe Agatha won. What a hell of a deal."

"Hell of a deal, is right. Pass the brandy sauce."

32

Oliver Stant did not appear to be clever, devious, or sly. He was, Melrose decided, all of those things, as Stant set about questioning his next witness, Annie Suggins. He began by establishing Mrs. Suggins in the Owen household, where she had worked for twenty-two years, she and Burt Suggins, her husband. In the course of the questioning, Mrs. Suggins told the court she had had little contact with the defendant, so could not attest to Lady Kennington's comings and goings. Yes, the Owens occasionally went to the Case Has Altered. *A very nice sort of pub, it is. Quite homey and frequented by pleasant decent folk, none of this disco stuff you see nowadays.* What happened the night of February first, she couldn't really say, as she'd been up late in the kitchen, and that's the rear of the house. She wouldn't have heard anything going on outside.

"All I knew was when Burt come into the kitchen and asked me did I see Miss Dunn. It was after eleven, after Major Parker'd left and after Mr. and Mrs. Owen had gone upstairs to bed. Oh, eleven-thirty or thereabouts. Well, no, I says to Burt, not since dinner. There was a bit of a commotion, naturally, when Lady Kennington got back and no Miss Dunn with her."

"And what was the reaction to this on the part of the Owens?"

"Naturally, Mr. Owen was puzzled. But he didn't bother Mrs. Owen with it, as she'd gone upstairs with a headache. Mr. Owen supposed Miss Verna just must've got in that fancy car of hers and gone back to London. But then more'n an hour later, Burt saw—"

"Don't mind about that, Mrs. Suggins. We'll be speaking to your husband a bit later. "They did not notify the police?"

"Why should they? It warn't as if Miss Verna never did nothing pecu-liar." She sniffed.

Stant smiled, nodded. "The Owens retired at about eleven?"

"I expect so; I mean they'd've gone upstairs. Mr. Owen, he liked to stay up to all hours, fooling about with those antiques of his, or up in his study reading up on 'em." Her brief laugh was indulgent; Max Owen might have been a child with a fancy electric train. "Mrs. Owen, like I said, she had a headache and went straight to bed and didn't know about it till the morning."

"And what happened the next morning with regard to Verna Dunn?"

"She warn't there for breakfast. Mr. Owen rung up her London house and no one—I think she has a housekeeper—had seen her. Well, now the Owens was in a real stew, you can imagine, after Burt told 'em about her car. That's when they rang up the police. Me, I still thought it was some trick or other. I was cook to Mr. Owen all the time he was married to her, and I don't mind saying anything's possible with that one." She squared and resettled her shoulders, posture conveying what she thought of Verna Dunn.

"I take it," said Oliver Stant, again with that smile, "you didn't much care for her."

"I did not. Why that woman was back in Fengate was more'n I could explain. But Mrs. Owen, patience of a saint, she didn't mind. Well." Mrs. Suggins shook her head, making the little fruit bouquet on her straw hat bobble. She was dressed in a bright blue suit, fitted tight and a little strained across the bosom. It was clear that witnessing to her was an occa-sion.

"You know the accused"—Stant turned toward the witness box—"Jennifer Kennington?"

Mrs. Suggins nodded. "Only by way of her being a guest, sir."

"And did you see her on that night of the first of February?"

"No, sir. I mean not except for a glimpse or two of the table when Dorcas was going in and out."

"By Dorcas, you mean the Owens' kitchen-helper and sometime maid, is that correct?"

"Yes, sir."

Stant turned then to the death of Dorcas Reese. Annie Suggins was in the process of lending a little shape, a little color to the image of the dead girl. "Moonin' an' moanin' about like a sick calf."

Oliver Stant smiled. "I like your description, Mrs. Suggins." He had already complimented her on her hat, which had really gone down a treat with her. It was new. "Did she tell you the source of this moan of hers?"

With an expression of one who thought her questioner a bit simple, she said, "Well, for heaven's sakes, thought 'erself in love, I expect. Don't they always, these girls?"

"I see what you mean. When it comes to that sort of thing, you know, men aren't as perceptive as women in—"

Pete Apted, used to Oliver Stant, was on his feet. "Your Honor, try as I will, I fail to perceive a question."

The judge agreed and once again gently reprimanded Stant who, once again, apologized and went his merry way.

"What I was trying to ask, Mrs. Suggins, is whether Dorcas ever confided in you."

The cook looked upward, as if the courtroom's vaulted ceiling might lend her inspiration. "Now, 'confide' might be too strong a word, sir. She told me things, it's true, you know, like as she just met some feller or t'other, and weren't he the cutest lad ever? Well that's all the lass thought about—men."

Stant said, "I know what you mean. I've a daughter myself." This earned him an indulgent smile from Annie Suggins, and severe glance from the judge. "My daughter seems to talk more to our cook than to us." Another look of displeasure came down from the bench, but Stant pretended not to notice.

"If counsel could confine his remarks to the matter at hand?"

Stant bowed slightly, mumbled his apology.

"Sometimes she did tell me things—mostly made-up, I'd think," said Annie, "but if you're talking about her being preggers and all, no she didn't tell me about that."

"We'll come back to that. But she'd not mentioned any man in particular."

"No, sir. One day it'd be that boy from Spalding she'd be going with; the next day it'd be—someone else. Ever so flighty was Dorcas. Got 'erself into this spot, and from all I could tell, she was expecting 'im to marry 'er. She warn't a comely girl, not in face nor figure. Nowt eyes, nor skin, nor teeth, nor hair had she a gift of."

Melrose found this unexpected little poetical turn rather endearing.

Having established that Dorcas was a mercurial, perhaps scatterbrained young woman, Stant asked the witness if there was anything in her behavior just prior to her death that the cook found different.

"Yes, sir, I'd certainly say so. For a while there—oh, maybe a couple of months before, she was happy as a lark. *That* must have been when some man walked in. Then, a week or more before she—got herself murdered, like, well, she'd turned round completely, she was morose and bad-natured. That's when I'd bet the man walked out. Same old story, been told dozens of times."

"Indeed it has. Mrs. Suggins, she had told a friend and an aunt that she was nearly three months pregnant. Have you any idea why she'd make up such a story?"

Annie shifted her weight in the witness box and looked grim. "Who says she made it up? There warn't much about the girl to make a person respect her, but I'd never known her to spread such a story. So I'll bet she thought she was." Annie drew herself up and in and seemed about to float up to the vaulted ceiling with her knowledge of this. "I must say, sir, I was that shocked, I was. But then there was all that time she spent at the pub, and lord knows what mischief she was getting up to. So much time, I thought she just might have an extra job at night. Starlighting, like."

Even the judge smiled at that one. Melrose wrote it down for future reference.

"And you discovered that she did, indeed, have an extra job?"

"Yes, but only a few hours a week. Not a proper job. But that don't account for all the time she spent there. I'd say it was more to hang around the men. There's nowt agin *them*, though, if Dorcas got herself full of ideas. There must've been some young chap or other she'd set sights on."

Oliver Stant paused, as if hesitating over his next question. Then he asked, "Did Dorcas ever speak of having particular feelings for anyone at Fengate?"

Annie Suggins reared back. "For Mr. *Owen*? Good lord." Here she laughed, couldn't help herself, even wiped a tear away.

"I was thinking more of Mr. Price."

Annie's brow furrowed, and she shook her head, slowly. "I'm afraid to say it, but, yes, I think she did. I told her straight out one morning when she was mooning about, talking on about how nice 'e was, I said, well, girl mebbe you're thinking o' '*im* but I assure you, Mr. Price ain't thinking o' *you*!"

This sent another titter of laughter through the courtroom; the judge simply looked his displeasure at the field of faces.

"And how do you know that, Mrs. Suggins? Did Mr. Price say anything to you about Dorcas?"

"No, 'course not. If she'd gone and left tomorrow, I don't think Mr. Price'd notice. Don't get me wrong; I don't mean 'e wasn't appalled by the poor girl's death, but not *personal*-like, you know what I mean."

Oliver Stant smiled and nodded. "Did she always stay out so late? Eleven-thirty or so?"

"No. Most nights she'd be back around ten. Well, she 'ad to get up early, di'n't she? Still, many's the morn I be dragging her outta bed by 'er feet. I complained once or twice to the missus, but Mrs. Owen, she'd never get rid of somebody just fer lyin' abed, or—"

Melrose noted the pause. Annie Suggins was no doubt thinking about her husband, whom Mrs. Owen had not seen fit to discharge, either.

"—personal habits. Long as it didn't interfere."

"Were you surprised when Dorcas's body was found in Wyndham Fen?"

The question was so abrupt, she drew back. "What a question! O' course I was! Whatever that poor girl done, it's no call for 'er to go gettin' 'erself murdered, no, she didn't deserve that! You think dead bodies turns up every day on Windy Fen?"

Annie Suggins spoke much more like a woman entertaining a visitor to tea in her kitchen than a woman in a witness box. But this, thought Mel-

rose, was simply testimony to Oliver Stant's ability to create the sort of atmosphere that turns a witness box into a kitchen chair.

His answer to the cook's question was, "I certainly hope not, Mrs. Suggins. And just before this, she was the same as always?"

"No, she warn't. That's what I told you. She was doin' more moanin'
than was usual. Said, every once in a while, 'I done wrong,' she says. "'I
ought not to've listened.'"

There was a bit of a stir in the court, quickly quelled when the judge's
head came up.

Oliver Stant, without moving from his place, seemed to draw nearer to
her. "'I ought not to have listened.' And 'I done wrong.' Is that exactly
what she said?"

Annie frowned. "Well, let me think a bit . . ." She put her fingertips to
her face, frowning in an effort to recall the words. "Now, what she said
was, 'I ought not to 'ave done it. I ought not to 'ave listened,' or, 'I
shouldn't've listened.' Yes, that's it." Satisfied, Annie again squared her
shoulders.

Stant repeated Dorcas's words, then asked, "Did you make anything of
that?"

"Indeed I did, sir, but it's speaking ill of the dead and all." Having put
herself on record with that, she was willing enough to do it. "Dorcas was
forever standing about doors, trying to hear what was going on t'other
side. Many's the time I caught 'er with 'er ear stuck-like to a door." Here,
the cook leaned as if in confidence toward Stant and whispered, "Right
nosy was Dorcas—"

It was the judge's turn to object. "Mrs. Suggins, you might feel you're
sharing a secret with counsel"—he smiled thinly—"but we'd all like to
share it, if you don't mind."

Annie blushed furiously. "Sorry, sir. Forgot where I was." She pulled
down her bright blue jacket, and possibly the corset underneath, and
straightened herself in a businesslike way. "Dreadful sorry."

"That's quite understandable, madam. I can see how you might think
you're having a good gossip in counsel's kitchen." He glared at Stant, who
bent his head to hide a smile.

"Did her demeanor suggest to you that she might have heard something to her disadvantage? Even something dangerous?"

Pete Apted's objection was routine: the witness was not a mind reader.

"Mrs. Suggins, how long was this before the poor girl's murder?" Oliver Stant was using his witness's words.

The cook had to think. "Right before, I'd say. I mean, a few days before, maybe a week. She was acting odd-like, I mean even for Dorcas— went about the kitchen mumbling. Kept sayin' she 'ought not to 'ave listened,' like I told you, and when I asked her what she meant, well, all sparky she gets—'Niver you mind!' she says, as if it's me making 'er tell an' not 'erself mumbling it out, and I says, 'There's all of us done wrong one way or another, so best forget about it and just carry on.'"

"'I ought not to have done it. I shouldn't have listened.'" Stant repeated it for the third time. "Did you conclude, Annie, that the two were related?"

Apted rose wearily. "Your *Honor* . . ."

But it was Stant who answered the implied objection, not the judge. "Your Honor, is this the sort of 'conclusion' that is objectionable? If my office boy came in scratching at a spot of jam on his shirt and saying, 'Damn that jam donut,' would it be risky of me to conclude the two were related?"

The judge's mouth twitched, but he still upheld the objection of defending counsel.

However, Melrose was sure it made no difference whether or not the point was allowed. The point the jury had most certainly taken: that Dorcas Reese had discovered, had overheard, something that had placed her life in jeopardy.

Oliver Stant said, "If we could return to the night of the first murder, Mrs. Suggins. To your knowledge, did the defendant ever have cause to pass through the mudroom off the kitchen?"

"Yes, sir. She'd come through that way once or twice. I recall one time she said her shoes were filthy from the footpath, and she'd not wanted to track dirt through the drawing room."

"And, again so far as you know, had she seen where the .22 rifle belonging to Max Owen was kept?"

Annie screwed up her face. "I expect I can't really say. But I do recall she was in the kitchen on the Saturday when Mr. Owen chided Burt— that's Mr. Suggins—for not keeping that rifle locked up in the case as he should 've done."

"Where would your husband leave the rifle when he wasn't using it?"

"Well, it sounds awful careless o' Burt, and I expect it was, leaving that gun just standing in a corner. The thing was that Burt used it so much. He loves his gardens, see, both flower and vegetable, and there was always rabbits and squirrels and things about to eat up everything in sight."

"I see. So anyone could have walked in, either through the kitchen or from outside through the mudroom door?"

Annie shrugged. "Yes, I'd have to say that's right."

"Tell me, did Mr. Owen own a handgun?"

She reared back as if one were pointing at her now. "Goodness, I shouldn't think so, sir! I certainly never seen one, and nor never heard about one. Well, it's too hard to get a license for any gun, much less that kind."

"So there were two guns in the house, a .22 and a shotgun—"

Apted made a display of getting wearily to his feet: "Your grace, we have a firearms expert. Mrs. Suggins can't testify as to what gun was, or was not, in the house beyond the ones she herself had seen or her husband had used."

"My point," said Oliver Stant, "is that the defendant had access to the .22 rifle."

"Your point is taken," said Apted. When Annie was turned over to him for questioning, Pete Apted said he had no questions at this time.

Annie Suggins was told to step down. She reacted as if someone were being rather rude, she'd not finished her tea yet, but suddenly recognizing just where she was, blushed and smiled at both Oliver Stant and the judge and removed herself from the box.

Then it was that Melrose remembered what Jury had said— indeed, what a number of people had said: *"Why do I keep forgetting Dorcas Reese . . . ?"* It wasn't the answer that was important; it was the question.

He left the courtroom in the brief shuffle of barristers and witnesses. It was a crowded scene, a crush of people who had found it a rather jolly break in the boredom of daily life to take in a murder trial. Double-murder trial. He looked around him in the corridor, registered three people sitting on a bench outside the door, clearly strangers to one another as they neither spoke nor moved. Witnesses, perhaps? And then he was stopped by the lettering on a cap that the sturdy-looking man was twisting in his hands.

Roadworks. Melrose stared at him for a moment, but the fellow was so deep into his own thoughts that he didn't look in Melrose's direction. The guard by the door noticed and shook his head as Melrose took a step toward the bench. A witness?

Melrose stared. He had never seen the man before, of course, but he certainly remembered now that detour he'd had to take outside of Loughborough to get onto the M6. He'd been only twenty or twenty-five miles from Northampton. After that, it was the A46. And if you kept on going past Northampton you'd come to the turn for Stratford-upon-Avon. . . .

Oh, *hell*, Melrose thought. *"Wednesday, I remember because it was me mum's birthday—"*

Did Apted know? He must. There was some sort of rule about disclosure or discovery, wasn't there?

☙

His name was Ted Hoskins and he took his place in the witness box, obviously nervous, for he looked round about him as if he were the one being charged. But he took the oath and told the court his name, his address, his position.

"Ah be ganger man on that job." He seemed quite pleased with this office.

"Is that the man in charge?" asked Oliver Stant.

"Well, not wholly in charge. That'd be the general foreman. Me, I'm in charge o' me mates, you know, some o' the lads."

"Mr. Hoskins, could you tell us about the job you were on that began on Wednesday, the fifth of February of this year?" Oliver Stant was looking pleased as punch.

"Yessir. It were on that part of the A6 near Loughborough, just t'other side going towards Leicester. We were tryin' to put in a new lay-by. That meant cars had to detour round on the B road for about a mile, nearly to Leicester, then double back a bit. Not too happy—" Ted Hoskins was cut off from having his little joke by Stant's interruption.

"Right. Now that roadworks operation began exactly when?"

"Like you already said, fifth February."

"That was a Wednesday?"

"Yessir, I believe so."

"Not on the Tuesday, February fourth."

"No, definitely on the Wednesday."

"So that anyone traveling that route on Tuesday the fourth would not have had to take the detour?"

"Well, no sir. It'd have been as usual."

"Mr. Hoskins, that's the way one would travel to Northampton, isn't it?"

"I'd say so, yes. It's only maybe twenty miles from that M69 junction."

"And if you were traveling to Stratford-upon-Avon, you'd also take that road?"

"Like as not. O'course there's always other—"

"The defendant claims to have driven that particular route to Stratford-upon-Avon on February fourth and to have taken the detour you describe."

Ted Hoskins gave a short laugh. "Well, I'm afraid she's forgot 'erself, 'cause for there was no detour on the Tuesday."

"So if she went the route you described, it would have to have been a day *later*, or at least no earlier than the next day, is that true? It would have to have been the Wednesday?"

Ted Hoskins nodded. "Yessir." His look at Jenny was a sad one.

ดง

I believe what you were about to say—before you were cut off— was that there are other routes to Stratford-upon-Avon?" Pete Apted smiled.

Hoskins nodded. "'Course there are."

"Can you say, offhand, what other way the defendant might have driven?"

"Yessir." Ted Hoskins breathed what seemed to be a relieved sigh; it was as if he hadn't liked calling Jenny a liar. "Shortest way'd be Market Harborough on to Leamington to Warwick—"

Before Stant could rise to object, Apted cut in: "I think we'll have to stay with the Leicester-Northampton route, as the defendant mentioned Leicester."

Hoskins rubbed his thumb across his forehead. "Well, now. She could've got off the A road somewheres round Syston or Rearsby. Could've taken a wrong turning, we all do now and again."

"There could, indeed, have been other roadworks going on at just about anyplace along this particular route, couldn't there?"

Oliver Stant rose quickly to voice his objection. This was mere speculation on the part of both defense counsel and witness.

Apted ate up the opportunity: "I'd agree, Your Honor. But given I wasn't informed about this witness until late last night, I didn't have time to look for a map."

The judge was severe. "Consider yourself fortunate, Mr. Stant, that I don't cite you for contempt. You know the rule of discovery means you must let prosecuting counsel know immediately."

"I do, Your Honor, but the witness was only brought to my attention yesterday afternoon. I assure you, I let defending counsel know as soon as possible."

The judge made a *hmphing!* sound and waved his hand for them to proceed.

Apted turned to Ted Hoskins again. "It's not like the motorways, is it, Mr. Hoskins? There were clearly a number of *different* A roads and, consequently, a number of different turnings?"

"That's right. We all make mistakes, sir."

Pete Apted smiled. "We do indeed. That'll be all."

✒

Court had recessed until two o'clock and the three of them—Apted, Charly Moss, and Melrose—were standing outside in the corridor.

"And now I'm off to have a quiet little think with my client." The words dripped acid. He walked off, black robe flying.

"I wouldn't want to be her at the moment," said Charly Moss, looking down the corridor.

"No." Melrose shook his head. "I wonder how the prosecutor twigged it. About the detour, I mean."

"Probably some slip on her part. Or it might have been accidental. Information does come one's way in the queerest manner." Charly turned her eyes from the corridor to Melrose. "What was she doing? Why did she stay Tuesday night?"

She was silent a moment, hugging her arms about her. It was cold in the corridor. Cold as marble could make it. Melrose looked at her, thought about the "cold ladies," a sobriquet that would never apply to Charly Moss or Flora Fludd. He frowned slightly. He was still pondering what Flora had said in the Blue Parrot.

"Where's Richard?" asked Charly.

"He said he was going to Algarkirk. To Fengate." Melrose looked off through a tall window. "I'm glad he isn't here, frankly." . . . *white first, the red last.*

Charly pushed her hair back out of her face, looked at him, asked, "Something wrong?"

"I was just thinking about the Red Last."

She looked puzzled. "I don't follow—"

"It's a pub. Was a pub, I mean."

"Named for shoes? Not very witty."

"You see, that's the point: automatically, one thinks of a last for a shoe, but—" Dorcas Reese's words came back to him. *That* was the connection.

"Heavens. You do look—lit up."

"Let's go somewhere ourselves and have a quiet think. I might have an idea Pete Apted should hear about." Melrose took her arm and guided her down the cold corridor.

33

Officially spring, thought Jury, but the day was returning to the winter light of the month before, and the wood where he walked, turning up winter's debris, was sodden with the rain that had just then stopped. He'd spent an hour on the Wash, a desolate hour, in the rain. A straight-down, relentless rain, pummeling like bullets—or perhaps that metaphor was suggested by his hoping he'd find one, a spent bullet, another casing, anything just to find something. Jury knew he wouldn't, unless the sands gave it up, like the hull of one of those buried ships.

Yet, he couldn't resist turning sand over with the toe of his shoe, hoping to find something. A shot in the dark. It still baffled him that anyone could picture Jenny Kennington with a rifle butted to her shoulder. But he knew this was a romantic defense on his part. Jenny had kept quiet about many things. Still, the kind of person she was . . .

Romance, again. He had been a policeman long enough to know that no one was, in the end, exempt. Not Jenny, not Grace, although it was equally baffling to think of her as a killer.

He was back at Fengate now. When Jury pulled up, Burt Suggins was tending the oval flower bed in front of the house. The gardener looked over at Jury's car, squinting into the sunless day, his face screwed up in a mask of puzzlement. Who could this be? And the master not here, nor the missus. Burt was easy to read. Jury told the gardener that he wasn't obliged to show him around.

That he had the power to grant a request or refuse it pleased the old man, unused to exercising any power. Thus he hesitated, thinking it over as he mopped the back of his neck with his neckerchief. "All them be over to Lincoln, even my missus."

"I know. Annie made a smashing witness."

That surprised him, knowing that witnesses had to put their hands on the Bible and swear to tell the strictest truth. Annie Suggins was never a liar, but she had been known to exaggerate a mite. "Well, Annie never did have any trouble speakin' her mind."

"Look, Mr. Suggins—"

"Oh, just you call me Burt, everyone do."

Jury smiled. "Burt. I'm not on a search. I think I'm really looking for inspiration—"

Burt Suggins frowned. He was more used to this lot looking for clues, such as footprints in his flower beds.

"—because this whole thing just doesn't sit right, you know what I mean? I'd like to see that gun room—"

"It's no more'n a little back room off the kitchen. You bein' a Scotland Yard inspector, well, I'd say it's all right."

Jury was used to being demoted by witnesses. Demotion was a fate that Chief Superintendent Racer often foretold, too. He didn't bother correcting the old man as the two of them headed for the house.

The room was as Burt had said, a small enclosure off the kitchen, crowded with wellingtons, rain gear, gardening tools, insecticides, lime for the soil. He turned to the steel cabinet bolted to the wall. The rifle it was home to was now in Lincoln. "This thing is kept locked, isn't it, Burt?"

"Yessir, but like I told them other policemen, I'll have it out times when I see them pesky squirrels and rabbits." Burt reddened. "Well . . . that night, I guess I left it . . . it's against the law, leavin' it out like that, but . . ."

"I'm not concerned with that, Burt. Only that anyone could have come to this outside door and taken it. The person didn't have to be someone with the key to unlock that cabinet."

Burt nodded. "I'm afraid so, sir."

"Didn't have to be anyone from inside the house, either. I assume that door is usually unlocked?" He didn't know why he was going through all of this. Oliver Stant had already made a meal of it.

"'Tis, sir."

They left the small room and walked back to the drive. Jury peered down the gravel. "You saw the Porsche sometime after midnight, did you?"

"I did. 'Bout half-past, it was. Wondered why it was parked at the bottom. Usually, that Miss Dunn parks it right near here, behind Mr. Owen's car. I go up to bed late, most nights."

Get in a little extra drinking time, thought Jury. Hard to blame him, out here in this unpeopled country. "They thought she'd returned to London."

Burt said nothing, just looked down the driveway.

But it was not Verna Dunn; it was Dorcas Reese he was thinking about. *"Why do people keep forgetting Dorcas?"* Or treating her as if she were an afterthought? "Did you work out who the man was Dorcas Reese thought would marry her?"

Burt was squinting, having a hard time even working out the question. "Can't say as I did. I never thought there was one, to tell the truth. Dorcas warn't near pretty, you know what I mean? Men, they'd not look twice at 'er."

It was the common assessment of Dorcas Reese and her chances with men. "You think she was making all of it up?"

Burt removed his cap, scratched his head, repositioned the cap. This took some thought. "Well . . . not making it *up*. Just making it *different*."

"Do you recall a period when Dorcas seemed happier than usual?"

Burt Suggins raised his cap, wiped his forehead, and readjusted the cap on his head. "Hard to tell if she was happy or just flighty, all that gigglin' like she'd got a secret. Pleased wi' herself, you know."

"When was that?"

Burt's eyes narrowed in concentration. "Not long ago, well, before that Dunn woman got herself shot."

That was what Annie had said. "Your wife Annie also said Dorcas's mood changed before she herself was murdered. Said she acted strangely. Morose, depressed—that sort of thing."

"Aye, that's true, that is. Not happy, not a bit of it." Burt looked off, shook his head.

"This man she seemed to think would marry her. Could he have given her the brush-off?"

"Coulda done, yeah. Like I said, she warn't a girl to attract the men. Any man'd mind."

"Perhaps one didn't." Jury was frowning. Had they all, with collective dimness, managed to turn this whole case the wrong way round?

⁂

I hope you don't mind my stopping in, uninvited."

Peter Emery smiled. "Wish more would. It gets lonely here." He paused. "Have you been watching the trial?" When Jury nodded, he went on. "'Tis awful." Peter frowned, shaking his head. "Crazy. Do you think she did it?"

It took Jury longer than he liked to say, "No. I don't think so." He paused and then asked, "You were here when Grace Owen's son died— Toby?"

"Aye. Nice lad, really nice. Horse threw 'im, they said. But it wasn't the fall killed him. It was this disease, this condition he had."

"Hemophilia. He bled internally. Verna Dunn was at Fengate when it happened."

Peter nodded. "Strange, her being here right after he married Grace. Mr. Parker said Max Owen divorcing Verna never kept her from stopping at Fengate. Mrs. Owen, she being the decent person she is, never raised a fuss."

Jury smiled. "Parker keeps you well informed."

Peter looked in Jury's direction and laughed. "Aye, he does that. If you'd ever spent a rough winter here you'd value a good fire and a chat, no matter who the listener or what the subject. I get to the point sometimes I'm talkin' to old Bob."

Jury looked around. "Where is old Bob? Where's Zel, for that matter?"

"She's outside with Bob. See one, you see t'other."

"Did you meet Verna Dunn through Major Parker?"

"Aye, but Fengate being so close, I'd've met her eventually, no matter who."

Jury smiled. "Fengate being close, or Verna Dunn being a wanderer? This was some time ago when she was Mrs. Owen?"

Peter's face clouded over, visibly darkening. "That's right."

"Do you know if Verna Dunn took a particular interest in Toby?"

Peter's face clouded. "Funny you'd ask that. I'll tell you this: Verna wouldn't care if the kid was fifteen or twenty years younger. He was a handsome lad. Looked like his mum . . ." Peter leaned forward. "Why you asking these questions, then? Are you saying Verna did something to cause that accident?"

"Just wondering."

Peter looked off in the direction of the windows and a failing light he could not see. His face was once again suffused with a dark anger. "I thought so," he said in a low voice.

"Did you? But you didn't say anything about what you thought, though."

Peter's short laugh was defensive. "Now, who'd've believed it if I did? And who was I t'say it to? Grace Owen? Would that have made her feel better?"

"No, but now, to the police——"

"Tell the police what? It's only my suspicion; I don't know anything. And it might make it look as if it was her killed Verna, as if it were Grace wanting revenge, and I'm not about to help police to thinking *that*."

"It would certainly be a strong motive. But a motive far more likely to occur at the time the boy died, not years later." Jury paused. "You have a .22 rifle, don't you?"

Peter nodded, getting up. "It's out back if you want to see it."

"Yes." Jury resisted the urge to help him. They walked back to the kitchen. "Police confiscated five different guns."

Peter laughed. "Well, now, I wouldn't call it *confiscating*. They're legal."

"Legal, all right. Shotgun and rifle certificates are thick on the ground around here. Max Owen has both. Can't imagine how he managed that."

"Suggins does a lot of rough shooting."

The room for rain gear and boots at the rear of the house looked much like the one at Fengate. Except here, the gun was locked into its steel box.

Without too much difficulty, Peter had the key out and had it open. He ran his fingers across stock and barrel, took down the rifle. "I expect in your line of work it's more handguns you see." Peter broke the barrel, handed it to Jury.

Jury looked it over, slapped it together, and opened the mudroom door. He raised the gun to his shoulder and sighted along the barrel. It was dusk, almost dark at five in the afternoon. Through the sight he could see a patch of the footpath and, way off in the blue distance, what he thought was the stone gate of Parker's house. He lowered the gun, broke the barrel, said, "It was black as pitch, I'd think, on the Wash." He paused. "You said Verna Dunn could shoot."

"Oh, yes. A surprising good shot, she was."

"You'd have to be to hit the target dead on in pitch-darkness."

Peter smiled. "That or awful damned lucky. Or maybe God was with them."

*

The air was as clear and sharp as glass. Zel was sitting on a log—lying, rather, across a section of bog oak that the farmers had dragged out of the ancient earth and hadn't got round to splitting for firewood yet. Her feet hung over one end, her head over the other. Her hands were laced across her stomach. Beside her sat the dog Bob, watching her and now Jury, who leaned against the crumbled wall, fallen into disuse.

Blood must be rushing to her head in that upside-down position. "Zel," he said.

She half raised up, enough to make out someone standing there. When she saw it was Jury, she said hello and let her head drop back down.

"What're you doing?" he asked.

"Waiting for stars."

The sky, a molten gray when he had entered the cottage, was turning quickly dark. "Mind if I sit down?"

Her head rolled from side to side.

"Can I take that as a No-I-don't-mind?"

"Uh-huh."

Jury knew that all of this must be rough on her. Two murders almost in her own backyard. Police come to question her uncle. Scotland Yard, even. How do kids deal with things like this? He sighed. The way they always have, he supposed. Deny it or turn it into something else.

At the moment, however, Zel appeared to be facing it head on. "I'm not sorry she's dead," she said suddenly and quickly, as if wanting to get the words out before she could assess the risk she was taking in uttering them.

Given her topsy-turvey position, Jury couldn't see into her eyes. "Who? You mean Miss Dunn?"

Impatiently, she said, "No, Dorcas."

"Did you know her well?"

For a moment she didn't answer. Then she raised her head again and said, "A little. She worked here some but then she stopped."

Jury was surprised. He didn't recall Plant telling him this. But perhaps Plant hadn't known. "Worked at what?"

"Cleaning and cooking. She was an awful cook. She couldn't even do boiled eggs right. And Uncle Peter likes boiled eggs done just right. He likes good cooking."

"You're certainly a good cook."

"Better'n Dorcas, anyway."

"But you didn't like her?"

Zel didn't answer except with a headshake.

"What was wrong with her? What didn't you like?"

"She was nosy. She—" Here she stopped, trying to puzzle out just what words would fit Dorcas's nosiness. "—wanted to *know* everything." Jury didn't immediately reply and she added, "She was always asking questions."

Nosy was the word Annie Suggins had used in describing Dorcas. Then he recalled Plant had said that Zel claimed to have seen Dorcas headed for Linus Parker's house. "Did she ask you about Mr. Parker?"

"Sometimes. She asked me things about myself, too."

"What things?"

"Where were my mum and dad."

"What did you tell her?"

"I didn't know, did I?"

The little shrug of her shoulders, the implication that, of course, she wouldn't know, struck Jury as infinitely sad.

"She told me I was an orphan. I said I wasn't because there was Uncle Peter. She said uncles don't count. She laughed at me thinking they did. She said if my uncle dies, I have to go to an orphanage." This had come out as though in one breath, hurriedly but with force. Then, on a less certain note, she added, "The Social can't make me do anything, can they?"

"No. Anyway, nothing's going to happen to your uncle."

There was a heavy silence.

Jury said, "I was an orphan, actually."

This was news that she seemed delighted to hear, for she sat upright. If it could happen to *him*, a Scotland Yard man, it could happen to anyone. And look at him; he'd turned out all right. Even Bob liked him; he was napping at Jury's feet. Still, Jury could tell she wasn't completely convinced.

She said, "The Social could make me live with some people I didn't even know."

"Zel, that's not going to happen."

"How do you know? Uncle Peter'll probably have to go for a witness."

"I don't think so, Zel. The people that the court wants as witnesses are more the ones who were at the house that night." Jury felt he wasn't making much of an inroad on her fear.

"Anyway," she said, her mind still locked on the dangerous doings of "the Social," "the Social can't get me because Mr. Parker will let me keep on living here. I know he will." She didn't sound so sure, though.

"You told Mr. Plant when he was visiting that day that you'd seen Dorcas go into Major Parker's house several times."

"I guess I did." She was sitting up now, batting a spitball-size piece of paper into the air. Bob had come sharply awake and was chasing the spitball.

"Why do you think that was? Could she have been doing the same work for him?"

"For Mr. *Parker*? Oh, don't be daft!"

Jury smiled. "That's daft?"

"But I just said she was a terrible cook! Do you think Mr. Parker would have her cook for him? She couldn't even make plum ice cream if her life depended on it."

"What about cleaning?"

"Mr. Parker has a proper char, and she's Dorcas's auntie. So why would he want Dorcas?"

Why, indeed. Jury was puzzled.

They were silent for a few moments, checking out the sky together. Then she asked, "Do you ever have to shoot people?"

"What? No. I don't carry a gun. Sorry."

She found this incredible. "You're a *policeman*."

"Sorry to disillusion you, but we only carry guns if we know we're facing a dangerous situation. And even then we have to sign out a weapon. Besides *that*, only certain of us are trained to use them. I'm in the Criminal Investigation Division. CID, we call it. There's a firearms unit and they're the only ones authorized to carry guns. And even *they* have to get permission from somebody higher up to use them." Jury wondered unhappily how long it would be until all policemen, down to the patrolling constable, would be forced to go armed. He turned to Zel. She looked awfully disappointed at this news about police. "Trouble is, you've been watching too many American cop shows on the telly."

Zel lay back again on the log, and Bob, wondering why the chase was done, came to sit again at Jury's feet.

Looking skyward at the stars, Zel pointed. "What's those ones?"

"Pleiades, I think."

"What are they?"

Jury searched through his meager fund of star-knowledge and answered, "The daughters of some god. They were turned into stars."

Zel was quiet, turning this fate over in her mind. She kept her gaze skyward. After a while she asked, "Where's that friend of yours?"

It was as if Melrose Plant were a constellation. "He had to stay in Lincoln."

Again, she was quiet. Then she said, "He kept trying to find out my name. He thought it was a nickname. You probably think so too." She turned to look at him. "You think Zel's a nickname." It was clear she expected better things from Scotland Yard than she did from her new garden-variety friend, Mr. Plant.

Silence fell as Jury discarded two or three obvious choices. Then he said, "Hazel."

That merited her full attention. "Hazel? *Haz-el?*" She thought this very funny. "That's not my name. I never knew anybody called *Hazel.*" She said this with a fair amount of contempt.

"It's a London name. It's popular there." Jury thought for a moment, then asked, "Did your mother have hair like yours, Zel?"

"Yes, only brighter." She pulled a strand over her shoulder, inspected it, and tossed it back. She could hardly have seen the color sitting here in the dark, but displeasure still graced her face. Not as pretty as mum's.

Jury said, "It's hard to imagine any hair brighter. Impossible." Carole-anne's perhaps, but then everything about Carole-anne was excessive.

"You're a policeman. You should be able to guess."

"Guess what?"

The look she gave him could have stopped a bullet. "My *name*. What we were talking about."

"I'll have to give it some thought."

She sighed. "Nobody will ever guess it."

Her sigh was truly disconsolate, as if the guessing of her name were the only thing to release her, as in the fairy tales she'd read, from the magic spell someone had wickedly cast over her.

34

$\mathbf{M}$r. Bannen, let's talk about Dorcas Reese now. What motive did the defendant have for getting rid of her?"

"That's even more difficult. Insofar as we know, the defendant and Dorcas Reese had never met before, and their relationship at Fengate was no more than that of guest and servant."

"That suggests there was *no* motive, doesn't it?"

"I didn't say that. None that we've discovered. Which is different."

"Do you believe the same person murdered both of these women?"

"I do, yes. Otherwise—"

Apted held up his hand, cutting Bannen off. "Then we should talk about Dorcas Reese, certainly, since, if we can show that Jennifer Kennington did *not* have any reason to murder Dorcas Reese, she would—according to what you've said—be innocent of the murder of Verna Dunn, is that not so?"

"I—"

"That is what you said, Mr. Bannen? That the same person committed these crimes?"

"Yes. I believe that to be true." For the first time, Bannen's face looked tight.

"Let's talk for a moment about this mistaken pregnancy. Dorcas Reese told her aunt and a friend that she was three months pregnant. Whether she was or not, if the supposed father of this child believed it and didn't want it, or didn't want to marry her—this person might well have had a motive, isn't that true? Especially if he were already married?"

"Yes, certainly. We've had no luck in determining just who this man is, though."

"I see. Then what about jealousy? Some other man who found Dorcas had been unfaithful?"

Bannen clearly didn't believe this, and said as much. "The Reese girl was not the sort who would attract many admirers, or inspire jealousy."

"Well, it doesn't have to be 'many'; one would suffice."

Melrose smiled at that. He looked at Jenny, then at Jury, who had returned from Algarkirk late last night and was now sitting beside him, unsmiling.

"Yes, of course," said Bannen. "But the witnesses we questioned—family, friends—were simply astonished to find the Reese girl was pregnant. The only one who suspected Dorcas might 'have a bun in the oven,' as she put it, was another young lady who worked at the same pub. Reese had told her aunt, Madeline Reese. And her friend, Ivy—"

"Ivy Enoch, the young woman who testified yesterday that she had no idea 'who the chap was'?"

"But that's not to say—"

Apted cut him off. The last thing he wanted was a freewheeling witness. Especially one as intelligent as the chief inspector. "You would not be inclined, then, to set down as a motive either frustrated love or a demand on Dorcas's part to marry."

"No, I wouldn't. I can't be sure, though."

"You're a fair man, Mr. Bannen. So we have a young woman who worked at Fengate strangled and dumped in a drain on National Trust property just two weeks following the murder of a well-known and glamorous woman, divorced wife and sometime actress, a name occasionally found in the tabloids. The second victim, Dorcas Reese, had for three days been given the task of taking tea or morning coffee to members of the household—the Owens, Lady Kennington, Verna Dunn. Now, put this together with Dorcas's strange words, uttered in the hearing of the cook, Annie Suggins: 'I shouldn't have done it; I ought not to have listened.' And Annie Suggins describes Dorcas as an overly curious, 'nosy' young woman. What do you make of all this?"

"I'd conclude that Dorcas Reese overheard something in the course of waiting upon Verna Dunn that was extremely dangerous. And that some third person caught her—Dorcas—at it, or found out in some way that Dorcas had overheard him or her. Understand, though, this is merely *one* scenario. There are others. Blackmail is always a possibility."

"Of course, except a person set on blackmail doesn't chastise herself because she's got the means to it. A blackmailer would hardly say, 'I shouldn't have done it.' Leave that for a moment. I believe you'd say that two things are still probably in any scenario: one, that Dorcas overheard something and, two, that she was murdered because she had this knowledge."

Bannen nodded. "It seems a reasonable assumption."

"Take the first point, Mr. Bannen. Your interpretation of 'I shouldn't have listened,' is that Dorcas overheard, in some way—perhaps standing with her tea tray outside Verna Dunn's door—she overheard a conversation."

Bannen nodded, but looked puzzled.

"Why?"

"'Why?' I'm afraid I don't—"

"Well, I merely wondered why you didn't interpret 'I shouldn't have listened' as meaning Dorcas thought she herself shouldn't have listened to a person speaking to her, giving her advice, possibly, and in taking the advice she wound up in trouble for it."

Bannen cleared his throat. "I see what you mean, yes. Well, of course that's quite possible."

"So Dorcas may not have heard anything at all related to Verna Dunn?"

"That's true. Yes."

"The second point—which, I admit, is not dependent upon Dorcas's having overheard Verna Dunn or anyone—the second point is that Dorcas was murdered because she knew something. She got in the way and had to be disposed of."

"I honestly think that's the most viable motive, yes."

"Again, why?"

Bannen was silent this time. And then with a cold smile said, "You tell me, Mr. Apted."

Pete Apted smiled. "Are you familiar with the hamlet of Cowbit?"

Bannen frowned, looked from the judge to Stant, who was also frowning and, Melrose supposed, would be on his feet in a moment. "Yes, but I don't see—"

"There's a cottage there with the name 'The Red Last.' A pub stood there once of that name—'The Red Last.' Now it's a private dwelling. What do you suppose that means, 'The Red Last'?"

Oliver Stant was up like a shot. "Your Honor, I can't see where this is leading."

The judge agreed. "Mr. Apted, is there a relevant question buried in your pub lore?"

"Yes, Your Honor; I just asked it. It's very relevant. If Your Honor could bear with me for a moment?" Without waiting to see whether the judge could or not, he returned to Bannen. "What does it mean?"

Bannen scratched his forehead with his thumb, smiling slightly. "Well, I expect it's something to do with shoes, Mr. Apted. The 'last' of a shoe. I don't know why the 'red,' though."

"Seeing the phrase out of context, that's a very understandable interpretation. It's what I said too, when I first heard it. But what if the word 'last' here means 'end' or 'the final one'? Say, in a game of chess, one might say 'The black goes first, the red last'?"

"*Mister* Apted, when you're finished . . ."

"I do apologize, Your Honor, but the matter of interpretation strikes me as all-important in this case. I merely wanted to demonstrate how things can get turned around. I'll proceed with the question—"

"We'd be much obliged," mumbled the judge.

"Chief Inspector, the question is: Why do you assume that the primary object of this double-murder was Verna Dunn? Couldn't it have been the other way round? That Verna Dunn was murdered because *she* knew something about Dorcas Reese, or Dorcas and another person; that it was Verna Dunn who 'got in the way'?"

"Yes, of course, that *could* be the case," said Bannen. His reluctance was evident in both his voice and in his posture. It was as if he couldn't comfortably arrange himself in the witness box.

"But you seem to have some doubt, Chief Inspector. Would it be fair to say this could just as *easily* be the case as the other? As the one you've so diligently put together?"

Bannen frowned. There was certainly more in that statement than he'd want to accede to—mainly that his entire investigation had got off on the wrong footing and it could easily walk off altogether. "Yes. I'd have to say that it could be either."

Apted smiled, standing squarely on his feet, arms akimbo, fists planted at his waist. Not precisely combative, not with that smile. "That rather alters things, wouldn't you say?"

Bannen's whole manner tightened, as if he'd subtly drawn himself in. For the first time, Melrose thought he saw the man repressing extreme anger. His control must be invaluable in his work, but was probably playing hell with his blood pressure. "If you're suggesting that I ignored evidence in the investigation of Dorcas Reese's death, I assure you, I did not."

"That was the farthest thing from my mind, Chief Inspector. I'm sure that your investigation into both of these women's deaths was thorough, that you in no way ignored other evidence that would have had you acting differently."

Bannen relaxed a bit, gave the court a rather cool smile. "Then I don't see it. I don't see that Dorcas Reese's being the primary target alters anything, really."

Yes, you do, thought Melrose.

"No?" asked Apted, feigning surprise. "What's altered, and *significantly* altered in the case before us, is the angle at which you viewed these events. What's altered is the conclusion you came to. The conclusion changes because now the defendant, Jennifer Kennington—" and here he paused rather dramatically as he looked at Jenny "—*has no motive,* at least insofar as this court has demonstrated. Jennifer Kennington had no reason to shoot Verna Dunn. If Verna Dunn had simply 'got in the way of' the killer, then she clearly was *not* murdered because of some alleged long-standing grudge or any fresh argument she might have been having with the defendant on the night she died. Perhaps Verna Dunn was murdered because of something she'd learned about Dorcas Reese."

"Further. If the defendant has no motive, then my learned colleague has no case. Your Honor"—quickly, Apted had turned his attention from the jury to the judge—"a question of law has arisen, which would best be heard in the absence of the jury."

The judge frowned, but gave directions to the court usher, who then led the jury from the courtroom. "Now, would counsel like to tell the court what's going on here?" His tone was acerbic and his smile icy.

Pete Apted returned a far friendlier smile. "Your Honor, I submit that there is no case to answer and that this case be dismissed for lack of evidence."

There was total silence as if the scene had been freeze-framed. Oliver Stant just stared at Apted, blinking. Even Charly Moss sat with her mouth open, astonished. *Dismiss?*

Impossible to say just how Pete Apted had done it, had broadsided them all, had pushed the chess piece to take out a rook and a knight and check the king. Oliver Stant seemed to have nothing to say.

Not only that, Apted had timed it perfectly, for it was by now four-thirty, time to get the hell out. The judge invited both counsel for the defense and the prosecution into his chambers, excused the jury, told the viewers to go home, and rose.

All rose with him.

Pete Apted didn't have to. He was already standing.

ઉ

Jennifer Kennington was discharged.

When the judge had retired to his chambers, Jury and Plant had retired to the Lion and Snake. They stood around one of the pillar tables where Charly Moss had just finished telling them what Apted had told her. Apted himself had returned to London.

The dismissing of the charges against Jenny Kennington did not mean that Chief Inspector Bannen was wrong; it simply meant the prosecution's case had been too weak to proceed. Oliver Stant argued that, motive aside, opportunity was exceedingly strong in both cases and that there was still enough motive resulting from the violent argument the two women had engaged in. Pete Apted had said the argument couldn't be characterized as "violent." Oliver Stant had tried to refute this.

There the judge had interrupted: *"I would suggest, Mr. Stant, that you discover the nature of this argument. We don't even know that. And absent that knowledge, together with the lack of proper procedure in that search of the defendant's house—I think the charges should be dismissed."* Charly was jubilant.

He had made it clear, though, that the case would be left on the court file; it could be reopened at such time as the prosecution would be justified in bringing further committal proceedings.

"Which means," said Jury, "that it isn't over. It's not an acquittal."

Charly took one of the cigarettes Melrose was offering and said, "I really think it's over for Jenny, Richard. *'Autrefois convict.'* What the Americans call 'double jeopardy.' Theoretically, the case could be reopened, yes. But it just doesn't happen that often in practice," she said, bending her head to the flame of Melrose's lighter. The fire suffused the hair she held back from her face. "Double jeopardy."

Melrose said, "At least one thing's been settled: she won't be going to prison for the rest of her life. Come on, Richard. That must please you."

Jury blushed. "Yes, of course it does."

Even as the pub appeared full-to-bursting, others jammed through its door. Plant had found a tall stool for Charly, but there wasn't enough space to use it.

Melrose shook his head. "She can't have done it. Even if she was lying about not going back to Algarkirk—" He stopped abruptly.

"'Going back'? Did I miss something yesterday?" Jury looked from one to the other.

"'Miss?'" said Charly, feigning wide-eyed innocence.

"Testimony. I have the feeling I missed something while I was at Fengate."

There was a silence.

"What?" Jury prompted them.

Charly fell to moving her glass around in damp circles. "Well . . ."

Melrose looked as if a memory suddenly struck him, unimportant as it might be. He snapped his fingers. "Oh, you mean that roadworks chap?"

And with a gesture, brushed the "roadworks chap" off the edge of the table.

"What 'roadworks chap'?"

Melrose lit a cigarette and studied it. "It was just something about Jenny saying she'd taken a detour. . . . A lot of boring testimony."

Jury looked at Charly. "Were you bored, too?"

Charly shook her head. Then she told him.

Jury said nothing for a while, then, "Pete Apted must have been mad as hell."

"Yes."

Why, he wondered, was he not really surprised? Because he'd suspected this after his talk with Jack Price. His friends both seemed to be waiting for him to explode, to do something. He only asked, "When will she be released?"

"She already has been." Charly was surprised they didn't know. "She said she was going back to Stratford-upon-Avon. I simply assumed—"

Jury's expression was tight, his voice harsher than he'd meant it to be. "No. We haven't seen her."

"I thought . . ." Charly dropped her eyes, raised them again, looking especially at Melrose, the one who was footing the bills.

"How does she intend to get to Stratford?" asked Melrose. "I'd assumed she could travel with me. As has been made painfully clear, we go the same route."

"I think she said something about the train."

"What time? There can't be more than one or two that would get her somewhere to make a connection to Stratford-upon-Avon."

"I don't know. She didn't say."

Jury excused himself, saying he'd be back in a bit. He made for the door.

"Where's he going?" asked Charly.

"My guess would be to the train station."

"He doesn't seem much relieved by all of this," said Charly, her head turned over her shoulder, watching Jury.

"Oh, he's relieved all right, but I can't say I blame him for being disappointed." Plant had his handkerchief out, mopping up a small puddle of beer from Charly's sweating glass before it ran off into her lap. "You did a wonderful job. Both of you." Charly said, "Thanks," but he thought that was probably more about wiping off the table than the "wonderful job." And she would turn every few seconds to watch the door Jury had left through, as if staring at it might bring him back. Melrose said, "I would have been glad to drive Jenny all the way home."

Charly Moss looked at him now quite squarely. "I know I'm asking a personal question, but both of you seem to be very . . . well . . . attached to Jennifer Kennington. Is this a long-standing friendship, or—"

"Love, you mean?" Melrose hoped he sounded convincing, to himself as much as Charly, saying, "No, we're old friends. Speaking for myself," he added.

"Speaking for Richard—?"

"Oh, I don't speak for *him*!"

35

The station was deserted. He could not find the stationmaster, could not find whoever was manning the ticket window, and when Jury finally managed to find the schedules tacked up on the wall, he could not make any sense of them. Train schedules, with their arrows pointing in both directions, might as well have been timetables to Hell or Heaven, his arrival at either purely arbitrary. If he ever got one of those cases in which a train schedule was the biggest clue, it would go unsolved.

He could make out that there were no trains directly to Stratford-upon-Avon; that didn't surprise him. So where would a traveler make a connection? Lemington Spa, Coventry? Warwick? All of these? Probably. She'd first have to go to London or Birmingham and change two or three times, he imagined. The trip would take over four hours; it was ridiculous. Especially since Melrose Plant was returning to Northamptonshire this evening and Stratford (as had been made obvious by the testimony about the detour) was veritably on his doorstep.

But that was the question, wasn't it? Why had she left this way? He told himself that there was nothing he should be doing penance for, that he'd done everything he could for her.

Why had he behaved so badly in the pub back there? Between them, Pete Apted and Charly had pulled off a coup. Jury knew that his ill-humor in the pub over the dismissal was caused by Jenny's not being acquitted; it had left all sorts of questions unanswered.

He understood now why Apted had wanted both charges brought, because to tear down one was to tear down the other. And it had been so simple, so obvious; oh, yes, that's always what people say once the trick has been exposed.

Jury slapped open the door to the train platform and stood in the gray evening looking up and down the platform. It was deserted too, save for a teenage boy down at the other end. Jury walked along the platform as if he were one more traveler impatient for his train. When he came to the end of the platform, he turned and walked back. Pacing, entertaining the notion of simply boarding the mystery train, the next train whose destination he didn't know.

What ingratitude on her part! With Melrose Plant footing the legal bills, my God, she could at least have said good-bye to him if not to Jury. He sighed. Indignation wasn't working.

The boy sat on the last bench, staring straight ahead, thumping his hands on the edge of the bench. His hair was sheared and dyed blue and purple; he was dressed in the usual teenage motley. Jury would have thought both haircut and clothes by now out of fashion. Beside him sat one of those boom boxes Jury was used to seeing in Oxford Street and Piccadilly. This kid had his earphones plugged in in an uncharacteristic gesture of consideration for those around him, but music still managed to leak out.

A wind blowing a gauzy rain in his face made Jury turn up his coat collar. He sat down on one of the fragile-looking benches and shoved his hands deep into his raincoat pockets, giving the impression of a man prepared to wait. *Determined* to wait, even though he knew she had probably already left. Inviting depression, as if he were doing penance.

As he reflected gloomily on Jenny's whereabouts, he became aware that the music in the background was actually a song being sung in French. He looked down the platform, toward what must have been the source of this music and saw the kid there had removed his earphones as if he meant to treat Jury to this *chanteuse*. It utterly surprised Jury that this kid with his wild clothes would be listening not only to such slow and mournful music but to mournful music in French.

Jury got up and walked slowly down the platform, confirmed that the music was coming from the kid's portable stereo. Beyond his phrase-book

French, Jury did not know the language. He listened to catch a word or phrase here and there:

". . . à l'amour . . ."

He could certainly understand that.

". . . Que je suis perdue . . ."

Lost. Yes, he could make that out. Plant should be here to translate, rather than back in the pub drinking beer with Charly. But he didn't really want it translated; it was actually this lack of understanding that made the song so poignant. The boy on the end of the other bench turned his head toward Jury, nodded, went back to listening. He was leaning forward, elbows on knees, his head down. Perhaps he thought they had this song in common.

He rose and walked back into the waiting room. Deserted as before. The music followed him, diminished slightly—the plaintive piano, the weeping violins sounded as if they'd taken up residence in Jury's mind.

"Je t'aime . . . adieu."

That was pretty clear. But the words in between might have been made on the moon. He stood staring at the pulled down blind of the ticket window, raised his fist to knock on the glass, then dropped it. What would he have asked, anyway?

". . . Que j'ai fini."

The end. The beautiful voice simply stopped, no longer offering whoever might be listening its protective warmth. Jury stood motionless in a moment of cold clarity. He knew the real source of the disappointment for both himself and Jenny: there had never been any declaration of innocence from her, just as there had never been any assurance from him, spoken with fervor, that he knew she was innocent.

Because he didn't know she was innocent, and she knew he didn't know.

And he still didn't know. *Amour. Adieu. Fini.*

Jury left the station.

ℐℐ

I owe you an apology, Charly," he said, back in the pub, which was less crowded now. They had found tall stools to park round the tall table.

Melrose Plant raised his glass. "I'll drink to that—"

Jury thought Plant did not seem to be focusing as well as usual.

"—and then we'll sing!"

Charly Moss giggled, coughed, aborted a sneeze all at the same time.

Melrose was trying out scales—"mi-mi-mi-mi-"—apparently tuning his voice.

"You're drunk," said Jury, in near-total wonder. "The both of you are drunk." He looked from one to the other. He had never seen Melrose Plant like this.

Charly made that sound through her nose again, as if Jury were the funniest thing in the world.

Jury shook his head, picked up his old glass, still with the dregs of ale in it, started for the bar, looked back and saw that the other two glasses were empty, and said, "Oh, what the hell," and walked back and picked up those glasses too.

He stood at the bar watching the pleasant, pretty, slightly overweight proprietress refilling the glasses. Then he turned and watched a sallow young woman feed some coins into the jukebox. Almost immediately, as if he'd just been waiting in the wings, out stepped Frank Sinatra belting out "My Way." Was there anyone more ego-affirming than Old Blue Eyes? Jury turned back to the bar, where the proprietress was topping up Charly's half-pint of Guinness. Drunker than a skunk that stuff would make her, *had* made her, he thought. As Jury was trying to get hold of the three glasses, Frank's voice was joined by others' that kept sliding in a beat too late to the close of the lines. Suspiciously familiar those voices sounded, and Jury saw that, yes, Sinatra's chorus was sitting at the table Jury had just left. He sighed and started back. Still hours to closing and they'd just got started.

> ". . . *each and every byyyyyyy-waaaay*
> *. . . dah dah dah* dahhh *. . . duh dah dah dahh . . .*
> *I did it myyyyyy waaaay.*"

Frank was out of a job in the Lion and Snake. The two did not stop upon Jury's return, only looked at him as if they had no idea who this was (this purveyor of drinks, this sober judge) and kept on singing along.

"People are staring," said Jury, drinking off a third of his glass and wondering how long it would take him to get to their level of drunk.

> "*I chewed it* up
> *And sssspit it* out!"

They certainly did. Jury got out his handkerchief and wiped his jacket. Actually, he rather liked the fact that the two of them were drowning out all of the unctuous talk of torts and codicils, deals and plea bargains. He had already finished his beer and was feeling, if not drunk, at least a little carefree.

Charly, actually, had a very pretty voice, almost professional sounding. Melrose was the laggard, the one who didn't know all the words and just *la-di-da'd* to fill in. Except he did know the finale, and when Frank socked it out, Charly and Melrose were halfway off their stools to join him. They collapsed, laughing. It didn't look as if Melrose would be leaving tonight for Northants.

Jury was surprised by the tap on his shoulder. It was the manageress, or bartender, or whoever she was, telling him *sotto voce* that his "friends" were being just a wee bit too loud, customers were complaining. Jury took out his ID, showed it to her with a smile, and said, "Look, they're celebrating. They've both just been acquitted of a really heinous crime—"

"Like singing?" She walked away.

36

He got to Stratford-upon-Avon shortly before ten P.M. and to Ryland Street fifteen minutes later. The town's one-way street system was more difficult to negotiate than most; make a wrong turning and you were halfway to Warwick. He supposed the town fathers had to work out something to accommodate the flow of tourist traffic, and this system was the one they'd devised. At last, he did find a parking space near the church and not far from Jenny's house.

Through the sheer curtains of the front window, he could see Jenny moving between kitchen and dining table. Late for a meal, he thought, but perhaps she'd missed dinner on the train or perhaps she hadn't been home long. She was wearing an apron and holding a glass of wine; in the next moment she was picking up a plate from the table where they'd shared a meal not long ago. Watching her as she carried the plate to the kitchen, he thought it was a homey scene, its domesticity almost a cliché.

Jury's coming here had been purposeful, at least he thought it had, but now he hesitated at the door, fell back into the misgivings he'd felt standing on the platform of the train station. Certainly, he had qualms about his reception. After all, if she'd wanted to see him, she would not have left Lincoln so hastily. He knocked.

When she opened the door and saw him there, her "Richard!" seemed spoken with delight, not dismay, but, he thought, with too much genuine surprise. Why should she be surprised that he had followed her? Her almost perverse refusal to acknowledge his feelings made him angry, but he tried not to show it.

Tried, but failed. "Why in hell did you run off that way?"

They still stood in the doorway. She was removing her apron. "Come on in. Have you eaten?"

He hadn't, but he was damned if he'd let a meal distract him. "Yes. Smells good, though." He felt the stiffness of his smile.

"*Pot au feu,*" she said, smiling and closing the door behind him. "Give me your coat. My lord, did you drive all this way . . . ?" The question trailed off, as if she wanted to ask him something but could only fall back on the obvious. She insisted on getting him some coffee and brandy, as if he'd caught a sudden chill. Perhaps he had. His fingers felt like icicles. He sat beside the fire, opposite the chair she'd obviously been sitting in before she got up to tend to the kitchen. In a moment she was back with two cups of coffee and a decanter on a tray.

"I wish to God I had a cigarette," Jury announced, taking his coffee and snifter. He sipped the brandy. Cognac, delicious. He might drink the entire bottle.

Jenny reached up to a shelf and took down a porcelain box. "You say it as if they'd stopped making them." Smiling, she held out the cigarette box.

Jury looked stupidly at the cigarettes and warded the box off with the push of a hand. "No, but I've stopped smoking them, remember?" He felt irrationally angry.

"I'd forgotten." She replaced the porcelain box. "Is that why you're so irritated?"

He nearly choked on the cognac. *Irritated!* When he'd recovered a particle of coolness, he said, "No, Jenny, that's not why. But I'm growing more 'irritated'—as you put it—by the moment. How can you smile like that?" The smile vanished, and that only stoked his anger, as if she were a mannequin, something soulless or mindless who only had to be told to do another's bidding and she'd automatically respond. "Jenny, why in hell did you run off that way?" He asked it a second time.

"I just wanted to get back here, that's all. Out of Lincoln. Surely, you can understand that."

Putting him on the defensive that was, making him appear a callous brute if he could make his own claim on her outstrip her own needs. And this was the problem, wasn't it? That his needs were not hers. She seemed honestly not to know why he—or Plant or Charly or anyone—would find it strange that she hadn't waited until she'd seen them. More than that, and perhaps worse, she apparently hadn't needed to see them. "There are some of us who were and are interested in your reactions to the trial." That was certainly pompous and stiff enough, he supposed.

"I'm sorry." She looked at her brandy snifter.

Did she fancy he'd driven from Lincoln to exact an apology? His hands were still cold, barely warmed by the cup or the glass. "We wanted to know how you felt. *I* wanted to know."

"It doesn't mean it's over," she answered with some trepidation.

"It's most unlikely the prosecution will bring further committal proceedings," he said, echoing Charly Moss's words, though perhaps not her certainty. For an instant, and against his bidding, a smile materialized on his face and quickly fled. It was the memory of Melrose and Charly out on the pavement, staggering along, still singing. He knew that image would stay with him for a long, long time. And that it would always make him smile. And he thought, further, about that unfortunate meeting of the three of them at Stonington, when Jury had come upon Jenny and Melrose by accident. Innocent as it all was, Melrose Plant had assessed Jury's state of mind in a heartbeat. No, more than that: he had *felt* Jury's feelings. He had simply known, in a way that Jenny hadn't.

"You're amused. Why?"

"What? Oh, just something about Melrose Plant." He asked, "Didn't you think Pete Apted did a remarkable job?" Was he criticizing her for not being grateful enough? Yes, he supposed he was.

"He's remarkable. It's just that I was hoping I'd be—" She moved her shoulders in a small shrug, bent her head over the glass.

"That you'd be acquitted, I know. Who can blame you? Short of that, though, a dismissal was the best thing that could have happened. I don't see how you could have been cleared in the absence of any other suspects."

She did not answer immediately; she gave him a speculative look.

"If I'd come up with anything, I'd certainly have passed it along to Bannen." He hated this feeling that he'd failed her.

Again, she was silent. Then she said, "I think I should go away from this place." A silly-looking shawl hung over the arm of her chair; she picked it up and wrapped it around her.

Jury felt the chill again. "I don't understand."

"I think it might do me good simply to leave here."

"Go away from here, well, possibly. Turn up, though, *where?* That's the problem. At least for me, it is."

Jenny pulled the shawl so tightly about her, it might have been a second skin. She seemed to want it to be, as if the first one were not enough to protect her. A log sparked, crumbled, collapsed, throwing embers on the hearth, which she shoved back with the toe of her shoe.

Jury felt a similar collapse of his resolve. Or, rather, of its strength to sway her. Behind her gentle, almost quiescent manner, she had great determination. He could sense, could feel her withdrawing in the same way he felt it years ago in Littlebourne churchyard where they were separated by the length of a grave. He was afraid they were still separated by a grave. He waited for her to return to the subject of the trial, but she didn't. They sat with their coffee and cognac on either side of the fireplace, she gazing into it; he, watching her. He wondered how she could so seal herself off from people.

And he counted back and realized he had actually seen her a mere handful of times in the ten or more years he had known her. He knew, really, little about her. It was with a kind of cold clarity he realized that this silence of theirs now was not the comfortable silence of old friends who had no need to speak in order to feel close to one another. He felt their separation acutely; the silence stretched between them filled with unspoken words—of blame, or hope, or desolation—like white noise.

But if these unspoken words bothered her, there was no way of knowing it. That was just the trouble. He was apparently not attuned to her feelings, when feelings were what he was very good at decoding. Had it always been like this? Probably, but obscured by his own willingness to talk about himself. There had never been from Jenny such a monologue as he himself had spoken just a few weeks before, about his childhood, his parents' deaths. It came with a small shock, the realization that he knew nothing about her that hadn't been immediately evident: that is, the death of her husband, the move from Stonington, the taking up of quarters here in Stratford-upon-Avon.

Jury drank off his cognac and sat looking at her, and if she knew he was looking, she gave no sign. She seemed totally immersed in whatever pictures the flames were casting up. Discomfort turned to desperation; he could feel whatever had been there slipping away, and he was at a loss to account for this and knew that if asked, she would look at him in dumb surprise. He could not rely on their long and close association, for it hadn't been long even though it had covered a number of years, and now he was forced to admit to himself that it hadn't been close. It was probably this desperation that got him out of his chair and in a step across to hers. He held out his hand and with a smile that was truly inscrutable, she let him pull her up and more than let him kiss her—more than "let"—then she sighed, reached her arms even more tightly around him, and laid her head against his shoulder. He had the strangest sense of her insubstantiality, as if she were not flesh and blood, but a figure in a Magritte painting, walking away through cloud banks.

Saying to him: "But there's no reason, is there, we can't occupy ourselves while you're doing all of this thinking?"

Even though her face was buried on his shoulder, he could sense her smiling. "I can't think of one."

Insubstantial as she might have been, still she led the way upstairs.

*

Physical love (he had told himself) would bridge the distance, but he hadn't believed it then and didn't now. On their backs they lay looking at the ceiling.

Not a word had been spoken except for a few endearments, and he wondered now if each of them was waiting for the other to speak. For the other to make something out of their being in bed together. To explain it. All he could think to say was "Don't go, Jenny."

"I feel I have to, after all of this."

There was no negotiating, no argument.

Yesterday, this morning even, he might have said, *Stay here and marry me*, but not now. "I don't understand," he said for the second time, and said it almost to himself as well as to her.

"I think you do." Her head turned sideways, studying him.

"No." He shook his head.

There was a long silence, and he again became aware of the problem: she had never, during the whole course of the trial, said she was innocent. He had never asked her. He thought it, but it was Jenny who said it.

"You'd never be sure about me; about my relationships to—other men. You'd never be certain that I didn't do it."

"That's ridiculous." He said this with great feeling, knowing he was lying.

"Then why don't you ask it?"

He paused. "I shouldn't have to."

"You mean, I should have told you."

Jury closed his eyes, letting the web of shadows on the ceiling go. "I mean, you shouldn't have to."

There was more silence, finally broken by Jenny. "The argument with Verna? Do you want to hear what that was really about?"

"Of course." He could not help the tinge of sarcasm. "I'd have liked to hear that the first time you told me."

His tone did not daunt her. "It began with Jack Price, you see. That's where I was; I wasn't on the footpath. That's why Major Parker didn't see me."

Hell, thought Jury. Then, the cop got the better of him, and he asked, "Why in God's name didn't Price *say* so."

"I didn't want him to. It had nothing to do with these murders, and it wouldn't have given me an alibi."

"God, you *amateurs* who make your own rules! If Bannen had known that, he would have had a completely different—" Jury stopped, heaved a long sigh. What difference did it make now?

"I just didn't want anyone knowing. I have that right, haven't I?"

The question was rhetorical. "And Verna Dunn?"

"Told me they were having an affair, had been for some time. Well, I imagine she was lying, Jack certainly denied it—"

"When you got together on the Tuesday night?" His tone was bitter.

"Yes. We met in Sutterton. I felt . . . I felt I needed—I don't know. Comfort, reassurance—I don't know. I've known him for a long time."

"Are you in love with him?"

"I . . . don't know."

Somehow, that made Jury angrier than a simple "yes." He sat up, put out his hand instinctively for the cigarettes on the nightstand, realized it wasn't his nightstand and that there were no cigarettes. He sighed. How was he supposed to get through such moments without one? He put his head in his hands, stupidly unsure which was the greater need: a disclaimer from Jenny about Jack Price, or a cigarette. "How can you *not know*, Jenny?"

She didn't answer. There was no answer. Instead, she lifted her hand and waved the question away, as if she were clearing smoke.

Jury raised himself. "Why all of the secrecy? Why didn't you say you knew Verna Dunn even if you didn't want to admit knowing Price? I can see her not doing it simply because deception seemed to be her meat and drink. But *you*—it just doesn't make sense. You don't play mind games."

"I wanted to find out what she was up to."

He knew that wasn't so; she'd just made it up. "I don't believe that, Jenny."

She sat up, threw an old chenille robe round her shoulders. There was a hard edge to her voice when she said, "You think I'm lying?"

"Yes." Jury lay there, looking at her, at her angry face.

Jenny said nothing; she got out of the bed and thrust her arms into the robe, tied it in front. Then she said, "You don't know what the answer is, do you? Whether I'm innocent or guilty."

"Listen, love: I don't *care* what the answer is. It's the fact you won't *give* me an answer—yes, that hurts." Jury pulled his legs from the bed, sat on the edge. He picked up the wrinkled shirt and pants that had fallen in a heap from a side chair. He pulled on the trousers, then socks. "You must not trust me very much," he said, feeling inexpressibly sad as he might do if he were about to lose something.

"Trust works both ways. You must not trust *me*," she said, not looking at him.

"No. I expect I don't."

That truly stung. "What happened to what they call *autrefois convict*? Double jeopardy, isn't it? I feel I'm being tried again."

He was sitting now on a little slipper chair, a shoe dangling from his fingers. Sadly, he shook his head. "No. You should know the difference, Jenny."

"Between what and what?"

"Between love and the law." He smiled a little, unsure of what he meant by that. *Amour, adieu, fini.* His throat constricted, felt crammed with unspoken words. He shut his eyes, tightly.

"I don't know what you mean." She pulled the tie of her robe tighter as if she'd cut herself in two. "Would you like a cup of tea?"

That did it. Jury burst out laughing. The British way of coping with love routed, with loss, with blackspot on the roses.

There'll always be an England, he thought.

Part IV

Helluva Deal!

37

"Permission to treat as hostile, Your Worship," entreated Mr. Bryce-Pink, solicitor for the plaintiff.

Oh, for heaven's sake, thought Melrose, just because he'd stonewalled old Bryce-Pink about his, Melrose's, questionable vision. And who wouldn't be hostile when it came to Agatha, except for that snake Theo Wrenn Browne? But then he had something to gain from all of this foot-in-the-chamber-pot business.

Melrose cast his eyes about the room. The court was in Sidbury. He saw most of Long Piddleton had turned out in flowery regalia as if the *Ardry vs. Crisp* case were ushering in the flower show. Melrose wriggled the well-shod foot that rested on his other knee and waited to be treated as hostile.

The magistrate, Major Eustace-Hobson, raised his drooping eyelids, waved his small, white hand at Bryce-Pink, giving that permission.

"Let me ask you again, Lord Ardry, as you were standing on the opposite pavement in direct view of Lady Ardry, who stood herself in front of the defendant's shop, with the dog theretofore seated on a chair taking the sun—"

Melrose turned to the magistrate. "Question! May I ask for the question, Your Worship?" Watching Pete Apted in action had taught him things.

Eustace-Hobson had been sitting with his head resting on his fist, eyes half-closed against the glare of injustice (Melrose liked to think), and nor did he change that position as he said, "Lord Ardry, try to remember you are not here as counsel, but as *witness*. However, as counsel for the defense sees fit to let any irregularity pass him by, yes, I judge it prudent at the moment to allow—"

What was the *matter* with these people? Couldn't they make a point within the time it would take to get to the Inns of Court and back?

"—you to ask for the question."

Marshall Trueblood was sitting beside Ada Crisp and looking absolutely spectacular in a three-piece pinstripe suit of fine wool silk by some Italian designer, not, for a change, Armani. Armani (Trueblood had told him) was too comfortable-looking. His shirt was actually white— Melrose didn't know he owned a plain white shirt—and he wore a gray tie of some exquisite silk dashed here and there with watery color. Trueblood had not risen once to object, not even when that asp Theo Wrenn Browne had sworn up and down he had seen numerous mishaps caused by the "rubbish" outside of Ada Crisp's shop and the dog barking day in and day out, snapping at passersby. *"A disgrace, a danger to us who use the pavement, a danger to life—"*

Blah, blah, blah.

Trueblood had let the maligning of the poor dog sail right by. The dog wasn't on trial, was it?

". . . and only twenty feet away, Lord Ardry?"

"Huh?" Melrose jerked himself back to never-never land. "Oh, you mean a clear and unobstructed view straight across the street?"

Bryce-Pink was wary. "Uh . . . indeed."

"Yes, well you must remember that this is the main street we're talking about and there are cars whizzing up and down it—"

"Poppycock!" exclaimed Agatha, half rising from her chair.

"Madam!" said the magistrate, with a bang of his gavel, "kindly refrain from these outbursts!" It wasn't the first time Agatha had shouted her objections.

"But he's just trying to muddy things," she said now. "He's just messing us about, don't you see—?"

"Lady Ardry, sit *down*." This was accompanied by some gavel-banging. "Bryce-Pink, please control your client."

She was as red as a beetroot, Melrose was happy to see. He said, "I was merely attempting to answer the question, Your Worship, as honestly as I could—"

Eustace-Hobson was not unimpressed with a title, even though Melrose had left his in the dust over a decade ago. But the "Lady" Agatha had adopted was, the magistrate knew, completely spurious. Melrose's uncle had been an "Honorable" but that was all. Eustace-Hobson nodded at Melrose to proceed.

Melrose found he was getting just like the rest of them; he forgot what his point had been, and so blamed the losing of it on Agatha's solicitor. "Please put your question again, Mr. Bryce-Pink."

Leveling a knifelike glance at Melrose, Bryce-Pink said they'd been talking about the witness's having a clear view of Miss Crisp's shop, and consequently of the "accident." And did he understand the punishment for perjuring himself?

"Oh, absolutely."

Bryce-Pink looked at him warily, again. "Continue, please."

"With what?"

The solicitor bared his teeth, reminding Melrose of the dog Bob.

"Your *position* in the High Street with relation to your aunt's. And don't"—now he was whining—"try to convince us that this was a dangerous intersection."

"Very well, only I've often thought there should be a zebra crossing right there. It would be a great help to the elderly and"—he smiled at Agatha, whose color was not improving—"baby prams."

Bryce-Pink, who had been keeping his distance from the witness, now got up quite close to Melrose. "Lord Ardry, I ask you again and, I hope, for the last time: did you or did you not see Lady Ardry stumble over a wooden chair left on the pavement by the defendant, stumble, and get her foot caught in a chamber pot?"

"Ummmm . . . Something like that, yes."

Bryce-Pink shut his eyes tight. "No, not 'something like that,' but *exactly* like that!"

Why wasn't Trueblood objecting, for God's sake? He'd hardly said *Boo!* since Bryce-Pink had started in. Trueblood just sat there beside Miss Ada

Crisp, smoothing his tie. Melrose took it upon himself to say, "Your Worship, I must protest at counsel's trying to put words in my mouth. Isn't that 'leading the witness'?"

"Kindly allow the witness to answer, Mr. Bryce-Pink."

Bryce-Pink groveled a bit, then said: "Perhaps, Lord Ardry, you will be good enough to answer 'yes' or 'no.' That's all. A simple answer will do. Now, did you see this accident to Lady Ardry occur?"

Melrose screwed up his eyes, as if thinking furiously. "Well, yeeee-yes, if you put it that way."

"Well, you either did or you didn't, so your 'yes' I shall take to mean you did. Again, a simple answer will do: you did see this lady"—he turned to indicate Agatha—"stumble, and her foot go into the chamber pot."

"True, but—"

"That will be all, Lord Ardry."

Melrose stepped down, but not before he leveled a black look at Marshall Trueblood.

❧

D<small>r.</small> Lambert Leach took the stand, pushed his thick spectacles up the bridge of his nose, and squinted out over the room. Dr. Leach was called upon by the villagers only if they were *in extremis*.

"Dr. Leach, you attended Lady Ardry, the plaintiff, shortly after this unfortunate accident, did you not?"

"I did." Dr. Leach looked out from glasses so thick they magnified his own eyes. He made a long scrutiny of his alleged patient. "Terrible shape she was in. Good thing they got to me when they did, even if it caught me square in the middle of my boiled egg; good thing, for I doubt she'd have lasted the ni—"

Realizing Dr. Leach had got his cases confused, Bryce-Pink rushed in to trample his words. "Quite so, quite so. Now, Dr. Leach, please describe Lady Ardry's condition. I mean the condition of her ankle."

Dr. Leach looked across at Agatha, probably trying to remember. Then he said, "Awful, it was. Terrible."

"Sprain, you mean?"

Trueblood, object!

Enlightened, Dr. Leach nodded vigorously. "Worst I ever did see. Worst."

"And what did you have to do in addition to bandaging it?"

"Give her pain pills. Oh, yes, she was awful bad. I told her to keep off her feet, put that foot up."

"For how long was she thus incapacitated, Dr. Leach?"

"Days." Dr. Leach bethought himself. "Weeks—" Before he could change that to "*months*," Bryce-Pink quickly excused him. "Your witness, Mr. Trueblood."

Trueblood rose, cool as a cucumber. "No questions at this time." He sat down.

Melrose was getting ready to throttle Trueblood. *Good God! You call that medical testimony? Ask about the X-rays, at least!*

But Eustace-Hobson decided they were all ready for their lunch, banged his gavel briefly, and looked with infinite kindness upon Trueblood, who, at this point, probably could have won by default.

♫

"Y̶ou didn't even call old Leach, for God's sake," exclaimed Melrose. The Jack and Hammer being out of the question in this instance, as were any of the Sidbury pubs, he and Trueblood were sitting in the Blue Parrot, chosen because no one else— in his right mind, Trueblood had added— would see them here. They were sitting as far from Trevor Sly as they could get. At the moment, he was back in the kitchen preparing their lunch.

Melrose went on, seeing he hadn't dented Trueblood's equanimity. "The man's memory has atrophied. At first, he wasn't even talking about Agatha; he was onto some case he'd probably had fifty years ago. His last case, no doubt—no, this is *his*—" Melrose said as Trevor Sly had put down their plates. Of something. Melrose shoved the Kibbi-Bi Saniyyi— the alleged Arabian dish—in front of Trueblood.

"Careful, hot plates!" Dangling his potholder from delicate fingers, Sly went humming off.

"You could have made mincemeat of him!" Melrose protested, pushing his fork toward Trueblood's plate. "You could have made Kibbi-Bi-blah blah stuff of him."

"Anyone could have," said Trueblood, ignoring his food and lighting up a turquoise Sobranie. "That's the point, old sweat. Why should I lower myself?" He inhaled deeply, then blew the smoke away from Melrose.

"Lower yourself? *Lower yourself*?" Melrose dropped his cutlery and raised his hands to heaven. "That's absolutely insane! You're Ada's legal representative!"

Trueblood flicked a bit of ash from his waistcoat. "It made me look the humanitarian, not driving questions into old Leach's heart like nails, don't you see? I mean, if I'd needed to tear his testimony to shreds, of course, I would have. But I didn't."

Melrose took a tentative bite of his lunch. Supposed to be a kind of lamb curry, it was instead, as he'd suspected, beef mince. "You're not cross-examining anybody! You're just sitting there! I need some ketchup."

Trueblood shoved over the plastic condiment bottle, shaped like a little Sphinx. "You haven't even heard my side of things, old bean-o; wait till this afternoon. I simply wanted to see how many irons old Bryce-Pink had in the fire. None, it would appear."

"None? He's got me! You can bet he'll bring me back!"

"Oh, don't get out of sorts. Have a Cairo Flame. Mr. Sly!"

38

The next morning Jury was sitting on a bench in Lincoln Headquarters, waiting for Chief Inspector Bannen to get off the telephone and summon him to his office. To his desk and assorted chairs, really, rather than "office." Finally, he hung up and waved Jury over.

"Mr. Jury. I'm surprised that you're still around."

"Why? It's the same old problem, but with a different spin."

Bannen smiled. "Perhaps different. After all, Mr. Apted could be dead wrong." He said this without any trace of irony or of anger.

"You're in a good mood, considering."

"Considering what? That I lost, you mean?"

"Not exactly. More an investigation going on for six weeks that you must have been glad to be shut of."

Bannen scratched the back of his neck with an index finger, more from habit than from discomfort. It was a mannerism he engaged in when he grew thoughtful. He didn't speak for some moments, and then said, "I shouldn't've allowed it to go to trial so soon. I was precipitate."

"*You* shouldn't have? It wasn't your decision; it was the court docket."

"Hmm. Yes, except prosecution would have considered a delay if I'd so indicated."

"Now what?"

"Well, of course, I keep on, don't I? It's a matter of realigning the facts."

"Do you still think Jenny Kennington is guilty?"

"Do you?" Bannen gave Jury one of his ironic little smiles. His eyes seemed opaque, impossible to read. They gave nothing away.

"You talked to the Reese girl's parents—?"

"Yes, initially, of course. They didn't inspire me with their testimony."

"Do you mind if I talk to them?"

"Not at all, just so long as you keep me apprised of anything interesting they might have to say. But I rather doubt it."

♫

Spalding, which lay some ten miles south of the Owens' house, was at the center of this tulip-growing industry; otherwise, it was much like any other largish town. Shops and businesses around a central square or at least a green piece of land, a complement of pubs and caffs, a post office, a hospital. The Welland, which coursed through part of the town, divided the traffic going to and from, and with its green banks leant to the scene the look of an esplanade, the sort one sees in spa towns, Harrogate or Leamington, where people go to immerse their weary limbs in healing waters.

The Reeses' house was semidetached with a high-pitched roof, the bottom part of which nearly covered the eyebrow windows. It was like the others on this side of the street, except for the goblins in the garden. Jury wondered what mind-set one must have to hanker after plastic gnomes and pink flamingoes, especially near beds of bulbs that would, this time next month, be a fiery glow of apricot, orange, and flame-red tulips.

He was met at the door by Mrs. Reese, with whom he'd talked that morning. She was a plain-faced, stout woman who could only have been the mother of Dorcas, so much did they resemble one another. She was one of those rigid housekeepers with rules to follow. She asked him to use the bootscraper and finish off with the doormat before he entered. He might be a Scotland Yard superintendent, but the same mud clung to his shoes as to other people's.

Jury had seen a hundred Colleen Reeses in the course of his investigations. Women with an inquiring eye, but not blessed with much intelligence; a combative or contentious spirit; red hands that had seen too many dishes and had always kept the house too clean for enjoyment. He looked around the parlor, feeling he had seen it all many times over: the faded flowered slipcovers, the shelves of painted china, the fringed lamp-shades, the flowered curtains, the imitation coals aglow in the clean, cold fireplace, probably turned on just before his arrival to save on the electric. The room was cold.

Once she'd told him where to sit, he did so and accepted a cup of tea and a biscuit though he was dying for strong black coffee. It was the house of a smoker, too, worse luck, for there were ashtrays on every surface. Given Mrs. Reese's inclination toward cleanliness, that surprised him. Or perhaps this room was the smoking-zone. Framed photos depicted Dorcas at various stages of her life, and Jury was once again brought up short by the transience of that life. The moments captured by the camera's lens were as insubstantial as shadows and as fleeting as light.

He had called the Reese home before he'd left Lincoln, and so she'd been waiting for him with the Sunday china and a tin of biscuits. He felt a little cowardly to be relieved that over a month had passed since the girl's death, and the worst of Colleen Reese's tears had been shed. Yet, she struck him anyway as a woman who wouldn't let emotions get the best of her.

She said she had told everything she knew about Dorcas "to that Lincolnshire lot" (the Spalding and Lincoln police), but that he—Jury—might be better able to make something of it, "you being Scotland Yard." This was a much more generous view of Scotland Yard than he was used to.

Sentiment far outweighs honesty in talking about a dead child, and Dorcas's mother was no exception. "She were a good girl, our Dorcas," had been repeated several times while Jury sat drinking tea. "A good girl, Dorcas," said Colleen, again. "Sorry I can't say the same for our Violet." Yet she smiled pertly when she said this, as if Violet had bested her sister in some way. Jury imagined that Dorcas's goodness and the other girl's lack of it had to do more with one being dead and the other living.

With that sentiment expressed, she handed Jury one of the several silver-framed photos, this one of the girls together. Violet was prettier, he supposed, but vapidly so. "'Dorcas shy, Violet sly,' that's what we all said." She pointed out to him that it rhymed.

Jury smiled and thought it might rhyme but it was hardly accurate. One thing Dorcas hadn't been was "shy." He carefully advanced on the subject of her daughter's saying that she was pregnant. Mrs. Reese's face went quite blank, scrubbed clean of emotion.

"That weren't like our Dorcas."

"I'm sure it wasn't. Probably it was just—" Just what? he asked himself. Just a one-night stand? Just an accident? Can the lost virginal world of childhood be "just" anything?

"Fate," he said.

Colleen was fully cooperative again. "It's what I told Trevor—that's Mr. Reese—'twas meant to be and who knows but what her saying she was preggers warn't the hand of Fate slapping sense into her. It's the good'uns gets caught, but I expect you know that, being in your line of work. I never wanted her autopsied because I didn't want it getting round that Dorcas—"

"But now we know she wasn't pregnant."

Colleen pressed the fist holding the balled-up handkerchief to her mouth. "No, but why'd she lie and say she was, that's what I can't make head nor tail of."

"Perhaps she wasn't lying; it could have been she really believed it. Or, it could have been wishful thinking or a lever to get whatever man she'd fallen for to marry her. It's hardly a new trick."

Colleen sniffed, pulled herself up in her chair. "Not very clever, that. Well, I don't wonder but that's the reason she got killed. I told Dorcas her making up stories would get her in trouble one day." A fresh wave of tears swelled, and Jury moved a box of tissues from the table beside him to the one at her elbow crowded with pictures of the past. She thanked him and dabbed at her eyes. "She was rebellious, was Dorcas. Tested the boundaries all the time."

Jury hid a smile. Colleen must have been reading books about adolescence. Dorcas was a little old to be testing her boundaries. "In what way, Mrs. Reese?"

"Things like not going with the family to Skegness. We done that every year for the last fifteen. Whenever Trevor gets his holiday. Vi, too, now she's been working. It's a sort of tradition, if you see what I mean. We're always down for the same rooms at Seagull's Rest every year. Mrs. Jelley says she always thinks of them as being our rooms, nobody else's, and she puts us down for next year while we're there. Same room and board for us, never more'n a hundred seventy quid. Can't do fairer than that, I always tell Trevor. . . ."

Jury let her ramble on about Seagull's Rest, reflecting on Skegness and how unspeakably dull it would be, as routine as home, especially for a young girl who'd be wanting discos or drinking beer on the terrace of a pub, all of these pastimes involving sex in some significant way. How pleasant it would be to stay home and not have Mum or Dad around to tell you what to do or Violet to compete with. He could hardly blame Dorcas for "revolting." Skegness. Even Jury thought he'd sooner stay home.

". . . and Dorcas wasn't like Violet. Our Vi always has some young man hanging about. I don't mean to speak ill of my own child, but Dorcas wasn't that pretty, you see. The men weren't after her like they are Violet. That's not her real name; it's Elspeth, after Trevor's mum. But she hates that name, always has, so she ups and tells us her name's 'Violet' from now on, and 'not a shrinking one, neither,' that's how she put it; Vi's the clever one." Here, Colleen set off on a cruise around Violet's many virtues.

Jury let witnesses take their own line. It was in such unguarded talk that they very often gave the game away. Violet with all of her boyfriends, Dorcas with none.

". . . and you can imagine that made Dorcas a mite jealous."

"Yet there was some chap, if not actually 'hers'—one whom she very much cared for."

Vigorously, Colleen nodded. "I don't think she was lying about that, Inspector. Why, she'd been ever-so-sprightly for weeks a while back, not like herself at all."

"That's what Mrs. Suggins said. The cook at Fengate. That Dorcas had seemed quite the happy girl, but recently rather glum and nervous. Can you think of anything that would account for these changes of mood?"

Smartly, she shook her head. "Not besides whoever this man might have been, I can't. And whatever he actually did, I couldn't say. And it's true, a week or two before she—died, she'd got awful snappish with us. More like the old Dorcas. What I thought was, her and her young man had a spat. I mean, if there *was a* young man."

"Yes, I'd say so. I can't believe it was all wishful thinking, but whether he was aware of her feelings, well, that's something else again." Out in the kitchen, a kettle sang.

Colleen looked over her shoulder. "Never mind, it'll turn itself off. Don't know what I ever did before we had this electric one."

"Don't let me keep you," said Jury, starting to get up.

Quickly, she motioned him back down. "No, no. It's finished and Trevor'll be home any moment now. And Violet with him. They always come back about this time for their tea." She paused and pursed her lips, considering. "Look here, we've plenty for an extra to tea, and police got to eat like the rest of us, so why don't you stay?"

"That's very kind of you, only—"

"Well, I expect your missus is a better cook than I am," she said with a particular look, a coy movement of her head.

Jury almost laughed. Here was a new straw to grasp at! Jury told her the good news. "I'm not married, Colleen."

She chirped out a few blandishments, "Good-looking man like you, girls must be blind!" She went on in this vein while Jury considered taking her up on her offer simply to stay longer and talk to husband Trevor and the sister. But the alternative to any talk of substance was they'd spend their time round the dinner table with the mum on and on about Violet's talents, thus far untried by marriage.

Jury thought for a moment, then said, "It's only just occurred to me. Not only could Dorcas have believed she was pregnant, but there is such a thing as a false pregnancy."

"A *what?*"

"Women can actually conjure up a pregnancy. They even have all of the side-effects that come with a real one: morning sickness, bloating, and so forth."

Colleen's hand was at her cheek, where a pinkish blush spread. "Does it go on, then, for the whole nine months?"

"I don't know; I rather think not."

"And you think our Dorcas was going through something like that?"

"I've no idea. If she deluded herself that she was pregnant, it shows how much she wanted a child."

A cutoff laugh from Colleen. "Not her! She was always complaining about her friend Sheila's nappies and her having to get up at all hours night and morning. No, Dorcas was never looking forward to being a mum."

Jury leaned toward her in his chair. "But she must have been looking forward to something, Colleen. Marriage perhaps. Getting this man she might have thought was the father." He was interrupted when the front door opened in a flurry of feminine giggles. The grunts (Jury imagined) came from Trevor, the father.

Violet breezed in—the expression really fit, thought Jury, not because she was lithe and limber, but because she seemed insubstantial. She fluttered and floated to various surfaces—the hall table where she roughed up the post to see what had come for her; to the dining room table to see if she liked the look of her tea; to the mirror over the mantel to see if she liked the look of herself. Yes. She tossed her flyaway, weightless light brown hair back over her shoulder. The face was pretty, yet without a hint of character, just as it appeared in the photograph. She was plump, but lacked density. Finally she fluttered to the sofa and fell softly into it like a sack of cinders.

Trevor, his face like a flatiron, had stopped in the doorway and been introduced. Unimpressed by Scotland Yard, he asked only if his tea was ready.

Not so, Violet. She was impressed enough for both of them. "You been talking about Dorcas, haven't you? I'd just like to say it's disgraceful that woman got off with not even a slap on the wrist! I just want to go on record." She must think Jury was the press.

Mildly, Jury said, "There wasn't enough evidence to convict her. She's probably innocent."

Violet made a dismissive gesture with her fingers. "It's them as has money that never gets convicted."

"Vi, we've been talking about"—Colleen looked round to see if anybody was listening—"about Dorcas saying she was pregnant when she wasn't."

"Maybe it was just another one of her stories is what I think."

"No, she could have thought she was." Here the mother lapsed into an explanation. She had got what Jury had said near letter-perfect. This surprised him; he hadn't given Colleen that high a mark for comprehension.

In her tremulous falsetto Violet said, "Want a baby? Dorcas? Don't make me laugh. Last thing she wanted. Couldn't stand kids, squalling and clobber, that's all they're good for, that's what Dorcas'd say."

"It doesn't surprise you, then," said Jury, "that it's not true, her being pregnant?"

"Nothin' surprises me about Dorcas. She was always making up stories. Made me tired, it did, not being able to sort out what was true from what weren't. Not that I lost any sleep over it."

Colleen said, tearfully, "That's a shame, Violet Reese, not caring about your poor sister."

"Oh, *Mum*." Violet sighed as Colleen's tears spilled over.

Wanting to avoid a family fracas, Jury asked, "Did she ever mention anyone, any man in such a way you might think she was intimate, I mean, that she was having sex with him?"

Vi slid down in her seat and laughed in silent heaves. When she finally righted herself, she said, choking on the words, "Since she was in the comprehensive, she had a reputation."

The scandalized Colleen said sharply, "Violet! Watch your mouth, now."

"Sorry, Mum." Looking at Jury she said, "She'd used to talk about nearly every man that way."

"I don't understand. I thought Dorcas wasn't, well, very attractive to men."

"'Attractive?' Whoever said you had to be 'attractive' if you was willing? She was just man-crazy. Sorry, Mum, I don't like to make you feel bad, but he *is* a rozzer—if you'll pardon the expression"—she made a little bow with her head—"and we can't be holding out on police." She leaned toward Jury. "'Poor Dorcas' is right. She was, I guess you can say, 'available.' What the kids used to say in school was 'willing.' 'Dorcas is willing.' They got that from a book by what's-his-name?" She screwed up her unlined forehead in a semblance of thought.

Jury supplied the name: "Charles Dickens. *David Copperfield*. It's 'Barkis' there."

"That's the one! Dickens. There's this old guy who hardly ever speaks. When he wants to propose to the nurse, he sends a message: 'Barkis is willin'.' Well, it sounds a little like 'Dorcas,' see?"

Colleen looked pale, pressed a tissue to her mouth, then said, "You've no business dredging all that stuff up, Vi. This is your poor dead sister."

Violet, having heard that enough in the past, ignored her mum. "I did feel sorry for her. It was the only way she could get a man to pay any attention to her. But I'll tell you truly, not even *that* could get her a man, I mean a permanent one." She turned her attention to Jury again. "But, see, I could name a few names but that don't mean I'd've named them all."

"Vi! That's a dreadful thing to say about Dorcas." A fresh flow of tears came; once wiped away, Colleen said, "I'd better go and see your da gets all his tea." She got up and left the room.

Jury thought the mother was the only one who was grieved by Dorcas's death and felt a renewed empathy for her. Violet could have told Jury in private about that harsh judgment on Dorcas's life. "Dorcas is willin'." Had Dorcas been pretty, or seductive, or even sweet and saintly it would not have been so sad; it was her lack of any of these qualities that made her beleaguered sexual history and death so awful.

"Why wasn't this in the information you gave Lincolnshire police— pardon me, the 'rozzers'?"

"You do learn quick," said Violet looking him up and down, coquettishly. "I can tell you one thing," Vi went on. "It wasn't no one local, meaning Spalding. You'd best look where she worked."

"You mean Fengate?"

"There and that pub. Case Has Altered. You know it?"

Jury nodded. "How can you be sure?"

"From the way she talked. 'Got me a real man this time,' she'd say, which pretty much lets out the ones round here." Vi giggled. "'I bless the day I ever took that job.' She'd just let go with these hints, you know? Now that sure sounds as if it was Fengate or the Case or somewhere around there."

"Your mother says Dorcas had been 'snappish' for the last couple of weeks. Did she strike you in that way?"

"Aye. Far as I was concerned, that was just Dorcas being Dorcas. I mean, she was in this really good mood for weeks before that, and then the mood changed."

"Any idea as to why?"

Vi shrugged again, said, "Probably the guy dumped her."

"If she honestly thought she was pregnant—"

Vi brushed that aside with a flutter of her hand. "Go on, she was lyin' about that like she did about what happened with all these men that was sweet on her."

Jury smiled at that old-fashioned way of putting it. But he wasn't at all sure of the truth of what she said. He was more ready to believe Dorcas was honestly going through a false pregnancy. "Who's your doctor, Vi?" Jury pulled a small leather notebook from his inside pocket.

"Dr. McNee. Only don't get the idea in your head that Dorcas went to him. Well, she wouldn't've done, would she?"

Just then Trevor, having finished his tea and rolling a toothpick in his mouth, had brought a heavy book into the parlor, keeping his finger in it to mark the page, sat down, and opened it. He did not look as if he were a man next in line to supply answers to questions put by police. The women were clearly used to his lack of social grace; Colleen asked if his tea had been all right.

"Aye."

Again, she introduced Jury as (as usual) "Inspector."

Trevor gave Jury a look over the top of the book. "Aye."

"He might be wanting to ask you a few questions. He's Scotland Yard, Dad."

Trevor merely nodded and went back to reading. Jury didn't take this personally, for he spoke to family members in the same abbreviated manner.

Vi kept trying. "He thinks we might've recalled something since that other policeman was here. You might know something."

"I know nowt." Trevor shook his head, didn't even raise his eyes from the page.

What surprised Jury was that he really did appear to be reading, instead of using the book as a shield against police. His eye movements showed this to be the case. Although Jury couldn't imagine he could really comprehend what he read, not with three people in the room trying to get him to talk. Jury had been going to offer some sympathetic comment, but decided not to, as Trevor Reese did not appear to need it. He was a small, spare man with dark hair and a toothbrush mustache and a Chaplinesque pallor. But without Chaplin's whimsical expression. Trevor seemed sober and somber and a man of few words. He was master of only three—*aye, no,* and *nowt*—and used even them sparingly, yet managed to convey, with his stunted vocabulary, that he wasn't about to let himself be intimidated by any rozzer. They could pistol-whip him and he'd still gi' 'em nowt.

Jury watched him wet his finger, turn a page, and keep on reading. The book was heavy, thick, looked hard to lift, much less hold and read. "You know that your daughter—Dorcas—wasn't pregnant after all."

Trevor still held the book, but lowered it a little. "Aye."

The "ayes" had various tonal shadings, this one suspicious, as if Jury were here to take it all back and tell him poor Dorcas's condition would be reported in the *Daily News.*

"Do you yourself go to the Case?"

That surprised him, as Jury meant it to. Trevor was enough taken aback to lower the volume to his lap. "Aye."

"About the regulars there: did Dorcas seem sweet on anyone in particular?"

Trevor pursed his lips, seemed actually to be giving this some thought. He surprised Jury by answering. "Aye. That Price fellow."

"Who lives at Fengate?"

"Aye." Hadn't he just said? Trevor shook his head and the book came up again.

Trevor Reese's voice was strangely melodic; his phrases had the upward swing of an Irishman, but the sheared-off consonants and resonant vowels of an old fenman.

"How did you know she liked Jack Price?"

"Usual way. Flirty." His eyebrows did an amusing little dance by way of illustration. Then he went back to his book, licked a finger, turned the page.

In her annoyance, Vi punched a pillow she'd been holding in her lap. "Ah, come on, Da! You know more'n you let on. And you can just put that book down, for god's sake." She turned to Jury. "Da loves to read. In winter he reads to us, sometimes. Mum's baking something, apples or pudding, and when it's near finished, she lowers the door of the cooker and all of us sit round it, listening to Da. Dorcas did a lot of it, too. Had a good reading voice, did Dorcas. Easy on the ears."

Surprising to Jury, this lovely description of a family scene. Reading aloud—how often did one come across that now? He said the same.

Vi merely repeated her words: "Da! Come on. You know things I bet you're not telling."

"Here, girl, and don't you be tellin' me what ah know or don't know."

Vi was standing now, shaking her head at such stubbornness. "Me, I'm having my tea, too."

Since Trevor's last answer had been close to being two whole sentences, Jury decided to push his luck.

"Anyone else she treated in that particular way, Mr. Reese?"

Again he contemplated the answer, but settled for another No.

"Look, I know you want to find out who killed your daughter—"

The book came down. "Ya know nowt, man. Ya think us wants t'be al-lus reminded by talkin' to you lot?"

"No, I don't think that. But aren't you forced to think about it more and more because Dorcas's murder hasn't been solved?"

Trevor made no answer; he shrugged and raised his book again.

"Did Jack Price show any interest in your daughter?"

"Not 'im. 'E just sits quiet-like. Keeps hisself to hisself. It 'oud pay oth-ers t'be like 'im." His baleful glance suggested one of those others was sit-ting on his sofa.

"Did you ever see them together?"

Trevor Reese sighed hugely. "Well, o' course. I jest tol' ya—"

"I don't mean while she was inside the pub. I meant, did they go back to Fengate together sometimes?"

He pursed his lips again, considering. "Hmm. Coulda done, ah guess. Well, they be goin' t'same place, why not?"

"Are you so sure there was no one else?"

This time he set the book aside. "Now ah don' want t'be speakin' ill o' me own daughter. But Dorcas, she just di'n't . . . chaps just di'n't take t' 'er, you know. Ah don't like saying it, but Dorcas was just a plain li'l thing. Just got left out in the looks department. It went 'ard wi' 'er, not bein' pretty like Violet."

"But what about her good humor for several weeks before she died. Your wife remarked on the change in her."

"Aye. She were lots different for a while."

"And Violet said Dorcas told her she had a 'real man' and that her life was going to change."

Trevor said, "Ah thought Dorcas was just dreamin'. Done a lot o' that, she did, an' no wonder."

"But if there was such a dramatic change in her manner, wouldn't that tell you that she did indeed have 'someone.' Even if it was all wishful thinking, the thinking was on some real and particular person."

Trevor did not answer. He was fanning the pages of his book.

"If Dorcas didn't come out with the identity of this man, it suggests that their relationship had to be kept secret; given her bad luck with men, I'd imagine she would have been dying to flaunt this. Certainly, if it were someone like Jack Price, she would be. He's pleasant, smart, and, if not handsome, has something far more valuable—he's an artist, a sculptor, who might become famous one of these days."

"And 'cause o' all that, not bloody likely 'e'd be leadin' our poor Dorcas on."

"No, but she might have been able to convince herself that he was interested. And if not Jack Price, well, who? Don't forget that Dorcas told people she was pregnant—"

"Ah ain't forgettin' *that*, God knows."

"So there had to be somebody."

Trevor turned on Jury a pair of canny eyes. "No, there di'n't. Ya forgettin' Dorcas coulda been makin' it all up."

Jury sat back. "That's possible, yes. But given her behavior, I doubt it. Did she say anything that made you wonder during those last days after she'd fallen off the pink cloud? About 'wishing she hadn't done it'? Or having listened to bad advice, or overheard someone talking?"

"No, nothing."

Jury rose and thanked Trevor Reese for his time and his patience.

"Ah, 'tis all right. It's just we're all o' us pretty bad over what 'appened t'our Dorcas." He also got up, tossing the book on the little table that shuddered with its added burden. Pointing to it, he said, "Now 'e's got out o' 'and, 'im. Don't see what t'bloody fuss is over this 'ere book. Damned Roosians, all they do is stand around jawin', ah could write this 'ere kind o' clobber meself."

"What is it? What book?"

"*War-and*-bloody-*Peace*."

39

Marshall Trueblood, by far the most elegant thing in the room, rose smooth as syrup to his feet. He fingered the watch pocket of his waistcoat as if he meant to bring out something—a calling card or a set of ciphers that would crack the case wide open. Actually, he had a watch in this pocket designed for it and he began to wind it with excruciating slowness. Everyone's eyes were clamped on him, waiting for him to do something, to save the day, for sentiment was altogether with Ada Crisp and her little dog. They had been fixtures in the village life long before Lady Ardry had set foot in it. An American, to boot, from Milwaukee, Wisconsin, who had the good luck to attach herself to Melrose's uncle Robert. Uncle Robert had been a happy ne'er-do-well who, probably after one of his nights on the tiles, had thought an American wife might be rather a jolly accompaniment to his gaming ways. He'd been dead wrong, poor man.

"The defense calls Theo Wrenn Browne."

Talk about your hostile witness! thought Melrose, who'd taken a seat at the back of the room.

Smiling, Marshall Trueblood pulled down his silky gray waistcoat and advanced on Browne. "Mr. Browne, you're the proprietor of a bookshop named the Wrenn's Nest. Is that true?"

"You know it is." This was said with a sneer.

"And this shop is next door to Miss Crisp's furniture shop."

Browne nodded, said sullenly, "It is."

"On the day of this alleged 'accident,' you have said that you left your bookshop and were standing just outside of it when Lady Ardry approached Miss Crisp's shop next door. You then saw the dog attack the plaintiff and saw her stumble and catch her foot in the chamber pot. Is all of this correct?"

Now, Browne tried for boredom, but didn't manage that either. "Yes."

"Why did you leave your shop?"

"To speak to Lady Ardry, as I've said."

"Right. And how did you know Lady Ardry was on the pavement in front of the shop next door?"

Browne sighed hugely. "Because I saw her pass by my own shop. Saw her through the *window*. As I've *said*."

Trueblood nodded. "Now, it's been established that Lady Ardry had been doing some errands round the village and had with her a string bag holding items she'd purchased that morning: these were a ball of twine, postage stamps, a half-dozen hot cross buns. Is that your understanding?"

Browne tilted his head and seemed to be studying the cobwebs on the ceiling. "Yes, yes."

"Which she was carrying when she passed your window?"

Lowering his eyes from the ceiling, he said, impatiently, "Well, I as-sume so."

"The window of your shop faces the High Street?"

"Naturally."

"And how many times did she pass by?"

Browne lifted his chin from the fist that had been cradling it in his as-sumed stupor at the banality of these questions. "What do you mean?"

"Did she pass once? Twice? How many times did you see her pass the window?"

"Uh . . . *once* . . . I mean, she wasn't parading her new hat back and forth in front of me!" Sharing this witty reply with the rest of the court, Browne looked about him, smiling richly.

Melrose looked around. Only his aunt wore a simpering smile. Theo Wrenn Browne was never a popular fellow in the best of circumstances.

"Then she must have been walking toward Miss Crisp's shop, as she obviously wouldn't be passing your window from the *other* direction, that is to say, *after* Miss Crisp's, after she'd had this accident."

Browne, to show his disregard of Trueblood's questions, slid down in his seat. "Obviously. She'd probably been coming from her cottage."

Trueblood smiled. "Oh, I don't think so, Mr. Browne. The two little parcels she'd dropped contained stamps, a ball of twine, hot cross buns, as I've said. She hadn't purchased those between her cottage and your shop. The ball of twine probably was picked up at the post office; the stamps certainly were. The hot cross buns were bought at Betty Ball's bakery, that bakery being the only place in the village where you can buy them. Both the bakery and the post office are *north*, not south of your shop. So she'd have to have been coming from the other direction; that is to say, she would have reached Ada Crisp's *before* she 'passed by' your window. Thus, as we've said, she couldn't have 'passed by' then, as she was in the throes of this grave accident." Trueblood waited.

Browne sputtered. "Well . . . well . . . what earthly difference does it make? Perhaps it was earlier, later . . . I don't know."

"But it couldn't have been either earlier or later, for you said she passed by immediately before she had the accident."

Theo Wrenn Browne scratched his head, looked around almost wildly. Melrose was enthralled.

Then Trueblood stood silent for a few moments, smiling all the while, and said, "What drew you from your shop, Mr. Browne, were the cries and yelps coming from Lady Ardry and the dog—"

Melrose loved that coupling.

"—and, quite naturally, you dashed outside to see what all the fuss was about—"

"All right, perhaps—"

"And that being the case, you didn't see what happened at all. You saw only its aftermath."

Yes! Melrose shoved his fists slightly into the air. *Bravo, Marshall!*

Browne simply blinked, as if Trueblood's smile were a little too bright for him. Then he began blustering again. "Well, the dog was running about, barking dementedly—"

"Oh, I've no doubt. But who is to say the little dog wasn't acting *defensively*? Who is to say Lady Ardry didn't go for the poor creature with a walking stick?"

Bryce-Pink shot like a missile from his seat, only seconds after Agatha was up from hers. *"Liar! Liar!"* came from Agatha. *"Objection! Objection!"*

came from her solicitor. The courtroom was noisy with small cheers and laughter.

Eustace-Hobson banged his gavel. "Madam, take your seat! The objection is sustained, Mr. Trueblood. You're *speculating!*"

Brightly, Trueblood said, "No more than was the witness, Your Worship."

More noise, more gavel-banging.

"I have no more questions." Trueblood bowed.

Browne's face was mottled with anger. He'd been caught out.

There, thought Melrose, was the prosecution's chief witness gone. The only other witness was he himself. And he himself wouldn't be much help.

Would Trueblood move to dismiss?

No. He was calling Melrose to the witness box.

"Lord Ardry," said Marshall Trueblood, wanting to imprint the title on the magistrate's mind, and then catching himself, followed up with, "Do pardon me. You prefer 'Mr. Plant,' don't you?"

"I do, as it happens to be my name."

"At the time that this incident occurred, you were on the opposite side of the street?"

"That's right."

Marshall dipped his head in a little bowing way. "And we—you and I—were having, as I remember, a rather lively discussion about the All Blacks, the New Zealand rugby team."

Melrose thought a bit. Yes, there had been a few comments about the team, but he hardly thought that constituted a "lively discussion." Still, it was close enough so that Melrose didn't have to perjure himself. "Yes, that's true."

"Mr. Plant, you've quite a solid knowledge of antiques, haven't you?"

Melrose jumped. Oh, surely *this* wasn't to come up again! "Oh, I wouldn't say 'solid.' I know a thing or two. . . ." That was indeed all he did know. His expression, he hoped, was properly modest.

"Let's for example take . . . oh, something like a *bonheur-du-jour.* Could you tell the court what that is?"

Naturally, Bryce-Pink was on his feet asking what the relevance of this was. Trueblood explained that its relevance would soon be apparent. The magistrate quite happily came down on the defendant's side because the plaintiff's had bored him to death. Mr. Trueblood could proceed. And so could Mr. Plant, who described, in relentless detail a *bonheur-du-jour.*

"Quite right. And what about . . ." Trueblood crossed his arms, resting his chin in his hand, a study in thought. "A . . . *secretaire à abbatant?*"

Oh, that what we found the dead body in, mate? Melrose smiled and, again, described it. Trueblood took him through his paces with two other pieces, one being the Ispahan rug Melrose had become achingly familiar with at Fengate. Bryce-Pink and his client sat at their table and smoldered. Agatha was, of course, completely furious at the loss of Theo Wrenn Browne, her partner in crime.

Trueblood, having established the witness's authority to speak on the matter of antiques, held up a book and asked him if he was familiar with it.

Melrose's eyebrows shot up when he saw on the back of this book the Nuttings' photograph in all its toothsome glory. But who was Melrose to question *Helluva Deal!*? Socrates here was on a roll, might as well play along. "I certainly am. Dipped in it more than once."

"And how, Mr. Plant, would you characterize this book? That is, if you had to describe it in a sentence or two?"

Melrose thought of a few sentences he probably couldn't repeat in public, and then said, "It's about auctions, primarily; secondarily, it's about scams."

" 'Scams'?"

"Well, yes, I'd say—" *Good God*, thought Melrose, *he isn't going to be so brazen as to suggest . . . ?* Melrose let the thought trail away, then said, with inward glee, "Scams, yes. The authors describe"—*and participate in, most likely,* he didn't add—"the various tricks people and dealers use—I shouldn't say dealers, really, most of whom tend to be at least moderately honest"—here he tilted his head toward Trueblood who gave him a razor-blade smile—"individuals who manage to flummox dealers, or auctioneers, let's say. Or simple, unsuspecting buyers. For example, there's the old 'bait-and-switch' technique."

"Ah, and would you tell the court what that is?"

Bryce-Pink was on his feet again, protesting loudly. Agatha managed to keep herself in her chair and fume. Eustace-Hobson didn't even bother to respond verbally; he merely waved Bryce-Pink down, looking irritated he'd interrupted what might be a promisingly sprightly tale.

Melrose picked a bit of lint from his jacket and continued. "It's basically an American term"—which was hardly surprising, he thought of adding—"wherein the owners of, let's say, some antique silver get swindled. There's the case of the Dewitt brothers of Kentucky, for instance." Melrose nodded toward the book. "The Dewitt brothers possessed a quite beautiful and valuable Georgian punch bowl. They'd take it in to some dealer—avoiding any real specialist—plop it on the counter, and say they wanted to sell it and an accompanying coffee service and a few other silver items. The shop owner would inspect the punch bowl, pronounce it fine indeed, and make a fair offer. The Dewitts would then bring in a box of other so-called Georgian silver, and, since the shop owner or jeweler or pawnbroker or whoever had inspected the punch bowl was certain of its value, he'd only do a cursory check of the other items. They, on the surface were quite resplendently polished up and looked the ticket. Turned out, of course, to be a mixture of odd bits and bobs—and of course, the Dewitts would beg off selling the Georgian punch bowl with some story it belonged 'to me old gramps,' or something like that, and they'd just sell the box of bogus stuff." Melrose smiled broadly. "I thought them rather jolly, really, especially since they were in their nineties."

So did Eustace-Hobson think them "jolly," apparently, for Melrose was actually managing to keep him awake. He gave a gruff chortle and looked pointedly at Agatha, who, Melrose thought, looked like her blood pressure had risen enough to have her pegging out right here in court. Wages of sin.

Trueblood leafed through *Helluva Deal!* and stopped at a certain page, then asked, "Mr. Plant, do you remember the bit about 'Piggy' Arbuckle?"

"Piggy? Oh, yes. Now, his favorite scam was what the Nuttings christened the 'fist-in-the-vase' scam. Mr. Arbuckle—whose name was 'Peregrine' actually, but he was called 'Piggy' even though he was thin as a rail and nearly ninety himself—anyway, Piggy would stop in some antiques shop or other, for a look round. He'd be in company with a lad, who would, upon a sign from Piggy, put his hand down inside some valuable piece and then not be able to get it out. Hysteria reigned. It just so happened there'd be a doctor in the shop, a 'Dr. Todd' who would proclaim they could either smash whatever it was or he could take the lad to his surgery and apply some ointment, some grease or other, and get the arm out with no damage to the Meissen, or whatever. The shopkeeper would yield to this plan. Well, they were a troupe, weren't they? I mean, they were all Arbuckles, the lad being a great-grand-nephew and 'Dr. Todd' some sort of cousin, and they traveled about like a little circus. The poor antiques dealer would understandably be so flustered and afraid for his Meissen or whatever, he'd go along with it."

Melrose was delighted. It wouldn't have taken an Einstein to see that the "fist-in-the-vase" trick could rather quickly be supplanted with the "foot-in-the-chamber-pot" trick—even though that was the only similarity in the two stories.

Marshall Trueblood said, "Where did you find this wonderful little book, Mr. Plant?"

Ah, *that* was it! Oh, how marvelous! Guilt by association! Melrose had a hard time keeping his countenance so that he could lend to his answer the gravitas it demanded. "Actually, I found it in the Wrenn's Nest, Mr. Browne's bookshop."

The courtroom broke into gales of laughter. Theo Wrenn Browne was out of his chair in a shot; Agatha was up and yelling; Bryce-Pink was screaming objections. And Miss Crisp, for the first time in weeks, was smiling. Not only smiling, but had her arms upraised, hands together in the "victory" gesture of a prizefighter.

Melrose was dismissed, smiling, too.

Eustace-Hobson made a great display of pounding his gavel.

When everything had quieted down again, Trueblood went to the table of "exhibits" where the chamber pot sat in lonely splendor, if one could call the rather mundane bowl with a greenish hue "splendid." Trueblood had mended it to near-seamless perfection. He passed it to Melrose. "Mr. Plant, would you turn this over and look at the marking, please."

Melrose did so. There was a rough, raised spot, but no name. He said this.

Trueblood said: "This particular mark places this piece in the Ch'ein lung period. It's one of the 'famille verte' pieces—hence its faint greenish cast—and quite valuable—"

Yes! thought Melrose, watching Trueblood open a price guide. Even Eustace-Hobson was looking eagerly at the two of them, having forgotten entirely that it was Plant in this instance who was supposed to be the expert.

"—nine hundred pounds for this bowl. Or, I should say, was *once* worth nine hundred." He fixed Agatha with a dire look. "I've had it authenticated. It isn't a chamber pot; it's a large bowl, possibly meant for fruit." Trueblood turned to look over his audience. "But quite definitely *not* intended for—" He paused. Everyone seemed to be hovering on the edge of a legal epiphany. "—not intended for anything else, if you take my meaning." He bowed.

The courtroom went wild; Agatha and Theo Wrenn Browne looked as if they might need the ministrations of "Dr. Todd"; and even old Eustace-Hobson was clearly delighted. He banged his gavel (more for appearances than any real desire to call for order) and motioned for Bryce-Pink and Trueblood to approach. He said a few well-tuned words to them, and when they'd returned to their respective places, he announced the case against Miss Crisp was dismissed. "Ridiculous business!" he said, forgetting for the moment his office. "Waste of the taxpayers' money! Shouldn't be surprised if there were a countersuit, Mr. Bryce-Pink, your client getting sued for slander! Either that or collusion or both!" And he humphed and grumphed his way out of the room.

Ada Crisp embraced Trueblood and did a little dance past the plaintiff's table, gave Agatha a little wave, and fairly skipped up the aisle toward her bridge club.

"Bloody *brilliant!*" said Melrose, clapping his arm across Trueblood's shoulder. "This calls for a Cairo Flame!"

40

In the Case Has Altered, Jury asked Julie Rough for the telephone tucked beneath the bar and dragged it and its long cord over to a table isolated from the rest of them so he wouldn't be overheard. Dutifully, he dialed Lincoln HQ. When Bannen came on the line, Jury said, speaking of Dorcas's moodiness, "I think this is important: something significant happened to cause it." Bannen was silent long enough to make Jury wonder if the connection had been broken. "Hello . . . you there?"

Bannen said, "We know 'something significant happened.' She thought she was pregnant."

"Besides that, I mean. *What* shouldn't she have listened to? What shouldn't she have done?"

"I'd say shouldn't have dropped her knickers for him. It would account for the change, wouldn't it, if he left her high and dry?"

Jury had to admit that was the case, only . . . It was his turn to be silent as the door opened and the woman he had seen here before walked in and took a seat at the bar. Madeline Reese, Trevor's sister and the person Dorcas had confided in. She looked so much like Dorcas that Jury wondered if their mutual lack of beauty might have created a strong enough bond between them to make Dorcas's confiding in the aunt even more understandable. Jury said to Bannen, "I don't get it, though. What we've been hearing all along is how unattractive Dorcas was. The mere *fact* of her 'pregnancy' surprised people. Who would find Dorcas attractive enough to go to bed with her?"

"Sorry, but I never heard a pretty face was absolutely *de rigueur* for that."

"You're right, except Dorcas simply wasn't physically appealing. Could we assume, then, just for the sake of the argument, this man she'd been seeing wanted something, but it wasn't *her*? Perhaps what he wanted was to keep her quiet."

"Why? The only man amongst the ones we've talked to who might conceivably suffer the consequences of this 'pregnancy' is Max Owen. Price certainly wouldn't; he'd be let off because he's 'arty' and everyone knows that type's eccentric and believes in free love. And Major Parker's a bachelor. Nor is he the type to put up with blackmail. And in the case of Dorcas, there's nothing to blackmail him about. So she's pregnant; so he's the father; so what?"

"That lad in Spalding?"

"Not a chance. The way he and others who knew him told it, their relationship existed primarily in Dorcas's mind."

Jury was silent, watching the solitary woman at the bar. The chaps at the end of it had greeted her, but no one had come to sit beside her. The door opened again, bringing the chill March air in with the old man who entered. "I'm missing something important. And I still think someone wanted her silence."

"He got that, didn't he?" Bannen rang off.

The old man was the one Jury had seen before in here. As he made his painful progress to the end of the bar, he put Jury in mind of a blasted tree. He sat down between Ian and Malcolm and laid his brier cane across the bar.

Julie saw Jury coming back; she smiled and pulled down her jumper, smoothed her short skirt. Jury ordered a pint of Adman's and told her to set up the three with whatever they were drinking. He was about to include Madeline Reese, but thought he'd better introduce himself first.

Ian—or Malcolm—Jury wasn't sure which was which, introduced the old man, whose name was Tomas. He said, "You be here 'bout these murders, ain't you?"

"I am, yes."

Tomas leaned uncomfortably close. "Interfered with, was they?"

"We don't think so." Jury smiled.

"It's usual, cases like that. Some pervert, like." He tapped his head. "Got sex on the brain."

"Speaking o' sex," said Ian, lowering his voice, "there's the perfect bird fer ya, Tomas." He winked at Jury, gestured with his head toward Madeline Reese.

Tomas squinted. "Who'd that be?"

"Down there."

"I can't see 'er, man."

"Well, get yer bleedin' glasses on."

Tomas fumbled a pair of wire-rimmed spectacles out of his jacket pocket and looped them behind his ears. "Ah, fer God's sake, it's that Reese woman. Better wifout me glasses." He took them off again.

Malcolm nudged old Tomas with his shoulder. "Go on, Tomas, you know you want to."

"Shut yer yob, Mac. You'd 'ave t'be blind. Stop takin' the piss outta me."

Madeline Reese looked tired; for her, Jury imagined, it was a chronic condition. Tired of exciting nothing more in men than foolishness or ridicule. He picked up his own glass and moved down the bar.

She appeared genuinely surprised when Jury sat on the stool beside her and offered to buy her another drink. Her looks did not improve upon closer inspection. Her straight brown hair was parted in the center and held back by her ears. Her light brown eyes were damp, the color of wet sand. A shandy, she said she wanted. He hadn't heard anyone order that in years. Like her dress, Maddy was out of date, a relic from an earlier time. There were some women the past clung to like a patina of dust.

Was Madeline what Dorcas would have grown up to be? The butt of jokes, the mock-solicitousness of men who could only look at her without her glasses. As Julie Rough set down the fresh drinks, Jury expressed his sympathy, told her he was sorry about her niece, and explained his position—that he wasn't part of the official investigation; he was trying to help out a friend. When Maddy discovered that the "friend" was the woman whose trial had been so thoroughly covered in the local newspaper, she said she was "thrilled." Here was information, first hand. She said she could hardly believe it'd happen to someone like "our Dorcas." Jury liked that proprietorial way of speaking, the same way the mother had. Maddy had read all the newspapers and was glad that this Kennington woman had got off. Jury took this as an indication of a warm and generous nature, since it left the murder of her niece unsolved. He said so. Unused to compliments, she blushed.

Her fear was that there was a serial killer out there somewhere, and Jury tried to assure her that this wasn't true. That the murders weren't random, that they were quite purposeful. She still wasn't sure police could eliminate a serial killer. Maddy seemed to hold that belief rather dear. Probably it made the whole thing that much more exciting. People were strange.

He noticed as they talked that her voice was especially pleasant. Like her brother Trevor's, her voice had that lilting Irish cadence that faltered only when coming up against her local accent. Despite her plain appearance, Maddy's voice might even have been seductive. Hadn't the father, or Vi, the sister, said that Dorcas's voice was so pleasant, it was she they elected to do a lot of the reading? Dorcas's voice was "easy on the ears."

Yes, Madeline agreed with her other niece, Violet. That Dorcas's mood had changed dramatically just a short while before she'd been murdered. "I make out," Maddy said, "somebody'd let her down, hard." She tapped the ash from her cigarette into a metal tray. "Hard," she said again. Jury thought she knew all about being let down hard.

He was about to comment on this, when he remembered that Madeline sometimes worked for Major Parker. Jury asked her how long she had been doing this.

"Years, on a regular basis. And also help out if he's giving one of his dinners. He's a grand cook, did anyone tell you?"

"Everyone's told me." Jury laughed.

"That's nice, I think, a man like him being such a grand cook. Most men, they wouldn't be caught dead. Imagine that lot there—" She nodded toward Malcolm and Ian and old Tomas. "—just picture them talking about cassoulets and soufflés. Makes me laugh, to think it. Major Parker now, the way I work it out is he's comfortable with himself."

Jury thought of Zel, what she'd told him. "Have you ever seen Dorcas there?"

"Dorcas? No. What business would she have there?"

"I was told that Dorcas visited Major Parker more than once."

"Dorcas did? Whatever—" Then she laughed. "Oh, no, you're not saying you think Major Parker—? Look, he'd never have anything to do with a scrap of a girl like our Dorcas. If you're thinking he's the one . . . no, never. Dorcas was never one to attract the men. I ought to know, for we look so much alike. Looked," she corrected herself, sadly.

There was no self-pity in her voice; nevertheless, Jury felt sorry for her. "'Attraction' covers many likes and levels. Then you think Dorcas's reputation as an easy conquest was exaggerated?"

Maddy shook free another cigarette. "I don't know. I *do* know she went with boys when she was still a schoolgirl."

"'Dorcas is willin''?"

She nodded. "Probably the only thing those kids came away with in all of their schooling. That line, I mean. And even then they can't remember who wrote it." She bent her cigarette over the match Jury held for her, inhaled deeply, exhaled a ribbon of smoke.

For Jury, the smell of the languidly drifting smoke was utterly seductive. He tracked its gossamer trail up to the ceiling, where it dispersed. He remembered how, on the roof of that hotel in Santa Fe, he had wanted to crawl into the arms of those lovely women who held martinis in one hand and cigarettes in the other. It wasn't sex he was after, it was smokes. Jury wondered if any scientific study had ever been done of the relationship between smoking and sex. "How much of it's sexual?"

"Dorcas's behavior?"

"No. Smoking." He imagined he looked as abashed as a little kid. Here were two murders committed and his mind was on cigarettes. "Trying to stop."

She looked at him sympathetically and blew the smoke away from him. "It's hard; I've tried." She thought for a bit, then said, "Maybe she was helping out. Dorcas, I mean."

Jury remembered what Zel had said about that. "It's not likely, is it, Dorcas would be helping out as sous chef. And the cleaning, well, you're still doing that, aren't you?"

"Once a week. All he needs, really. He's a very tidy man. And a lot of the house is closed off, so it's not as big a job as it seems. And, anyway, if Major Parker decided he needed more help, he'd've had me doing the searching out."

"You have no idea why she might have gone there?"

Maddy shook her head. "Whoever told you that, anyway?"

Jury did not want to say it was Zel. Although he believed in what she'd said and seen, others might dismiss information coming from an imaginative little girl. "Did you know Verna Dunn?"

"No. Except to see; I mean I know what she looked like. Way I heard it, she wasn't very nice."

Jury shook his head.

Maddy said, "Did you think your friend would get off?"

Again, Jury nodded. "Her barrister and solicitor are very good."

"What I wonder is, why couldn't it've been two different people—the killers I mean. It would make more sense."

"Why do you think so?"

"Because I just can't see a person with reason to kill them *both*. Like, I can imagine Dorcas going to this man and telling him she's preggers. And if he says no, he won't marry her, her getting shirty about it and saying to him she'll tell the world. If he's married, he wouldn't want that. Even if he's not, but he has kind of a social position, well, he might want to, you know, get rid of her. Awful as that all is, I can imagine it."

"I can too."

41

There's nothing at all sinister in it, Superintendent," said Parker. "Dorcas was a terrible cook. So for a few weeks there I was trying to teach her some basics. All right, I should have told this to that Inspector Bannen, about her coming here, but I simply couldn't see why. It was all so innocent."

"I'm sure it was," said Jury, taking another sip of what was arguably the best cup of coffee ever made. "The trouble is, what has the appearance of being irrelevant to a case often is quite important."

"How was my teaching her a few basic things about cooking relevant to her death?"

"I don't know."

Parker returned the pipe to his mouth and kept his eyes on Jury.

"The point is, why? Why would Dorcas want to learn how to cook?"

"She didn't tell me," said Parker. "Just said it meant a lot to her. She couldn't even follow a recipe in a cookery book. Oddly enough, I never asked her the question, you know? I expect I assume everyone wants to cook, or would do, if he knew any better."

"Not Dorcas Reese, not from what I've heard."

Parker sat silently smoking his pipe. There were times when Jury thought everyone else in the world smoked except him. "I see what you mean," said Parker.

They had talked about the trial. Parker observed that all of them, himself, the Owens, felt great relief when the case was dismissed. They all liked Jenny Kennington so much. He had never believed she was guilty, nor had Max or Grace. The prosecution had a weak case to begin with, Parker said.

"I see what you mean about her. Dorcas wouldn't be wanting to learn anything unless she had some unstated agenda." He removed the pipe from his mouth, looked thoughtfully at the bowl. "You know, I went to one of those *cordon bleu* cooking schools years ago. Most of the students were men, just two or three women. All except one of them wanted to be chefs. Two of the women took the course because they knew nothing about cooking and were getting married." He looked doubtful when he said, "Perhaps Dorcas—?"

"Yes. How often did she come here?"

"One or two afternoons a week. Five or six weeks, I'd say."

"Right up to the time of her death?"

"No." Parker rubbed at his temple with the stem of his pipe. "She missed a couple of times. Actually, I was surprised. She was so determined. Nor did she call—" He shrugged. "I expect it'd been a week, perhaps ten days since her last lesson."

"I've been talking to the Reeses, including the aunt, Madeline. She didn't know Dorcas had been visiting you."

"Maddy, ah. She wouldn't have known, no. Dorcas came on days when she wasn't here. Coincidence, perhaps; or perhaps Dorcas wanted her cooking lessons kept a deep secret."

"More than her supposed pregnancy? She told her aunt about that. And you. Why?"

"I've no idea." Parker shook his head. "All right, I should certainly have told that Chief Inspector Bannen. But I imagine you can see why I didn't. As you say, why would she have told me, unless—?" He left the question unfinished. "Dorcas was pretty much a lightweight in the brains department," Parker went on. "Scatty, couldn't keep her mind on the hollandaise. She always had her eye on the finished product—a mousse, a soufflé—but couldn't manage the steps involved in getting it. That picture-perfect cassoulet or pear confit *à la Parker*." He looked sheepish. "Sorry, I do tend to get a little precious about cooking."

Jury smiled. "Sounds good." He turned his head. "Smells good, too. What are you making?"

"A ragout. Lamb. You should join me. 'Us,' I should say. Zel's coming to do the dessert. Are you sure you can't stay for dinner?" It was the third time Parker had asked him, done so with a near-childlike tenacity.

"I wish I could, but something is going on in my mind, some glimmer of an answer that might get lost in the middle of a ragout. Assuming, of course, you're as good as they say you are."

Parker laughed. "Probably I am."

Jury's look at Parker was speculative. "Could Dorcas have said any-thing at all that might have seemed—again, irrelevant, but indeed might not be?"

"Well, you can't put it that way, old boy." Parker laughed. "If it seemed irrelevant, I wouldn't know, would I?"

"No, of course not. Just tell me anything she said you wondered about." Jury leaned forward. "The thing is, if we knew who this man is, we just might know who killed her. I keep thinking of what she said: '*I shouldn't have listened. I ought not to have done it.*' Listened to whom? Done what? Was she talking about her pregnancy? Suppose she told the man she was pregnant—"

"But she wasn't."

"That makes no difference, as long as she thought she was. The so-called father would have believed her, finally. Dorcas would have con-vinced him if he'd had any doubt. She was determined."

"And finding out, he'd have got rid of her?" Parker rubbed at his tem-ple again with the pipe. "That just doesn't strike me as much of a motive. Not these days, not when everything is so accepted. Hardly any kind of behavior fazes us anymore. Unmarried mothers would hardly qualify. I don't know why Dorcas chose me as her confidant in all of this. But then I didn't know why she'd ask me to make a cook of her, either. I hope you believe me; I had no relationship at all with Dorcas; I have no idea why she told me she was pregnant. She blurted it out one day. She was quite upset."

"Could it have been you she 'shouldn't have listened' to?"

"I don't know what you mean."

"Did you give her any advice at all when she told you she was preg-nant? Thought she was, I mean."

Parker shook his head sadly, removed his glasses, and set them on the table, and fell to contemplating the silver smallwork there. Picked up and set down again the snuffbox, mull, salt trencher. He said, "I don't give advice, I'm not good at it. I'm uncomfortable in the face of crisis, which is probably why I'm alone, why I live here alone." His eyes swept the room, played over the elegant mismatched pieces—the Oriental cabinet near the mahogany étagère, a Venetian mirror above a Georgian kneehole desk, the Russian rosewood, the eighteenth-century pine cabinets.

"Perhaps she told you because you give the impression you can be trusted." Jury got to his feet.

Parker rose, retrieved his glasses, massaged the bridge of his nose, and put the glasses on again, looping the metal around his ears.

Jury stared at him. The glasses looked much like the ones old Tomas had put on to see down the bar to where Maddy sat. *"You'd 'ave t'be blind."* Jury felt dazed. Dazzled with the clarity of it. He repeated to Parker, "I have to go, sorry."

He did not have to go; he needed to be away so that he could think.

♪

He stood on the footpath, stopped in the purple dusk, going over it. It had to be Peter Emery. Peter was the one man who wouldn't be put off by Dorcas's looks, and who would be taken by her voice, reading to him. Jury stopped at the sound of an early owl, listened to small rustling movements coming from the hawthorn, then walked awhile on the footpath.

Dorcas had thought she was going to marry him. Deluded girl. What stood between them were years of calcified emotion. Bitterness at his blindness. He was a hundred years older than Dorcas Reese, if emotional journeying were the yardstick of age. He might have had a fling with Dorcas, if that quaint word explained it, but together with her for the rest of his life? Jury didn't think so.

He drew in a deep breath and stood motionless, listening, hearing the blessed nothing, thinking how Wyndham Fen was beautiful in its restoration—for that was what it was; it had been reclaimed in much the same way Max Owen or Parker might have restored a piece of furniture. And what he wished for—even though he knew it was romantic nonsense—

was to step back in time and see the whole shire like this, when the old fen tigers had wrested their living from it. Or even before that—imagine how this whole countryside must have been when there were only islands: Ely, Ramsey, Whittlesey, March. Cities and towns surrounded by water, when it was bog and reed-bed and little else. Romantic, for there were also the rivers breaking banks from the raging streams and rivers, the merciless water. ". . . . *And even the weariest river,/Winds somewhere safe to sea. . . .*" He heard Parker reading that poem by Swinburne.

Jury sighed. He was only thinking these thoughts to avoid thinking others. Jenny was innocent, and now he knew it. *"You'll never be sure,"* she'd said. But now he was and now it was too late because neither one of them had voiced their fears. They had held one another at bay; they couldn't depend on one another. They hadn't trusted one another, not even in the very simple way that Dorcas had trusted Parker. *". . . And even the weariest river,/Winds somewhere safe to sea."*

That glimmer of an idea suddenly became a glare. It spread out before him like water flooding the fen. It was as if it weren't really himself, Jury, who was doing the thinking, but some force doing it for him.

He could not act alone. He would have to ring Lincoln HQ; he would have to speak to Bannen and do whatever Bannen said to do. He turned and started the walk back to the footpath and to Parker's, feeling extremely sad.

⁂

Aha! Gave more thought to that ragout, did you?" Parker opened the door wide, and gestured for Jury to come in with the hand that held a glass of wine.

Jury smiled. "Actually, what I need is your telephone. I have to call Lincoln." Parker led him to a small room that looked pleasantly worn with constant use. His library, judging from books not only on floor-to-ceiling shelves, but sitting stacked on the floor and spilling from surfaces. Parker turned to leave and Jury stopped him. "Would you have a map of this area? Maybe an ordnance map?"

"Oh, yes, I've a hundred of the damned things." Parker pulled some maps from one of the shelves. "What part of the county did you want?"

"Here, this area—the Wash."

Parker gave him a speculative, raised eyebrow and sifted through the maps. "Here you are." He handed the map to Jury. "You've an idea, have you?"

"First in a long time, I can tell you." He smiled. "Swinburne helped."

"Did he?" Parker laughed. "Swinburne does get one through some tight spots, I've found. We're having an excellent Medoc." He raised his wineglass. "Want some now?"

"Later, thanks."

"Ah! You will be staying. Good, take your time."

Jury shoved papers and magazines out of the way and spread the map over the large desk. As he studied all of those fen-waterways—there were so many of them, wide and narrow, cross-hatching the land—he traced the flow of the river Welland, which, he saw, coursed through Spalding and the land nearby. All the way to the Wash.

⊙⊙

What? You're, well, one hesitates to say 'mad,'" said Arthur Bannen from his office at Lincoln headquarters. "One hesitates, but one will. You're mad, Mr. Jury." Bannen laughed a humorless laugh.

"I don't think so. If you stop to consider it, knowing Emery, it's perfectly reasonable. He grew up knowing the waterways."

"Peter Emery is *blind*, man. Now, it's quite possible a blind man could garrote a person. But a shot in the heart? Apparently on the first go?"

"But I didn't say he shot her."

Bannen sat in Lincoln in dead silence as Jury explained himself. Then he said, "Maybe you aren't completely mad after all. It'll take us an hour to get there. And you're to do nothing *until* we get there."

It was bluff-anger, Jury knew, coming from Bannen's wounded pride. Of course, the man was thinking he should have known it; he'd grown up around these ditches, drains, canals—all of this water. He had seen, as well as Jury had, that punt leaning against the cottage. "You can depend upon it, Chief Inspector, I don't *want* to do anything." Jury hung up, feeling a wrench at the thought of Zel. And then as if the name were some magical incantation, he turned at the sound of a demanding voice.

"You've *got* to stay for supper! I cooked a lot of it."

It was Zel. She was holding a wooden spoon and wearing one of Parker's *rondeaux*, even though it was as long as two yards of good ale and had to be folded several times to keep her from tripping. The back corners made a train when she walked.

"Zel! What are you doing here?" Then he remembered she was coming to "do" dessert. There were few times in his life when he'd been so glad to see anyone as he was to see Zel, safely here at Toad Hall.

Parker, wearing his own *rondeau* and waving a carving knife about like a scimitar, said, "We mean business around here, Superintendent. You have got to stay!"

Jury laughed. "I hope you don't need that knife to cut the lamb."

"Wait 'til you taste my dessert! It's chocolate soufflé!" As she turned, Jury thought that Dorcas Reese would have absolutely had to learn to cook, for she could hardly let a ten-year-old child show her up. Zel ran across the marble tiles, racing back to the kitchen, her apron hem flying, and streaming behind her, her incendiary hair.

Rapunzel, thought Jury. Had to be.

42

The two men, Jury and Bannen, stood on the saltings near some inlets whimsically named "The Cots." Near the place where the body of Verna Dunn had been found, they looked out over the Wash, its silt and sand, at the waters that were part of the North Sea. Bannen had parked his police car near Fosdyke Bridge. They had trudged the rest of the way, for reasons obscure to both of them. They would have said, if asked, that it was a crime scene. It pulls one back.

Bannen said, "Desolate place, isn't it? Or peaceful, I suppose, depending on your turn of mind."

"For God's sake, tell me how he discovered it was Verna Dunn? After all these years?"

"Yes. Well, she made a little slip. Naturally, she went to the cottage when she was at Fengate that weekend. Verna Dunn could never leave anything alone. Emery said they were sitting there talking about wetland shooting, and whether Peter had tried the steel shot in place of lead—you know, the whole business of poisoning the water with lead—and, naturally, the dreadful accident came up. Verna Dunn made a stupid slip. She told Peter he shouldn't have been wearing that 'dark Barbour jacket' because another wildfowler wouldn't be able to see him. The thing is, he'd just acquired that jacket, only the day before. It was new. There was no way she could have seen it unless she'd been there. I thought that 'accident' rather peculiar; I mean, no one coming forward to admit responsibility."

Jury shook his head. "She hated him that much because he dropped her?"

"The Verna Dunns of this world don't take to being dumped. No. Well, thank the lord that's over," Bannen went on. "And I'm glad I was wrong, you know. About Jennifer Kennington."

"I wondered sometimes if you really believed she was guilty." Jury looked up at the hazy sky. He wondered if there was going to be a storm.

"It was very hard connecting her with the murder of Dorcas Reese, certainly." Bannen shook his head. "If she'd only told the truth. If she'd been straight about things. If she hadn't lied, I doubt very much if I'd have charged her." He scraped his thumbnail over his chin, across the unshaven whiskers. Strange how the dead silence of this place augmented the sandpapery rasp.

Jury said, "I suppose you can't really blame her for not wanting it known that she'd stayed here an extra day because of Jack Price." But Jury did blame her. In part, he blamed her as Bannen blamed her, for running out on the truth, for not sticking. And she had confided in Jack Price, not Jury. *Oh, get over it, man.*

"She never has said just *what* their relationship was. One assumes—" Bannen stopped abruptly.

It was nice of him, Jury thought, to consider Jury's feelings. He said it for Bannen. "One assumes they were lovers, I suppose."

"Is it just part of her nature, this secretiveness? It certainly worked against her. It wasn't difficult to turn up the place in Sutterton where they stayed Tuesday night."

"I think it's part of her nature, yes," Jury said, grimly. "It could be she learned at an early age not to tell things because she was always in danger of Verna's taking away anything she valued." He turned up his coat collar and shoved his ungloved hands deeper into his pockets. "But that's mere amateur analysis. And it wouldn't explain her behavior. I'm not sure what would."

Bannen seemed to be untroubled by the bitter winds, the North Sea air. His arms held back his dark brown topcoat, as if he were warming himself before a fire. "I'm not at all glad to know Peter Emery's guilty, I don't mind telling you. It's the little girl, Zel. What will happen to her? I hate foster care."

"Oh, I don't think that's going to be a problem."

"No?"

Jury smiled. "No. She and Linus Parker are quite matey. I'm sure Parker can take care of the Social."

Bannen smiled, considering this. "You know, she'd be better off with him, anyway. The burden of having to live alone with a blind man, well, that's rough for a child."

They were silent for a while, thinking their separate thoughts. Jury's were gloomy ones. The landscape matched them.

Bannen turned to look behind them, back up the narrow channel that the Welland had become at this point in its travels. "They put the punt boat in a stream near Wyndham Fen and from there used streams and canals until they got to the Welland."

"Peter's an old hand with a punt. And it explains why he chose the Wash. It had nothing to do with the tides. He could get here by boat. How did they get *her* here, though?" asked Jury.

"'They' didn't. It was Peter who persuaded her; he said Verna Dunn thought it all a game, enjoyed the intrigue of meeting someone in such a godforsaken place. Everyone said she was impetuous. I believe he thought it some sort of poetic justice: shooting Verna from a punt. A lot of trouble though."

Jury said, "Not for him, probably. This way, there'd be no footprints, would there? That's difficult for even a sighted man to avoid, in this muck." Jury looked out over the mud flats. "And he certainly wasn't worried about poor Dorcas leaving prints. Look at the way it went: Dorcas takes the Owens' gun. Dorcas is the shooter. Dorcas drives the car back. My God, Emery himself is like smoke, invisible."

"And yet he killed her."

"Perhaps he simply got sick and tired of her. He had no intention of marrying Dorcas Reese, that's certain."

Bannen shook his head, looked toward the mouth of the Welland. "It must've been there the boat put in. She shot from the boat."

"It's the way fenmen used to shoot wildfowl. Except then they had a punt gun. Well, neither one of them could have done it alone. He needed her eyes; Dorcas needed his planning and his nerve."

"I forgot to tell you," said Bannen, "I had a look round up in Scotland. I went to Perthshire. To my way of thinking, Emery probably *was* guilty of murdering that lass. The bridge was one of those wooden footbridges. The water was deep enough, but there's no way the girl could accidentally fall into it. No way that I could see. She had help."

Jury was astonished. "You suspected Emery? But you seemed so dumbfounded when I suggested him."

"Oh, I was. I didn't see how he could've shot Verna Dunn, for the obvious reason of his blindness. But he still bothered me. I remembered his lady-love in Perthshire, pregnant and dead. Like our Dorcas."

Jury smiled. Even Bannen sounded proprietorial. "Poor girl. It must have taken quite a bit of persuasion on Emery's part to get her to do it."

"Surprisingly little, according to Emery. She'd have done anything to have him. And she wanted Verna Dunn dead. She was, understandably, jealous. That caused her change of mood."

"That, or the realization that she 'ought not to have done it.' Shooting another person would be enough to change anyone's mood." Jury shoveled up a layer of silt with the toe of his shoe. "Only one bullet? She must have been a damned good shot."

"Perhaps, perhaps not. I think there must have been at least one more cartridge buried in these sands. And, remember, they got the boat in close." Bannen rubbed his thumb across his forehead. "It's all a rather grotesque version of a lover's tryst, wouldn't you say?" For the first time, Bannen seemed to feel the cold. He blew on his hands. "Lord save me from love, if that's how desperately it works itself out."

Jury said nothing.

"Let's get out of here. I don't know why we came. It makes me think of the war. I was always warned against the beaches." He said it again: "I don't know why we came here. Why did we?"

"I suppose there are some scenes that pull you like a magnet, that you can't exorcise until you look on their harmless aspect."

"Lord, that's almost poetic."

Jury smiled slightly. "I try."

As they made their way to the seawall and the car, he turned and looked back. The chalky sky took on the glow of pearl, and the sun, smoking behind a haze of cloud, threw off a light of burnished pewter. Mysteriously lit, it was as if the watery, colorless land refused drabness, stood determinedly against diminishment.

Bannen slammed the door, started up the engine. "Christ, but I'm glad that's over. Let's put paid to it. Let's say *fini* to the job and go to that godforsaken pub and have a pint."

Jury nodded. "I'm with you. *Fini*."